KHAMSIN

The Devil Wind of The Nile

A Novel of Ancient Egypt

by

Inge H. Borg

* * *

Cover Design by Diana Wilder

* * *

CONTENTS

KHAMSIN

The Devil Wind of The Nile

Book 1

"Legends of the Winged Scarab"

Foreword

At the dawn of the great Egyptian dynasties, before any Pyramids were built and the camel was introduced to the Nile regions, certainly long before the royal title of *Pharaoh* came into use, Aha rules as the second King of the First Dynasty (ca. 3080 B.C.). His triumph and tragedy plays out centuries before the Greek colonization of the Two Lands. The famed temples of Thebes, Karnak and Amarna have yet to be built.

To this day, our vague answers are drawn only from relics and mummies of much later dynasties, their cities wrenched from the hot red dust driven into the verdant river valley for fifty days by the Khamsin, the dreaded Devil Wind of the Nile.

In *KHAMSIN*, the reader is immersed in the life of the fertile Valley of the Nile, as flesh and muscle have been molded back onto those brittle bones. The author gives authenticity to her work by having researched often conflicting archeological outpourings, and by using ancient Egyptian names for the earliest known settlements, as well as most gods—rather than the customary Greek names in use today. A few, however, have been adhered to for easier identification.

This novel is not meant as a dissertation on the dawning of Egyptian history. It was written for pure reading pleasure of a multi-layered epoch, and it is hoped that it might give its readers a better understanding of, and renewed curiosity in, the beginning of an astounding civilization and of those enigmatic Ancient Egyptians.

* * *

i

Inge H. Borg

Prologue

Rih al-Khamsin!"

It was an eerie howl rather than a cry. It multiplied, and it traveled fast. The urgency of the warning sent the inhabitants of the far-flung settlements scurrying. In great haste, children were collected, drinking wells covered, and home sites secured. All against the onslaught of the feared wind whose turbulent airs had gathered strength from far away.

Its father, the Sirocco, was spawned over the hot desert. Before it abandoned its cyclonic origins to reach across the vast stretches of the Great Green Sea, clawing young islands along the way, racing toward the densely forested virgin coast of the primitive Northern Continent, it gave birth to its unbridled son Khamsin, the Devil Wind of the Nile.

This new turbulence then grew into adolescence over the desolate sandy expanses of the great desert, gathering strength and hot dust, reaching merciless maturity as it slammed into the broad Valley of the Nile. With the Khamsin's arrival, the populace knew to expect accompanying sand storms; and swarms of vermin covered the ground bringing widespread devastation to the already parched land.

Only when the Great Wind's hot fury was spent, did its evil spirits seem appeased, and the land and its people could breathe anew, and anticipate the life-giving flooding of their river once again.

Just as once again, the principles of *Ma'at* would be adhered to. It was their cornerstone of all life, of all culture. Its teachings were to suppress all chaos stemming from ones emotions, feelings and reactions. To keep life in absolute order. No deviation was permitted. Those who offended its strict laws were severely punished—often by a cruel death.

But during those enervating days when the incessant wind raged, *Ma'at* was often breached; usually calm tempers flared; violent crimes were committed. And it was said, that people vanished without a trace.

*

Only one other queen occupied these chambers before her; King Narmer's beloved Royal Wife Neith-hotep. After her sudden death, the royal wing had stood empty, awaiting yet another royal occupant.

Mayet shivered in the dark. Throughout the royal palace, a damp smell of the swamps lingered. As if the buildings were not yet cured enough for their mud-brick walls to retain the day's dry heat. Would he come this night? Her women-slaves were asleep, her loyal Amma spending a time of privacy somewhere else. The young queen ached with longing. And with fear. For her beloved. For herself.

"Mayet?" The voice drifted into her small ante-chamber from behind a wall-hanging. The young lovers had discovered that it hid the entrance to a secret passage. Cut into the thick wall, it led into an overgrown pomegranate grove.

"My Love." Mayet rushed toward the dusty weaving and reached out for her nocturnal visitor. "I cannot bear him any longer." She buried her sobs in his shoulder, lest she wake the slaves blissfully dreaming nearby. After a fervent embrace, she pulled him into her chamber.

"My sweet heart, my life," he soothed. "I know you are lonely. Everything is still strange to you. The court, this palace. Even Aha. But he is your husband. And, he is the King. Whatever happens, I shall be there for you." His hands soothed as did his firm lips. He cupped her face and covered it with his kisses until the fear drained from her and she responded to his ardor. Now, her mouth was eager to meet his, her whole being pressing close to him, urging his desire to burst upon her.

"What if he finds out?" Her voice again was laced with concern. "I feel he watches me. And, sometimes, I think, he knows."

"My darling kitten," he whispered back and pulled her onto the soft quilts. "He does not know, believe me. Just let me love you, Mayet."

His passion engulfed her as he enveloped her in his arms, his breath, his tall lean body. She strained toward him, ready to receive him, her forbidden love mounting to match her sorrow.

"How I love you." He repeated his words as she clung to him and pushed upward. When he could reach into her no farther she rose with him, like Horus soaring toward the skies. At last, they sighed in wondrous fulfillment, their love one of total abandon; of total happiness. Of total hopelessness.

The life Queen Mayet conceived that night was new; but its eternal soul was old, for it was a reawakened *Ba*; an essence, that had lived through paradise and cataclysms. It was a soul destined yet to live through many other storms for it was a sinner's soul that had not yet found atonement on this earth.

* * *

Part I

The Two Lands

Chapter One

Darkness hung over the Upper Region of the Two Lands, near the Kharga Oasis. To the east, the first of the six roiling Falls rendered vast stretches of the great river Hapi unnavigable. Above the Falls lay the lands of the Wawat and the Kush and, further south, the Kingdom of Nobatia where the legendary King Ogoni ruled over his Black and Red Noba tribes.

A good two hours' donkey-ride from the main encampment of King Aha's Fourth Army, three small tents huddled in the lee of a barren hillock. The entrance flap of the main tent was thrown open allowing the cool desert air to cleanse the dark interior of the pungent smell of passion.

The man had spent himself with unhurried maturity, savoring the ebb and flow of his pleasure.

The girl, as usual, had clawed and defied and ensnared him. She was a beautiful desert girl, and he knew that she was greedy.

But how she could harden the pillar of his *Mehyt*. In the end he always triumphed over her coy taunting, their intertwined skirmishes making him fight more ardently than on the battlefield, his hollow victories over her so much sweeter than any enemy's defeat.

General Ali el'Barum, Commander of King Aha's Fourth Army of Amun, enjoyed his occasional visits with its entanglements on the soft lion pelts, away from his smelly army camp, the clanging of war implements, the rough language of his men. Here, he escaped for a few sweet hours from the heavy burden of his responsibilities.

At thirty-five, he had weathered the seasons well and his muscles rippled forcefully in the moonlight. There was only a trace of thickening around his middle yet his face was deeply lined from the desert sun and the incessant gritty wind; even more so from the concern for his legions.

On these brief outings, Barum was accompanied by Keheb, his Aide-de-camp, who also served as his Quartermaster, Regimental Seal-Bearer and Scribe. They arrived with three laden jackasses. When they returned to their army camp, their saddlebags were empty. Still, Barum never felt that he left the tiny outpost empty-handed. He stretched in the cool night air and smiled at the beneficial bargain he had struck in this inhospitable desert. Naked, caressed by a light breeze, his thoughts dwelled on soft brown arms and smooth thighs. Yes, he was much taken with the unruly young woman waiting in his tent.

There was an added value to his slender temptress. By the complicated ties of the nomadic desert dwellers she was supposedly related to the tall tribesman with the sharp eyes and excellent memory, who spoke their language, and who was endowed with the appropriate greediness so that his tongue could be loosened by generous gifts.

It was well worth it, Barum thought. Whenever he visited this hidden encampment, the tall man would ride up on a scrawny ass and tell of his latest travels. He spoke with great flourish, his eyes blazing like the daytime sky. Pressured for details, the tribesman insisted that the hot wind from across the desert whispered all this to him. And while the wind was free, the man's interpretation of its murmurs was not. For their combined services, the tribesman and his obliging relative invariably found the general's appreciation neatly stacked in the smallest of the three tents. Sacks of grain, bowls of fresh fruit, and an occasional well-sealed jar brimming with sweet date wine. Colonel Keheb always saw to that.

*

Barum slipped back into the dark tent and groped his way toward the soft cured lion pelts. A sleepy gurgle welcomed him. No sooner had he reawakened his young beauty with his newly stirring urgings than there was a scratching on the tent wall. With a lusty curse, the seasoned warrior roused himself again. He wrapped his kilt around his wide flat middle and stepped outside. Keheb, carrying an oil lamp, pointed to the second-largest tent. Without a word, the two men strode toward it.

When his aide threw the flap to that tent open Old Barum, as his men called him, sensed someone in its depths. A second lamp was lit and its pale flicker danced across the small space. There were the usual floormats, a trunk and, unusual for this location, a writing box, a chair and a rough-hewn stand. The general's visits were frequent enough for him to keep a few of his professional necessities on hand. Sometimes, in the early morning hours, alone again yet no longer lonely, he would work out the details of his next maneuvers or compose a reassuring message to his wife. The scrolls he sent to her from this small camp were always filled with unaccustomed tenderness.

The tall tribesman unwound the long strip covering his head. Rid of the obscuring cloth, his long hair fell in dark matted tangles. His bearded face had the look of well-cured leather and a beaked nose separated a pair of piercing blue eyes. Barum recognized his nightly visitor at once. It was Yadate, his young beauty's supposed relative, one of his hired spies.

To all appearances, Yadate was a simple desert herder whose scattered tribe roamed the barren wastelands. They traveled from one oasis to the next, in search of water. According to Yadate, he had come north years ago from the far reaches of the mountainous Land of Punt in search of better grazing for his scrawny herd of goats and donkeys.

"Yadate!" Barum touched his lips and forehead, emulating tribal custom. "It is good to see you." He motioned to a pile of mats. Over his shoulder he called, "Keheb, some libation for our friend."

"I greet you, el'Barum, and I ask your forgiveness for disturbing your night. I trust you are well," Yadate said as Keheb poured wine and left.

Both men settled onto the mats. The tribesman comfortably with his legs crossed, Barum reclining on his side supported by his right elbow. He would never get used to this awkward crouching down and winced as he tried to find the least numbing position.

"I am well, thank you, my friend. I trust that your travels led you to bounty-filled oases, that your flocks are fattened, and that your water-bladders are full. Yadate, I appreciate seeing you day or night," Barum replied with the same formality, neither man betraying his suspicion of the other.

Barum detested having to go through these lengthy rituals, although he knew better than to press his furtive visitor into undue haste lest he offend the valuable spy and risk the other's information to dry up like a dying spring.

"I am certain you will find my news of great importance." Yadate scratched his matted beard. In contrast to the people of Kamt, as the southerners called the Two Lands, desert tribes kept all their body hair throughout their life. In the enclosed tent, Barum vividly smelled the differences of their cultures. Much too eager to hear the man's information he forgot to be offended by his visitor's appalling lack of personal hygiene.

"Due to the dry season my tribe moved into the greener pastures of the Kush and Noba. We heard that a new lode of yellow nub was discovered between their lands. A rich vein. King Ogoni is claiming all of it for Nobatia." Yadate paused to let his news sink in.

"The mine is located somewhere between the river and the Crystal Sea. Where the Hapi tumbles over the rocks a fifth and sixth time from here. *Red* and *Black Noba* warriors are moving north. I believe to combine forces with the Kush and the Wawat."

Barum's mind raced ahead. If the Noba had unearthed a new mine yielding precious yellow nub, King Ogoni could outfit huge tribal armies, in addition to enticing foreign mercenaries to fight his battles. He could then push the timing of a long-feared confrontation months ahead. Barum had to inform King Aha at once.

"Yadate, if I draw for you the river's course, can you show me the location of this mine," Barum asked.

"And where the Noba might be by now?" He took a piece of papyrus from his document box and spread it on the floor, reaching for a lump of charcoal. Despite the crudeness of his drawing, the well-traveled nomad easily recognized the snaking of the river. Yadate studied the image and pointed to a site east of the river, between the fifth and sixth Falls. It gave Barum a fair idea of the location and his military mind weighed at once the possibility of taking the mine by force. They would have to decimate the enemy first, of course. A confrontation was overdue and King Aha wanted to extend their borders further south at any rate.

"Yadate, your news is interesting. Although, a mine that far south does not concern us, you understand." Barum hoped his feigned disinterest would throw the nomad off.

Yadate inclined his head. He understood; the general was lying. He, too, kept his face impassive.

"As usual, you will find my humble gifts for your valued services. They should compensate you for your long journey. Shall you need a place to spend the night?"

The provisions in the adjacent tent could hardly be called humble. Still, custom had to be observed even in the harsh desert. For the tribes, outward courtesy toward visitors was paramount. It being understood that at any moment a gracious host might slit his guest's throat, or the other way around.

"My people sleep by day and travel by night," his nocturnal visitor grinned thinking of the sweet wine, the sacks of emmer wheat, fresh produce, and shining copper implements.

"I must leave." Yadate jumped up as lithe as a panther and slipped from the tent. Before Barum could struggle to his feet and follow him outside the tall tribesman had already vanished into the indigo night. Barum called for his aide. The valuable man appeared within the blink of an eye and the two of them stepped back into the working tent where the scribe reached for his writing materials.

Pleased to sit down like a decent man, Barum fell into his chair. He disliked having to endure the cramping in his legs during Yadate's visits. Keheb, with the ease of a professional scribe, arranged himself on the very mat which had been occupied by the tall nomad. He only hoped not to catch too many of the sand fleas that no doubt had escaped from the sweaty folds of their visitor's rough-woven robe.

Barum realized the news had to reach the Grand General

in Ineb-hedj with utmost speed. His very message might become the signal to push the campaign against the enemy forward, the reason for the King to journey to Nekhen. War could be declared only by King Aha, Supreme Commander of all armies. On the other hand, Aha's official arrival at Nekhen would also signal for the combined forces of the Wawat, the Kush, and the fierce Noba to march against the Two Lands.

Sending messengers was dangerous business. They could be intercepted by enemy spies. With the river now at its lowest, most boats were unable to make a swift journey downstream. Barum's messenger would be forced to take the slower, even more dangerous, route through the western desert.

"Scribe," he nodded to Keheb, letting his loyal Aide know that he appreciated his many talents. "Begin: To Chancellor Makari, Grand General of the Four Royal Armies, at the Royal Palace in the Court City of Ineb-hedj. Maneuvers of the Fourth are progressing well. However, I urgently request supplies for our *New* War Games. May Horus, the great Fighting Hawk, give us his protection now, without fail."

Within the ambiguous language lay the pre-arranged signal; the push into the south, described as the *New* War Games, could commence as soon as Hor-Aha arrived upriver to lead his armies into battle.

By now, the Wawat were accustomed to large masses of armed men near their borders. Repetition and non-aggression by the Fourth Army had lulled them into believing that these were mere maneuvers. The growing enmity between their nations not yet having turned into open hostility, both sides kept a tenuous peace, allowing their caravans to travel beyond each other's borders where traders exchanged exotic wares from the south for much needed foodstuff from the Two Lands.

After Colonel Keheb finished writing, Barum took the document and placed it in a sturdy leather tube. Deep in thought, he fingered a cylindrical object around his neck, but ruled against sealing the scroll with his personal mark just yet. His messenger had to memorize the simple words. As the scroll needed to be authenticated by the recipient, a matching stamp was to be worn by the messenger—indelibly burnt into his skin. The necessary utensils for this procedure were at the main camp, as was the messenger yet to be chosen. Barum went to the large tent to take tender leave from the sleepy girl while Keheb rounded up the hobbled donkeys.

*

It was still night when they arrived at the Great Oasis where the vast encampment of the Fourth Army of Amun hugged barren desert terrain. There was a good supply of water from the Oasis and in three days, a trek of donkeys could bring fresh supplies from the old southern capital city of Nekhen where a desert-weary warrior could find a bit of amusement during his leave. There, parched for drink and affection, a man could head for the House of Pleasures to dip his swelling pillar into the costly honey pot of a whore while others, given to fierce wagering with the city's less alluring denizens, could bet on anything from river-frog races to rolling the ivory dice. Officers often preferred to wager heavily on the outcome of *Senet*, a board game played by favored masters.

As they drank sweet date wine, they often increased their bets beyond their ability to make good. It was of little consequence. Montu, the God of War, hovered around the next hillock. They might not see Nekhen, or their debtors, ever again.

*

Fresh clothes were laid out for him and a jug of water was brought. Barum quickly quenched his thirst without losing precious time to remove the desert's tenacious dust, nor the musty aroma still clinging to his loins.

"Keheb, find a messenger with courage, cunning and endurance!"

His Aide, equally dusty yet without his general's pleasant memories, left to have the watch captains select a man for the dangerous mission. He returned with a young warrior.

"This is Pase, my General. His captain thinks him best suited for the mission. He is an excellent archer."

Barum assessed the young soldier who stood motionless before him. The lad was pleasant-looking and appeared extremely fit. His gaze was unflinching, his expression eager, without being over-confident.

"Who is your captain, Archer Pase?"

"The Watch Captain Nebah, my General." His voice was

steady. His muscles rippled tensely despite his rigid salute.

"Ah, Nebah. A good officer." *If you keep him away from the board games*, Barum thought. He had heard of the man's outrageous wagering in Nekhen.

"Archer Pase, I am dispatching you to Ineb-hedj. While speed is of the essence, the successful completion of your mission is paramount. Can you read?"

"No, my General, unfortunately, I cannot," Pase replied, his regret sincere. Barum directed Colonel Keheb to read the message aloud.

"Memorize it, Archer. Guard the scroll with your life. You are to deliver it to Grand General Makari only. His working chambers are in a building adjacent to the palace."

"Yes, General. I am familiar with the palace grounds. I trained with the Palace Archers in Ineb-hedj until six moons ago. Under Captain Veni."

"Excellent. Before you leave, Pase, there is one other thing," Barum said quietly.

Pase knew that the seal had to be authenticated. Without this, the Grand General would never set Aha's complicated war machine in motion. Before entering Makari's tent, Pase had seen the foot soldier stoking an open flame and knew the painful process ahead of him. As they passed by, Keheb had commanded the man to throw on more dried donkey cakes and ordered him to call for the camp priest and his special healing salves.

Barum laced binding loosely around the scroll before he knotted the strands leaving the two ends dangling. From a small wooden box, he poured fine clay onto a saucer and added water from a flask. With an ostrich quill he stirred the soft mixture before rolling it into a ball which he pressed over the two loose strings. As he rolled his cylindrical seal over the round ball the soft clay flattened out. Imprinted on the resulting disk were intricate marks. Once the clay hardened, it left a perfect impression of Barum's personal identification seal.

Colonel Keheb reached for a long-handled implement as Barum handed him his seal to be heated on the fire outside. This time, the cylindrical seal was not to be rolled over soft clay. When Keheb re-entered the tent with the heated cylinder, Pase removed his protective leather flap and stripped his short kilt from his loins.

"Are you prepared?" Keheb asked and handed Pase a small roll of cured leather.

"I am prepared," Pase replied and sank his teeth into the sturdy piece. He would endure the pain without a moan. His searing skin protested. Acrid smoke rose from the burning flesh. Tears welled up inside Pase's lids and his breath became belabored. True to his resolve, he did not flinch.

Keheb pulled the hissing seal away. General Barum's distinct mark flamed on Pase's abdomen. The young colonel checked it carefully. A perfect match. He stepped outside, thankful for the fresh air. He hailed the waiting priest-surgeon and led him back into the tent where the portly man applied a thick layer of aloe salve to Pase's raw mark, dressing it with a length of clean linen.

Barum handed the archer's kilt to Keheb who fastened it carefully around the young messenger's waist as a sign of respect for the stalwart warrior.

Although he still felt dazed from his ordeal, Pase recovered quickly and took the leather holder from his General, proud to have been chosen. This would most assuredly bring him a quick promotion. Assuming he survived the journey.

"I shall leave at once, General."

"One more thing," Barum said. "Tell the Grand General that the Noba found a mine with much of the yellow nub. They are pushing north to combine forces with the Kush and the Wawat." Barum looked quizzically at the archer and added emphatically, "Tell Makari that he must prepare for war at once!"

After saluting his commander smartly, Pase turned and left as quickly as he could. The desert route would be long and dangerous. He was determined to succeed.

For now, Ali el'Barum, Commander of the Fourth Army of Amun, could only wait and hope, banishing all thoughts of soft embraces and languorous hours of sweet semi-sleep.

Barum, the seasoned warrior, had replaced Ali, the lusting man.

* * *

Chapter Two

Two days after Barum's secret meeting in the desert, a man swathed from head to toe in protective cloth rode up to the enormous walls of Nekhen, and without so much as reining in his plodding ass he passed through the imposing gates heading for the Temple of Horus. A whispered word to a passing priest, and he was permitted into the vast courtyard. Immediately, a young acolyte ushered him toward Chief Priest Rahetep's chambers.

Rahetep was entrusted with a most sacred responsibility. In the House of Life, earnest temple acolytes copied confusing rows and columns of light and dark squares from grass-weavings crackling with age. As one generation finished their papyri, another followed to repeat the tedious tasks. From time to time, Rahetep thrashed them soundly demanding excellence.

"Yadate!" Rahetep turned from his writing stand. The Chief Priest was a tall slender man, although age had begun to curb his height and he squinted against the onset of myopia. "May our gods protect you and your tribe, and lead your herds to ever better grazing grounds."

"And may these gods of yours listen to you, Chief Priest, when you ask for such splendid protection for me and my tribe."

Rahetep was never certain whether the nomad mocked him or whether he appreciated to have a good word put before the gods on his behalf. What might the nomad be willing to share with him today? For a price, of course.

"I have news of great importance," Yadate said and touched his lips and forehead, then bowed, not very deferentially.

14

"I am listening, son of the desert," Rahetep replied as he touched his own lips and forehead. He, too, gave a slight hint of a bow and asked his visitor to make himself comfortable. "You look as if you rode all night." With the quiet assurance of his class, Rahetep pointed to a pile of mats near his own chair, calling to an acolyte, "Bring juices, fruit and cooked fowl for our guest." The cultured priest sank into his chair in such a graceful manner that he did not appear to hover above his visitor whose robes sent up clouds of dust as he dropped effortlessly onto the finely woven floormats.

Yadate retold his information about the mine and its location. Then he described the massing of the Noba toward the First Falls.

Rahetep listened intently. When the refreshments arrived, he offered Yadate juices from glimmering cups followed by an array of fruit arranged on a platter of hammered copper. Succulent pieces of cold fowl lay piled high in a woven basket.

Yadate lustily tore great strips from the proffered meat. While he ate copious amounts, the nomad's calculating eye surveyed the temple's obvious wealth. What should he ask for today? Other than the sweetness of a woman his beloved desert did not yield such splendid comforts. Yadate briefly thought of the girl in Barum's tent. This day, he did not wish for worldly goods, however. The army general had already been more than generous for his information, and for the girl. Today, the superstitious man hoped to gain the goodwill of these priests' powerful gods. If Rahetep could promise their protection, it would be Yadate's price.

Besides, there was another benefactor whom he visited from time to time, and whose new price the cunning tribesman had decided should be a kir-full of the yellow nub from the jungles of Nobatia. Yadate looked slyly at Rahetep. Northern upstarts! In all his years of supplying information to their generals and priests, they never commented on his strange name. And how he loathed their careless use of it.

'Yah-dah-tey.' The tribesman silently caressed his name.

That was how it was pronounced in the Land of Punt where he was born. His parents had come from the other side of the Crystal Sea after crossing the dangerous narrow stretch that separated a large peninsula from this land. Not without reason, they called the passage Bab al Mandab, Gate of Tears. Perhaps that was why Yadate's eyes shone so unusually bright and why his skin was not as dark as that of the natives of the Land of Punt.

Having satisfied his hunger and his asking price, Yadate took his leave.

*

Rahetep stared after the vanishing tall figure with faint uneasiness. Could the nomad be trusted? Reaching for his writing implements, Rahetep began to compose a precise note to the Venerable Badar at the Temple of Ptah in Ineb-hedj. He purposely addressed his message to the retired old High Priest, confident that the High Priest of Ptah, Ramose, would be informed of its urgency at once. However, should it be intercepted by foreign spies, its importance was lessened.

Rahetep rolled the scroll up with deliberate care and prepared soft clay to seal it. Just as carefully, he selected a heavy copper holder to protect the delicate papyrus during its long journey. Now, whom should he send to Ineb-hedj? He decided on his most promising priest-surgeon. The ambitious young lad would strive to succeed in his mission at all cost. Almost from the beginning, Rahetep had recognized this youth's great talent. It warranted to be brought to the attention of the High Priest. Only in Ineb-hedj could this lowly-born priest vie for a brighter future. The important message was an opportune introduction. Rahetep added a second scroll with high commendations regarding the messenger's exceptional promise and hoped Ramose would remember his own good judgment in the future.

"Find Tasar," he ordered a young acolyte.

Within moments, an eager youth bowed deeply before him.

"Tasar. I have chosen you for an important mission." The Chief Priest stepped forward and extended his hands toward his disciple. Even standing straight, the young priest did not match the older man's height. Of medium build, Tasar's physique was sinuous, his face handsome.

"May Horus be with you, Rahetep. I am honored to have been chosen." Tasar's ready smile exposed two even rows of large white teeth. His voice had a rich timbre. His clear eyes rested with interest on his aging mentor. Thick eyebrows could not obscure the high forehead evidencing great intelligence. His well-shaped closely scraped head showed a hint of black hair.

Tasar was not of noble birth yet his bearing bespoke of natural nobility. He was born in these Upper Regions, the only son of an embalmer who worked for the minor noble houses of Nekhen. His mother was a weaver whose intricate patterns were still prized funeral shrouds for the departed wealthy. From an early age, young Tasar wanted to learn all there was about the human body, about its failings, how to cure its maladies and wounds.

Recognizing his ambitions, his doting mother had managed to bring him to the attention of the local head priest. At twelve, Tasar had entered the priesthood. A formidable education included training in desert survival. He was taught to handle bow and arrow. He studied the stars. His interest in the human body propelled him toward the art of embalming and he dissected many a cadaver. Later, hypnosis became part of his curriculum and his proficiency was exceptional. Silently, he congratulated himself that he had not become besotted by a particular temple chantress like so many of his peers although he had tasted the sweetness of one or two wily temptresses without allowing their soft arms to ensnare him.

Tasar listened to his Chief Priest and replied quietly, "Your message will be delivered as fast as humanly possible. I will not disappoint you, Rahetep."

"I have every confidence in you to get through to Badar. And, assuredly, you will also meet the High Priest of Ptah," Rahetep said and then added quietly, "As far as I know he is not preparing anyone as of yet to succeed him."

Tasar gasped at the audacious implication. "It will be quicker to travel by boat. A few captains are still stranded here, waiting for the upper river to rise sufficiently." Awed by the possibilities before him, he added, "It will be less conspicuous than were a priest to rush along the narrow shore on a stubborn ass without so much as stopping at the temples along the way." He would have to bargain hard with a captain willing to risk being stranded further downriver.

"Tasar, are you prepared to bear my seal?" Rahetep already held a long-handled copper plate over the open flame.

Tasar removed his wrap. Nothing mattered but success.

"Look into my eyes, Priest Tasar ... You are far away ... Your body is devoid of pain ..." Rahetep's monotonous voice droned on as he led his messenger into a deep trance. Confident that Tasar would not feel any pain, he withdrew the plate from the hot flame and pressed his glowing seal onto his protege's exposed abdomen. Flesh seared. Acrid smoke stung Rahetep's nostrils. Tasar had not moved. From a small turned wooden jar, Rahetep applied a special salve to the angry burn and dressed the wound with long strips of fine linen. He then clapped his hands together. "Tasar! Awake!"

Tasar's consciousness ebbed to the surface. He touched his belly and flinched. When he saw the fresh bandage, he nodded, "I did not feel a thing," and retied his wrap, careful not to brush against the wound.

"You will, though, over the next few days. Here, take some bandages and the rest of the salve. Redress the burn every two days without disturbing the scab or the marks will not heal to match those on the document. Your life depends on it."

Rahetep handed Tasar the copper document holder. "May Horus protect you."

Rahetep prayed that he was sending his brilliant student toward a glorious future in the distant capital, and not into a misbegotten death on the capricious river.

*

Tasar was elated. To have been chosen was the rarest of chances to meet Badar, the legendary Father of Ptah; and once at the great temple in Ineb-hedj, he would surely manage to attract the attention of Ramose. Determined to begin his journey immediately, he clenched his teeth against the fresh burn's surfacing pain and went down to the riverbank.

Fortune was with him. An old river captain was willing to take a gamble—and the promised profits—against the advice of his more cautious peers.

The experienced man was confident that he could navigate the silt-banks, and the two men struck their bargain.

Once aboard, Tasar removed his priestly sash and stretched out on deck leaving the intrepid riverman to negotiate the treacherous stream.

Rarely stopping along the way, their progress was swift. Late on their sixteenth day, they approached the First Royal Mooring Place.

Tasar thought it beneficial to visit with the Chief Priest of the new Temple of Horus. With his pleasing manner, he easily endeared himself to Tuthmose and his son Khentika, while the riverman fell into a deep, restoring sleep.

*

They pushed off just after daybreak the next morning, not more than half a day's travel upriver from the capital.

Stretched out on deck, Tasar pulled the gritty sail over him. Downriver, boats relied on the swift current and his captain would not need to hoist the dusty cloth. The burn had healed well and without distortion. Tasar fell into a deep self-induced slumber that would allow him to arrive at his destination unfatigued.

When the swift falucca bumped against the Ineb-hedj dock, the river captain shook his passenger awake. He had well earned the promised trinkets. Tasar sat up and rubbed his eyes. He marveled at the imposing sight before him. He was safe now and could afford to be recognized as a priest. Carefully, he tied his sash across his chest.

*

Unbeknownst to the elated Tasar, the Archer Pase, General Barum's messenger, had bullied his exhausted jackass through the royal palace gates not more than an hour earlier. Having left his army camp near the Great Oasis two days before Tasar had started his river journey, Pase's travels over the arduous land route had taken that much longer. At last, he also had completed his mission, too exhausted to be awed by his commendable feat.

* * *

Chapter Three

Nefret! Safaga!" Amma cupped her hands over her toothless mouth. "You have been out here long enough." She squinted against the harsh sun hoping to spy her charges through the dense hedge of the palace garden.

"Nefret," she called again. There was a rustle, followed by unmistakable giggles. With her hands on her ample hips, Amma talked into the greenery, "I know you two are there."

Still giggling, two adolescent girls fought their way through the lush thicket. While Safaga pressed her hands against her mouth to suppress her laughter the taller of the two held hers cupped in front of her budding breasts.

"I brought you something, Amma," she said and opened her palms under Amma's face. The little frog looked stunned, the moisture from his bright-green hide evaporating rapidly. First, a large ladle had scooped the tiny fellow off its lotus-leaf. The contraption perpetually poured river water into reed-lined ditches that sloped toward the palace. For the little frog, the journey ended when eager young hands had groped for him. Out of its element, it did what it did best. It jumped.

"Ayah! Really, Nefret! Sometimes, you behave as if you were still a child! And you, Safaga, the way you carry on, one might think you fancy yourself a princess as well. Don't you forget, girl! You are her slave. Now, go and clean up. Both of you. You smell like water carriers before the days of the *Shaduf*."

When Amma had come to Ineb-hedj with Aha's child-queen Mayet, the new palace obtained its river-water from buckets handed along an interminable line of slaves. By the thousands, they labored, blinded by their sweat, passing buckets hand over hand, day after day, season after season, until the *Shaduf* had replaced the sweat-dripping multitudes. The constant ladling of the new invention replenished the farmers' irrigation canals with much greater efficiency, vastly increasing their yields of grain and vegetables. Also, Amma found, it notably decreased the salty taste of human sweat in the palace's household water. Now, the reassuring clanging of the *Shaduf* all along the great Hapi represented the life-giving rhythm for the Two Lands' prosperity. If the sound stopped the populace had reason to fear the coming of the Great Wind, and a terrified wail would shatter the foreboding stillness.

"Rih-al-Khamsin!"

The very thought of the dreaded wind made Amma shiver. The two girls sauntered ahead of her, one tall and fine-featured, the other smaller, pretty, older. Their heads hung in demure penitence as they shot mischievous looks at each other from under lowered lashes. Amma could hear their suppressed giggles and shook her head in mock-dismay. What a time she was having with that willful royal child! And how much she loved her!

"You are going to look like Dokki if you stay in the sun all day," Amma admonished.

"Like Dokki?" Renewed spasms shook the two girls. "How can I look like Dokki? Really, Amma!" Nefret glanced back at her Royal Nurse and rolled her eyes the way her good-natured, dark-skinned slave did after she broke something, which was quite often.

"Don't I look more like Zeina?" Nefret stopped. "Or, rather, Zeina looks a lot like me."

It was true. The third of the Royal Heiress's women-slaves, tall Zeina, could easily be mistaken for her mistress. Sometimes, the two played tricks on old near-sighted Amma, switching places and vanishing into dimly-lit corridors.

"That's enough, Nefret," Amma scolded. "When your mother—may Osiris guard her eternal *Ba*—was your age, she was already betrothed. And quite the lady!"

Ah, her lovely *kitten* Mayet. After fifteen years, Amma still mourned her dead Queen.

The moment passed, and she continued to scold Mayet's child. "Imagine! Here you are, Royal Heiress to the throne of the Two Lands, and you still gallop about like a desert goat.

And with just as much hair!"

"Oh, Amma! Your comparisons are hardly fit for a royal princess," Nefret laughed and, without thought to her expected royal bearing, flung her young arms around the old nurse.

Protesting outwardly, Amma let herself be enveloped by Nefret's affection. The girl's effusiveness softened her as she remembered that Nefret never knew a mother's gentle touch. Almost at once, she resumed her exaggerated posture of authority.

"I swear, Nefret. I am at my wits' end. Ramose needs to have a talk with you. It is time that you behaved as befits the daughter of our King."

The mention of the High Priest of Ptah brought the desired reaction from the two girls. Quite earnestly now, they walked toward Nefret's private chambers where Zeina and Dokki waited, ready to amuse their restless mistress during her noontime repose. Amma insisted that Nefret spend the hottest time of day inside, lying almost naked on soft quilts. After that, she might resume her studies or receive trades people delighting her with finely crafted wares.

Nefret's thoughts turned to the jewel-maker's next visit. He had fashioned a new neck collar for which she had chosen rare lapis lazuli and red carnelian. A sprinkling of turquoise with beaded yellow nub would further enhance her glowing skin. She planned to wear the new ornament for her father's Jubilee. This afternoon, however, Nefret would have to endure hours of boredom while her slaves fitted her with new wigs which she was to wear as soon as they cut off her hair. The prospect made her anxious.

"Amma?" Nefret asked, "When am I going to be introduced at court? Officially, I mean?"

"Soon, child, soon," Amma replied.

"Too soon, I suppose. For then they will cut off my hair," Nefret sighed. She did not want to be a grown-up. Her slender fingers traced the outlines of her budding breasts. A delectable shiver cursed through her as her nipples firmed.

Still, it was wonderful to be revered as the daughter of the god-king Hor-Aha, successor to Narmer, son of the great Queen Neith-hotep.

*

22

The Catfish, Founder of the First Dynasty, Uniter of the Upper and Lower Regions, had been dead now for more than two decades. During his reign, the broad river valley saw many changes. Until then, nomes were ruled by powerful nomarchs. At last, a glimmer of unity pervaded the region and Narmer succeeded in uniting the powerful districts under his rule, creating *The Two Lands*. He built a new northern capital for this united kingdom. When the palace and its temple were completed, a whitewashed wall was erected around them. Narmer named his new court city Ineb-hedj, the City of White Walls.

The new settlement sprawled along the western bank of the great Hapi, south of its expansive Delta. Thousands labored to divert the river and to drain the swamps of the Upper Delta, others spending their lives in quarries to shape round boulders into square building blocks. Most of their basic building materials were cut from alluvial mud. The bricks were sun-dried and, if destined for use on the inside, glazed. The workers built their mud huts at the edge of the wall, adding rings of hovels to the spreading metropolis.

When King Narmer's beloved Queen Neith-hotep suddenly died, his natural exuberance appeared to have died with her. Despite an onset of the feared Khamsin, he went hunting on the river. Legend had it that he was carried off and devoured by a sacred crocodile. No trace was ever found of him. However unfortunate for Narmer himself, the occurrence was regarded a supreme honor; his death a fitting end for a true son of the great Hapi.

Young Aha ascended the Horus-throne. He would have preferred to rule the Two Lands from Nekhen, the old southern capital. His first Queen Mayet was from there, he himself having been born in Tjeny. But the threat of an uprising by the powerful Delta nomarchs demanded his royal presence in the north and he moved his court—and his reluctant Queen—to Ineb-hedj.

Aha then took a second minor wife. Hent's dowry was to be the renewed loyalty of the Delta nomarchs. Whereas Aha learned to like his new surroundings, Queen Mayet never adapted to her new life.

*

After enjoying a decade of relative peace, Aha was faced

with the threat of war. From deep within the unexplored southern territories, King Ogoni's *Noba* armies were reported snaking toward the First Falls, gathering legions from among the querulous Kush along the way.

Over the past years, these southern trading partners brought yellow nub, ivory and exotic hard woods in return for grain, fresh fruit and copper implements. Now these nations coveted the vast granaries of the productive river valley for themselves. So far, the Royal Fourth Army of Amun had deflected several skirmishes along the southern border but military confrontation loomed. It was a matter of time. Victory was paramount! Aha had already commanded Grand General Makari to convene a war council with his generals. Instead of discussing this portent decision with his Vizier, the King had sought counsel from the learned High Priest of Ptah. Perhaps because rumors of insurrections had reached Aha, and strife and corruption tore at his kingdom from within.

* * *

Chapter Four

The Temple of Ptah was built from alluvial mud mixed with straw, molded into standard bricks, then sun-dried, with mud slime the masons' mortar. Sandstone or granite columns with intricate alabaster borders attested to wealth. Still, large offering tables encouraged the populace to remain generous in the feeding of the gods. The priests ate well. With its well-trained bowmen, lusty butchers, snobby scribes, bustling priests and lowly acolytes, tall silos burst with grain. Hidden larders stood stuffed with dried waterfowl and tender lotus shoots, aimed to carry the self-contained community through such hard times as wrought upon the land by the Great Wind.

Separated from the Temple by the Sacred Lake loomed the Royal Palace. This afforded the High Priest of Ptah often unofficial access to the King. Years of maneuvering layered in sincerity had elevated the priesthood to unprecedented heights under Badar, the Venerable Father of Ptah. Ramose, his protege, found himself closely involved in the intricacies of ruling The Two Lands. Ramose's counsel was sought by a king who depended on it more than he heeded the conniving urgings of his Vizier.

The fenced pasture of *Hapi*, the sacred bull, lay toward the south. This was yet another form of the river god, also called *Hapi*. Solely a black bull-calf with a white diamond on its forehead, two white hairs on its tail, and the image of a vulture across its back could be a sacred bull. A feat rarely achieved by nature.

When the bull Hapi died or was put to death after twenty-five years, its huge bulk was drained of all blood. Bound in strips of cloth, the dead animal was buried with only its great horns left to protrude from the sand. So far, two pairs of horns bleached under the sun near the empty royal *Mastabas* at Saqqara.

Wrapped in their leopard skins, it fell to the *Sem*-priests to scour the countryside for a new calf. Once they located a suitable animal, it was kept in seclusion for forty days. Mainly to allow the priests and the little beast sufficient time to endure the torturous pinching, shaving, and tweezing to achieve the required images.

Then the new Hapi was introduced with great pomp, its godly markings awing a generous populace into offering their lovely cows for the young bull's pleasure.

*

At high noon, in concert with the last vibrating peal emanating from the man-high copper disk suspended from two pillars within the Temple of Ptah, in strode the most illustrious servant of the gods—Ramose, the munificent High Priest of Ptah. He conducted only the most important rituals. Requests by lesser nobles for an intervention with the gods were left to Wazenz, the portly Chief Priest. After succeeding the extraordinary Badar, Ramose continued to seek counsel from his aged mentor. Not only did he enjoy their animated discussions, but Badar was the only person to whom Ramose entrusted his innermost thoughts.

The appreciative sighing from the tightly packed crowd was more that of an expectant audience at the royal plays than from worshippers humbling themselves before the gods.

The High Priest's regal bearing was not an affectation. It was second nature, stemming from his princely breeding. Ramose traversed the columned nave with long strides and ascended the Altar of Ptah with grave dignity. Once above the crowd, he extended his arms as if in private supplication to the gods. Silence gained over the scraping of sandals and the expectant clearing of throats as the worshippers settled down.

A lean man, Ramose stood almost four cubits tall and his thirty-eight years rested lightly upon his square shoulders. His face was clean-shaven, a perfect oval. His hair had been so closely cropped that it formed a halo-like effect when the light was behind him.

Only the priesthood wore its hair in this fashion, in contrast to the court where everyone was shaven clean of head and body hair in early adulthood.

A superficial glance might have suggested a lassitude about the High Priest's handsome features. Upon a closer look, however, his thinker's high forehead dispelled such. Shaded by strong brows, his deep-set eyes blazed forth with startling deep-blue irises, a feature most unusual in his dark-eyed world. With his unflinching stare, Ramose was said to discover a man's treacherous thoughts, yet he looked benignly upon those who sought his counsel or begged him for favors from the gods. From all, however, his lapis eyes demanded truthfulness. The firm chin was divided by a short cleft. Full lips hinted of a sensuality that belied his tempered countenance.

Usually, Ramose wore a white linen waist wrap of comfortable knee-length customary for nobles and commoners alike. If he ventured out into the market place, he added a linen sash slung across one shoulder which identified him as a priest. It enhanced successful barter with foreign caravans—an unpriestly pleasure Ramose afforded himself in acquiring rare cloths and potions without anyone's knowledge.

For his special noon-time service, Ramose had added a chain woven from thin strands of yellow nub. It hugged his slim hips five fingers wide, brilliant against his glowing copper skin. His considerable height was extended further by the tall headdress fashioned after the carved images of ancient temple columns from the south. From his neck hung two glittering chains, one entrapping a large crystal cupped in a basket of yellow-nub filament. It rested on top of a disk of yellow nub attached to the second chain, a square hollow at its center. Ramose and Badar were the sole humans who knew of its special application.

Around his shoulders, the High Priest wore a floor-length cape of a shimmering material that cascaded over his shoulders, an ornate neck clasp holding it in place. Such fine threads were unknown in the people of the Two Lands whose farmers were acquainted only with the production of flax to weave their linen. Even more than the material, it was the garment's color that had stunned everyone when Ramose first wore it and it had aroused more than a little envy. The color of a ripe fig, it shimmered in an array of different hues with every movement. No one had ever seen, much less worn, anything so splendid. Not even the King.

Ramose had spied a bolt of this unknown material among the wares of a foreign trader who had lashed his caravan to the Two Lands from the far reaches of the vast northeastern continent. He surreptitiously carried it back to his quarters. Swearing his cowering temple slaves to secrecy, Ramose designed the full-length cape himself. Having been endowed with a fine sense for the dramatic and being aware of his land's superstitions—most of them fed to the impressionable populace by his priests—Ramose knew that the mysterious cloth would enormously add to his exulted status.

He had worn his new garment first during a past Festival of the New Year.

The entire populace of Ineb-hedj appeared to have crowded into his temple. When he strode in, everyone had been awed into submission. By now, however, the cape was accepted as another symbol of his godly service, part of his sacred insignia. Following Ramose's persuasive counsel, King Aha decreed purple the Sacred Color of Ptah to be worn by the High Priest only.

*

Hushed silence pervaded the vast temple. Below the Altar of Ptah, facing Ramose with virginal expectancy, lithe temple chantresses occupied two rows of the wide steps. Below them, sistrum players positioned themselves next to those playing various other instruments.

The Venerable Badar stood alone opposite Ramose, although a step below him. The aging sage tried to ease the pain of his bent body by leaning on a thick pillar. While his arthritic limbs protested the rigors of prolonged ceremonies, his parched face was illuminated by an inner peace; looking up at his brilliant successor, his heart became light with joy, and his physical pain receded into his subconscious.

Lower, the Temple's portly Chief Priest Wazenz stood motionless drinking in the ritual with rapt attention. As the second-highest officiating priest, he hoped for his great chance should Ramose retire in favor of research, as Badar had some years ago. Still, no rumors of his becoming the next High Priest cursed through the whisper-absorbing halls, and nagging doubts about his own aptitude for the rigors of such an exulted calling plagued the jocund man.

Several steps further down crowded the other temple members, many of them well past their youth. The old half-blind Prophet of Ptah touched sandals with the solemn Chief of Altar. Next to them, the studious Chief Lector willed his older acolytes into silence. The well-fed Counter of Grain in the Granary of Ptah leaned surreptitiously against the pale Scribe of Divine Offerings who in turn stood thigh-to-thigh with the self-important Overseer of the Temple Granary. The elf-like Bearer of Floral Offerings stood alone having lost his jostle for a place next to the pale scribe.

Their ambitions shone in their faces and their eyes sponged up each of the High Priest's movements while they defended their places against the upsurge of the newest acolytes. Their constant maneuvering was not confined to temple steps alone. As they watched, they learned. As they learned, they dreamed. One day ... they vowed secretly, and craned their necks so as not to miss a single thing.

Worshippers, mostly nobles of the court, crowded the deep temple nave. Some had come on foot from nearby villas, fanned with bundled ostrich feathers by servants tripping after them. Some had chosen to be carried in their sedans with the advantage that they could remain seated during the lengthy service. By whatever means they had arrived, all were glad to escape the oppressive heat outside.

With expectant stillness at its height, Ramose intoned the old sacred chants, his rich baritone echoed by the pure high voices of his temple chantresses. The simple notes of a lonely flute rang out, a harp adding its melodic strings. Sistrum-players rattled their papyrus stems. The beat quickened. With nothing more than belts around slim waists, the undulating chantresses mesmerized the crowd; it often fell to these lithe servants of the gods to keep the beer-drowsed audience alert.

As the chanting ebbed, then ceased altogether, the High Priest lowered his outstretched arms. Through a side-door, an acolyte approached, a long reddish-yellow staff clutched in his nerve-iced hands. Coming to a trembling halt two steps below the greatest servant of Ptah, he proffered the staff to Ramose. Crowned by the gleaming *Ankh*, it surpassed even Ramose's great height by three full hands.

To everyone's concealed relief, Ramose at last descended the wide steps signaling the end of that day's worship. Ptah had been duly served. As head of all the kingdom's temples, Ramose planned to devote the afternoon to messenger instructive scrolls to chief and head priests of temples situated along the river.

The most important link of this well-planned network was Rahetep, Chief Priest at the Temple of Horus in Nekhen, followed by Tuthmose who was completing a new Temple of Horus at The First Royal Mooring Place, south of the capital. Chief Priest Seka at the Temple of Osiris in Tjeny also served as *Ka*-priest of Abdju where Queen Neith-hotep began her eternal journey through the *Field of Rushes*.

While Ramose, Badar and the assisting acolyte exited through a side door, the main pack of priests, followed by the nobles and their bearers, were pushed into the harsh midday hour through the temple's great portals like bread loves into ovens. Under the hot sun, the crowd disbursed as expediently as possible, most of them anticipating a languid afternoon repose. The soothing chants and the undulating bodies of the temple virgins had heightened their urge for pleasant relaxation. Those who could not expect to find sweet diversion in their own sleeping chambers headed for the House of the Concubines.

* * *

Chapter Five

Once the door closed behind them, shutting off the main temple from their private chambers, Ramose and Badar quickened their pace enough for the young acolyte to have to lengthen his youthful steps to keep up with his energetic elders.

"I should see the King soon. The New Year is approaching and there are extensive arrangements to be discussed," Ramose said. "For instance, the *Sed*-festival, his Jubilee ceremony. Even though Aha has not reigned for thirty years he feels a need to prove to himself—and to others—that he is still in full vigor. Also, there is still talk of *Sati*. I thought we had abandoned this abominable practice of human sacrifices. A wasteful insanity that must be stopped. I should like the King to issue an official decree."

They reached Badar's chamber where the old priest now spent most of his time studying, researching, and resting.

"Will you come in?" Badar asked.

"Thank you, Badar, I would like to." Ramose turned toward the acolyte. "Here, take these." He handed over the long staff and whirled himself out of his purple cape. Pulling off his wide sash, he also removed the chain from his waist. He handed all to the temple servant who carried everything off with great reverence. Now, except for his two necklaces, no outward sign betrayed Ramose's status as the priesthood's most powerful prince; yet his regal countenance could not belie his noble birth.

Badar broke the silence. "You are concerned with more than the King's Jubilee. Is it our young Nefret?"

Badar's unfailing sensibility did not surprise Ramose.

"It is indeed our willful princess who concerns me more

than usual," Ramose sighed. "She is coming of age. She is past her fifteenth year and it is time for her to be initiated into court as the Royal Heiress. Should anything happen to Aha, Hent would be a useless co-regent, especially in her advanced state of pregnancy."

"There is always the Vizier." Badar watched for a reaction.

"Indeed. There is always al-Saqqara." Ramose did not mask his dislike for the ugly official.

Ever since Aha's first queen made him swear that he would protect her child, Ramose took on an almost fatherly role toward the young princess. The heavy responsibility placed on his young shoulders by the dying Mayet had affected him deeply. Overnight, the carefree young nobleman transformed into a dedicated servant of the gods, destined forever to wrestle with painful memories of his forbidden youthful passion.

Motherless from birth, Mayet's daughter grew into a precocious child. As her primary tutor, Ramose had been unrelenting. As her mentor, he tried to guide her wisely. As her spiritual guardian, he worried over her as a true father might. Aha, in contrast, paid little attention to his first-born child.

The two friends—one so old and wise, the other in his prime, so powerful—discussed diverse matters. Not all of them pertained to the service of the gods.

Realizing that his venerated friend might need to rest, Ramose took his leave. Clad in his simple kilt, he left Badar's chamber and traversed the sun-drenched courtyard. He exited the temple grounds onto the Royal Road hemmed in by the palace wall on one side and the river on the other. Ramose thought of the right approach to get Aha to listen to his proposal about Nefret's future. As of late, the King appeared preoccupied, with his attention span decreasing. Not that it had ever been great.

*

The royal palace stood on its own knoll. The grounds were set well back from the highest remembered waterline of annual inundation.

A whitewashed wall, as high as two men, encircled the vast property. An imposing double-towered bulwark twice as high as the wall dominated the main entrance overlooking the river. The flat-roofed towers were accessible only from the inside. From this vantage point, sentries could scour the city as well as the river.

Between the wall and the river ran the Great Road. It had witnessed many magnificent processions. The villas of the rich court nobles lined the broad promenade where the palace grounds ended; the first the Vizier's magnificent home. Adjacent stood the more modest home of Chancellor Makari, who was Grand General of the four Royal Armies, and often absent from Court. Happily so, it seemed to some. Next were the dwellings of other magistrates who served the kingdom's new extended bureaucracy.

A busy landing downriver gave barges easy access to the city promising to transform it into a busy crossroad of trade. Wheat and cattle from the Fayum, schist, natron, and precious yellow nub from the Wadi Hammamat, wooden caskets from far north, and innumerable other supplies were continuously unloaded at the city's public ramp.

In front of the palace another stone ramp reached deep into the river. Here, the Royal Bark was moored with its tenders, their lines slackened by the shallow waters, as the flat-bottomed vessels rested on the soft river mud. There was a shorter, higher ramp next to it belonging to the temple. Its smaller boats with shallower drafts swung freely on rough lines.

Inside the palace wall, winding gravel paths connected the extensive grounds with the main palace and its many side buildings, and high-hedged orchards of mature pomegranate, date and fig trees extended far into the walled royal settlement.

Away from probing eyes, a small military camp housed an elite troop of Royal Archers where they tried out their prowess with the latest weapons. Its recruits were either of noble birth or were found to possess above-average skills. From their ranks, the rotating Palace Guard was drawn.

The massive palace was also built of mud brick, whitewashed like its surrounding wall. High bushes crowded its three facades. On the inside, the palace walls were lined with large glazed tiles and renewable reed matting covered the floors. The building was shaped into a perfect square, its principal entrance opening toward the river which, of course, was hidden from view by the high wall. Protected by a columned portico leading into an inner courtyard, several columns opened onto a veranda from which a small hedge-covered path led to the working wing of the court's highest magistrates.

The palace's inner courtyard opened onto the Grand Foyer which, at its farthest wall, led to the balconied *Window of Appearances*. From there, seated on his throne, King Aha dispensed rewards and special rations to deserving officials during his rare audiences. And on days of an important public trial, the Vizier and his *Kenbet* of ten judges presided over the great hall filled with curious city nobles. For much of the time, the Grand Foyer stood empty, its gleaming alabaster floor merely a transition chamber for the numerous passages dissecting the great palace. They connected a vast number of royal suites, kitchens, work niches and silos at the back of the compound with its enormous stores of grain and fat mice.

The palace's no less imposing back entrance was built into the west wall. High pylons opened to a large outer settlement of workers. At its gates, the Royal Paymasters faced the milling hordes once a day, dispensing anything from daily bread and beer rations from the royal bakeries to gritty emmer wheat from the silos; from carefully measured allotments of oil wicks, honey and beeswax to cured leather. It was through this entrance that huge quantities of supplies were carried into the palace. In a constant stream of coming and going, thousands of bent workers passed by the harsh overseers and alert guards to rest briefly in front of the scribes who scrupulously kept record of the King's wealth.

The vast royal gardens and orchards were tended by free serfs who lived in mud hovels crowding *Hapi's* banks upriver, suitably removed from the villas of the nobles. Their lives, like everyone else's regardless of status, belonged to the King. Many worked in the huge bakeries to produce this most-eaten staple. The ovens were erected well away from the palace and the white villas of the nobles so that the prevailing wind could deposit the sooty smoke elsewhere. Usually onto the hovels of the poor. By the thousands, flat loaves of unleavened bread were pushed into the gaping ovens on mud-trays, while innumerable cylindrical pottery molds lay strewn about from earlier use for ceremonial narrow loaves, baked from leavened dough. The bread was so gritty from sand mixed in with the flour that it scratched the throat and wore down the teeth. The entire city and the nearby headquarters of the Second Army received their rations from these bread factories.

Next to the ovens, vast brewing vats were lined up. As yeast was needed for both bread and beer, the two were always produced in the same location. Beer was regarded as a food rather than looked upon as an intoxicating drink. However, as the gruel-like liquid spread such pleasant feelings through tired limbs it was a sought-after complement to the daily diet. So much so, that the priests included warnings against its effects into their lengthy sermons.

*

Ramose approached the palace gates. Not hesitating for even the blink of an eye, he strode toward the closed portals. As if by magic, the massive gates swung open. He, of course, knew the guards had seen him coming. He also knew that they feared his magic powers. There was not one among them who would have dared to deny the High Priest access. As he walked through the entrance, he paid them no attention. Had they seen his face, they would have spied a flicker of bemusement as Ramose chuckled to himself, 'One day, these fellows may be dozing and I will ram my face against the gates.'

He traversed the Grand Foyer and headed straight for the private chambers of the King. Not until he reached the King's study did the Royal Steward bar his way. Aware of his trusted, powerful position, the muscular man stood his ground.

"High Priest of Ptah, I greet you." Beir bowed.

"Beir. May Horus place his protecting wings upon you." Beir was accused to cling secretly to the old Osiris-cult, as did wonderful old Amma. When it suited him, Ramose liked to remind these two devoted servants that they could not hide their innermost beliefs from him. It was always done with kindness and his jesting held no barbs. He liked the astute Steward and often enlisted his help to gain an audience with his reluctant King, when neither the Vizier, nor the Chancellor, nor the whining Hent succeeded.

"I am sorry, Ramose. The King is resting. He cannot see anyone right now. Perhaps in an hour or two ..."

With Hent's advanced pregnancy, the King's afternoon

35

reposes among the Queen's women had become more frequent and extended, and well-known. These interludes left the King in a mellow mood and the prospect of a more relaxed listener suited Ramose well for his delicate mission. *The gods are smiling upon Aha,* Ramose thought.

"I will gladly wait for the King to wake."

The two men looked at each other, too loyal—and much too wise—to add a knowing smile.

"I will take a walk in the garden, Beir. It should be cooler there by now. And the exercise will clear my mind. Please send for me as soon as the King can see me."

*

Tasar jumped from the unstable boat onto the stone ramp. At once his attention was caught by a tall man emerging through the temple pylons. He almost hailed him but the older man's stride was purposeful, his countenance seemingly unapproachable. Tasar hesitated long enough to lose the commanding figure from sight as the other turned to enter an enormous gate that opened up before the man as if pushed by invisible hands. For a moment, Tasar stared with nothing more to see, uncertain of his next step.

"The Temple of Ptah is right in front of you," the seasoned riverman called in parting to the youth, and shook his head. *The youngster must still be half asleep,* he thought, and pushed his falucca off the sloping ramp glad that this journey was behind him. Humming, the simple man looked forward to seeing his family before he would sail upriver again. No matter how often he arrived back home, there was always another journey awaiting him, testing him and his sleek craft.

Tasar walked up the ramp onto the wide quay. He fingered the copper holder to reassure himself that the important scrolls were still there. Satisfied, he set off toward the towering monument to Ptah. Passing the great pylons, he crossed into the open courtyard. The temple's porticos gaped with a young apprentice sweeping desert sand from the wide steps.

"Direct me to the Venerable Badar."

The young temple servant stared. No one ever came up simply to ask for Old Badar. Despite the stranger's priestly sash, he was uncertain what to do and decided that it would be best to let someone else take the blame for ensuing trouble.

"Please, wait a moment. I shall find someone to help you. Who is asking for the Venerable Badar?" The youth looked expectantly at Tasar who hesitated. Temple pillars were known to have ears growing out of their stony sides.

"Tell the Venerable Badar that I come from Rahetep. He will recognize the name." The acolyte tried to think who this Rahetep was. Failing in his mental search, he shrugged his thin shoulders, dropped his reed-broom and sprinted off.

*

"Any messenger from Rahetep is always welcome at the Great Temple of Ptah." The voice belonged to a short man who pushed an ample stomach in front of him as he approached the waiting Tasar. "I am Wazenz. Come."

Unimpressed, Tasar did not move and watched as the acolyte re-emerged behind the portly figure. The youth rolled his eyes at Tasar, mimicked a bow and then spoke with great emphasis. "I was fortunate to find the Chief Priest of Ptah to welcome you."

Tasar caught the hint and hastened to bow to the important temple servant whose appearance had so deceived him. After he exchanged formalities with Wazenz, Tasar reiterated his urgent need to speak to Badar alone. Wazenz bade Tasar to follow him into the unfathomable depths of the great temple. Opening a side door he led them down a short corridor from where they entered a small chamber containing the usual assortment of chairs, stands, trunks, and document boxes. An unexceptional room, a corner also held an old sedan, possibly belonging to an ailing priest.

Tasar glanced at the worn carrying chair and hastily followed Wazenz who opened another door, beckoning to the young traveler. As soon as Tasar saw the old man he knew that he was in the presence of the revered first High Priest, the Divine Father of Ptah—Badar, the living legend of the priesthood. Tasar stood transfixed by the burning eyes. Then, as if being pushed by an invisible force, he sank to his knees, his eyes held captive by the other man's dark stare.

He is testing me, Tasar thought. It took all of his training and concentration to break the binding spell. The study of hypnosis was one of his favorite subjects. Smiling, though sapped by the trance, Tasar forced himself back to his feet.

"Quite good for one so young." Badar looked up at Tasar, the hypnotic stare gone from his deep-set eyes. He had been taller once, before his sixty years claimed their toll whereas his mind was still as sharp as a finely honed blade.

"Wazenz tells me that you come from Rahetep. I hope that my old friend is well and still where I last saw him. Your ride through the desert must have been exhausting; yet you do not appear tired. Ah, the inexhaustibility of youth."

Badar motioned to one of the chairs and sank down into another. Tasar sat and began to feel more at ease. While Badar's questions were polite and innocuous. They could be cleverly disguised snares. He decided to play the old man's game. "I am the Surgeon-Priest Tasar from Nekhen's Temple of Horus, Divine Father. I can assure you that the Venerable Rahetep is still where you left him. He is well and continues to wield his reed over his young acolytes."

"Acolytes? Anything in particular that they study?" Badar questioned with a disinterested shrug.

"They copy the mats and fill papyri after papyri with the dark squares with absolute exactness, albeit without comprehension."

Badar nodded, and Tasar continued, "As for my *inexhaustible* youth, my message is too important to have arrived half dead. My journey took fifteen days."

Badar raised an eyebrow and Tasar hastened to explain, "I entrusted my luck, and my temple's reward, to a seasoned riverman." He handed over the copper holder and after Badar examined Rahetep's seal, Tasar lowered his crumpled kilt. The burn had healed well, its mark matching the scroll's seal perfectly. Rahetep had committed the barest essentials to the scroll, its main purpose being its identifying seal; without it, Tasar would be deemed an imposter. The important message would have gone to waste; as would have his life. Badar chuckled. The correct parameters were established. This young priest had indeed been sent by Rahetep.

Tasar elaborated on the message and Badar's interest grew into rare agitation. The news was momentous, and he wished Ramose had not gone off in such haste. He must have missed the messenger by mere minutes. Badar was tempted to go to the palace himself. As his sudden appearance would have caused immediate and unnecessary speculation, he reined in his impatience. Should he send Wazenz? He decided against it. The rotund man was much too slow.

Badar read Rahetep's glowing recommendation of the young priest and looked more closely at Tasar. If he showed the temple seal of Ptah to the guards they would allow him quick passage to look for Ramose.

"Tasar, the High Priest went to the palace to confer with the King. You must go and find him. Here, take this seal and show it to the guards. Tell only Ramose what you have told me. No one else." In a whisper, Badar added, "Not even the King."

Tasar's eyes widened with incredulity.

The old man smiled reassuringly. "The High Priest will do that. And, Tasar, ask for a new kilt and sash on your way out. Ramose is fastidious." *And somewhat vain,* Badar smiled to himself.

Tasar surmised that the tall man he saw earlier was the High Priest Ramose. What an opportunistic day. Meeting Ramose one-on-one with an important message would bear significantly on his future. He planned to make the most of it.

* * *

Chapter Six

When I am queen, I shall appease *Nekhbet* by having your limbs fed to her vultures, you issue of an unworthy concubine!"

The vituperative outburst of the adolescent Princess against her slightly younger half-brother Dubar shocked Ramose.

"And when I am king ..." The young voices trailed off.

Ramose sank onto one of the many stone rests along the hedge-bordered garden path. Over the past seasons, his duties as High Priest of Ptah had become increasingly demanding. He was tired. Mentally blocking out the heat of the day he settled into a semi-trance.

*

The Venerable Badar was the true architect of the early dynastic priesthood. The middle son of a little important nomarch from Badari, young Abou al-Badari was conscripted into King Narmer's military forces. Rather than mindlessly wielding a battle ax, the youngster became interested in the new sciences emerging from the priesthood where he could learn about curing the sick, the preservation of cadavers, and the mysteries of hypnosis. With foresight and planning, young Abou joined the priest-surgeons of the Badari garrison as a healer-apprentice, thus absolving himself of his military duties. He took the name of Badar.

High cliffs border the Hapi across from Badari and one day, some settlers poked through the many caves where they stumbled upon a bundle of woven mats. Brittle to the touch, the corners gnawed away by rodents, apparent great age and dust had stiffened them so that they could not be unrolled. With little interest in the unusable discovery, the settlers might have left the weavings in the dark cave when out of one of the tight rolls tumbled a fist-sized stone. Translucent with symmetrical proportions, it shone brilliantly in the sun.

The superstitious men took their find to Badari and asked the garrison's resident healer-priest for an explanation of this strange stone. The busy surgeon-priest asked young Badar to placate the primitive river dwellers with sacred murmurings and some beer.

Once, when Badar transported surplus bodies to the mass graves at Abdju, he had listened to an old *Ka*-priest who spoke of a far-away honeyed land that floated on an endless sea until an ancient god caused a horrific cataclysm. As their island sank below the waves, those who had saved themselves onto huge floats reached land and fled into another endless sea; one of grasses, divided by a great river. The old man called it the Sahari. Remembering the legend, Badar sensed a connection between the stricken island nation and the fifty tattered mats, as well as the translucent stone.

The young apprentice-priest soaked the brittle mats until he could unroll them. They were woven from different-colored grasses; small light and dark squares arranged in innumerable rows. Light, light. Dark, light, dark. Dark, dark, light. This had to mean more than counting *kirs* of grain filling a royal silo. He was certain that each row, or grouping, represented something. A particular sound perhaps? Time had blended the subtle hues almost into each other and it was difficult to see where one square ended and the other began. Badar suspected a form of communication. He stared many hours at the squares hoping somehow to break through the ancient code. No matter how he strained his eyes and foraged in the corners of his mind, the riddle eluded him.

Not easily discouraged, Badar placed the puzzling mats into a large wooden box and took leave from his garrison temple. He journeyed upriver to Nekhen where he prevailed upon the Chief Priest of the Temple of Horus to assign him as the Guardian of the Ancient Mats. He was convinced that they were the key to his rise within the priesthood little realizing that they would become his magic wand.

Badar chose ten of his new temple's youngest sharp-eyed acolytes whose task it was to copy the squares from the mats onto papyri. It was excruciating work. After a few hours in

41

the diffused light of the working chamber, the faint marks would flow into each other. By the time papyrus copies of all fifty mats were drawn up, the ten boys had grown into young men.

Badar was named the Envoy of the Temple and as such he was permitted to approach Narmer, the first Horus-King, who took great liking to the intelligent priest and appointed him as the Two Land's first High Priest. This elevated the new priestly sect into unprecedented heights at the court of Nekhen. Though it carried a price. The priesthood's vast knowledge was to be disseminated among the nobles, their children and children's children. Badar obeyed reminding his priests not to be too zealous in their tutoring. He set up training programs for the royal army, its lay-healers receiving good instructions in the use of special salves and potions and how to set simple breaks. He never, however, taught the army physicians proficiency in leading their patients into deep trances. Hence, only priest-surgeons performed serious operations with any measure of success using this method.

Badar also established the Great Library of Nekhen and, near the Sacred Lake, built the House of Life to contain the Ancient Mats.

*

After King Narmer's new *City of White Walls* was completed in the north, he and Queen Neith-hotep moved the royal court to Ineb-hedj.

Badar followed his king and built a great temple to Ptah, Creator God of All. He became the High Priest of Ptah. His priests were feared as magicians, revered as interceders with the gods, being more than a little hated by those whose powers they usurped. By then, having gained great respect as healers the priests were a force onto themselves. The High Priest was elevated beyond the reach of the judges of the *Kenbet.*

When Aha succeeded Narmer as King of the Two Lands he, too, moved his court to Ineb-hedj. While Aha was not half the man Narmer had been, Badar served him tirelessly, if not mindlessly.

*

As Badar reached the pinnacle of his calling in Ineb-hedj, an exuberant young prince from Nekhen's second important house was called upon to absolve his obligatory military service. Prince Rama's family connections kept him away from active battle duty and when Aha became King, Rama was permitted to accompany the new court to Ineb-hedj. Because of his quick wit, his placating demeanor and his flawless retention of complicated messages, he spent several years as intermediary between nome administrators and the King. Only those of princely birth as well as the Vizier and the Grand General were allowed to approach the Horus-King directly. This was the young opportunist's perfect chance. His responsibilities expanded from interpretation of petitions to more tenuous duties of confidant and advisor to the King. The two men developed a closeness that could have been regarded as friendship though it could only grow as close as the teachings of *Ma'at* prescribed.

The young prince was fascinated by Badar's extensive knowledge and he contrived to meet with the High Priest on a regular basis. Badar became his tutor and, more importantly, his mentor. It was only a matter of time before Rama felt compelled to enter the priesthood where he took the name of Ramose. It suggested strength, wisdom, and solidarity, all of which were to become synonymous with him. Training under Badar at the Temple of Ptah, Ramose achieved highest proficiency in healing and embalming, in mathematics, astronomy, and metallurgy.

Second cousin to Aha's child-bride Mayet, Ramose was a frequent visitor at the palace where he humored the homesick young queen. As his charm made her forget the musty palace, her longing for Nekhen, and her insensitive husband, she naturally fell under Ramose's spell. Her tears flowed freely when she learned that Ramose asked to be sent back to the Temple of Horus in Nekhen.

There, he insisted, a well-established library afforded him more extensive training. After seven months there, he excelled in logic and the military sciences, and his preeminence in mathematics equaled that in astronomy. He became proficient in the practice of deep trances. He also studied the Ancient Mats. Knowledge was his elixir; learning his vehicle for his lofty goal to be the next High Priest of Ptah.

Only during the idle hours of the night, when loneliness

stole into his heart and his young body fed on dreams of bygone caresses, did Ramose wonder if this was his true calling or did he merely seek refuge in the service of the gods. Solitary in nature, others sensed a great age about him. As if he came from an eon long lost in the desert sands.

One day, a courier arrived in Nekhen for Ramose with word from Queen Mayet. She feared for her life, she wrote in a secret note. Also, she was soon to have a child. She implored him to return to Ineb-hedj.

Ramose, having left the northern capital a mere eight moons before, returned to the city of White Walls within twenty days. Upon his arrival, Badar took him aside and warned him against disquieting rumors that shamelessly assaulted the Queen's fidelity. Ramose was advised to stay aloof, to disengage himself from his blood-relation with Mayet.

It was the only time Ramose acted against Badar's counsel. He stood by his royal cousin and solemnly promised to protect her unborn child. A heavy responsibility for one so young, not completely above the King's suspicions himself.

*

Ramose sighed and adjusted his tall lean body to the hard stone under him. His thoughts again reached into the past to the fateful day of Princess Nefret's birth a little over fifteen years ago. He had been at Queen Mayet's side for several days when the semi-conscious woman implored him to protect her unborn child. The Queen grew weaker, and both lives seemed lost. Too much pain endured, too much blood lost. Amma diagnosed the child's position as unfavorable.

*

Amma was Mayet's wet-nurse from the day Mayet was born into a major noble house in Nekhen. Barely sixteen herself, the slave Amma had just given birth to a healthy son and her milk flowed amply enough for her son Khentika, and for the infant Mayet who—at the age of seventeen—was to become Aha's Queen. Forced to move to Ineb-hedj with her new husband, the young Queen granted Amma freedom and provided a small dowry; the slave accepted both. Still, Amma would not leave her beloved Mayet and begged to be taken along to Ineb-hedj with the court. Her heart, however, remained behind in Nekhen, as did the father of her son.

The priest Tuthmose, thirteen years older than Ramose, had served in the royal administration as well before joining the promising service of the gods. Now an important Chief Priest himself, he was supervising the completion of the new Temple of Horus at the First Royal Mooring Place, barely a day's travel upriver from Ineb-hedj, where his son Khentika served as Chief of Altar.

*

On that tragic day of Queen Mayet's difficult labor, all hope for her survival vanished and Badar was sent for to begin the death rites. Instead of wailing and imploring Osiris to welcome their *Ka*, the imperturbable Badar ushered everyone except Ramose from the Queen's birthing chamber.

Badar spread the contents of a bulky length of linen next to the weakening Queen's bedstand. He lifted her head from its padded rest holding a slim vial to her feverish lips. Anxious moments passed. Mayet's head rolled back. She fell into deathlike slumber. Badar pulled the covers off her and with ground kohl, a cosmetic used to circle the eyes, he drew a cross onto her extended stomach. "Hand me her dagger," Badar whispered.

Ramose found and unsheathed the ornate dagger which only members of the royal family were allowed to carry. Its ivory handle was inlaid with deep blue lapis lazuli and red carnelian. Badar looked around and then dipped the double-edged copper blade into a jar containing a thick natron solution that had been readied to receive the child's royal placenta.

In speechless shock, Ramose witnessed a procedure that Badar had secretly perfected on deceased pregnant women after they were brought to the temple for their *Opening of the Mouth* ceremony. By dissecting their cadavers, Badar discovered that an unborn child could be lifted from the mother's abdomen provided the cuts were placed correctly, and not too deep. He reasoned that the procedure could also be applied to a living mother to save a child in a bad position. 'Now is the time to find out.' Ramose could still hear the fateful words. Why did it have to be his gentle Mayet? There had been no time to rile against fate. Badar extended long cuts across the abdomen and parting the wall of the uterus he reached into the womb. The sight of the lifeless child, wrapped in its protective membrane, awed them both. With a sigh, Badar lifted the whole thing out as its watery cradle burst. Bits of bloody afterbirth fell away.

As Badar severed the umbilical cord, he said quietly, "I am sorry for you, little one, for I am not able to save your Royal Placenta. May the gods, and may you, forgive me for this."

Acutely aware of such a foreboding omen, the two priests looked at each other across the lifeless Queen. Badar reached for the prepared placenta jar and sealed it tight with melted beeswax. Only he and Ramose would ever know that the beautiful container held nothing but its saline solution.

For the first time that day, Badar prayed to Ptah. He asked that the drug would not wear off before he finished the doubtful procedure. For once, he had not trusted trance to keep the Queen sedated and hurriedly wove the long cuts on her stomach back together.

Ramose, in the meantime, tried to swing life into the newborn child. When her tiny cry filled the birthing chamber it hung in the air as frail as a wisp of smoke. Was this to herald life? Or would its innocent *Ba* be called to the Netherworld all too soon? Ramose peered at the wizened face. He felt that an ancient soul, rather than a new one, lay in his arms.

The King paced outside the heavy curtain. Upon the weak sound from within, he was no longer able to contain his anxiety. Whatever suspicions he had harbored vanished. He rushed in.

"A daughter, my King," Ramose told him, tears of joy veiling his blue eyes. If she lived, she would inherit Aha's throne.

Momentarily forgotten in favor of her gift to the young dynasty, life ebbed back into the Queen. Ramose called for Amma and handed her the baby. While the nurse cleansed the frail newborn princess, she noticed a discoloration on the left upper thigh. The ragged patch, imperceptibly darker than the surrounding skin, startled the superstitious woman. She pointed at the offending mark. How could his gods allow this, her look demanded from Ramose. He shrugged and returned to his cousin's side.

"Keep her safe, Rama," the Queen whispered after the King and Badar left. She used the name she had known him by when they were young, and carefree; full of life—and love. "Keep this child safe. Promise me, on the life-giving breasts of Mut. Promise me that, Rama."

A great, longing pain stirred in the young priest's heart and he took her cold hands between his long warm fingers, "I shall love her like a daughter, Mayet," he promised.

"That you must." Her breath waned into nothing.

He drew closer and whispered his tearful oath. "I shall guard her with all that is sacred to me. In this life. And in the next. I solemnly promise you that, my heart, my *Ak-ieb*." He looked at the graceful amphora, its foreboding emptiness driving spears of premonition through his heart.

Despite the doting care from her servants and nurses, despite the strong love from Amma and Ramose, and despite the thin cries from the small basket, Mayet was not strong enough to triumph over the internal infection that set in. Osiris called to her exhausted spirit and her *Ba* followed the irresistible beckoning. The embalming process took seventy days after which Mayet's casket was placed aboard the Royal Bark to take her upriver to Abdju, as she had not wished to lie alone among the still unoccupied royal *Mastabas* at Saqqara.

*

With Aha's enemies forever ready to wrench his sixteen-year rule from him, he had to guard against all eventualities—even his death. His heirs still so young, he elevated the lowly Hent to his rightful consort forcing his nobles to recognize her as queen and co-regent with the Royal Heiress. Hent was, after all, the mother of his two young sons Dubar and Djer. Since neither of them was his first born child, succession to the throne would fall to Nefret, the royal daughter born to Queen Mayet.

Conceivably, Aha still harbored deep-seated resentment against his only daughter. Had not her birth wrenched his beloved queen from him? Worse perhaps, there had been vicious rumors of infidelity before Nefret's birth, the child reminding him of Mayet's alleged betrayal. He was never able to forget, nor forgive, his dead queen for such a bitter insult.

With the passing years, it became apparent that his second wife Hent and the daughter of his first queen hated each other. As did Nefret and Hent's son Dubar. It was the girl's fault, Aha insisted. She was such a willful, headstrong child.

*

Ramose surfaced from his bitter-sweet ruminations. The sun was still high; too little time had passed. The King would still be unavailable. With very little effort, Ramose slipped back into the past.

After Mayet's funeral, Badar announced that he would retire, and reasoned with the King that he wished to devote himself to documenting the collective teachings of the priesthood. Before he rendered his great power, the abdicating Badar guided the vacillating King toward the all-important decision to appoint Ramose as the new High Priest of Ptah.

Ramose still wondered if Badar came to his decision as a way to save his brilliant protégé from the King's suspicions. Instead of sending Ramose into hiding, the wise Badar thrust him into Aha's presence. The risky gamble paid off. Over time, Ramose was able to renew his tenuous friendship with his weakly monarch. Ramose had fulfilled his early promise. The future of the priesthood seemed assured.

Ramose and Badar still conferred on matters of life and death, on war and peace, and their calling. Ramose had become untouchable. Because of this he also became a monumental obstacle to the Vizier's designs on undisputed power which drove the ambitious magistrate to bitter enmity toward the High Priest of Ptah. Undeterred, Ebu al-Saqqara watched and waited for his chance. And Ramose was well aware of it.

*

A cooling breeze rustled through the leaves overhead. Ramose pulled himself from his nostalgic journey, once more concerned with the present.

Aha, already aging at thirty-five, was plagued by threats of war and, upon the Grand General's counsel, had divided his large but hitherto much too concentrated military force into four separate armies. Each was given the name of the particular god worshipped in the region it patrolled.

The *First Army of Sutekh* secured peace in the East and the Lower Delta. The *Second Army of Ra* guarded the tenuous peace in the Upper Delta near Ineb-hedj. The *Third Army of Ptah* patrolled the Central Region, whereas the *Fourth Army of Amun* was encamped near the Kharga Oasis.

All were under the command of Grand General Makari, a veteran of many successful campaigns.

The Army of Amun was being readied for confrontation. The eventual push into the southern lands of the aggressive Noba had to be swift. However, general alert could only be sounded by the Horus-King himself. Only he, as Supreme Commander, could lead his troops into battle. And therein lay the problem, Ramose mused. The King would have to travel to the oasis encampment. News of his arrival had to be carried to the army commander without interception or falsification of crucial words by enemy spies. Sailing upriver took a good eighteen to twenty days. A royal envoy was too recognizable if by nothing but undue haste—unless someone posed as an innocent traveler delivering the fateful message undetected.

Ramose's arm brushed an overhanging branch laden with figs. He plucked one and fondled its velvety ripeness. Pulling it apart, the fruit's pink inner juiciness was reminiscent of a woman's cleft. A smile played on his lips until he shook himself free of thoughts more suited to a strapping youth than a worry-burdened priest. As so often in the past, the pain of long-quelled suspicion pricked his heart. Had she not been a queen would she have lived? Or had Badar been commanded to let her die? By the gods? By his King? The laws of *Ma'at* were clear. In his early civilization justice was dealt out unforgivingly.

Ramose never intimated his recurring doubts about Mayet's death to Badar; certain confidences could be dangerous for either of them. Their closeness remained a delicate balance of knowledge and power, of trust and survival.

With a soft plop, the two fruit halves yielded to his ruminating pressure, spilling deep liquid onto the front of his white linen wrap. Splattered with the color of blood, Ramose struggled from his reverie.

* * *

Chapter Seven

An hour before Ramose enjoyed his moment's peace under the fig tree, a parched dust-covered courier had entered Ineb-hedj on an even more dust-caked donkey driven to exhaustion by its rider's determination to absolve himself of his pressing mission.

The journey had been long and dangerous, and the royal palace was a more than welcome sight to General Barum's secret envoy. Pase would have much preferred to have been carried down the river on a light falucca. The Fourth Army was encamped a three-day ride from Nekhen where he could have caught a boat if he had found a willing river captain. Instead, he had chosen the slower more dependable desert route and endured the endless bumping and chafing on the backs of slow-plodding asses, most of which had collapsed along the way. He had rested at a handful of small oases and acquired his fresh animals from friendly tribesmen, only to press on sparing neither himself nor any of the poor beasts forced to endure the dusty trek with him.

A few months earlier, the Archer Pase had traveled upriver from Ineb-hedj by barge, together with a contingent of the King's Palace Archers, ferrying new weaponry to the Fourth Army. Before that, they trained within the palace grounds and often provided a welcome diversion for court officials and their bored ladies, as well as their attentive slaves. Pase smiled thinking of the self-assured pretty girl who always accompanied the Royal Princess and her brother. His surreptitious glances had not been lost on the alert young woman.

By sheer luck, Prince Dubar's interest in one of their new bows provided a perfect chance for Pase and Safaga to get to know each other as he tried to teach the stiff-limbed prince to grip the heavy bow correctly.

Pase smiled through his cracked lips. Safaga's nightly admiration of his manliness lay deeply etched in his subconscience. He looked forward to holding her again. Perhaps tonight. If he could keep awake.

*

Vizier Ebu al-Saqqara was also the kingdom's premier magistrate, Chief Justice of the *Kenbet*, and Regent in the King's absence from the capital; as he would be in the event of Aha's death. Amply occupied with administrative and judicial matters, Ebu al-Saqqara additionally served as Quartermaster of the Royal Armies, and his hordes of scribes enforced the unpopular levy of new taxes throughout the united nomes.

The increasingly short-tempered Vizier had been buried in papyri to tally up the royal wealth disgorged from fertile lands along the Hapi. Innumerable trunks crammed full with royal accounts lined his musty working chambers. Many stood open for easy access to their contents, their heavy lids leaning against thick mud-brick walls. Most of the unadorned trunks contained neatly stacked papyri attesting to the riches of King Aha. Every force-fed pig, every fattened hyena and crane, every head of cattle was listed, as were goats and ducks, and the farmers' children.

Saad, Ebu al-Saqqara's Chief Scribe, interrupted the important man's impatient thoughts. "My Lord, forgive the intrusion. I had hoped to find the Grand General with you. Or Colonel Khayn."

"It should be quite obvious that I am alone," al-Saqqara snapped. He had removed his conical headdress but still wore the long shirt customary for a high official although he would have much preferred a shorter waistwrap in this heat. He wondered why his usually astute Head Scribe was looking for the two high-ranking officials. "Saad, what's so urgent?"

"A messenger, my Lord. From General Barum. He insists that he see the Grand General at once."

"From Old Barum, eh? Well, what are you waiting for? Bring the man before me."

"His message is for the Grand General alone, my Lord. The messenger insists upon it," Saad replied calmly.

"Saad! One day, I swear, I shall feed you to the vultures! Either this message is urgent, or is it not! Either I am the Quartermaster of the Royal Armies, or I am not!" Al-Saqqara stretched himself taller. "If Makari and Khayn choose not to work like the rest of us, their important messages have to be taken care of by those who are. Get the man in here! Now!" A bluish vein on al-Saqqara's forehead welled up like an angry cobra. Saad knew better than to oppose his Vizier further and hastened to fetch the new arrival.

Despite mounting anticipation, al-Saqqara rolled up his three papyri with deliberate slowness. He gently replaced the inked reed in its holder. A bureaucrat by nature as well as by calling, he treated the tools of his profession with care.

Saad reappeared and the dust-covered man behind him stopped in surprise when he recognized the Vizier. Near collapse, Pase clutched the leather holder tighter.

"I am the Royal Archer Pase, Great Vizier. I am honored to be in your presence. Forgive me, my Lord, my message is for the Grand General alone," he rasped and tried to steady himself.

Al-Saqqara smiled thinly. "The Grand General is absent from court. So, naturally, I shall take care of this. However, your conscientiousness will be remembered, Archer."

Pase reluctantly handed over the container to al-Saqqara who examined the seal. When his look met the courier's weary gaze, Pase lowered his stiff waistwrap. The burn had not healed well. Dust, sweat, and constant movement had caused it to become inflamed. Green-yellowish pus oozed from beneath the thin scab.

Upon a signal from the Vizier, Saad stepped forward and took the container. He peered at Pase and then back at the seal comparing it against the angry branding on the archer's skin.

"They are the same, my Lord," he said at last and handed the container back to his master.

Al-Saqqara seated himself and motioned to the swaying archer to do the same. "So, you are from the Fourth? How serious is the situation in the south?"

Pase sank onto the proffered chair and stretched his legs before him. Having clung to the rounded bellies of a succession of stubborn, flea-ridden jackasses for the past seventeen days, he feared he might never walk with straight legs again.

"It is serious, my Lord. General Barum needs weapons and reinforcements. Fast. The Noba are marching north, combining forces with the Kush and the Wawat."

The Vizier reexamined the seal. It appeared undisturbed. After barely a moment's hesitation, he broke it and shook the scroll from the container, unrolling the coarse papyrus. Glancing over the first few lines he instantly interpreted the portent words. There was no mistaking the implications. He listened to the tired messenger whose report was extensive and precise. Satisfied, al-Saqqara grunted and, for the first time, looked closely at the courier. "What was your name again?"

"Pase, my Lord. I am the Royal Archer Pase and..." The words trailed off, and al-Saqqara realized that the exhausted man was close to losing consciousness.

"Saad!" al-Saqqara shouted. "Ah, there you are," he added more subdued when he realized how close Saad had stood all along. "Give this man drink and food. Tend to him yourself. His presence is not to be divulged to anyone for now." For an instant, he lost himself in thought. Reaching a decision, he turned to the messenger, "Get some rest. I will need you later."

Clearly being dismissed, the young courier remained in his chair, unable to move. Saad proffered his arm. With great effort, Pase pulled himself up and, with equally great effort, bowed to the Vizier.

Steadied by the Head Scribe, Pase left with the uneasy feeling of somehow having failed in his mission after all.

*

Al-Saqqara rubbed his hands together. "I must seek an audience with Aha at once," he whispered to himself.

He was to be the very first to bring an overwhelmingly important message to the King. He pressed his head-dress back onto his shaven skull and rushed from his chambers. Choosing a small side path instead of the official gravel road, he reached the veranda off the Grand Foyer without being observed by the guards. A private audience with the King this late in the afternoon had to go unnoticed lest it arouse the curiosity of those who had no need to know.

*

King Aha reclined on his four-legged day-bed. It resembled an ordinary sleeping platform except for the missing headrest. Approaching his thirty-fifth year, he already tired easily with the draining heat adding little to improve his temper. This afternoon, he had spent a pleasant hour with one of Hent's willing maidens and his vigor was much restored. Despite these pleasant interludes, Aha did not easily tolerate interruptions prior to his evening meal. When his Steward transmitted such sense of urgency regarding the Vizier's request for immediate audience Aha was left with little choice but to admit the annoying official whose appearance usually spelled bad news. Aha did not particularly like nor altogether trust his Vizier.

"My great illustrious and godly King," Ebu al-Saqqara bowed deeply. "Only moments ago, I received a messenger from the Fourth." Al-Saqqara savored every word.

"A messenger from Barum? Well then, where is the man?" The King propped himself up, his interest aroused.

The ugly man gloated, "He is practically dead from exhaustion. However, he told me everything in detail before he collapsed." Ebu al-Saqqara's explanation as to why he had not brought the messenger with him came easy. How could he have brought the man? Or the scroll? Both made it evident that Barum's message was intended for the Grand General. No one else. Al-Saqqara was not about to squander his big chance to cull favors with the King.

"I can repeat every word of Barum's message, Great Hor-Aha."

"Then do so. No! Wait," Aha added suddenly. "Ramose should hear this as well. My Steward said he was in my ante-chamber just a while ago." Aha motioned to the attentive Steward and al-Saqqara's stomach twisted in silent fury. Could this feeble-brained monarch do nothing without that confounded charlatan? He would have only a moment longer with Aha.

"Great Hor-Aha." The spiteful man sank to his knees, desperate to be heard. "They found a vein of yellow nub, lots of it. They are arming mercenaries. The King of Nobatia, pushing north, toward our army. Barum wants to conquer ... a new mine for the Two Lands. You have to be there." Stale breath belched in belabored gasps. The words tumbled over themselves. Aha grasped the gist of his Vizier's garbled outburst. He sat up and sharply fixed his prostrate magistrate with an exasperate stare. "By Horus, Vizier, get up! And find Ramose. Wait! Best get Makari, too. I shall meet with the three of you in my study chamber. Have Beir inform me as soon as you are assembled."

Al-Saqqara frantically searched his mind for a way to gain favor before he would have to justify his breach of protocol against Makari. Before he could stop himself, he sputtered, "A word on another subject, my King."

"When the others are here, Vizier!"

"No, Great Aha. I couldn't. Much too delicate. Very private."

"Then make it brief," Aha waived his hand as if to rid himself of a pesky fly.

"I....eh, I thought perhaps that, eh..., for a long time, now..."

"Oh, out with it, al-Saqqara," Aha grunted.

Al-Saqqara wished that the insane thought had not jumped into his mind. It was madness. The thought of it was revolting. Yet, there were advantages to be gained, and great power. He could deal with the stubborn girl.

"As you know, Nefret is coming of age, and ..."

"Don't drivel. Of course, I know that my daughter is coming of age," Aha roared, increasingly annoyed by the ugly man's unpleasant presence.

Determined to force the King to listen to him, al-Saqqara stretched himself as high as he could. He filled his meek chest with noisy gulps of air and blurted, "Nefret and I! She and I should marry." If anything, he expected bemusement from Aha as the King never took much heed of his first child's apparent fate. He had never thought Aha capable of such speed, such vehemence and, above all, such outrage. What fatherly feelings had he suddenly stirred awake? Al-Saqqara bit his tongue. Fool, he raged against himself. Fool! Fool!

Aha rolled off his daybed. His kilt caught and was half ripped from his thick hips. It was the only thing that prevented him from wringing the Vizier's scrawny neck as he needed both hands to hold onto his unraveling wrap or risk standing naked before the presumptuous upstart.

"Have you gone mad! By Horus, you are older than I am and haven't produced even one bastard to prove you are a man!" Al-Saqqara realized that Aha's rage was not generated by his suggestion as Vizier. After all, he was also Regent and as such a most suitable match for a royal heiress. No, Aha's rage came straight at him, al-Saqqara, the son of a lowly father. At last, the King exposed his true feelings toward him. That is unwise of you, my feeble king, al-Saqqara seethed. He forced himself to control his own outrage, resigned to grovel and to turn the unfortunate moment around. You fool, he cursed himself again.

"Forgive me for offending you, Great King." He sank to his knees and placed his head on the floor, hating Aha with every heartbeat. "So rarely are we alone to talk freely, man to man. I imagined that such a union might strengthen your Horus-throne. No outsiders to seize power through our lovely Heiress."

Aha realized that it was unwise to expose his intense dislike for the groveling man. True, he had not overseen Nefret's upbringing as much as he should have. She could be fiercely annoying, and never acted pleasantly toward Hent. But this caricature of a man he would not wish on any woman. Least of all Mayet's beautiful child. Ah, Mayet, if only you had loved me.

"Get up!" he commanded as he turned away in disgust.

Al-Saqqara scrambled to his feet vowing to deal with Nefret when the time was ripe. He thought of Prince Dubar. His thick lips stretched over his pointed teeth. White flecks of spittle seeped from the corners of his mouth. Yes, the time would be ripe soon.

"Forgive me, Aha. Nefret has grown into such a beauty. Right before our eyes."

He inhaled with that annoying gurgling sound Aha detested, whining on, "Can you fault a discerning bachelor to spy the lotus blossom among the reeds?"

Aha forced himself to calm down and responded, "This is perhaps not a good time to discuss my daughter's future, Vizier. Not with the news you just brought. Let's leave it for later. Barum's message is too urgent. And, al-Saqqara," he hated to sound grateful. "Thank you for bringing this to my attention. It was wise of you."

He could not wait to rid himself of the annoying official and hoped that he had squelched the preposterous man's hopes for a royal union. He would have to talk to Ramose about this, and let him deal with it.

*

"Find the High Priest!"
"Find the Grand General!"
The royal commands reverberated throughout the palace grounds.

*

Grand General Makari, the King's Chancellor and second-highest magistrate after the Vizier, was a military genius. During times of war, by royal decree, he became his king's Premier Minister. A proud veteran of many successful campaigns, he held himself upright for his fifty-five years. It was not that he so much towered over other men rather that his squareness obliterated them. His face ended in a square chin and his like-shaped head was embedded on broad shoulders. The angular impression was broken only by thick brows that practically circled his black eyes. The nose was prominent and started high between those brows. The trend of wideness again emerged in his torso, and his hands with hard fingers could grip painfully.

Not all of the strong man's victories were achieved by force. Makari was also an enthusiastic husbandman, and many an animal had been tamed by his cajoling and infinite patience. Lady Beeba, his wife of many years, had been won over by true love.

Makari was born into a well-established family of traders and his mother had been a talented woman who hammered sheets of yellow nub into intricate neckwear. Since she had accompanied her husband on extended trading forays into foreign lands, young Makari was raised among the large brood of an uncle who managed a prosperous oasis farm west of Ineb-hedj.

The youngest daughter of the proprietor visited the farm oasis often where Makari showed her the animals he had domesticated. Soon, the pretty Beeba shared the youth's interest in experimental breeds. Encouraged by love and driven by ambition, Makari's aspirations soon extended beyond his uncle's farm. He sought out the priesthood for his training and concentrated on military strategy. Excelling in his studies, he won the approval of young Lady Beeba's family.

Makari's advance through the military ranks was rapid and he fought many battles. During a successful campaign on the small eastern peninsula, he was severely wounded in one leg. A slight limp would remain with him for life.

After his marriage to Lady Beeba, they took over his by now deceased uncle's farm, a three-hour donkey ride from Ineb-hedj, while maintaining their home in the capital where they often had to entertain nobles in the river-side villa.

A most capable woman, Beeba ran the two large households like well-supplied army camps, a trait not lost on her proud husband.

Makari quartered a battalion of loyal warriors on the farm. None had families, and all were of extremely small build.

Vast rush fences were erected to shield a training ground, and guards were placed all around the oasis garrison. Makari had raised and cross-bred an astonishing herd producing an animal that could carry a grown, albeit lithe, man and attain incredible bursts of speed while traversing the sand easily on two-toed muscular legs. Despite his excitement over his success, Makari had not reported his experiments to the King, nor the Vizier, nor the High Priest. His *Special Forces* were Makari's secret.

His garrison's official duty was to guard an old mysterious structure. Near it, a small temple housed a contingent of dedicated priests living in virtual isolation. Upon the bidding of the High Priest they tunneled underneath the enormous monument which reached many cubits into the azure sky. No one knew when the colossus had been carved, or who wrested the human features from the bedrock. Despite its body of a fierce lion a kind of peace exuded from the *Guardian of the Desert* as it faced the rising sun.

*

Makari and his Aide-de-camp, Colonel Khayn, were returning to their working chambers from the Grand General's villa. The luncheon meeting with General Sekesh of the Second Army had lasted two hours, and Makari was pleased with its outcome. After their meeting, the younger general left for Makari's oasis to attend a War Council meeting, while Makari and Khayn planned to follow the next day.

"Grand General Makari..." The cry had reached the Chancellor long before he saw the caller. "Grand General, my Lord, you are needed at the palace." The muscular young guard skidded to a halt on the path's loose pebbles, glad that at least this venerated warrior did not have to be roused from an afternoon repose. Breathing hard he thought of the bad tempers he often had to endure summoning the King's various sleepy ministers.

"What's the trouble, soldier? Is your squad not able to guard the King so that you now call for an old man?"

The young guard turned crimson. Perhaps his words were not precise enough. Find Makari! That's what they had said; well, he had found 'Old Silver-Tongue' and told him he was needed. He shifted from one foot to the other.

"All right, soldier. The King sent for me?" Thankful nodding assured Makari of this, and he continued, "For me alone? Do you know?"

"We are to find the High Priest as well."

"How about the Vizier?"

"He is already in the King's study chamber."

"Ah, well. Run along now." Makari saw the young man hesitate and waived him on again. "I assure you, I can find my way. As long as I can remember where I left my scull-cap."

In the heat of the afternoon, Makari had removed his cap. He detested the tight headdress. Made of leather, it fitted his square head too snugly, the wide flaps covering his ears and neck with the top part ringed by a glittering band of yellow nub. It was the only outward sign attesting to Makari's high military rank. The King's summons, he thought, might be as good as any opportunity to divulge his secret. He knew he would have their undivided attention. What he needed was their unanimous approval. So he had better be prepared to present an irrefutable argument for keeping his secret this long.

Exuding calm despite his fastened pace, Makari arrived within minutes in the King's study chamber.

* * *

Chapter Eight

Oh, let's ask Ramose!" Out of breath, the royal siblings emerged from a thicket and headed toward the High Priest. Of the two, Ramose favored the Princess, and always tried to give her guidance and freedom alike; too frequently, Nefret ignored one and partook freely of the other.

Still too young, Nefret was yet to have her head and body hair shaved to wear the customary wig. Among the nobles, such practice was exercised as much as to distinguish them from the common people, as it was done for personal hygiene and freedom from body lice.

Ramose watched as they rushed toward him with the impatience of youth. Tall and slender, Nefret was quite different from her half-brother Dubar, and her fine features were accentuated by unusual blue eyes. They mirrored his own.

"Are you two alone? Where are your women, Nefret?"

"I am not a child who needs constant supervision, Ramose," Nefret replied vehemently. "Do I always have to be surrounded by my slaves? Anyway, I have no idea where they are. They must have left while I took my boring noon-time rest. When I awoke, I went looking for them but only found Dubar in the garden. He always runs around alone!"

"That's because I am a man," Dubar challenged only to have his leg kicked by his sister.

"I swear, one of these days, I'll get you good," he howled.

Ramose sighed. His adolescent Princess still acted more like a tempestuous child than the Royal Heiress. She had not yet been reined in enough by life at court, by her slaves, by her priestly teachers. Nor, alas, by himself. Her budding forms belied the youngness of her spirit. For no apparent reason, Ramose remembered the unusual mark on her left thigh and wondered if it had grown darker with the years. He was also concerned by Nefret's childish delight to cause a scene. She could hurt her slaves with no remorse. After her initiation ceremony into her official court life—during the King's Jubilee—would she mature into her prescribed role, or would she lack compassion and sensitivity? A fruit that ripens too quickly will rot from within. Ramose shook his head.

"What happened to you?" Dubar stared at the High Priest's stained kilt, not so much in shock, as with glee. A few months younger than his half-sister, Dubar's stocky frame was supported by bowed legs, and his head seemed to grow straight from his shoulders. Already, he was tending toward fleshiness. The youngster shook his princely lock which stuck from the left side of his head in defiance of his slave's combing. Except for it, Dubar was clean shaven, and soon, his sidelock of youth would fall prey to a priest's sharp knife during his manhood rites; as would his prepuce. The special day of losing his foreskin was not far off. It worried the youngster whose countenance was intensely dark; his eyes as black as his stubborn hair.

Too taciturn for one so young and he lacks royal bearing, Ramose thought. No wonder, with his graceless, thick-limbed mother whose race was darker, built more compactly than the refined southerners from the Upper Regions.

The Lady Hent was first chosen by King Aha as a minor wife when his first queen Mayet was still alive. While bigamy was not forbidden, it was nevertheless unusual. The King's second marriage brought assurance of renewed loyalty from her native Delta nomes. By taking up residence in Ineb-hedj, having abandoned his preferred domicile in Nekhen, Aha proclaimed his strong commitment to the Delta regions.

"I squeezed a ripe fig too hard ..." Ramose smiled.

He was patient with his King's second-born, despite the prince's sad lack of protocol. The boy was not important. Yet.

A ripe fig; a ripening maiden. That was it! The girl could be the unsuspecting, and unsuspected, courier to the Fourth Army in the Kharga. The proximity of the army camp to the great Temple of Horus in Nekhen would serve a deception well. Coded messages could be divided to be carried by different trusted members of royal entourage. A cleansing rite at the Temple of Horus prior to Nefret's court initiation was a perfect reason for the long journey. Ramose smiled, amazing himself by the word-association games his agile mind often played, though this plan had taken a rather circuitous route.

"What's so funny," Nefret demanded. Still annoyed about her never-ending squabbles with Dubar, she could not yet manage a politer tone toward her adored High Priest. He meant more to her than anyone. More than her aloof father. More than her beloved Amma. Certainly more than the three slaves she regarded as friends even though she kicked them on occasion.

"I was just thinking of your future, my child."

"I am not 'your child'." She stomped her foot to hide her apprehension that her carefree days were soon to change into the stylized rituals of the royal court. Most likely, she would be forced into a marriage with the unsavory son of some useful noble.

"No, of course not, Princess. Please, forgive me. Which is why we must prepare you to behave like a lady," Ramose soothed.

"Like a queen!" Nefret stretched herself above her shorter brother and shot the youth a haughty sideways glance.

"Quite so. Hence, I have decided to ... Nefret! Are you listening!" Ramose's firm retort was not a question. His rare reprimand carried a cutting edge although his sharp words did not penetrate past Nefret's sudden new interest.

*

The young man approached them in haste. He wore a simple knee-length waistwrap and a sash across his torso marking him as a priest. He was in such a hurry that his papyrus sandals caused the gravel to shift noisily as if the pebbles protested their displacement on the wide path. Ramose had not seen this particular priest at the temple and wondered who he might be.

Nefret stared openly at the handsome stranger.

Ramose saw it with alarm. Was the child turning into a woman before his very eyes? Unconsciously, perhaps, she was signaling her budding womanhood to the young man. Ramose decided to prepare her for the journey as soon as possible.

Every noon, the sun was closer to its zenith. In a few weeks, the helical rising of Sothis, the Dog Star, would signal the beginning of the New Year, bringing with it the annual inundation of the river—*Akhet*, the most anticipated of their three seasons. It would take nimble temple faluccas close to twenty days to sail upriver. At certain places, the lateen-rigged boats had to be paddled if the northerlies were too weak. Still, it was easier than a hot trek through the desert, chafing atop a sweaty donkey. Allowing for a week's preparation, departure could be soon, just in time for Hapi to be navigable again, its current not yet too torrent to impede their progress upriver.

Once in Nekhen, they could await *Peret*, the season when the land reemerged from the flood, and celebrate the *Festival of Opet*, before heading back down on the flooded river. Then, during *Shomu*, with the water at its shallowest, they would be back in Ineb-hedj where Nefret was to be initiated into court during the *Sed*-festival.

It was a good plan. To convince the King of its viability was not the problem. To persuade the headstrong Princess that her cleansing rites were to be performed in Nekhen would be more difficult. Ramose decided to confide in Amma, Nefret's trusted nurse since birth, as well as in Safaga, Nefret's intelligent older slave and companion since early childhood.

*

Ramose recalled when he first saw the Sumerian slave. A dusty trade caravan from the north had pulled into Ineb-hedj. Their beasts of burden were laden with much sought-after sycamore lumber which his tree-less country required for building and for the manufacture of furniture as well as boats.

This particular group of traders, however, offered another commodity—slaves, captured in the skirmishes between the tribes of Babylonia and Persia. They were brought to the great city of Damascus where the caravans traded them for metals and precious stones.

Among their human cargo was a young girl. Ramose judged her to be about eight. She must have spent most of her young life among the caravans. To have survived this far she had to be of sturdy stock. Her eyes were bright, her reactions quick, and she held herself straight and proud in her dirty rags.

Ramose continued to wander around the marketplace in search of the rare royal-blue lapis lazuli. He was also on the lookout for the red carnelian to be fashioned into seals, to attest to a document's authenticity. He remembered how, on impulse, he turned to the bearded slave-trader and asked the girl's worth. She was too young to fetch a good price as a workslave and the sly trader saw his chance to unload his young burden on an eager priest. A knowing wink left nothing to the imagination. If the godly man was looking for inspiration in what better form to find it than in a young girl. Although, in the trader's experience, those who served the gods most often preferred boys.

"This one is Sumerian," the Syrian pointed out. Accompanied by vigorous nodding of the grizzled head, it was meant to increase the girl's value. No one knew of the true origin of her ancestors who were thought to have come from the mountains of the northeastern highlands, far beyond the realms of Babylonia. Settling with the old Uruks into the great two-river valley, they grew into a sturdy intelligent race. Isolated, their language bore no affinities with any other.

Ramose glanced again at the young slave and settled on a generous price. With the wide-eyed girl in tow, he left the rancid trader to his insidious suppositions.

"Ramose," he pointed to himself and repeated his name several times.

"Ramose," the girl repeated and poked him in the stomach. She turned her outstretched finger toward herself and said several words he did not understand.

"Safaga," she said with emphasis.

Safaga. Like the settlement on the Crystal Sea. Her acquisition, followed by good training, had a purpose. She would do nicely to keep a three-year old company. It would also be useful to have another friendly pair of eyes and ears in the palace and with careful tutoring she would be a vital link to the palace's rampant rumors before they became general knowledge. Ramose smiled down at her.

When the unlikely pair passed the high-walled palace entrance, the girl's eyes brightened with delight. She had traveled far, with many caravans. She saw much and stopped at many places. Along the way, she was made to serve the traders, some of whom had shown more interest in her than her young manual labor could provide. This man's interest was promising. At least he did not reek and seemed of a kindly disposition. She tugged at his arm. He returned her silent question with a reassuring smile.

In the Grand Foyer, Ramose hailed a passing slave and asked him to call the Royal Head Nurse. The ample woman appeared quickly and, after one look at the grubby girl, whisked the barefooted waif away. Looking back over her shoulder she smiled at the High Priest, "We shall be back as soon as I have cleaned her up. Then you can tell me about her. I shall have refreshments brought for you."

The marketplace always parched his throat and Ramose nodded thankfully. He moved to an alcove where he settled in to wait. A slave padded along on bare feet. He carried a hammered copper jug and a glittering drinking cup and poured him some refreshing pomegranate juice.

Ramose counted on Amma to acquaint the other women with Nefret's new companion. Mayet's former wet-nurse had transferred her loyalty without hesitation from the dead queen to her newborn daughter. Just as she had been in Nekhen, the old woman was a formidable force among the women-slaves in Ineb-hedj.

Safaga took to her small mistress at once. Under Amma's tutelage, she learned their language quickly. And she possessed a natural aptitude and grace. This endeared her to the other slaves and even won acceptance from the sour Hent.

Relieved of the bothersome royal toddler, Hent could now devote all her time to her own small son. Dubar, who just began to discover his walled surroundings and, in his insatiable curiosity, explored every nook and cranny, was forever reported missing and needed to be found. He had, of course, his own wet-nurse as Hent always feared for his safety, notably from the loyalists of Mayet's line who might gain access to the grounds.

Djer, the youngest prince, was not yet born, being seven years younger than his brother.

The Princess Nefret and the slave Safaga grew up together. Safaga became an ever-present attendant to the Princess. A close confidante and teacher in many things. Both had grown into dark beauties, with the slave's womanly forms more pronounced since she was five years older. Over the last year, Nefret grew taller than her slave who was now fittingly shorter than her royal mistress. Safaga must be just past twenty by now, Ramose mused.

There was another servant, Zeina, a year older than Nefret. With the girls still wearing their natural hair, cut shoulder-length, their resemblance was startling.

His thoughts of Nefret's women slaves reminded Ramose of his stained robe. More often than not clumsy Dokki, a *Black Noba* brought down the river years ago, spilled things during his lessons with the royal siblings when she was told to serve refreshments. The slave's hands would flutter in fear and her dark face would screw up in anticipation of an imagined flogging; instead the High Priest always gave her one of his rare smiles. In devoted gratitude, the well-developed nineteen year-old slave would do anything for him.

'Poor Dokki,' they called her. With her dark skin and thick lips, her share of the work seemed larger than anyone else's. At times, she thought herself excluded from the fun and hushed whisperings of the young group. Nefret often took her meals in the intimate privacy of her bed-chamber with her slave-attendants joining her. It was better than having to face her father's questioning looks, her pregnant step-mother's whining, and her two half-brothers' disgusting table manners.

While Safaga and Zeina arranged the eating stands and chairs in a circle, Dokki was cajoled into serving them. It fell to her to rush along the corridors to bring the simple meals from the communal kitchens while they were still hot.

When she was gone, the others giggled about her dim wit and her exasperating clumsiness. Once she returned, though, they made room for her and liked her for her good nature.

A carefree hour of chatting and laughing followed until Amma dispersed the giggling foursome with stern orders for Nefret to learn her lessons and for all to wash themselves and fold their clothes, and say their prayers to Ptah. They would giggle some more. It was believed that Amma was a fervent Osiris-cult worshipper. The ancient sect was rumored still to engage in cannibalism.

While such beliefs should have brought Amma in direct opposition with her worship of Ptah, no one could discern any conflict that the old nurse might have with her often loud and fervent prayers to the Creator God.

Slaves were important. They served their masters. They made life bearable during hot days. They knew how to sweeten a master's lonely night. Ramose, on the other hand, appreciated them for their knowledge of court gossip and the gauging of royal moods. Most had an instinct for intrigue and were useful carriers of secret messages to and from the palace. Dark, clumsy Dokki was safe as long as she continued to be true to herself, and loyal to him.

*

"Forgive the intrusion, High Priest of Ptah. The guards said that I might find you here."

"Who are you?"

"Priest Tasar. I just arrived from Nekhen with a message from my Chief Priest Rahetep for the Venerable Badar."

"The Divine Father of Ptah is not with me." Ramose raised his eyebrows.

"I already saw him, High Priest. He urged me to find you. It is a very important matter. And absolutely private. A subject for your ears only," Tasar replied with a meaningful glance at the two adolescents. The boy was half turned away with a sullen look. The girl was beautiful, and his cheeks warmed as he caught her appraising look.

Tasar was so thrilled to have met the High Priest that he rushed his words without thought to ceremony. He had anticipated his first meeting with the great man to be quite different. Having forgotten to bow, he quickly did so now. At the same time he noticed the High Priest's spotted waistwrap. Recalling Badar's comment about the High Priest's fastidiousness, his astonishment at the stained garment showed plainly on his face.

This one still has to learn to mask his reaction, Ramose thought amused. As well as his feelings. He observed the flush on Tasar's handsome face. Ignoring the shorter Dubar, Tasar's eyes had rested a bit too long on Nefret, Ramose thought.

With a brief bow in the direction of the two adolescents, Ramose drew Tasar far enough aside to keep them out of earshot. Over his shoulder, he apologized, "Excuse me for a moment. Important temple matters."

Tasar assumed the young pair to be the children of some

noble. Most likely, the High Priest was instructing them in the natural sciences. Tasar refocused his attention on Ramose and repeated Rahetep's important message choosing his words with clarity and precision. How fortunate that old Badar had not insisted that he rest up from his long journey or he would have missed this great opportunity to speak to the High Priest alone. Opportunities like these were rare and one had to be brought to the attention of the right people. Badar and Ramose were certainly more than 'right.' They were the answer to his secret offerings to the god of good fortune. His words had a greater impact on Ramose than Tasar could have imagined.

Ramose at once realized the implications of the message. Not only for his priesthood. But for the Two Lands. In uncustomary agitation, he took the young priest by the arm and led him back toward Nefret and Dubar who still watched, curious about the stranger's unannounced appearance.

Ramose had no time for explanations. He already visualized a different meeting with the King than he had originally planned. He nodded to Tasar, "Would you kindly escort these children back to the palace. I must see the King at once," and rushed off, his gait sprightly for one usually so temperate. In his excitement, he called the royal siblings *children*—which they still were to him—and overlooked to present Tasar to them.

Dubar seethed. Nobody took him seriously! If only, of late, his voice would not break into uncontrollable squeaks every time he opened his mouth. Then he could tell this stranger off properly. As it was, he managed to startle his throat into a loud croak, "I don't need a nursemaid!" His childish chin high, in emulation of his father's most defiant mood, the young prince vanished into the hedge leaving behind a tremble of leaves.

Because Dubar never fully faced Tasar, his princely lock was not revealed. It would have alerted the young priest to the sulking youth's royal standing.

* * *

Chapter Nine

Ramose strode through the empty palace vestibule just as Beir hurried toward him.

"Beir! I must see Hor-Aha at once!"

"It is now the King who calls for you, High Priest."

"Indeed?" Ramose said.

"He also summoned the Grand General. The Vizier is already here." Beir hesitated. "He must have had important news, for he came without bidding, in a greatly agitated state."

That man is like a hyena, Ramose thought. He smells blood from afar. Considering the fateful news Tasar just brought him, al-Saqqara could have received word through one of his own spies. It would explain why the King called a meeting after al-Saqqara spilled his early knowledge, obviously to cull favors. Ramose decided to be on his guard. Of course, he always was concerning al-Saqqara.

"Beir, look at this! I could use a new wrap. A fig."

"Most unfortunate," Beir nodded. He had already spotted the soiled garment and signaled to a slave. After he and Ramose traversed several chambers, he bid Ramose into an alcove. Moments later, he reappeared with a fresh kilt draped over his powerful arm and silently helped the High Priest to change into the shorter, more voluminous waistwrap. Ramose suspected it was one of the King's. Wisely, Beir had chosen a simple wrap. Not one of the newer pleated ones the King wore as of late, mostly to hide his expanding girth. He hoped the King would not notice the unauthorized loan of one of his garments as all of the god-king's possessions were sacred objects. Ramose straightened the ends of the ample waistband as Beir ushered him into Aha's spacious study chamber.

Several chairs were grouped around stands, and beautifully

inlaid trunks lined the glazed tile walls. Along one side, on a long table, alabaster vessels stood filled with juices and imported wines, and polished copper trays reflected the colors of fresh fruit heaped upon them. The inimitable Beir had anticipated this to be a lengthy meeting among the four most powerful men of the Two Lands.

An ornate sedan waited in a corner, ready to carry the King on a rare outing. Several white quilts and robes lay draped over a tall stand to shield their god-like owner from the elements and from the furtive glances of his subjects. A few of the robes were adorned with bright ribbons, a sign that the King was yielding to progress, no longer averse to add a little color to the traditional white of his clothing.

"Vizier, may *Safekht* look upon you," Ramose said. And curdle your avaricious ink, he added silently in a rare uncharitable mood. He purposely did not invoke the protection of *Ptah*. Instead, he commended his opponent to the favors of the God of Writing. Not *Toth*, the God of Writing *and* Learning! But to *Safekht* alone, thereby inferring that he deemed the Vizier a glorified scribe. And not a learned one at that.

Al-Saqqara swallowed hard. May the vultures pick your skull clean, he thought and his dour expression deepened. Aloud, he said, "I return your greeting in kind, High Priest." No bow accompanied his greeting which fled his tight lips only forcibly. Still, he could not suppress a triumphant gleam in his bulging eyes. At last, he had learned of a great importance before Aha's priestly lapdog had had the chance to snatch it from him.

He reeks of death, Ramose thought. No wonder. His father chose the family name from his native village, Saqqara, which had become the new necropolis for the rich and powerful of Ineb-hedj. It befitted this cadaverous official. Al-Saqqara was as thin as a reed. As he stood there he appeared of greater height than Ramose only because a conical headdress hugged his egg-shaped head perfectly but emphasized the large pointed ears as they fled outward from the weight pressed upon them. The hooked nose almost met the thick upper lip rimmed by a dark line. No matter how closely Ebu al-Saqqara's barber scraped the ugly face each morning, he never managed to eliminate the last traces of a heavy growth. Ebu al-Saqqara was not only extremely ugly, he looked positively malevolent.

The realization of such unfortunate features drove young Ebu into a permanently dour disposition. Already thirty-six, he still was not successful, or perhaps had never tried, to woo a willing maiden into being his wife and hostess and it was generally assumed that he spent his celibate passion in the pursuit of power.

'What is taking the old goat-farmer so long,' al-Saqqara seethed. He wished Makari arrived so that Aha would join them. Then he could astonish these two with his momentous news, just as he had startled the King earlier. Al-Saqqara anticipated well-earned recognition for his involvement and began to gloat again. His lips stretched exposing a row of surprisingly small, almost pointed teeth. A fleck of foamy spittle bubbled in one corner of his mouth.

"Makari! Where have you been all day? And what took you so long now! Don't tell me your useless stump held you back!" Accusingly, the Vizier rushed toward the entering Grand General, stopping abreast with the waiting High Priest.

Makari was taken aback by the Vizier's rude informality as well as the unwarranted reminder of his slight lameness. He exchanged an imperceptible glance with Ramose before he bowed in the direction of both men, not favoring either.

The door to the inner chambers swung wide open.

Beir sang out, "Hor-Aha, God-King of the Two Lands."

The three men bowed deeply.

"Hail, Hor-Aha."

"Hail, Supreme Commander."

"May Ptah smile upon you, and may Horus circle above you."

"Sit down, my friends," Aha sighed.

All, except Ramose, settled into a semi-circle.

Without further social preamble, Aha continued, "Al-Saqqara brought stupendous news which we need to discuss among ourselves. There are hard decisions to be made." He paused to reach for the gleaming cup handed to him by his Steward. Beir had filled it to the brim with sweet wine. After serving the others, the Royal Steward glanced at Aha and with unfailing instinct heeded his master's unspoken signal. Silently, he closed the heavy door behind him.

Al-Saqqara was the first to take a big gulp, swallowing his wine greedily, and then cleared his throat several times to gain attention. He had just opened his mouth when Ramose, who was not yet seated, lifted his arms high above his head as if he were facing his altar.

Eyes turning vacant, Ramose swayed. Seemingly in a trance, he intoned, "A vast cavern, laced with thick veins of yellow nub was discovered in Nobatia. The Noba are massing in war against us." He blinked and suddenly his blue eyes blazed down on his rapt audience, "The gods foretell that we shall be victorious."

His words stunned everyone into silence until al-Saqqara jumped up as if stung by a scorpion. He fairly splattered the remnants of his last mouthful of wine onto himself. His face had turned bright red.

Makari drew his breath in, surprised at the commotion, and his brows curled themselves into even higher circles over his steadfast eyes.

Aha fixed the High Priest with a sharp, questioning look, his ample chin jutting forward. "What you say is true. But how do *you* know about this, Priest?" he challenged.

"I read it in his thoughts." Ramose pointed at his ugly opponent. "It is written in his eyes." Not a trace of mockery tainted his words.

Makari smiled bemused. Leaning back in his chair, he was beginning to enjoy himself. Would the animosity between these two powerful adversaries erupt into open feud as they vied for the King's favor? He felt like the sole audience of a palace pantomime play.

'Seth's wrath upon the treacherous shaman! And upon Aha, too, the gullible old fool! Believing the driveling magic-maker can read things in my eyes!' Al-Saqqara's thoughts raged, bordering on treason. Ramose had just deprived him of his delectable surprise, his due recognition, his moment of triumph! The scheming baboon must have more hired spies than stolen emmer wheat filling his granaries. Perhaps, al-Saqqara suspected, they bribed the same spies. 'I shall have to question the messenger in depth.' His red face flushed into purple. He knew how to make a man talk.

So, his guess was correct! Ramose lowered his hands. He sat down wearily, as if exhausted from an enlightening trance.

The other's outburst confirmed what he had not already been told. Somehow, the Vizier had gained knowledge of the portentous news. How? And when? It had to have been this very day for the power-hungry bureaucrat could not have kept such a secret to himself for any length of time without running to the King. Ramose would have the palace guards questioned about any unusual arrivals.

He gazed at the agitated Vizier through half-veiled eyes. First, the thin image was blurred. Then it sharpened into a lance with himself as a deflecting shield. From a distant past, the future took shape: Victory. Tragedy.

While he appeared attentive to the conversation, Ramose attempted a cursory interpretation of his vision. Knowing that al-Saqqara harbored lofty ambitions, did this mean danger for the King? For Nefret? For the royal family from hired assassins, from poisoned wine? He must thwart any attempts on the royal lives. One way was to remove them from Ineb-hedj as soon as possible. Secretly, of course. Yes, as soon as possible.

Only seconds of actual time elapsed while a plan took shape in his thinker's mind. Ramose shook himself free of the ominous visions and forced himself to relax, refocusing on what was being said.

"So, you know about this, Ramose," the King said quietly. "That surprises me. However, the Grand General presumably has not yet had a chance to see the urgent message from his Commander of the Fourth. Am I correct?"

"A message to me from Barum?" Makari sat up straight.

"Indeed. Vizier, why don't you repeat what you told me a while ago." Aha took a sip of wine, watching his three advisors over the rim of his cup. "Just so that everyone knows what I was told. Then, perhaps, I might learn what else there is to know!" Aha's words carried a sarcastic undertone. His dinner hour, as well as his future, was being unpleasantly rearranged; it started to upset him.

Makari's hard eyes gazed squarely at the squirming Vizier. Barum would never send a single message to al-Saqqara without sending a duplicate scroll to him. He staked his life on that. While he did not consider it wise to make an issue of it in the presence of the King, he would take the matter up with al-Saqqara privately. By his *Special Forces*, he would get to the bottom of this!

Extremely uncomfortable, al-Saqqara bowed to Aha and offhandedly repeated the message. Without openly accusing him of having tampered with a private message, Ramose and Makari managed to extract the truth from the nervous man whose pacing increased everyone's loathing for him.

When the Vizier finished with his sputterings, the King said curtly, "Sit down, Vizier. You agitate me!" He looked at his brilliant old commander. "Makari, our four armies must be readied at once." He thought for a while, before he continued, "I suggest that we arrange for my court to journey to Nekhen. Ostensibly, to attend the *Festival of Opet*. Luckily, the timing is right."

"Indeed. And the river is beginning to flood," Makari agreed.

"Whereas, in reality, I shall head for the Kharga to take the Fourth into battle," Aha finished his thought.

"Preparations for an official trek will be observed and reported by enemy spies," Ramose said and al-Saqqara added, "To the Ruler of the Kush and the King of Nobatia, undoubtedly."

"Undoubtedly," Makari said. "We know that the Wawat will side against us, which forces us to fight against a combined larger army." A brief silence enveloped the room.

Aha looked at Makari. "Have your battle plans drawn up within three days." Turning to al-Saqqara, he ordered, "Vizier, you are to receive your final instructions after I confer with Makari. In the meantime, arrange for the war barges to be loaded with provisions. Makari will outline his troop movements for you."

"The Fourth stands in readiness," Makari confirmed. "And, coincidentally, I summoned our other three commanders for a War Council at my Central Command. I am planning to leave tomorrow for my garrison. We were going to discuss strategies for our Annual War Games. Now, we must concentrate on the real campaign against the southerners."

Aha nodded, and again turned to al-Saqqara. "Have the Royal Bark prepared to leave within fourteen days. Troops of the Second are to accompany my convoy. They can sail behind in the war barges."

Exhausted from the mental effort of such portent decisions, Aha sank back into his chair. His well-oiled war machine was set to roll toward the south. He looked at Ramose. "And what shall you contribute to all this, my good priest?"

"I shall pray with you, my King.

"To Horus, to lend you his swift wings for speed.

"To Ptah for protection.

"But that I may do so effectively, I beg you, Hor-Aha, grant me a moment's prayer with you after this meeting. Alone."

"Very well. You and I shall pray."

The King rose.

The audience was over.

Al-Saqqara took a few steps then hesitated. He turned to bow to the King. Makari, too, rose and moved toward the door. Trying to avoid the suddenly bowing Vizier, the stocky Grand General had to step aside. As he did so, he bumped into the High Priest.

Apparently aghast at his blunder, Makari immediately apologized.

"General Makari, perhaps you wish to atone for your unintentional offense. If your Supreme Commander assents, please remain behind and pray with the King and me," Ramose suggested.

The two men understood each other perfectly.

If the Vizier guessed any hidden meaning behind the High Priest's invitation, he could think of no excuse to linger. It was common knowledge that he was not a pious man; but neither was Makari. Grudgingly, he took his leave. Once again, he felt slighted and out-maneuvered by the detested priest. One day, he swore to himself. One day soon, Ramose!

According to dynastic edict, Ebu al-Saqqara was also Acting Regent. Were something to happen to Aha, Queen Hent's co-regency with the young Royal Heiress would be no cause for concern for the ambitious Vizier. He could handle the whining woman and the girl, even if he had to marry her. The thought made his skin crawl. He would easily subdue the immature, unruly Dubar. Already, the boy had turned into his willing pawn. He saw to that some time ago. But Ramose had become too great a danger; as had the entire priesthood. The ugly official sneered at his tall opponent who waited calmly for his exit.

When al-Saqqara passed Beir in the ante-chamber, he exchanged a sly look with the Royal Steward who did not bow but nodded imperceptibly.

*

"Great Ptah, Omnipotent Creator God of All, safeguard us. We are your children.

"Almighty Maat, Goddess of Truth and Harmony, protect this land from devastation, dissent and defeat.

"Lofty Horus, Name-Giver of Kings, lend Hor-Aha your wings for swiftness and good purpose.

"Hawk-headed Montu, Mighty God of War, bring us victory.

"Sacred Hapi, Protector-Bull of Ineb-hedj, support the King with your strength so that he may return from battle unharmed."

As he intoned the beseeching litany with practiced ease, Ramose thought of Nefret, so like a daughter to him. A child still, she was much too quickly turning into a beautiful young woman. He appealed silently to Ptah on her behalf. Then he continued his supplication to several of the lesser gods to protect the royal family, the four royal armies and, again and most importantly, their earthly equal, their God-King Hor-Aha.

Listening to Ramose with only half an ear, Aha tried to conjure up a soothing answer to Hent's anticipated whining against a long journey south. He admitted to himself that, this time, her protestations would be justified. Her third pregnancy was not an easy one. Best if she remained behind with their two young sons, Dubar and Djer. He suddenly recalled al-Saqqara's unexpected suggestion that he marry Nefret, and wondered if he should bring this up in front of Makari.

As Aha ruminated about his domestic arrangements, Makari envisioned the movements and provisioning of the Four Royal Armies. A gargantuan task calling for sleepless nights and long busy days. He also thought of the tremendous chance to reveal his *Special Forces* at long last.

"Osiris, God of the Dead, satisfy your hunger from amongst the enemy.

"Do not lust for our living on the battlefield."

Ramose lowered his arms and bowed to the King.

Aha grew impatient and wished to retreat to his private chambers. He had been alert enough to sense that Ramose's request for Makari to stay behind had nothing to do with atonement. He sighed and waved his hand toward their vacated chairs. "Let us have more wine, my friends."

He sat down reaching for his cup. When he lifted it, his disappointed look showed that the gleaming vessel had to be empty.

Makari hastened to refill it.

Ramose, too, sat down, still not touching his wine. "Hor-Aha," he began, "the gods gave me a plan that would allow you to surprise the enemy." The two others looked expectantly up as he continued, "Of course, all depends on your assent. And a great deal more on the Grand General's ability to ready his armies even sooner."

"We have been ready for a long time," Makari emphasized.

"I am talking about immediate readiness, Grand General. More than anything else, secrecy is paramount for success. On the other hand, failure will spell tragedy for all of us."

Aha was tempted not to let the High Priest continue. All this talk of war and tragedy turned his stomach into a roiling monster. "Well then, Ramose, what is this plan of yours?"

"For a considerable time now, Badar has wanted to return to the Temple of Horus."

"The one in Nekhen? Or are you talking about the new one at the First Royal Mooring Place?" Makari asked.

"No, our old temple in Nekhen. He wishes to devote himself to some advanced studies there."

"Does this have anything to do with anything, by any chance?" Aha growled.

"It does indeed, my King," Ramose smiled, sensing Aha's deteriorating mood. "Three of my temple boats could leave the capital within a week to take the Venerable Badar south. Of course, I plan to accompany him."

Aha rolled his eyes and exhaled.

Ramose was not to be deterred and continued his explanation without haste. "We can deliver a secret message to General Barum to signal the beginning of the campaign."

Makari glanced sharply at the High Priest. He liked him. Indeed, he had received his early training through the priesthood. But why was the High Priest suddenly concerning himself with a soldier's task? His priests already had a stronghold on every segment of the sciences. They experimented with unknown metals and powerful poisons. Did they want to dictate strategy and tactics to the military as well? Makari felt a twinge of uneasiness as he thought of the excluded Vizier. Al-Saqqara would question him about this meeting. He listened with heightened interest to Ramose's next explanation.

"I thought of asking you to send Nefret on my temple boats to Nekhen with a message. Officially, I would accompany her to consult the *Oracle of Isis* while she begins her cleansing rites. With her court initiation imminent, it is a plausible reason for the journey."

"Go on." Aha sighed.

"It could still be the real reason for her to go. However, she should be accompanying you, my King. *Officially*. Both of you are sailing on the Royal Bark to attend Nekhen's *Festival of Opet*."

"No, no. Nefret at that musty palace in Nekhen? Or even cloistered safely at your Temple of Horus, at a time of war? Much too risky! Besides, you know how willful she is. Who knows what mischief she will get into without proper supervision," Aha interrupted; perhaps for the first time genuinely concerned for his young heiress.

"Great King, I cannot explain it. But I have a strong premonition that the Princess is in danger here in the capital were she to be left behind while you journey to the south," Ramose argued with unusual insistence.

"So you want me to send her into the midst of war, what?" Aha's chin jutted out again, a sure sign that he was turning argumentative.

"Please, hear me out, Great King." Ramose leaned forward and looked at Aha who was unable to break the blue gaze. "In about six or seven days, the temple's *Kariy* boat, accompanied by two unassuming faluccas, leaves from Inebhedj. I am on board as, *supposedly*, is the Venerable Badar, hidden from view in the *Kariy*. Several temple chantresses, as well as a few priests shall serve as escort on this pilgrimage."

Ramose lifted his right hand. "Only those concerned and the three of us here in this room must know that in Badar's place, you, Great King, would travel hidden in the sacred deck shrine. Nefret and her women would pose as temple chantresses on the accompanying boats."

Ramose saw Aha's look change to an amused grin. He had often observed as his sensual King followed the undulating nakedness of his temple chantresses intently rather than paying attention to his own invocation of the gods.

"Of course, the girls will be covered by light capes. The mosquitoes can be annoying along the river," Ramose added.

Aha guffawed as he imagined his daughter posing half naked on a simple river falucca.

"The supposed priests will be well-trained Temple Bowmen. Not only will they wear priestly sashes, they will carry spears and knives."

Aha opened his mouth.

Ramose was not finished and held up his hand, begging Aha's indulgence. "In two weeks, the Royal Bark then leaves with the official convoy. With Badar in your place. And one of Nefret's slaves to pose as her."

"And just how do you propose to manage all this deception?" Aha asked, then added half amused, half incensed. "This is preposterous!"

"My King, Zeina, one of Nefret's servant-girls, bears great resemblance to your daughter; if you forgive my saying so."

Again, Ramose gauged Aha's mood. Seeing the chin recede, he felt safe to continue. "Of course, Amma would have to travel on the Royal Bark, as should Beir; neither you nor the Princess would travel without them, and their absence from the Bark would arouse suspicion."

The daring plan evolved as Ramose spoke. The more he explained it to Aha and Makari, the more feasible it became to all three.

"You say that neither I nor the Royal Heiress would travel without our closest servants. But you force us to do just that, my foresighted High Priest of Ptah." Aha's sarcasm resurfaced. He and his headstrong daughter, traveling upriver on simple temple boats without their capable servants! They, instead, would comfort the impostors on the Royal Bark!

"This is preposterous!" Aha repeated.

"Only for twenty days, my King. Most importantly, you would arrive in Nekhen so much earlier without anyone expecting you there. Including the enemy. It is paramount that we keep this our secret. And if the Grand General ..."

Ramose glanced at the seasoned soldier who listened intently to the clever ruse "...and if General Makari could have his troops ready earlier ..."

"I already said that it is done," Makari muttered.

"... then the Fourth Army can stage a surprise attack, with your remaining three armies rapidly pushing toward the south. Victory would be ours for certain."

"If I am not here, at the palace, until the Royal Bark leaves, the whole thing blows up in our faces." Despite his weak objections, Aha was fascinated by the convoluted charade. It would be a miracle if it worked. He could use a miracle right now. His life, and his kingdom, might depend on it. So might his daughter's future. At least, it would distance her from her disgusting suitor.

"I have considered that as well." Ramose continued. "Nefret would *officially* go into seclusion until she reaches Nekhen, with only Amma allowed to serve her. The old nurse, of course, will know that the veiled figure is the tall slave Zeina. There could be no fooling Amma."

"And what about me? Whereto am I supposed to have crept until my *official* departure?" Aha relished throwing Ramose another challenge.

"You could fall ill. Too ill to see anyone until the Bark's departure, though not ill enough to have to abandon your planned journey during which only Beir would be at your side, tending you. Or Badar, as it were."

Aha grimaced.

Ramose knew of his King's distaste for illness and quickly added, "It is the only way. Otherwise, the Vizier and others would insist to confer with you on one matter or another prior to your travel. Again, this is why it is of utmost importance that we keep this plan absolutely secret. Only a trusted few with a need to know must be taken into our confidences."

"That would be your Venerable Badar, my Beir and Nefret's Amma and her slaves, I suppose," Aha said, caught up in the plan at last.

"Anyone else?" Makari asked, looking straight at Ramose.

"No one else," Ramose replied firmly. "No one!"

The inference against informing the Vizier was clear and Makari hoped that his later military action would make up for his divided loyalties against the Royal Quartermaster. Though he would have to explain to al-Saqqara why the troops were to be armed and supplied with such undue haste. As a bureaucrat the man would accept a call for expediency. However, regarding other inconsistencies, the ugly man was anything but a fool.

"I shall have to think about this, High Priest." Aha pretended to waver in his approval for the undertaking even though he had already decided to follow his old friend's advice.

"Allowing Nefret to travel on an unprotected temple boat could prove disastrous. What if we are attacked? She has no idea how to protect herself against anything, except perhaps Dubar's verbal mud-slinging." He sighed, recalling his infrequent and invariably unpleasant family dinners. "She is spoiled. I blame her stubborn nurse for that, you know."

Ramose knew, and took some blame as well. At this moment, however, he did not wish to digress into Nefret's lenient upbringing.

Instead, he envisioned the worst that could happen to their small convoy was an attack while they camped on the shores of the *Hapi* at night. If by chance the women managed to escape, they had no survival training and no knowledge of how to find their way back through an unforgiving desert. And only a pitiful few days remained to accomplish much.

"Hor-Aha, would Beir instruct Amma to bring Nefret to the temple tomorrow morning, and each day after that? She and her women should be taught rudimentary survival in the desert. I have an excellent tutor in mind as I shall unfortunately be quite occupied myself," Ramose asked.

"When do you tell Nefret?" Aha did not intend to be the one to break the news to her.

"At the end of a week's training, Amma can instruct the girls in their roles. Not before we leave, though. We cannot have our plans revealed through idle chatter."

The King clapped his hands together.

Beir appeared at once. Highly trusted, he was

indispensable to his King.

"Beir!" Aha motioned for the waiting Steward to approach. "Where is the Queen's dagger?"

Beir knew at once which queen, and which dagger. He nodded, "It has lain in its sheath waiting to be worn by a royal princess."

"Fetch it!" Aha commanded and, as the Steward left the room, he turned toward Ramose, "If my daughter has to be exposed to more danger than I care to wish upon anyone, at least she should wear that dagger. After all, it is her royal right." Quietly, he added, "It was her mother's."

Ramose's throat tightened with secret long-borne pain.

Beir entered proffering a simple leather scabbard to Aha. "Here it is, my King. Just as the Queen had worn it."

"Yes, yes," Aha rasped and blinked to mask his latent sorrow for his first, and only, love.

The astute Steward handed the reminder of lost love to his King and disappeared noiselessly.

Aha pulled the short dagger from its sheath. Unlike its humble husk, the weapon itself was finely crafted. A jewel-encrusted clasp held the sharp blade securely to the carved ivory handle. For a moment, he lost himself in the mists of his memories fondling the ceremonial weapon. Then he slid the dagger back into its scabbard and handed it to Ramose. "Tell her to wear it from now on. Someone should teach her how to handle it." Taking a sip of wine, he asked, "What about my sons? What about Hent?" He answered his own questions. "She is too heavy with child to travel. Djer is still too young, though I suspect Dubar will not want to be left behind. The youngster is beginning to flex his muscle."

"Dubar could accompany you on the Royal Bark, my King. Of course, without being allowed to speak to you during the journey," Makari suggested without much interest in the make-up of the royal entourage. His thoughts already raced ahead. The fantastic opportunity to display his *Special Forces* gratified him! He deferentially bowed to the brilliant High Priest who favored the small assembly with one of his rare smiles.

After several minutes, the King consented. "All right, Ramose. I am placing myself in your hands for now so that, with your gods and the strength of my armies, victory shall be ours. Of course, much of that depends on you, Makari. I need not emphasize that we have to win this war; or we shall all die without dignity."

The words hung heavily in the room.

"Yes," Ramose said, "we all need to win our next confrontation." An ugly face appeared to his inner eye.

Aha surprised them as he announced, "I shall accompany you tomorrow morning to your War Council, Makari. Your generals need to know that their Supreme Commander is at the fore of his armies. Ramose, you should come with us as well."

Startling himself by his sudden decision, Aha realized that his presence at the War Council would lift the morale of his seasoned army leaders.

"Beir," he called loudly.

Again, the Steward materialized at once from an adjacent chamber.

"I am leaving early tomorrow with Makari. Tell Captain Veni, I want a squad of archers and one standard-bearer. No other fuss. We shall be back in two days hence."

"What am I to tell the Lady Hent?" Beir asked.

If Aha was aware that his long-time servant never referred to his second queen as such, he never chastised Beir for it.

"Oh, well. Tell the family, ah, tell them, yes, that I have gone to hunt for ostriches," the King said flippantly.

Makari smiled. If Aha only knew how fitting an explanation this was.

Their audience with the King was over.

Not so their working day.

Much had to be accomplished in a very short time. With much foresight and even greater secrecy, plans were to be solidified, strategies forged, and the 'who-could-know-what' was to be sorted out.

More importantly, the various plots had to be precisely remembered by each participant as the next meeting was to include the Vizier. There could be no slip of the tongue.

* * *

Part II

Ineb-hedj, City of White Walls

Chapter Ten

Zeina rushed toward Safaga readying Nefret's sleeping alcove for the night. "He's back!"

The sun dropped lower toward the horizon but dusk had not yet spread its softness over Ineb-hedj. Safaga liked to do her chores early. Nefret's suite was comprised of her own sleeping chamber with a granite-lined bathing room. Adjacent to it was an ample stone-lined waste drain although the spoiled Princess did not like to use it in the dark. Safaga placed a glazed wide-mouthed clay-jug next to the recessed bedstand to collect the royal night soil, one of her least desirable duties. Whenever she could manage, Safaga delegated the emptying of the smelly jug to Dokki.

Nefret's three personal servants were housed in a room connected by a windowless ante-chamber, whereas Amma slept in one of her own off the inner courtyard letting in air and light.

These parts of the palace were originally the assigned quarters of the reigning queen. Nefret's mother, Queen Mayet, had briefly occupied them, as had Queen Neith-hotep. Queen Hent, however, chose to be nearer to the King's large royal suite. Much to Nefret's relief.

Despite its previous illustrious occupants, Nefret's room was simply furnished. Soft woven mats covered the floor. Still, it would have been unthinkable to sleep on them because of the invading hordes of vermin and crawling insects. One of the thick walls was stepped back creating a sleeping alcove for Nefret. Her bed was lined with straw mats, and flax had been woven into the softest white linen sheets. All the beds at the palace were of the new kind, standing on four posts rather than slanting from two legs at the head. The royal household deemed itself progressive and of late preferred to sleep completely horizontal. Most of the time, a thin white linen coverlet was enough but a warm quilt always lay folded nearby. During hot times it was stored in one of the numerous trunks that held garments and adornments, wigs as yet unworn, and fresh linens.

With deliberate contrast to Zeina's excited rush, Safaga took the folded quilt from her mistress's bed and placed it on an exquisitely adorned trunk. Its ornate top was half covered by a quilted, most unusual, garment. No matter how finely flax could be spun into soft linen, this quilt was finer yet. Its most stunning quality, however, was its color which matched the deepening hue of the evening sky.

White was the prescribed color of the court. Yet Nefret had secretly conspired to have Safaga acquire a bolt of the unusual material after the slave once smuggled a sample of the blue cloth into the palace from one of her forays to the market place.

Fascinated by its lapis lazuli color, Nefret planned to have the cloth made into a cape for herself. To break from strict tradition, she required the King's consent to wear colors and the determined girl devised a clever ruse. During one of their rare family dinners she impulsively announced that she would have her women sew Aha's *Sed*-Festival robe.

While the Royal Jubilee called for the King to wear a special robe, Nefret neglected to point out the color of her intended present. Pleased with her for once, Aha accepted her gesture and assured her that he looked forward to her offering. Outdone by her young step-daughter, Hent sniffled that she had planned to present a robe to the King herself while the two young princes listened without much interest and stuffed their mouths with honey-sweetened cooked grain.

Nefret boxed and cajoled her women-servants into starting the King's promised festival robe at once. They cut, and sewed, and quilted the blue bolt into a wondrously hooded garment, its flowing folds sweeping the floor. The King chilled easily and Nefret was certain that he would be pleased with the robe. As well as its color, she prayed. His acceptance would pave the way for her to wear new colors. After all, the High Priest already wore a purple mantle. And he was only a priest.

Safaga caressed the soft Jubilee robe, recalling the shocked arguments Amma screeched against Nefret's breach of well-established custom, but smiled as she thought of the cunning and persuasiveness her young mistress had conjured up to sway the Royal Head Nurse. In the end, Nefret won and she, Zeina and Dokki were kept busy sewing the King's intended quilt, under Amma's chiding guidance.

Opening a trunk, Safaga carefully placed the blue garment inside ready to be offered to the King in all its breathtaking exotic beauty.

"Who is back, Zeina?" Feigning disinterest, Safaga closed the heavy lid, barely pausing in her routine. She knew the easily excitable younger Zeina would spill her secret all too soon. Most likely, about some palace gossip burning to be shared.

"Pase! He is back." Zeina strained to see the impact of her words. She was not disappointed.

"Pase, back?" Breath held captive for a heartbeat exploded into Zeina's face as Safaga shook the taller slave by the arms. "Are you certain? Where is he? How do you know?" Safaga's words tumbled over each other slurring into foreign sounds.

Zeina smiled slyly. Whenever the Sumerian became agitated, she broke into some unintelligible gibberish.

The handsome Archer Pase became Safaga's lover when he was garrisoned with the Royal Palace Archers. Six moons ago, he was sent to the Fourth Army near the Kharga Oasis. For him, without family connections to help further his career, it was a grand opportunity. While Pase and Safaga were trained from childhood to bow to those who rearranged their destinies at will it had been difficult for them to accept being torn from each other's passionate embraces.

Zeina shook herself free from her older friend's tight grip and laughed, "Patience, Safaga! I will tell you, if you let me. Besides, you have not exactly been starved for a man's affection during the past moons. Or did Beir not do so well by you?"

"Forget the Steward! Zeina, please! Tell me about Pase!" The mischievous grin spreading over Zeina's pretty face grated on Safaga's nerves. *How much she resembles Nefret when she tries to be clever,* she thought, annoyed with her friend's coyness.

Zeina knew how to fuel Safaga's anxiety with just the right pause. It gave her a rare advantage over the older slave and she savored her brief moment of triumph. "I happened to be across the grounds, near the Vizier's working chambers, when I saw a disreputable looking traveler kick his jackass through the gates. I thought how strange it was for a dusty beggar to gain entry, so I lingered for a moment. Suddenly, Saad appeared. He seemed in a great hurry."

You were loitering about for Saad, you little vixen, Safaga thought. *Cavorting with your lover, instead of helping me in here.* Too eager to learn more she decided not to chide the smitten girl lest she became sullen and refused to say more about her discovery.

"And?" Safaga urged the taller girl.

"And, Saad seemed in a great hurry." Zeina relished the moment.

Safaga expelled an exasperated breath. Rotating her hand in front of Zeina to hasten her to speak, she brought her face close to the other slave's so as not to miss a word.

"...As I said. Saad seemed in a hurry," Zeina repeated, picking up the thread of her story, unperturbed by Safaga's anxiety. "He stopped to speak to me."

Of course he did, Safaga thought.

"And?" she urged Zeina once more.

"And," Zeina took her time. "And, he told me Pase had returned with an important message. And that he, Saad, was on his way to request an audience for the Vizier to see the King at once. Saad also said that the poor man had ridden his jackass so hard day and night that the animal was near death. As was the messenger."

"Near death?" Safaga, used to Zeina's tendency to exaggerate, grew nevertheless alarmed. She would breathe easier only once she reassured herself that he was still alive. "Where is Pase now?"

"Saad said he collapsed somewhere within the Vizier's chambers."

"Zeina, do you think you could persuade Saad to let me see him? You said yourself that the Vizier went to an audience with the King. No one would need to know." Safaga's tearful plea moved the mischievous but compassionate Zeina.

"Well, I do have my ways with the big Scribe." Zeina swayed her slender hips and winked.

"I daresay that you have caused his reed to stiffen more than once," Safaga shot back, her eyes alight with hope.

"And what about a certain Steward? He won't be too happy to give up your honey pot while Pase dips into its sweetness once again?" Zeina countered.

"Zeina, please! Can we go and ask Saad?" Safaga pleaded anew, ending their good-natured sparring. "Nefret is in the garden. Amma, too, is gone. We will not be missed until the evening meal."

"What about Dokki?"

"Oh, for Horus' sake, Zeina. What about Dokki!"

As if on cue, they rolled their eyes and giggled. Poor Dokki. Clumsy and slow to comprehend their little jokes, she would not betray them. Despite it all, Dokki was immensely loyal and happy to be a part of their group. With them, her darkness did not matter. They were friends even if they chided her or if Nefret slapped her in one of her nastier moods.

After a furtive glance around, the two servants hurried from Nefret's chamber. They crossed their own quarters quickly and sashayed across the Grand Foyer with studied nonchalance.

Moments later, they reached the small side-veranda and stepped onto the path from which al-Saqqara had come just minutes earlier. Hoping themselves unobserved, the two slender figures broke into a trot, each urged toward a magnetic pole of her own, the unattended chambers of their young mistress forgotten.

*

Zeina's coy pleas softened the studious Saad as soon as they found him. The Head Scribe placed his index finger on his lips and led the two along a passageway. After they passed the double-portal of the Vizier's working chamber, Saad opened a small adjacent door.

Safaga pushed Saad aside and tiptoed into the dim room. She gasped at the dust-caked, bearded man lying prone on thin floormats. Tears welled up in her eyes and she looked back at Saad. The Scribe nodded sadly, guessing her intentions. In a hushed voice, he called for a slave to bring a basin with fresh water, clean linen, and a shaving blade. Then he took Zeina's hand and pulled her from the room. The two vanished into the Scribe's private chamber. He knew he should not be with Zeina this time of day but the tall slave made his loins burn and he figured it would not take them long.

*

Safaga knelt and gently touched the drawn face, kissed the closed eyes, traced the aquiline nose. It was her Pase all right. Even in exhausted sleep, he seemed tense.

An old scribe with useless gnarled fingers shuffled in and placed a large copper basin on the floor together with clean linen strips and shaving utensils and then retreated quietly.

Safaga soaked a strip of linen in the gleaming basin and methodically started to wash the sleeping man's chest. Desert grime came off his skin in dark blotches and she had to change the linen often. She untied Pase's belt and threw the dirt-stiffened kilt open.

At first, she thought a piece of red clay was stuck to his abdomen. As she squinted closer in the dim light of the smoking lamp, she cried out, guessing the mark's true origin. She cleaned the festering wound and promised to remember to bring a healing salve as soon as she was able to return. Having loosened the oozing scab, she squeezed the puss from the burn. Then she dressed it. Even when she rolled Pase from side to side to guide the bandage under and around him, he did not stir.

She longed for him as she washed his well-formed flaccid *Mehyt*. Stroking the soft folds, she smiled. Her loving ministrations apparently reached through Pase's heavy dreams for his tense muscles relaxed and a smile appeared on his cracked lips.

His stalk filled her palm, and she sighed. Her stay with him was running out too fast, and she still had to shave the dark stubble off his face. A less delicious task, yet one she rendered no less tenderly.

* * *

Chapter Eleven

Tasar bowed to the young woman who had been left alone with him in the vast gardens.

She smiled sweetly at him. "You can accompany me, priest. Come, I shall show you the way." She kept her eyes demurely on the path.

Not an inexperienced man, but a stranger to her ways, Tasar could not be aware of the sudden change in her from her earlier girlish willfulness. Her appraising sidelong glances along his bronzed body did not escape him, and he realized that his ample youthfulness pressed plainly through the borrowed knee-length wrap. Her natural shoulder-length hair reinforced his assumption that she was the daughter of a palace noble having blossomed into pleasing early womanhood. About eighteen, he gauged. A quick warm welcome might be just the thing to melt away the monotony of his journey.

Nefret felt reckless. Above all, she felt free. The unexpected chance to be alone with a stranger excited her. He obviously did not realize who she was. She decided to keep up the innocent charade a while longer before she told him. A mischievous tingling cursed through her as she led the stranger toward some bushes. Only minutes earlier, the lush branches had swallowed the rebellious Dubar. Under the pressure of her slender arms, the leafy branches widened into a reluctant gap revealing a narrow foot path between high hedges. Seeing the young priest hesitate, she smiled alluringly, "A shortcut."

The band of gravel led them through a pomegranate orchard, its trees gnarled by age and the constant fight against the desert wind. When the dreaded Khamsin blew, these ancient sentinels would groan and struggle, though never snap, under the pressure of the cursed wind.

Justifiably, King Aha chose this tenacious tree as the emblem for his young dynasty's standard; branches reaching out, blossoms ripening into prodigious fruit issuing forth new seedlings to grow into another orchard; an ever-growing maze, firmly rooted in place against the onslaught of outside forces. Indeed a fitting symbol added to the Red Horus-crown of the Lower region, and the high White Seth-crown of the Upper lands.

"Oh!" A hiccupped cry escaped Nefret's full lips and she closed her eyes against the pain of an anticipated fall. She and the young priest walked side by side. Suddenly, her left foot caught an exposed root that snaked its way across the unused path to seek moisture in the softer soil of the adjacent underbrush. Instinctively, Tasar's right arm reached across her body to prevent her from a nasty stumble. Her imprisoned left foot propelled her away from him and his long fingers, intending to grasp her arm, glanced off and instead found hold around the gentle mound of her left breast. Their combined momentum pivoted them face to face. She moved closer to him, as he stood, unmoving, perhaps consternated by the unpriestly crimson rush to his cheeks. His left hand encircled her slim waist and she noticed a firm bulge that parted the folds of his wrap bridging the narrow gap between them. By now, her own cheeks burned with an inner fire, and her breath plummeted into her stomach to pulse through her deeper still. Despite the delicious moment, Nefret saw concern sweep over Tasar's face. She remembered Dubar. Could her dark sibling still be nearby? Overwhelmed by youthful rushes she pushed all worries aside. If she mentioned Dubar's propensity for spying on his half-sister, the Nekhen priest would break the delightful snare she knew she had laid out for him.

Her tight linen wrap did little to guise her spilling forms, her wrapper stopping just below her heaving breasts, leaving her nipples barely covered by thin shoulder straps. Playing out her innocent charade, Nefret had no idea of the mind-numbing turmoil she caused in the loins of her young stranger. Seemingly to steady her, he pressed hard against her in a headlong rush of sudden need.

Nefret sometimes pretended to be asleep among her sewing maidens in order to listen to their whisperings. The giggling slaves spurned her imagination and her curiosity, as they spoke of clandestine trysts with palace guards and archers. At other times, they discussed the discomforts of the female moon-cycle. Or, they talked in hushed tones about a man's *Papyrus Clump*, the sheer wonders of a man's pillar and its prowess, and how it could pleasure a woman's honey pot. She had listened breathlessly, licking her lips and swallowing hard, without understanding all of it.

Here now, unexpectedly, was her opportunity to find out for herself. She smiled her most alluring smile. Spied off Safaga, she had secretly practiced it.

"Come, priest," she breathed into Tasar's ear. "It is hot out here. I know a place with fresh juices to quench your thirst."

Tasar heard a veiled promise. "Then take me there," he rasped. His throat was parched. His loins throbbed. He had to quench his thirst. All of it!

Nefret led the entranced priest toward an ancient mulberry bush. Parting its ample branches, a dark opening stood revealed. She had come across the overgrown entrance by accident while hiding from Dubar. Tasar followed without hesitation, glad for the cool passage.

Outside, the air shimmered hot and still. Near the hidden entrance, the leaves of the low laurel hedge rustled curiously in the windless afternoon but neither of the anxious pair noticed the unfounded disturbance. Their breathless attention was focused ahead. They spilled from the low passageway into a small alcove just off Nefret's own ante-room that separated her private bed-chamber from her slaves' quarters. A faded double-woven hanging, stiff with age and dust, its purpose long forgotten, hid the inner opening to the passage. As the furtive pair slipped past the musty curtain fine sand trickled noiselessly onto the floor. The two edged toward a newer hanging that led into Nefret's bed-chamber. No one was in sight. With young urges rawed by anticipation, caution was dispelled. As was any shyness, usually inherent in the young, and the innocent.

Unfamiliar with the surroundings, Tasar brushed against a small cosmetic stand. A slim-footed amphora tottered precariously before it crashed onto the floor to spill its precious oils over the woven mats.

"Shhh," Nefret cautioned. His ardent carelessness annoyed her.

As Tasar's eyes adjusted to the semi-darkness he saw the outlines of a recessed bed and he put his arms around the girl. Not much taller than Nefret, he smiled at her. "You provide a fitting welcome for a weary traveler who is dying of a great thirst."

All at once, Nefret felt unsure of herself. She also realized the grave risk she was taking. It frightened and excited her.

"Oh, yes! I promised you something to drink." From a readied jar, she filled a bejeweled cup with ruby pomegranate juice. "Here, this should quench that great thirst of yours."

He took the cup and smiled at her over the rim. "It will. But not all of it." After he drank he held the precious vessel to Nefret's lips. "Drink to the goddess of love with me, my beautiful enchantress."

Nefret pretended to sip as he steadied her hands around his. "What do you mean, not all of it?" she asked.

"Only you can quench all of my thirst," Tasar whispered into her ear. He emptied the rest of the cup and replaced it on its stand. Then he propelled her toward the recess.

His forcefulness startled her.

He smiled and coaxed her on, until the bed barred their retreat. When he eased her onto the soft quilts he sensed resistance. All at once, his young temptress appeared less experienced and eager. What had his experienced temple chantress teacher once said to him? 'Women require coaxing, and sweet whispers, and ardent entreaties.' This was the time to practice what he had been taught.

"I have never seen anyone lovelier than you," he whispered and pressed his burning lips over hers. Increasing the pressure of his mouth, his tongue at last caressed her full lips into parting. Her eyes widened into blue stars. Momentarily startled, Tasar thought they were much like the eyes of the High Priest. He stopped his kisses. "Close your eyes, my beautiful. I will still be here when you open them again."

He mumbled sweet nothings and explored her slender body with his hands. Not like a surgeon seeking knowledge through his touch, but like a man anticipating pleasure. Tasar's waistwrap became inadequate by his rising urges. It parted and his throbbing pillar stood revealed.

Nefret opened her eyes and gasped. Her women had joked and giggled about a man's pillar but her breathless eaves-dropping did not prepare her for this unsheathed man. Water collected in her mouth, as if she were reaching for a long-awaited delicacy. Blood pooled in the very depth of her, rushing toward her pink privacy. *My Honey Pot!* At last, she grasped the meaning of her women's sly descriptions.

Up to now, only her women had touched her hidden place as their tender ministrations with sweet-smelling oils pleasured her into tantalizing day-dreams while they soothed and cooed, and exchanged knowing glances. But this was far from that gentle semi-drowsiness. Excitement pushed her into urgent nearness with the handsome stranger. She could resist him no longer. Closing her eyes again, she instinctively arched toward him.

Tasar assumed her willing. His rigid member homed. Suddenly, Nefret's eyes stared at him transfixed with anxiety and he knew that he needed to be gentler still.

"Sweet lady," he whispered, his breath hot on her face. "Don't fight it. Let it happen. You are so beautiful, so soft, so rare. Be mine."

Nefret only heard that he thought her beautiful and this pleased her immensely. His words carried reverence, instilled trust. *If he finds out that I am not a woman yet, he will leave me in disgust. I might never have another chance,* she thought. Sensing rather than knowing the purpose of his urgency, she clenched her teeth and pulled her tight wrapper higher exposing her long legs and slender hips. Then she slipped her arms out from under the restraining shoulder-straps, freeing her nipples for his moist lips.

Shivers cursed through Tasar as he tasted her hardening pink buds. He followed a primeval force until he was hardly aware of the girl under him. His stiffness moved over her silky mound to probe below her furry friction until his *Mehyt* found her pink cleft. He pushed into sweet release.

Nefret's pained cry urged Tasar back into reality. Before he fully regained his senses, ecstasy swept over him so that it took another moment to become aware of the struggle under him. She was pushing him away, sobbing. Tasar withdrew from the tight embrace of her warmth.

Freed from his passion and his weight Nefret broke into heart-rending sobs.

Surprised, Tasar took her face into his hands. How had he upset this willing maiden? Mellow and replete, he realized that she might not have been a woman yet. Remorse gripped him. As did fear. What could he say to this girl-child? Who was she, anyway?

"There, there. Shhh, my sweet. Be still. You are so beautiful, and I am the luckiest man for having loved you first." He rocked her in his arms and stroked her tangled hair, and thought of what to do. How could he have let this happen? Had the long days on the river parched him so that he had to slacken his thirst, and his lust, with the first woman—no, girl—he laid eyes on? Or had the sun baked every ounce of good sense and caution from his brain? He had to leave this place! And fast!

Calmed by his gentleness, Nefret wondered why her slaves always whispered so deliciously about a man's hardness. As if it was something to be coveted. Then, why did they not whisper of that searing pain, when the sweetness was so brief. Yet, she wanted him again.

Unaware of Nefret's emotional recovery, Tasar cupped her unblemished cheeks. "Sweet girl, you must forgive me." He pressed his lips onto hers and she responded ardently until a faint sound reached them. Nefret pushed him away, listening for the padding of bare feet. Alarmed by the girl's intensity, Tasar shot off the bed and hastily wrapped his waistcloth over his flat stomach.

Nefret noticed the red mark on his lower abdomen. Not daring to offend him, she asked instead, "Tell me your name."

"I am the surgeon-priest Tasar from Nekhen," he whispered as he smoothed the borrowed kilt.

"And yours?"

"I am, ah, I am Zeina."

"Zeina. What pretty name." Too common for anyone important, he thought.

"Are these your chambers?"

"Yes. Well, not really," Nefret corrected herself,

wondering what best to tell him.

"Then whose are they?"

"We are in the wing of the Royal Heiress." She enjoyed the blanching of his cheeks.

"By Horus! Don't tell me that this -" he grew whiter yet, "that this is a royal bedstand?"

"Indeed it is."

"You little fool! If I am discovered, I am as good as dead. Besides, I believed you to be too old to be untouched. If I had known, I would have never..." His knees trembled.

"But you did," she smiled, took his hand and added impetuously, "I am consecrated to the High Priest of Ptah."

Tasar jerked his hand away and stared at her, aghast. Nefret feared she had gone too far. "Consecrated? To the High Priest of Ptah? To Ramose?"

"I am not to talk about it," she pouted.

"Who was the boy?"

"What boy?" she asked, wondering what Ramose might say to her newest brainstorm; or her behavior, for that matter.

"The one you were with. Outside," Tasar pressed.

"Oh, him. That was Prince Dubar. My, ah, pupil. I teach him court manners." As if I could, she thought. Tasar's anxiety was infectious and she, too, grew anxious. "If they find you here, Priest Tasar, we are both dead. You have to leave. Now!"

Nefret wondered where her women were and swung her long legs onto the floor to push herself upright. Moist warmth trickled down between her thighs and the angry red stain on her rumpled sheet startled her. Had he cut her? She had seen no dagger. A musty odor clung to her as she pulled her wrapper back over her slim body. Crumpled and distended, her garment bore accusing witness to the fulfillment of the young man's urges. She would have to hide it from her slaves.

Tasar's mind raced. Apparently, he was not in a side building as assumed but in the main palace. How could he have missed the fine furnishings? If the chamber's royal occupant were to return to find the bed desecrated by a lowly priest, having defiled the High Priest's maiden, he was dead at best.

"Tasar. Tasar!" Nefret's urgent whispers reached him

from afar. "I think you, too, are beautiful," she smiled and pressed against him with trusting young intimacy.

Tasar had only known a few women after his practiced temple teacher and hoped that this beautiful girl would be wise enough, or afraid enough, to hide the tell-tale signs of their young passion. With luck, and the gods' compassion, his transgression might go unnoticed when the High Priest claimed his due. Only after that would he have a chance at his ambitions, and at life. For now, he had to gain the girl's trust. He sank to his knees. "I beg of you, lovely Zeina, forgive me. Your beauty blinded me." He hoped his abject apologies were convincing, and continued, "I was unable to resist you. Your beauty simply overwhelmed this sun-crazed traveler." He watched her expression soften into a girlish grin.

"Tasar, get up. There is nothing to forgive," she said.

He breathed easier and hastened to assure her, "I shall forever remain in your debt. I must get back to the temple before I am missed. Can I leave these grounds unseen?"

Nefret thought for a moment and then nodded, "There is a little-used entrance. After you leave the secret passage, turn left to find the main path. Then walk toward the great pylons as if you belonged. Do not look furtive. Walk tall. Close to the main gate, swerve to the right and go along the overgrown wall to a small side-gate. It lets out onto the Royal Road. Be careful of the patrols." Was he listening? "You are rather visible in your white wrap though it must be almost dark by now." She spied the ornate trunk. Following the impulse of youth, she rushed toward the sturdy piece, threw its lid open and pulled out the indigo robe. "Here, quickly, put this on."

Startled by the incredible color of the proffered garment, Tasar fondled its cascading folds. Soft as a gosling's down they shimmered like the night sky. He shook his head in wonder. He had never seen the like nor touched such softness; except for her.

"Quickly," Nefret pressed.

Tasar shook his head. "I cannot wear this. Colors are forbidden. Whose is this?"

"The King's," Nefret said casually and again enjoyed the shock in his eyes. "Listen, Priest," she said with mock sternness. "Either you wear it, or we are both in trouble." She placed a slim finger on his mouth sensing his renewed protest. "If you appear suddenly behind the guards and surprise them, they will be too startled to stop you."

"The King's robe?" Tasar mouthed, thunderstruck.

"Yes, the King's robe. He does not know it yet. It is his daughter's gift for his *Sed*-festival. The High Priest is the only one for now allowed to wear anything of color. He has a cape of almost this hue. The guards will think it is he who has sprung upon them out of nowhere." She chuckled, envisioning the superstitious men. "You must walk tall. Keep your stride purposeful, like Ramose."

Tasar wondered briefly if she was lying. Perhaps the High Priest had come through the secret passage to prepare her for her sacred duty. With that uncomfortable thought, Tasar wrapped himself in the pliable cloak and drew the hood deep over his face.

Magnificent, Nefret thought. Quite regal. But she dared not delay his flight another moment. "I shall miss you, Priest Tasar."

Tasar had no illusions. The success of his escape would be his path into renewed life; its failure a tumble toward a most unpleasant fate for the lowly priest who defiled Ptah's consecrated virgin. The High Priest's wrath would prove worse than death. He reached for her again, wanting her, detesting himself for his weakness.

"I want to see you again," she whispered fervently. "Now leave!" she urged and pushed him toward the ante-chamber's old curtain, waiting until the narrow opening had swallowed him.

*

The young lovers were completely unaware that their sudden disappearance had been observed by a young adolescent prince whose own forays into carnal pleasures left him with little doubt as to why the young pair had rushed off.

When his half-sister and the stranger were swallowed by the huge bush, Dubar did not dare to move in closer. In this part of the garden, the hedges were not as high and they would not hide him sufficiently. Thinking the couple behind the dense greenery, he decided to sit down and simply wait. His discovery elated him although he realized that he would need more proof before he could convince anyone of his observation. Even his doting mother might ask stern questions before she used this knowledge in corralling the King's waning favors for him. From now on, Dubar would watch Nefret twice as closely.

He hunkered down vowing to find out about the stranger. His thoughts drifted off.

*

About six moons ago, during one hot noon-hour, Dubar rough-housed with several half-grown sons of some court nobles. Their lessons concluded for the day, they charged about the grounds in wild glee, play-acting out games of their over-active young minds. Dubar had come upon a small clump of boys. Their heads almost touching, their arms around each others' shoulders, they formed a secretive circle and Dubar could hear them whispering. He wanted to join them, curious, but they cast furtive glances and retreated into silence. Stung by their reluctance to include him, Dubar cornered Hem, the youngest of the group, and pressed him into submission.

Hem was pretty for a boy and his tears flowed easily during the rougher games. Thinking him a nuisance, Dubar never paid much attention to the eight-year-old. That day, he took a closer look at the small lad. The child appeared tired and drawn, thinner than he remembered him, as if he might not be well. Wanting information, Dubar was determined to obtain it, and when sly cajoling did not work on the stubborn child, he resorted to threats. "I have a good mind to tell Father," he glowered.

This had the desired effect on Hem. The small son of the *Privy-Councillor of the Two Diadems* broke into tears. "They'll kill me if I tell," he wailed. In his vivid imagination, he conjured up the gruesome oath his peers had made him swear in his high thin voice. In sudden resolve, he stretched himself. "Dubar, promise you won't say anything to anyone. I will tell you, and you will be pleased with me. With me." The younger boy had long learned that it was more rewarding to please those who were stronger. Like the forever fawning members of his father's large household.

"I won't tell anyone, Hem-Hem," Dubar said with a conspiratorial wink, calling Hem by his nickname. The boy stammered, repeating his words, and the other youngsters had been quick to dub him Hem-Hem.

101

"Now, let's hear it." Dubar shook the child. "First, where do you boys go during the noon-hour? I can never find any of you just when the grown-ups are occupied with naps or noon-time offerings, or whatever. We could have all sorts of fun without their supervision."

"That's why we do it during that time," Hem whispered importantly. "We go outside the palace-palace, through the small gate. You know the place I mean-mean."

Dubar leaned closer, "And where do you go-go, Hem-Hem?" he sneered.

"We sneak into his villa. Nobody must see us," Hem said. "It's part of the rules. When we reach the dark room, he serves his special brew. At first, I didn't like it. Now, I can hardly wait to drink more. I don't know why because it doesn't taste all that good." Hem stared into the distance with a queer smile and smacked his lips. Then he added quietly, "But it makes me feel so-so good."

"Really?" Dubar was interested. Could someone be serving these small boys unwatered wine? On several occasions, he had smuggled a stoppered jar into his own chamber. Always observant, Beir caught him and insisted that he give the wine back.

"Yes. Really!" Hem's small voice drifted through Dubar's anticipation of the sweet, numbing taste he had grown secretly to like.

"And?" he bored into Hem.

"And then we play lovely games." Hem's tears had dried and his pale face became animated.

Dubar put a hand on the youngster's shoulder and urged him on, "What kind of games?" The more Dubar pressed, the more the frail boy withdrew into his reverie.

At last, he drifted back. "The games start after I have drunk a cup. Some of the boys get two-two."

Dubar grew impatient with the child's stuttering. "A cup of what, Hem! Wine?"

"Oh, no," the small boy sighed. "Not wine. I am quite sure of that. When we finish our cup, there are leaves at the bottom. I ate some once. Piuh!"

Little by little, Dubar pieced together a scene of hushed fun and secret games. Hem would not elaborate further and from his furtive glances, Dubar realized that Hem was not telling him everything. He shook the *Privy-Councilor's* young son roughly, "Who is it you visit, Hem-Hem. I am waiting." In a wide-legged stance, he stared darkly at his young informer.

"Perhaps, if I ask the others, they'll take you with us to visit him."

"Visit whom?" Dubar asked, exasperated.

Hem backed a safe few paces away from his stocky tormentor and turned to leave. Looking back he whispered, "Uncle Ebu."

*

Dubar never forgot his first visit to *Uncle Ebu*. The cautious approach through the backways of unfamiliar orchards, his fear of the unknown. His deep shock after the other boys pushed him into the darkened room.

"This is our special friend, Uncle Ebu. Prince Dubar," the eager group chorused.

Before Dubar's eyes adjusted to the room's dim light, a gruff voice hissed from a dark corner. "So I see." Dubar could not know that the Vizier was trying to mask his own numbing shock. As the intrigue-versed man recovered over the prince's unexpected—and potentially quite dangerous—appearance, his demeanor changed into one of gracious welcome. Perhaps, the apparent calamity could be turned into good fortune, the ambitious man thought, angered by his carelessness.

Slowly, *Uncle Ebu* accustomed the ever-thirsty Prince to his dream-inducing brew. With great patience, the older man would steep the leaves and let Dubar sip his fill. The dried hemp was pandered from close-mouthed traders who brought it to Ineb-hedj over arduous caravan routes from the cooler, damper climes of the northern steppes.

Dubar came to prize the wondrous promise of hashish. Floating on the haze of his hallucinations, the pubescent Prince learned pleasures that made him forget his mother's dutiful maidens.

The older man proved an exquisite master of the senses. With infinite cunning, and the help of his mysterious elixir, *Uncle Ebu* turned the haughty Prince into his malleable puppet.

*

A rustle disturbed the stillness of the descending dusk. Dubar's head jerked up. Despite his potentially exciting discovery, he had nodded off. As he rubbed his hot forehead he noticed a slight movement out of the corner of his eye. He could scarcely see the dark figure emerging from the middle of the mulberry bush. In the diffused light, it was almost impossible to distinguish between the waving branches and the fast-moving shadow. Then he recognized the dark mantle.

Dubar's mouth fell open. The Prince sat still as though he had grown roots. Hot rushes of blood flooded his dark face. Ramose! What was the High Priest doing here? And what had happened to the stranger? Dubar stared after the disappearing shadow. He did not dare to follow it. Nor did he think to explore the space behind the bush. Fear swept over him. What if it had been the High Priest all along? Could he change his shape at will? Was he aware of Dubar's presence behind the hedge? If so, Ramose could turn him into fodder for the vultures; just as Nefret had threatened to do with him once she would be queen. Which she never will be, Dubar swore under his breath.

Fear of Ramose's magic constricted his throat. The thought of the High Priest's ubiquitous power terrified the superstitious Prince. He left his hiding place, crashing carelessly through hedges, his mind racing. All he wanted to do was to hide from the all-seeing, all-knowing High Priest of Ptah.

The guards were used to Dubar's headlong rushes through the Grand Foyer. His sudden spurts of energy and secret forays were well known, and usually ignored.

Dubar reached his chamber and flung himself onto his bedstand.

Whom could he tell? Accusing the High Priest was like accusing Ptah himself. Who would believe him? Mother! No, he decided, she would whine and lecture him, and most likely box him behind the ear.

An ugly face appeared before his inner eye. Yes, he would speak to the only one who would listen to his story, and believe him.

Dubar had long discovered the powerful man's disgust for the priesthood in general, and his hatred of Ramose in particular. Embroiling the haughty High Priest of Ptah in a scandal could be a delicious diversion during these boring days. Dubar rushed out, forgetting all about the young stranger from Nekhen.

* * *

Chapter Twelve

After anxious moments, Tasar reached the end of the secret tunnel and listened for any sound before he parted the hidden passage's leafy sentinel. Its branches caught the indigo robe and held its hasty wearer fast. Tasar's breathing became belabored as he worked to free himself from the mulberry bush's vindictive grasps. Calling on his training he concentrated to summon self-control. At last, he was free and quickly slid into the warm dusk.

Stretching himself taller he walked down the narrow path in measured steps despite the urge to flee like the swift gazelle of the flood plains. In what seemed an age, he reached the overgrown opening in the high wall. Taking a deep breath, he slipped through praying to Horus that it would spew him safely onto the river quay.

The girl had been right. It did. Tasar glanced around to get his bearings. To reach the temple, he would have to pass in front of the palace gates. Ahead, two guards patrolled the Great Road. Their backs were turned toward him as they, too, headed for the boundary between palace and temple. Tasar took another deep breath and stepped into full view, his stride purposeful, as she had told him. Wrapped in the color of the night, he pushed through the two guards, and before they could react, his billowing apparition disappeared into the misty dusk.

"Murderous Seth! Where did he come from?" one of the startled guards blurted, his eyes bulging.

"We should have stopped him," the other ventured, not convinced at all. The river mist lifted for a moment and they saw the shadowy figure vanish through the temple pylons.

The first guard, his face drained of color by superstitious

fear, shook his head, "I wager you my next ration of beer that it was the High Priest himself."

"How would you know?" his companion challenged with false bravado.

"Only Ramose wears a robe of color. If we had stopped him, he would have turned us into hyenas."

Their hackle rising, the pair turned on their heels and hurried back toward the palace gate.

*

Tasar groped his way along the temple steps. The main entrance was closed but he found an open side door. Semi-darkness stretched in front of him. His short time with the Venerable Badar did nothing to prepare him to find his way through the temple's maze of halls and chambers. An oil lamp flickered at the end of a side passage and he decided to follow its soft glow. He chose a small door and entered recognizing Badar's study by the old sedan that he had noticed when he spoke with Badar, although he could not recall the long passageway. Shivering, he pulled the robe closer around him.

The robe! He had to rid himself of it. Reluctant to give up its warmth, he took the unusual garment off and was at once assaulted by a humid chill. He wished he could keep the cape around him a little longer yet knew that its comfort was deceptive. The sentence for wearing such an unauthorized adornment would be severe; not to speak of the deadly punishment for his earlier unspeakable transgression against a virgin consecrated to Ptah. He felt trapped.

As his eyes adjusted to the dimness, he glanced at the old sedan. A simple upright wooden box with two handles in front and in back, just far enough apart for two bearers. Opaque linen curtains were turned back to reveal a wooden seat that was softened by a large cushion. Tasar reached for it. A perfect hiding place for the robe! At least temporarily.

He folded the quilted mantle into a square smaller than the cushion. Then he placed the blue package on the wooden slats. Judging its size against the circumference of the cushion he placed the cushion back on top. Well done, he thought and sat on it, bouncing up and down a few times to flatten the hidden robe.

"Comfortable, my son," a voice mocked from the doorway to an adjacent chamber, its owner half-hidden in the shadows. "I can imagine that, at long last, you have tired. I wondered where you were so long but assumed Ramose kept you. Did he return with you?"

"Oh, Venerable Badar. No, he did not." Tasar scrambled from the unsteady chair. "If the High Priest has not yet returned, he must still be with the King. I came back alone."

The young culprit tried to be appropriately vague as to his latest whereabouts. Hoping to avoid further questioning, he added, "I apologize for my presumptuousness, Divine Father of Ptah. The sedan looked inviting to my tired bones."

"Yes, you have come a long, long way. It is I who must apologize. I have offered you neither food nor drink since you arrived, nor have I given you time or a place to rest. You have done extremely well to bring us Rahetep's important news. Come with me, young Tasar."

With a last glance toward the sedan, Tasar assured himself that none of the blue material spilled out from under the old cushion. He suddenly felt drained. Not from a pleasant afterglow of the past hour but from fearful anticipation. Only a short while ago, he had thanked the gods for this opportune day. Now, he wondered if it would end ignobly. Would his unpardonable transgression against *Ma'at* be revealed? Possibly by the girl?

*

Dusk had settled over Ineb-hedj when Safaga and Zeina hurried back to Nefret's chambers.

Relieved to see no sign of Amma, Zeina rushed to finish her chores and Safaga slipped into her mistress's bed chamber, past the pretty cosmetic stand that held slender flasks and finely chiseled alabaster jars, kohl used as eye mascara, and precious scented oils. A hunched figure knelt in front of the stand busily gathering up the shards of an amphora.

"Dokki! Now what have you done!" Safaga scolded.

The dark girl crouched deeper into herself. Her full lips began to quiver. "It wasn't me," she wailed.

"Leave her alone, Safaga. I broke the stupid thing."

Safaga was startled by her mistress's cold voice. She had not seen Nefret lying on her recessed bed.

After having pressed Tasar into hasty departure, Nefret racked her brain how she could deceive her observant slaves about the telltales of her afternoon. She did not dare to leave her bed, afraid that they would see signs from which they would guess what happened while they had been out. Fear now rendered Nefret imperious when she would rather have cried and flung her arms around her three women for comfort and assurance that everything would be all right.

"Nefret, why are you in bed? The evening meal is to be served soon."

"I am not well, Safaga. I only wish some fruit served to me here. Pomegranates and figs. Now." Nefret's stern voice faltered, "And something cool to drink. I am very thirsty. Please, Safaga. Please?"

Safaga rushed toward the prone figure. It was not often that the willful girl pleaded for anything. She must be feeling badly. "Amma warned you not to stay out too long in that hot sun," she lectured.

"Oh, I shall be all right. I am just a little dizzy, and not very hungry. Some fruit sounds good to me, though. Please bring it right away," Nefret waived her off.

Safaga was relieved to escape any uncomfortable questions regarding her earlier whereabouts. She and Zeina should not have left the royal quarters in Dokki's care. While the poor girl was always willing she seemed unable to cope with anything alone and required constant supervision and prodding. Most likely, she had been asleep somewhere. At least, she would not be too eager to reveal their absence during the afternoon. Especially not to Amma.

It seemed that time stood still for Nefret until Safaga returned with a polished copper tray with buffed pomegranates and sweet figs interspersed with delectable *Nabkh* berries from the sidder tree. Nefret was thankful for Safaga's bright smile when her slave removed the white linen square which kept the flies away.

"This fruit looks as good as it comes," Safaga showed off. Concerned about Nefret's sudden malaise, she sat down on the bed and selected the ripest of the pomegranates. Guiding a copper blade between her fingers, she split the red globe and just in time caught its purple juices with the linen cloth marring its whiteness with crimson stains.

Nefret stared at the red blotches. She looked slyly at Safaga who placed both fruit halves back on the tray.

The slave was about to cut into a plump fig when Nefret reached across for one of the pomegranate halves and brought it to her lips. Then, as if feeling faint, she let go of it. The spilling sphere rolled toward the lowest point on the soft matting and came to rest against her hip. As if she tried to snatch the escapist, Nefret rolled forward only to crush the pulp beneath her. Red ooze covered the crimson circle that had so accusingly invaded her sheet earlier.

"Oh no!" Safaga jumped up and removed the tray. "Nefret, you will have to get up. These linens must be changed at once. And just look at your wrapper, it is all stained and wrinkled. If Amma sees this ...""

Dokki, who continued to sponge up oil from the floormats, was torn from her private reverie by Safaga's urging. She roused herself heavily and went to rummage in the depths of an inlaid trunk re-emerging with new linens and a loose night-robe.

"Dokki, hurry up!" After what seemed an eternity to Safaga and the shivering Nefret, Dokki shuffled over to them with clean bed sheets. She held the long night garment out for Nefret. It was not often that the others allowed her to attend to the Princess directly and she meant to take her sweet time, relishing the rare occasion.

Safaga pulled the soiled sheet off the bed. Just look at these spots, she thought. Mixed into the pomegranate's sweet aroma was a curiously familiar scent. She brought the sheet up to her nose—and breathed in the heady smell of semen. Her eyes widened and she met Nefret's cold stare; it was the haughty look of a mistress defying her knowing servant. Safaga was treading on dangerous territory. One wrong move now and the ground could give way under her to open into an abyss from which there would be no escape.

Without a word, Safaga clutched her weighty burden and fled toward the outer chambers. Her thoughts tumbled through her shocked mind. What had happened while she and Zeina were gone? Who could have gained access without being challenged by the guards? No one that she could think of. Except Dubar, of course. She gasped. Dubar was known to have come into premature manhood long before he would outgrow his sidelock. Mostly with his mother's women-slaves. Although, during the last six months, his rough visits to

Hent's slave quarters had been few. What then had replaced his young curiosity? Pursuit of his sister? Perhaps to wed her to share the falcon throne with her? Both were of royal blood, related only through their father. Or not at all, if old rumors were to be believed.

Or had someone else been here? Only the King had unquestioned access. As did Ramose. Safaga almost fainted from sudden shock. No! No! Her mind screamed. Not the munificent High Priest of Ptah! Everybody knew that he did not keep virgins as did many other priests. She should tell Amma. How could she tell without endangering herself? She would pray to Ptah. His punishment upon her worthless head might be severe after she was dead. At least, it would not be as fierce nor as immediate as Amma's fury, or as relentless as the King's wrath, if they were told. Think, Safaga, think!

*

"Dokki, see where Safaga is. And then leave us." Nefret's first reaction toward Safaga had been defiance. As she watched Safaga scurry away in horror, her contrived haughtiness vanished to be replaced by young anxiety. She needed to confide in her loyal friend. Who else would give her insight into her confusion. There were so many questions. And she wanted to see the handsome Tasar again, for which she needed Safaga's help. Already, she yearned for more of this new pleasure. There had to be more to it than the sweet pain. According to her women at least, there was. The thought of him sent her body tingling again.

"Ah, Safaga. Come. Sit here by me."

The Sumerian was usually not intimidated to approach the sacred daughter of the god-king of the Two Lands. Every day since Ramose brought her to the palace, she served Nefret, guided her, comforted her. And, no matter what the subject, she tried to still the young child's, and later the growing girl's, curiosity. They shared hours in hushed gossip talking about life outside the palace walls.

All this had changed within the last moments. Safaga edged closer, her head bowed. Nefret patted the fresh sheet under her gleaming in white innocence.

"Come, Safaga, please, sit down beside me." Whether it was the mellow afterglow of her first encounter with young womanhood, or the relief of having decided to confide in her

111

trusted friend, Nefret could not say. She broke into tears. "Safaga, I need you," she sobbed. In an instant, she was the child again, confused about this adult world into which she had been flung without forewarning. She felt great guilt, as well as hurt. She was intrigued, and very curious, and already anticipated her next meeting with the handsome priest.

The sudden outburst tugged at Safaga's heartstrings. She folded her royal friend into a comforting embrace. "There, there," she rocked. "Tell me, my sweet, who was here with you?"

* * *

Chapter Thirteen

Lost in thought, Makari returned to his working chambers in the long side building that stood at right angles to the main palace. Despite his eagerness to immerse himself in his battle plans, he had to face the Vizier first. His report would have to be essentially truthful to appease the suspicious man. At the same time, Makari was to uphold the oath of secrecy he had sworn to the King and Ramose. The choice was easy. It was its execution which would be rather delicate.

The Head Scribe admitted him at once into the ante-chamber of the Vizier's inner sanctum. Makari liked the learned scribe and returned his greeting with a nod, "Evenin', Saad." He was about to inquire as to the scribe's wellbeing, when a door was flung open and al-Saqqara rushed toward him to propel him personally into the private study.

"Makari! How do you suppose he knew, eh? I'll have that hyena of a messenger dismembered if he wagged his tongue at the priests before reporting to me. Saad!" The agitated Vizier half ran after his retreating Scribe. "Get that messenger in here!"

Saad saw the cruel intent on al-Saqqara's distorted face. "Great Vizier," he bowed, "as you ordered, I gave the messenger plenty of restoring beer, which sent the exhausted man into a deathlike slumber. He might not be coherent if I rouse him now."

"My Lord," Makari intervened, "why not let the man sleep. He must be half dead from his long trek. He is not going anywhere. Not with Saad watching over him." Makari knew that the Vizier's barely contained rage still smoldered from having been excluded from the pretended prayer meeting, and that he was about to vent it on the innocent courier. There were better uses for the man than to torture him for nothing. Makari turned to the Head Scribe, "Saad, who is he?"

"His name is Pase, Grand General. He used to be attached to the Palace Archers here, under Captain Veni, before he was dispatched to join the Fourth at the Oasis. His message from General Barum to you ... " Saad stopped, appalled at his own blunder.

Makari nodded and turned to the Vizier who no longer towered over him after having taken off his imposing headdress. Very quietly, Makari asked, "Ebu al-Saqqara, do I understand that the courier's message was addressed to me? Personally! How is it then, Vizier, that it came into your possession first?"

Al-Saqqara had hoped that the Grand General might overlook his interception of the scroll in light of its portent message. He squirmed under Makari's glare. There was nothing righteous about the general's demeanor; nothing that openly challenged. Still, al-Saqqara did not like the square man's forceful presence, emphasized by the poignant quietness of his steady voice.

"Well, you see, ah, you could not be located. We inquired everywhere, didn't we, Saad. Then we looked for your Aide-de-camp but could not find Khayn either."

"And?" Makari breathed. His eyebrows circling higher.

"And, as I said, we could not find either one of you. According to the courier, immediate attention to Barum's message was imperative. I had to intervene. Now, I grant you, Makari, I did overstep my bounds a trifle. What you must understand, my friend, is that we are practically at war and I had to inform the King."

"Indeed, Vizier. Of course, the King was to learn my army commander's observations from me."

Al-Saqqara realized that he had lost ground with the steadfast general. Still, he felt that his early knowledge was worth Makari's reprimand. Once peace was restored, he would again be the more powerful of the two ministers. Right now, though, he needed to apologize. A small shrug with upturned palms was all the ugly man could muster.

Makari dismissed the incident as something else occurred to him. Reverting to his normal tone of voice, he said, "I am taking the messenger to my desert camp tomorrow. He will provide valuable information for my troops concerning the desert route he has just traveled. I can then determine where his loyalties lie. Should I find them wanting, the man will be dealt with accordingly."

"Oh, very well, Makari." Al-Saqqara managed to regain his calm and he waived Saad from the room. When they were alone, he turned back to Makari, "Now tell me, what happened after I left?" He meant to sound disinterested but could not hide his eagerness to hear what he had missed.

"Oh, we spent about an hour praying, the King and I on our aching knees, while Ramose stood entranced, his hands upraised, invoking Ptah and a half dozen other deities, most of whose names I don't recall."

"Don't I know these endless supplications," the Vizier growled. "Ramose slips in and out of his trances the way I slip in and out of my headdress. I guess we have to avail ourselves of all possible gods to be successful in this campaign. And to capture that yellow nub for our people."

Makari grimaced at the Vizier's suggestion that any of the heavy ingots were to find their way to the people.

Al-Saqqara, who did not catch the irony of his own words, continued, "Believe me, Makari, I am determined to find out how he knew about that mine. You don't believe this I-saw-it-in-your-eyes palaver, do you?" It was obvious that al-Saqqara was not about to give up on the subject.

Makari sighed and replied, "Who is to say, My Lord. Ramose has powers we cannot fathom. By the way, I shall leave very early in the morning. There are important things we must discuss, and I hoped that we could do it now."

Al-Saqqara stored his venom for another time. He bade Makari to sit down and fell into his own chair. "I will have the supply tallies brought to me at once," he said. "Our stores should be in excellent shape. Have you had an opportunity to decide what we must do first?" He leaned back in his chair and placed his hands together, finger-tip to finger-tip, awaiting Makari's reply.

"I have, My Lord. Ramose and I did what we both do best. While he prayed, I planned," Makari answered.

A thin smile stretched the Vizier's lips toward his prominent ears. Neither he nor Makari were known to be avid followers of the gods. If Makari bowed to any one god, it was to *Montu*, the God of War. Al-Saqqara's most revered deity was Power.

"As I mentioned earlier," Makari continued, "I shall leave tomorrow morning for my desert camp. I asked three of my generals to assemble there at my Central Headquarters for a briefing on the Annual War Games. A fortuitous coincidence. I can now outline the actual battle plans and discuss strategy and tactics with them. General Barum, being in the south, will be given his final instructions by special messenger. He is our most important link. A pity not to have him here for the discussions. As you know, I like to work with my people's input."

Al-Saqqara's face widened again into a depreciative grin. He knew how Makari operated and doubted that any of his four generals ever voiced serious opposition to a planned campaign.

If there were any protests, Makari was known to joke ominously that the malcontent might want to change occupation; perhaps to that of a stone cutter toiling in the dust-laden royal quarries. Or a Gatherer of Fire, which meant collecting monumental heaps of dried cattle paddies and donkey manure. Nevertheless, Makari had a reputation for being quite the diplomat and after each discussion, he would leave his officers with the impression that he had solicited, and duly weighed, their valued opinions. 'Old Silver-Tongue,' they called him, loyal to the death.

"Colonel Khayn will accompany me to compile the supply lists," Makari's calm voice reached the Vizier. "I'll be gone for no more than four days."

"That long?" Al-Saqqara's curiosity was aroused.

"Most likely. I'll send Khayn back sooner with the lists and he can discuss our needs with your scribes. You will receive a time-table with the planned movements of the four armies." After a moment of silence, Makari bowed to the Vizier and added, "Oh, one other thing, My Lord. At the end of the, ah, prayers, the King decided to come with me tomorrow to attend the War Council himself. He wishes this to be kept quiet, naturally."

"Naturally," al-Saqqara mimicked.

"Officially, Aha is to be on a hunting trip." Makari did not feel compelled to add that the High Priest would join them as well. He was after all a military man and could justify such an omission that he was only concerned with matters of the army.

Al-Saqqara was not surprised that Aha would want to be present at the War Council where the fate of his Four Royal Armies, and of his own, was to be cast.

"I trust you will agree with me, for security's sake, that Colonel Khayn will not be privy to our strategy sessions. All he will be able to bring back to you are the supply requirements. Although I know him to be fiercely loyal, it is a precaution. The possibility always exists that he could be intercepted on his way back by enemy spies. Some may have infiltrated the north by now. The Kush are recruiting lighter-skinned Wawat, so we can hardly tell who is friend and who is foe any more."

Makari hoped that it would not occur to the volatile Vizier that the Chancellor wanted to prevent Khayn from being forced to divulge information. Al-Saqqara's threat to torture the messenger caused him to take this added precaution. Khayn had been his trusted Aide-de-camp for a long time and to exclude him from any part of the meetings was unthinkable. The more so did Makari need to protect the valuable man and his intimate knowledge of their plans. It saddened him that he should have to do so from his powerful equal in the realm.

Al-Saqqara was taken aback. He managed to respond with seeming grace, "Excellent suggestion. I look forward to your return when you must tell me everything. I mean everything."

Both men knew that Makari did not have to abide by the hidden order. Makari bowed as al-Saqqara continued in a lighter tone, "Meanwhile, I'll have the Royal Bark provisioned for the King's convoy upriver. Would you say he is to leave in two weeks' time?"

"A fair estimate, I'd say. One more thing: Aha wishes that the Royal Heiress accompany him to Nekhen," Makari added without lending it too much emphasis.

"Oh? What for?" Al-Saqqara's face showed open surprise.

Makari hastened to explain, "According to the High Priest, his gods," Makari raised his eyes toward the ceiling, "I mean, *our* gods gave him a sign. A special cleansing ceremony for young Nefret is to be conducted at the Temple of Horus. Ramose will seek an answer from the *Oracle of Isis*. He can only do so with her there, at Nekhen."

Al-Saqqara squinted as he listened to Makari continue, "The King decided it was time to prepare her for her Court Initiation to be celebrated here in Ineb-hedj at the time of his own Jubilee, when everyone is back."

"Who is 'everyone'?" Al-Saqqara looked disinterested.

"It is still uncertain if the Queen and the Princes will be on the convoy. Hent's time is nearing fast. And," Makari sounded as if he wished to confide something, "of course, we cannot have the King's Bark arrive without my armies in place for the campaign. Coordination of the timing is imperative. I will know more once I get back from the Council."

Makari got up and, with a slight bow, took his leave. He was glad to return to matters more suited to his soldier's mind, and hoped to have left al-Saqqara with enough tasks and bits of information for the suspicious man not to have any time to pursue unwanted inquiries, such as the departure of three temple boats, for example. Ramose was to announce his and the supposed Badar's journey up the *Hapi* during a special ceremony to be held the day prior to their departure. Should al-Saqqara suspect Makari's involvement in the secret plans, it could mean trouble. Even for a Grand General.

On his way out, Makari beckoned to the waiting Head Scribe and whispered, "Saad, rouse the messenger and house him in a cell next to my chambers. What was his name again?"

"Pase," Saad said.

"I don't want anything to happen to this Pase. Do you understand!"

Saad nodded. As was his habit, he had listened to the conversation through a small crack in the door. He understood.

*

When Makari entered his working chambers, his Aide-de-camp rushed up to him. Despite the late hour, Colonel Khayn had waited up.

"Greetings, Grand General. I have messages for you. Several petitions from various posts, as well as ..."

Makari raised his hand to silence the conscientious man. "Later, Khayn, later. Sit down and listen carefully." Makari seated himself and motioned his aide to take another chair. "We have to make plans for a new campaign."

Colonel Khayn drew his breath in. "Against Nobatia, I assume," he uttered, then added, "What do you need me to do first, Grand General?"

"There is an enormous amount to be accomplished in the shortest time possible. Have supper with me here; and bring your writing materials. We shall be busy until well after midnight. Tomorrow, at sunrise, we leave for the garrison. By the way, Aha and Ramose are to ride with us. To hunt ostriches, as the King put it."

Colonel Khayn's eyebrows shot up, "He knows?"

Makari shook his head. "No. A lucky choice of words."

Khayn's face broke into a smile of relief, and Makari continued, "We are taking a courier with us. He arrived this afternoon with an important scroll from Barum."

"I received nothing from the Fourth," Khayn interjected, alarmed at a possible oversight on his part.

"His message precipitated all of this," Makari waved his young Colonel's concern aside. "The man came by the desert route and will therefore have crucial observations about the best way for our push south."

"Who is he," Khayn asked.

"His name is Pase, a former Palace Archer. Saad will bring him. Let him sleep until the morning; the man arrived near death. It took him only seventeen days. Not bad at all. Which reminds me. Mekh needs to be informed of our earlier arrival."

"As soon as I have your instructions, I shall send a dispatch to Colonel Mekh. Should I announce the King, and Ramose?"

Makari thought for a while and then shook his head, "No, Khayn. The King wants it kept quiet."

The Colonel nodded. "May I take the liberty to send word to the Lady Beeba? She might appreciate to learn that you will be at the farm much sooner."

"She might indeed," Makari smiled.

Khayn looked for the archer-on-duty to order their evening meal. "And bring some watered wine," he called after the disappearing man.

"Al-Saqqara expects you to return within two days with the supply tallies. I told him that you would not be attending our sessions. Should he plan to press you for information, you could not possibly know anything."

Khayn understood the inference and was grateful.

"I did not have a chance to reveal the existence of our *Special Forces* to the King this afternoon. If you were to be asked by anyone about who trains at my garrison, you must feign ignorance." Makari's eyebrows drew ominous circles. "Is that quite clear, Colonel Khayn!" His voice had a sharp edge.

Khayn nodded and a wry smile appeared on his hard lips. He was about to proclaim his total ignorance on the subject when a slight knock stilled their exchange. The archer-on-duty entered with a large tray. On it were two earthen plates of food, two copper cups and a flagon of watered wine. The two men ate in silence as each mentally organized the many tasks ahead. When they finished their simple fare, they removed their plates from the stands but kept their wine cups within reach. Khayn went into an adjacent chamber to fetch his writing box to ready himself to take notes. Makari leaned back in his chair. Without realizing it, he adopted al-Saqqara's favorite finger-tip to finger-tip posture.

"This is a list of overnight stops for the High Priest's river journey. You alone are to act upon its instructions, Khayn. No one else is to be told about this schedule. No one! Understand!"

Khayn looked up and raised an eyebrow at the particular emphasis, "Absolutely *no one*, Grand General?" He thought it odd. The Vizier was also the Royal Quartermaster and thus expected to be privy to any military plans.

Makari's round head bobbed up and down. "Correct! *No one.* Only the King, the High Priest, and I know what I am about to tell you. And, as you just acknowledged yourself, you have become selectively forgetful of late."

The young Colonel had served under the Grand General long enough not to ask further questions. If his general did not mention anyone else as a need-to-know, he had done so on purpose, not by oversight. Khayn would follow his instructions precisely. The spoken ones as well as those left unsaid.

"In seven days, the High Priest and the Venerable Badar plan to travel to Nekhen on three of their own temple boats. Accompanying them are several priests and three temple chantresses. Well-trained Temple Bowmen will provide the on-board escort, under Chief Senmut, whom you know."

Khayn listened. Interesting, he thought. But what does this have to do with the army. And why would the two priests venture south with war imminent in that region.

Makari noticed the puzzled look on his intelligent aide's face. "Be patient, Colonel. I shall explain. We, the army that is, are to provide protection for the priestly pilgrims during their overnight camps along the river."

"I see," Khayn said and again wondered why the military was being pulled into this. Most temples supported their own complement of trained forces to protect the priesthood. As a matter of fact, most military leaders were trained under temple forces to gain valuable knowledge from these excellent tacticians.

"You are to give Ramose a schedule of nightly stops. With any luck, and with Ramose's prayers, the waters will be high enough to adhere to it. I will dictate orders for the Third Army to have several squads meet the travelers at these designated landings. I expect General Teyhab to be at the camp tomorrow. Therefore, the message will have to be addressed to his Aide-de-camp. Who is that, Khayn? Do you remember?"

"A certain Colonel Mayhah."

"Ah, yes. I remember him. Only too well, I am afraid. Wasn't he attached to the Palace Archers at one time? A bit of a windbag, as I recall. Vain, too. And I seem to have heard that he fancies himself an independent thinker. A good soldier, otherwise." Makari shook himself to dispel the image of the strutting colonel. "It is paramount that he follows my orders to the letter." Makari looked up. "Where was I?"

"The message to Colonel Mayhah, Grand General."

"Yes. To continue: Ramose plans to spend the first night at the new Temple of Horus being built at the First Royal Mooring Place. The second, third and fourth nights, they will have to camp ashore. And that's when three separate squads from the Second Army must protect them. Remember to tell

General Sekesh tomorrow. He, too, will be at the Council."

Khayn jotted down a note on a scrap of papyrus.

"It never should be the same squad that follows them along the shore; too obvious. Tell the Second and the Third to deploy three different squads, each to reach their designated spot from deep within the desert."

Makari reflected for a while. In his mind he envisioned the course of the river. "Their fifth night can be spent at Khnumu. Not much there except for a small temple, sufficient though to provide protection."

"The boats must pass through the Narrows after that," Khayn added.

"Right. For their sixth and seventh nights ashore, between Khnumu and Badari, two different squads from Colonel Mayhah's Third are to come downriver. The eighth night, at Badari, the travelers can be quartered at Mayhah's garrison."

"It has a small temple, I believe. Ramose may prefer to have a tented encampment set up closer to the river with Mayhah's troops on guard," Khayn suggested.

"I leave that up to him and Mayhah," Makari replied as he continued to visualize the journey. "The ninth night, again, they camp on shore. With one of Mayhah's squads having gone ahead, upriver. The tenth night, they can spend at Tjeny, at the Temple of *Khentiamentiu*."

"Osiris," Khayn corrected without thinking.

"What?"

"The Temple of Osiris," the Colonel repeated. "The old God of the Dead seems to have *Gone West* himself; the priesthood has renamed the temples at Tjeny and Abdju after Osiris, their new God of the Dead."

"I thought the worship of Osiris was forbidden."

"The old Osiris-cult is forbidden as it calls for human sacrifice. The worship of Osiris as an omnipotent God of the Afterlife is not," Khayn explained.

"Whatever." Makari shrugged and turned back to more pressing concerns. His arrangements for adequate protection of the temple boats could not fail, at any price. Precisely why, he dared not confide even to Khayn, lest the truth be tortured out of him.

"It is the eleventh night that worries me. There is a long stretch past high cliffs from which marauding tribes have been known to attack river travelers. It will be imperative that Mayhah's fourth squad is there to meet the boats that night. This is the farthest from Badari. I do not want them to tramp blithely along the shore to meet the boats. An easier trek, for sure. But they must head into the desert first and circle back unseen. Make that clear in Mayhah's orders."

"I shall, Grand General."

"After that, villages and temples are strewn all along the river. The nineteenth day should see them safely sailing into Nekhen. I hope," Makari concluded his instructions.

"In essence," said Khayn, "the priests' safety hinges to a great extent on Mayhah. Did you know that he is no admirer of the priesthood?"

"He better attach importance to this," Makari growled, and his fist hit the stand in front of him. Their cups jingled. "Now. To the war plans. I need to arrive at Central Command prepared."

The two men set to work. They composed dispatches and after having sealed the last Colonel Khayn called the archer-on-duty back. "Send for Captain Veni. Tell him, to bring two of his best messengers. Let us know the moment they arrive."

Makari and Khayn turned their full concentration to formulating the preliminary battle plans. They filled several papyri only to discard them onto the floor. The archer reappeared to announce that his captain was standing by outside. Khayn asked Veni to enter.

If the stocky soldier was awakened from deep sleep, he showed no trace of it. Standing at attention, he looked alert, without undue curiosity. He had served Makari for years and supplied many of the messengers the busy man required in his duties as Chancellor and Grand General.

"At your service, Grand General."

Makari liked Veni. Moreover, he trusted the man.

"Ah, Captain Veni. Good to see you. You've brought two of your best?" He strode toward the loyal soldier.

"Yes, General. Two of my very best."

"Excellent. Do you remember a young archer named Pase?"

"Pase? Yes, I do. Now, there was an extraordinary messenger. The reason I could not bring him with me tonight is that about six moons ago, I dispatched him to the Fourth."

"So you did," Makari nodded. "This afternoon, however, he returned with a message from Old Barum. Made it through the desert in seventeen days flat. Your training, no doubt."

Veni pulled his shoulders back with pride.

It did not escape Makari as he said, "I want to use your Pase for a while longer, Captain Veni. Would that be acceptable?" Once again, Makari solicited an officer's assent when opposition would have been unthinkable.

"Colonel Khayn has the documents for your other two messengers. Thank you for coming so quickly, Captain." Makari returned the Archer Captain's bow.

Khayn left the room with Veni to instruct the messengers and to alert Veni that he would need him to attest to the burning of the discarded plans later on. When the young Colonel returned to Makari's chamber, the two men resumed their work. More discarded papyri floated onto the floor as one plan was superseded by the next. As if by prearranged signal, both men looked up. "Tomorrow," they said in unison.

Makari rolled up the three final documents and strode toward a corner where he took a woven bedroll from an unadorned chest. With a sweep of his arm, he unrolled his thin sleeping mat and, without any further word, placed it on the floor. The three last papyri, he kept tucked between him and the wall. By the time his Aide gathered up the discarded scraps and stuffed them into his large writing box, Makari was asleep.

With the box under his arm, Khayn left the stuffy working chamber. Outside, he summoned one of the archers. "Send word to Captain Veni."

Soon, the archer was back to report. "Captain Veni awaits you, Colonel."

Khayn clamped the document box tighter and followed the archer to the outside of the administration building. Veni stood motionless in the dark. When he saw Khayn, he saluted.

"Colonel."

"Captain."

The two men walked to the far palace grounds where the Royal Archers were quartered. A small kiln spewed acrid smoke. Khayn opened his box and, one by one, handed a papyrus to the Archer Captain. Veni took each scroll and called out its number. They fed one discarded war plan after another to the flames. "Seven," Veni sang out as the last turned to ashes.

Khayn requested that a signed statement attesting to the burning be brought to his quarters first thing in the morning. As he passed the archer guard on his way back to his own chamber, he left instructions to be awakened before the break of daylight. Then he entered his dark room.

"Tomorrow," he murmured willing himself into a brief period of restoring sleep.

* * *

Chapter Fourteen

Safaga, believe me, I don't know," Nefret sobbed into Safaga's shoulder.

"Nefret, I know someone was in here with you." Safaga patted her distraught mistress on the back. "Did he hurt you? Tell me. Who was it, my sweet?"

Nefret searched for the right words to share her dangerous secret. Looking into space over Safaga's shoulder, she spied Amma followed by Zeina and Dokki.

"Nefret, girls, quickly, gather 'round," Amma clapped her hands together. At forty-eight, the plump Royal Head Nurse still moved with precision. She stopped in front of the huddled twosome, a frown on her broad face. "What's the matter with you two?"

Nefret straightened up, pushing Safaga away. "I don't feel well, Amma. Safaga says I stayed in the sun too long. She thinks I have a fever." She sighed and sank back onto her freshly sheeted bed. "I just need some rest." A sly kick from Nefret's knee reminded Safaga to get off the bed.

"By Osiris! I mean, by *Horus*," Amma caught herself.

Zeina glanced from Nefret to Safaga for one of their conspiratorial grins. They always exchanged a delighted wink when Amma's tongue slipped in her godly loyalties. But this time, neither of the two seemed to notice. Nefret had to be feeling badly to have let this pass. Zeina felt a nudge. Dokki behind her clicked her tongue. The tall slave looked at the sly dark face, amazed that the slow girl had caught on. Perhaps she did so more often than they all assumed. Zeina would remember to mention this to the other two. Dokki was, after all, a *Noba*, and rumors about war with her people abounded at court. Of course, the dark girl hardly remembered her origins and had been accepted as one of their own long ago.

"Well, then. You better get some sleep. For we are to be at the Temple early tomorrow. Ramose wishes to see us," Amma said and went to Nefret's side. She motioned the others closer before she plopped down on the bed. "Listen up. And not a word of this to anyone, you understand." Amma's stern gaze fixed upon Safaga and Zeina. "I mean, *anyone*! That is meant especially for you two. You have been about the grounds too much of late."

The two blushed. Instead of unleashing her wrath upon their hung heads, Amma continued, "Nefret's initiation is to be celebrated soon. It is time for her to begin acting like our Royal Heiress. And," Amma paused to stroke Nefret's thick shoulder-length hair, "soon, a princely consort will be chosen for her." When she saw the shock in the eyes of Mayet's beloved child, her toothless mouth stretched into a smile. "My innocent *Seshen*, I shall pray to the gods that the chosen one be gentle with you."

Never before did Amma call her a Lotus, innocent or otherwise. Nefret looked at Safaga who flinched at Amma's words. Legend had it that the water lily closed at night to open again at dawn. It was their symbol of creation. Nefret wondered why her old nurse used the name now. Was it because she somehow sensed her transformation from girl to woman? On the other hand, the Lotus was also the symbol of the Upper Region, where her family came from. Could Amma be thinking of that?

Amma continued to stroke Nefret's head and gave a big heave from deep within her pendulous breasts. Pity, she mused while she fingered the glossy strands. It will have to go, replaced by an ill-fitting wig of peasant hair. "There will be a special ceremony for your initiation," she said. "Most likely, it will be combined with your Father's Jubilee. First, you have to present offerings, not only to Ptah but to all the gods. Especially Horus, to bestow your throne-name upon you, once you are queen. Such festivities have not been held for many years. Not since your father came of age in Nekhen." Amma peered at Nefret's pale face. "Ramose will instruct us in the complicated rituals."

Nefret and Safaga exchanged another panicked look. Now they feared that Ramose somehow knew about their respective afternoon activities. For them to have been summoned to the Temple, other than for normal services, was unusual. If the omnipotent High Priest of Ptah knew already, his powerful god had told him. Safaga trembled. A terrifying thought leaped into her young mind. She remembered hearing about *Sati*, the secret practice that offered human sacrifices at special jubilees and funerals. Could this be the reason for the High Priest's summons? Years ago, Badar and Ramose hoped to have persuaded the King to abolish these wasteful human offerings. Still, their counsel had not yet become one of Aha's *Authoritative Utterances.*

Unaware that half of the young women in the room were terror-stricken, Amma smiled at Nefret, "Rest now, my precious. Tomorrow, you will feel much better." Noticing the large empty clay pot next to the bed, she nodded at Dokki, "For once, you managed to do your chores without reminding." Then she wagged a gnarled finger at the dark slave, "Dokki, make sure Nefret's sedan is free of dust. It will be needed in the morning. And you, Zeina, alert the bearers of our outing in good time. Now, we all better get some sleep."

Amma ambled from the chamber. How quiet the girls are, she thought. Usually, following her last admonition to go to sleep, they giggled and jostled for a while until Dokki extinguished the lamps. This evening, they were strangely subdued. Perhaps they were anxious about the meeting with Ramose.

She was not entirely satisfied with the given reason for this visit. Earlier that evening, the King's Steward sent for her and told her in confidence about the King's secret meeting. Then he passed on Ramose's orders: The Princess and her three servants were to be in the High Priest's private chambers by mid-morning the next day. Something was amiss. In her many years of unflinching service, Amma had learned not to ask questions and had developed a wily sense of intuition. She felt that this concerned more than future initiation rites and jubilees, but she also knew that in due time she would be told.

At last, Amma reached her room and, with a great sigh, fell onto the simple bed. Tonight she felt the age in her bones more than usual. Her mouth hurt. She should not have eaten so much bread. The loaves are grittier than ever, she grumbled to herself. The high sand content in the flour could wear the healthiest of teeth into stumps. She was one of the luckier ones. Her decayed teeth had fallen out so that she did better with her hard gums than she would have with painfully exposed roots.

*

"Nefret?" Safaga had not been able to fall asleep and when she was assured that Zeina and Dokki were no longer awake she had groped her way back into Nefret's chamber and now gently shook the slender form curled up on the recessed bed.

"Nefret, are you awake?"

"Oh, Safaga. I hoped you would come back." The whisper reached Safaga together with two searching arms pulling the shivering servant under the light quilt. For a while, the two lay still in the dark.

"Do you think they know?" Nefret whispered.

"Who?"

"Amma and Ramose, silly!" Nefret hissed.

"Shhh," Safaga calmed her. "Not so loud." In a hushed decisive tone she added, "Nefret. You must tell me! Who was here this afternoon?"

"No one you know."

"Tell me. Who was it."

"A stranger."

The trite answer exasperated Safaga. "Nefret! Stop it. We both know that no stranger could pass through the Grand Foyer without the guards spearing him." She took a deep breath and lowered her voice to a whisper again, "Do you know what I think? I think it was Dubar."

"It was not! I would have killed the little swine!" Nefret exploded with such fervor that Safaga believed her. That left Ramose. How can I say this, she wondered, without having my head chewed off. It was going to be difficult for Nefret to confess whoever the intruder was. She decided on a different approach. "All right; so he was a stranger. At least tell me, was he tall and handsome?" She reached out and caressed Nefret's smooth cheek with her fingertips.

The simple gesture accomplished more than her verbal

urgings, and Nefret's response to her friend's gentle touch was immediate. "Safaga. You have been with a man before. I heard about the Archer. Was he your first?"

Safaga laughed aloud, a derisive sound, full of latent rage. She pulled herself back into the present. If she was to learn the truth about this afternoon's events, she needed to take advantage of the opening Nefret gave her. "No, my sweet," the twenty-year old slave sighed, "the Archer was not my first. You forget that I was sold to the caravans when I was seven. I don't remember my first time because the man beat me unconscious. I was so young that I did not know what he wanted at first. When he lurched at me, stinking of too much drink, grabbing me, I bit him. Hard. He hit me. I don't remember anything after that. Only, that I hurt for days. Down there." Safaga's hand slipped along Nefret's rigid body. When she reached the young bruised mound, she cupped it with her cool hand, as if to protect it from further harm.

It was Nefret who now reached for her friend, appalled at Safaga's past sufferings. She pressed closer and they comforted each other.

Nefret never thought about Safaga's other life. The Sumerian slave was a part of her life from as far back as she could remember. It was impossible for the pampered Royal Princess to imagine poor Safaga's raw survival among the caravans.

"Then it hurts each time?" Nefret asked, dismayed.

"No. They say only the first time—if it's not done gently. Or if his *Mehyt* is too ample for a small honey pot."

"What do you mean?"

Banishing her enraging memories, Safaga smiled in the dark. "I mean, if his papyrus clump is well endowed his filling pillar can grow big," she whispered and giggled despite her resolve to be solicitous. "When he pushes himself too deeply into your honey pot, it can still hurt. Even after several times."

Annoyed, Safaga thought that Amma should have talked to this royal child months ago. Why should she, a slave albeit presumably with a lot more sweet experience than the old Nurse, have to explain these things to Nefret in secret.

Dawn had almost succeeded to push the night over the western horizon. Safaga sank back, exhausted, content. She had explained things quite well, she thought. The dusty caravans from Babylonia had turned her into a savvy courtesan by the time she was eight, when the tall priest had bought her from her last cruel trader. After that, her life blossomed into a comfortable routine of safety. True, while she had to endure tantrums from her temperamental child-mistress they passed quickly. Safaga asked herself again: Who had defiled this royal child into forced womanhood?

"That is about all there is to know. This closeness to another person can be a beautiful feeling as long as the two people involved care for each other deeply. No stranger can evoke that."

"Tasar does! He does!" Nefret covered her offending lips. "Oh, very well," she conceded. "His name is Tasar." It was a relief to have spilled her secret at last.

"I never heard of anyone named Tasar," Safaga said, relieved it was no one she had suspected.

"He arrived in Ineb-hedj today and came looking for Ramose who was in the garden with us. Ramose rushed off like a stung bull after he talked to this stranger. Dubar left too."

"Dubar? He knows about this?" Alarm shrilled Safaga's voice.

"Yes. No! I mean, Ramose asked the young priest to see us back to the palace but Dubar felt insulted and stomped off. You know how he is. So, I was left alone with Tasar."

"So how precisely did this lead to you two being in here, alone?" Safaga asked, ready to have the impertinent man picked up by the guards.

"I brought him," Nefret replied, her chin jutting like the King's when he felt challenged. After a moment's pause, she added, "And, if you must know, he *is* handsome. Not very tall, though."

Despite her anxiety about Nefret having been observed by Dubar, Safaga was tempted to ask about the handsome stranger's more intimate attributes. Used to chatting freely about men with other women-slaves, she held her curiosity in check. It might not be wise to press the traumatized girl too soon.

Far from being bothered, Nefret twittered on, now that she could share her secret, "Safaga, if I show you something, promise me that you will not tell anyone."

What else could there be, Safaga thought. Her head began to ache as she stared into the grayness of the young dawn. When Nefret told her about the hidden entrance, she sat up, "I had no idea. Imagine, our own secret way in and out." It opened up untold possibilities.

"Promise, you won't tell," Nefret whispered again and Safaga vowed somberly that she would not tell anyone. As if she could. Well, except perhaps Pase. "I still can't believe this Tasar of yours had the audacity to come into your Royal chambers.

"He had no idea who I was," Nefret chuckled.

"He must have realized you were somebody!" Safaga stated.

Nefret guffawed and boxed Safaga on the arm. "I told him that I was the consecrated virgin of the High Priest of Ptah."

"What!" Safaga almost screamed. This was outrageous! And so like Nefret. She suddenly shook with hysterics, trying to smother her laughter behind her hand. Nefret joined in. Not that the thought of Ramose having a virgin tucked away in the royal bedchamber was that hilarious, but they needed a release from their fear. Exhausted with suppressed laughter, they fell asleep in each other's arms.

When daylight invaded the royal sleeping-chamber it found two young women in a comforting embrace.

Dokki padded in on bare feet. For a while, she watched the two friends, sleeping peacefully together. Sadness, born of her deep loneliness, engulfed her. Yet there was no envy in her heart. She knew that she was different and, although they let her be close to them, she realized that she would never truly be a part of such intimacy.

* * *

Chapter Fifteen

He woke with a start. Captain Veni hovered over him thrusting a papyrus scroll into his sleep-slackened face.

"The official certificate, Colonel, attesting to the burning of the seven scrolls," the Archer Captain announced. "It was witnessed by my Second-in-Command."

Khayn blinked as Veni dropped the small document onto his chest, turned, and left. He stretched; the new day had not yet broken the darkness of the preceding night. Still, he rose from his bedroll and after he had completed his brief morning routine, he took the certificate of the burning and went toward Makari's quarters. He met the square-built man as the latter emerged from his own chambers, rushing the new dawn. "I trust you slept well, Grand General," Khayn saluted.

"Well, yes. Although not long enough for a tired old man." Despite his derisive words, the fifty-five year old general looked fresh and ready for the trek to his oasis garrison.

"The burning of the unused plans was completed last night. Here is the certificate from the Archer Captain. I am off to assemble the Honor Guard and the Standard-Bearer. Are you ready to leave?"

"I am, Colonel. However, I shall stop at the temple to give Ramose the schedule we prepared for him. He promised me a small morning meal before we leave. The King's company and you can catch up with us. And don't forget to bring along the messenger. Did Saad bring him over last night? I hope the man has recovered enough to undertake this trek?"

"I am going to check on him now, Grand General. By the way, I plan to bring two of our best scribes to note down the

Council meeting. My own speed may not suffice anymore for so important a gathering," Khayn added, counting on Makari's approval.

The older man nodded, "Good idea, Khayn. This could be a stormy one." He strode from the building. Behind him, two soldiers carried boxes and heaped them onto the pack donkeys until their swayed backs could not take any more. Khayn called for an archer and questioned him as to the messenger's whereabouts.

The beer-drugged Pase had spent the rest of his night in a tiny room near Khayn's chamber dreaming of gentle hands; of soft caresses easing the ache from his exhausted limbs. Awakened by a guard, he looked down and saw that someone had indeed attended to his wound.

"Messenger! Hey, Messenger! Wake up!" The voice cut through Pase's dreams. He blinked his eyes open and looked into a youngish man's chiseled face.

"I am Colonel Khayn, the Grand General's Aide-de-camp. Are you the messenger Pase from the Fourth?"

"Yes, Colonel." Pase's training took over. He forced himself to emerge from his gentle thoughts and bolted from the cot. When he tried to stand at attention, the walls, the door, and the stern colonel, all spun around. Pase groped the air.

"Take it easy, Archer. They fed you much beer last night," Khayn laughed and pushed the dizzy man back onto his cot. "Here, take my arm. Now try again. Slowly."

The colonel's gesture was benign. Yet Pase could not help but wonder what else there was in store for him. He forced a cautious smile. His belt loosened and his kilt slipped down. Khayn looked at the freshly dressed wound and said nothing.

"A small price to pay for a great honor," Pase shrugged.

"You deserve to be commended for your speed," Khayn conceded and clasped Pase by the shoulders.

A feeling of accomplishment swept over the young Archer. He was safe with this young officer; something he had not felt in the presence of the Vizier, especially when the ugly man violated the seal of the message addressed to the Grand General. Pase had seen the greed in the high official's eyes. And something else he was not able to define. He wished he knew how to explain this better, and that he could share his observation with the young colonel. But how could a simple soldier express the merest dawning of suspicion against the land's highest judge?

*

"Nefret! Girls! The sandal-maker has arrived." Amma clapped her hands at her tardy charges. She ushered a bowing man heaped with bundles like a donkey into the antechamber.

Nefret and her three companions abandoned the remains of their morning meal. They always enjoyed being fitted for new sandals and liked the bent craftsman whose clever hands transformed strips of tough leather into beautiful supple footwear. With much excited chatter, they rummaged through his wares. Amma kept rushing them through their decisions and fittings and, much too soon, she bid Dokki to show the sandal-maker out again.

"What's the rush, Amma? We haven't finished our gruel," Nefret pouted.

"Oh, my Princess! Has your pretty head already forgotten that we have to be at the temple this morning?" Amma shook her head in feigned exasperation. "Have Safaga comb your hair. And, Zeina," she called to the tallest slave. "Are the sedan-bearers ready?"

"Oh dear." Zeina put her hand over her sensuous mouth. "I shall call them right away!"

Amma grumbled and muttered. She slammed the soles of Nefret's new sandals together with finality. "Hurry up. The High Priest will not wait forever; not even for you, my Princess!"

Nefret darted back into her chamber. Safaga rushed after her to prepare her for the short trip. No bejeweled neck-collar for this visit, no arm-bands, just a simple white wrapper with a short light cape over the shoulders. She fetched the small alabaster container with crushed malachite from the cosmetic stand. As Safaga outlined Nefret's eyes, the Princess mused, "I wonder what he really wants." Her idle speculations about Ramose's summons were cut short as Zeina returned with two muscular slaves to carry Nefret's small sedan. A royal standard bearer accompanied them.

Their group caused little stir among the guards as they traversed the palace grounds toward the main gate. Two Royal Archers left their station and fell in behind the women.

135

As soon as they did, two others replaced them from a nearby station.

"Please, in here, Royal Heiress." Chief Priest Wazenz had waited for the small group on the temple steps. He scraped and bowed before he directed the two bearers to a small side door where he told them to set their light burden onto the stones and to wait there. A brief scuffle among Nefret's guards caused Wazenz to raise his hands, "You must not accompany the Royal Heiress any further. She and her women are expected by the High Priest who wishes to pray with them. I can assure you that they will be safe within Ptah's temple." The short man pulled his protruding stomach in and tried to stretch himself to greater height as he led the women into the temple's inner sanctum.

The High Priest's study chamber was filled with beautiful trunks, glittering objects and stacks of document holders, some made of hammered copper, others crafted from sturdy hides. On an elevated dais, framed by fine linen draperies, stood an ornate chair resembling a throne. Against it leaned Ramose's tall staff and over one of its armrests, draped the sacred purple robe. Secured in a small precious box lay the top piece for the staff: The *Ankh*; Badar's legacy. Some day, it would be part of Ramose's legacy to his successor.

Comfortable chairs and stands where placed throughout the room. It was a large chamber, bright and airy. Four large openings led into a secluded courtyard filled with lush palms and flowering plants. Lotus blossoms exuded their sweet perfume from a little pond where stone rests beckoned to savor the serene retreat.

"Nefret!" Badar advanced with outstretched hands. He was draped in a simple kilt over which, however, he wore a wide belt of woven yellow nub, just like Ramose did during temple services. This addition to his appearance heightened the formality of the visit. "You haven't been here for some time, my child."

"Venerable Badar," Nefret bowed. The opulent study had always been a source of wonder to her. Its display of great knowledge, awe-inspiring decor, and the many mysterious objects actually intimidated her. She faced the Divine Father of Ptah and smiled at him. She also tried to read his eyes. Did he know anything? And where was Ramose? Nefret cast a shy glance around.

"You were expecting Ramose, of course. He was called away and asked me to introduce you to your new tutor. At least, he will be that for the next few days."

Oh, bother, Nefret thought. Then she caught her breath and her hand flew to her mouth. A figure had darkened one of the courtyard openings. Even against the filtered light she recognized the youthful outline at once.

"Tasar," Badar said. "You startled our Royal Princess. Come in and show yourself, my son." He turned back to Nefret and continued in a voice that carried well, "Ramose has asked me to beg your forgiveness. He confided that, in his unpardonable haste of yesterday afternoon, he overlooked to present this newest addition to our Temple to you. This, Princess, is Tasar, a brilliant and courageous surgeon-priest from Nekhen's Temple of Horus. But no doubt," he added, "Priest Tasar introduced himself yesterday." Badar briefly wondered why the two young people stared so intently at each other. "You must understand," he continued, "it was of utmost importance for Ramose to seek an immediate audience with the King."

Nefret released her breath. Badar's effusiveness was unsettling. Even Safaga's sly wink did not alleviate her chafing nerves. "Yes, of course, he did," she said and turned to introduce her women, glad for the pretense of common courtesy.

"This is my Royal Head Nurse, Amma. And Safaga, and Dokki – and, ah, Zeina. They are my loyal women."

Dokki beamed, loving her mistress for public recognition to her loyalty.

Tasar bowed, "It is a great honor to meet you, Royal Heiress. Officially." He bit his tongue not to ask if the tall slave Zeina was indeed a consecrated virgin. Reminding himself not to be reckless, he added with another bow toward the small entourage, "I am very pleased to meet your loyal ladies."

Dokki could have fainted with pride; after her initial fear to be herded to the temple, she was beginning to savor this.

Silently, the two forbidden lovers prayed that they might not betray themselves, or each other. Their heads and their hearts pounded with the rush of young desire, their cheeks were aflame. Tasar realized that his transgression was worse than he had feared. If the others noticed the rising color on his handsome face they all, except Safaga, attributed it to his awe of their beautiful princess. Nefret's equally flushed face was thought to be caused by her girlish innocence assaulted by the unexpected appearance of this handsome stranger.

"Nefret. Ladies," Badar smiled. "Please, seat yourselves. You too, Tasar. You'll be standing enough later."

They formed a half-circle around the former High Priest who intoned as if in prayer, "The Royal Heiress Nefret, of the great House of Horus of Nekhen, can no longer remain the royal child."

Shivers ran down Nefret's spine. Safaga, too, felt a sudden chill. Here it comes. They both slumped lower in their seats while Amma instinctively crossed her thick arms in front of her as if readying to fend off an unknown threat.

"Soon Princess Nefret's Initiation Rites are to be held in Ineb-hedj. After that, her new duties at court will foreshorten her formal education." The old priest looked at Amma. "I believe we have done a creditable job of stuffing knowledge into the royal craniums." Amma nodded, gratified, and leaned closer toward Badar to catch his every word. "However, we have been remiss in paying attention to a more practical side." Badar had to catch his breath before he continued, seemingly addressing Amma. "I have been told that the Royal Siblings are fine swimmers. However, survival skills in a harsh land are also paramount. We are a nation which not only lives on the shores of the life-supporting *Hapi* but in the surrounding desert.

The girls jostled Nefret. Amma cast a warning glance.

"Our priestly tutors have not acquainted their royal charges with the desert. Nor did they explain the usefulness of the stars which rise above us each night." Again, Badar paused. No longer used to expansive speeches, he needed to replenish his waning breath. "Ramose and I will be occupied for the next few days. Therefore, Tasar has been chosen to interpret the stars for you. He will explain the mysteries of this new science. First, from a design painted on papyrus; then, one evening you will look up and recognize the positions of those stars you have studied."

I wish he would get on with it, Amma thought and sighed.

"Also, our temple bowmen have been told to show you ladies a few techniques, should you ever find yourselves in the desert without the appropriate escort. Not that this will be likely, mind you. Still, it is prudent to be prepared." Badar leaned back in his chair and silence pervaded the room until Nefret pointed out the obvious.

"What about Dubar? Is he not to be included in these lessons?" Not that she wanted him to be but they had always been tutored together.

"Ah, yes, Dubar." Badar rubbed his clean-scraped chin. "While Dubar and Djer will receive their training from the Palace Archers, our lessons here are tailored to you ladies."

"Why?" Nefret asked with little interest.

"Young boys are a bit of a, shall we say, deterrent. Their attention span wears thin much quicker. We think their tutoring is best left to the bolder Archers."

Badar caught Amma's look and knew that someone had better tell the old woman soon what this was all about. He could see with one glance that she did not believe his convoluted story. Hoping her to be patient, he gave her a nod before he picked up his explanations again. Ramose had not given him much time to think and Badar had become unaccustomed to dealing with female inquisitiveness.

"For the first two days, Tasar will instruct you here. Then, perhaps a brief outing, say to Saqqara, to locate certain stars and to practice how to survive a cold desert night."

"Night, you say, Venerable Badar?" Amma shuddered.

Long ago, she had been a member of the old secret Osiris-cult which practiced human *Sati* and sacrificed virgins with great fervor. The memory of the bloody practice leaped into her mind at the mention of the necropolis. A nightly foray into the dark god's *Realm of the Dead* was a frightening thought, particularly when it concerned her darling virgin Princess.

"Why not? There is nothing to be alarmed about. Now, I shall leave you to your knowledgeable tutor, and I look forward to seeing you here again tomorrow."

"Will Ramose be back by then, Venerable One?" Nefret asked in a girlish voice.

"I am not certain, my child," Badar replied, mustering his patience. "Tasar, your eager pupils await you." He turned again to Nefret, "We will serve you a simple noon-time meal. I trust that you honor the temple by partaking of our humble offering, Royal Heiress."

While Nefret had not missed anything Badar had said, she was still confused. Why would Badar leave her in Ramose's private study with a young, and unknown, priest?

Their lessons went on all day. Nefret and Safaga listened with rapt attention. Zeina sat frowning. Dokki played with her fingers trying not to stare at the handsome priest. Amma had long given up and had retreated to the courtyard from where she could see the outlines of the girls and Tasar as he paced in front of his pupils, explaining the intricacies of the skies.

"You mean you can actually find your way back from a spot in the desert just by looking up into the sky?" Ever the inquisitive pupil, Nefret was caught up in this new heavenly world. She was fascinated and wondered how soon they would be allowed to look at the night sky over Saqqara. She would love to do that. Preferably alone with Tasar. Alone. Entwined.

Tasar caught her languid gaze and held it for a moment. Desire welled up in him. It was sheer torture to remain composed and act aloof. He sensed that he had to avoid attracting Amma's watchful stare. He also noticed that the slave called Safaga had tried to catch his eye several times; Tasar wondered if she knew. Slaves were often more than servants; they were confidantes and he could not shake the uncomfortable feeling that Safaga was one of the latter. She was pretty, though, and probably experienced. He imagined her warm welcome of a man's desires.

"I feel stiff all over." Dokki's loud whisper brought Tasar back into the present.

He clapped his hands to tear himself from his sweet stirrings. "You have been patient long enough, Ladies. We covered so much of the sky today that we could be at the end of the desert and still find our way back. Your undivided attention was a great honor."

He inclined his head toward them and went to fetch Amma from the courtyard where he broke into his most sincere smile bowing to the toothless nurse who brushed by him without a word to gather up her charges. Tasar again resolved to be very careful in her presence. She was an old lioness protecting her unweaned cubs, and not one to be trifled with. He had to win her over. A sudden idea struck him. "Royal Heiress, the High Priest would wish me to offer you the protection of Ptah. Allow me to accompany you back to the palace. It must be dusk by now."

Before Amma could protest, Nefret inclined her head and replied with regal formality, "We appreciate your concern, Priest Tasar. Amma, let the bearers go. We sat around all day. A walk in the cool air will do us all some good."

When they exited the temple, Amma and Dokki somehow fell behind since they had to deal with the waiting bearers. Safaga and Zeina kept pace with Nefret at the head of the small procession, while Tasar walked respectful a step behind them.

A gust of wind danced Nefret's cape off her shoulders. The light fabric fluttered into the evening breeze to settle itself onto the Royal Road. Zeina dashed back to pick it up; love-attuned Safaga turned quickly back to help her dust it off.

"Tomorrow! Come with us again to let the guards get used to you. Later, use the small gate. I shall wait inside the tunnel. Bring the robe!" The words sprayed from Nefret's lips as Amma and Dokki caught up and were only a few steps behind.

"Here we are," Amma said. "Thank you for your lessons, young priest, although I for one did not comprehend much of what you said. Tomorrow, you must excuse me. The girls' young minds will keep you busy enough without my dried out old brain having to be tortured."

She marched her charges through the palace gates like any conscientious goose-herder. There is no escaping this flock, Tasar thought. The massive doors swung shut behind them as Tasar was left outside, alone.

He would have to retrieve the blue quilt from under the sedan cushion. But how to carry it back? Perhaps he could hide it under his sash? Better yet, he would borrow a longer kilt so that he could wrap the blue garment around his hips underneath. In anticipation of his foray, he was tempted to rub his hands together when he sensed the guards' boring eyes and caution forced him into a measured walk back toward the temple. Life was looking good again. She had seemed friendly, even amused. And still interested. By Horus, the Royal Heiress! It was treacherous terrain. On the other hand, it could prove fortuitous.

'Tasar, High Priest of Ptah and Royal Consort.' It had a most pleasing ring.

Late that evening, two nimble shadows hastened toward the Vizier's working wing. An Archer barred their way. When Zeina asked that Saad be called, she was told that the Head Scribe was still with the Vizier, even at this late hour. Safaga cut into the whispered conversation, "Do you know the Archer Pase?"

"No, I don't," the guard replied, not caring.

Safaga explained whom she meant and the Archer suddenly nodded, "Oh, you mean the messenger from the Fourth." He checked himself and added, "I never saw him." Safaga's tearful look softened him and he bent down to her, "No one is supposed to know that he was here. He left this morning with the Grand General." His sly wink at the pretty slave left no doubt about his willingness to console her. "Sorry about Saad being busy," he added and looked at Zeina. She was quite pretty also, though a bit too tall for his taste.

Disappointed, the two women returned to their quarters with their young spirits depressed, their hearts aching, and their longings once again left unfulfilled.

As soon as she believed Zeina and Dokki asleep, Safaga crept into Nefret's bedchamber.

The young Princess had waited impatiently and now pleaded for her slave's help during the next evening's planned clandestine meeting with Tasar.

"And what do suppose I tell Amma?" Safaga argued against the dangerous idea.

"Please, Safaga. I just want to talk to him. Alone."

"But what about the others," Safaga tried again.

"What others? Amma goes to bed early. And Zeina could go and see Saad."

"What about Dokki, then?"

"Oh, Dokki! I know. We need fresh oil to replace what was spilled yesterday. Send her to the sesame-seed gatherer," Nefret grinned, proud of her suggestion.

"At night? Oh, Nefret, you are something else," Safaga

whispered. "Oh, I'll think of something," she consented.

Nefret flung her arms around her loyal slave.

"This one time only," Safaga relented and shook her finger at her young mistress who smiled back, confident that it would not be so. The two clung to each other. One anticipating a lover's embrace, the other remembering a sleeping man's response to her caresses.

* * *

Chapter Sixteen

It was noon when the small group drove their well-fed donkeys into Makari's desert garrison. The colossus of the lioness loomed near and beyond, through the shimmering heat, the riders saw a fenced corral. Whatever it held was well hidden from view by a high matted reed fence. Guards watched their approach and when they recognized the standards, a group of them drew toward the small convoy raising their lances over their heads in a respectful salute. Others turned and sped toward some low-lying buildings to announce the high visitors.

"Great Hor-Aha, Supreme Commander of the Four Armies, I humbly serve you. And, welcome back, Grand General. High Priest of Ptah, Colonel Khayn, it is an honor to have you with us." Colonel Mekh, the short lithe commander of Makari's Special Forces, greeted them. If the thirty-one-year-old colonel was surprised to see the King and the High Priest, he did not show it.

The newcomers, except Aha, bowed to him in turn. Those who had never met Mekh, hid their astonishment at his small stature. While the colonel was by more than a cubit shorter than everyone else his sinewy torso bespoke of great endurance.

"Mekh! Good to see you! We bring news of great importance. As well as a great deal of work. Have the others arrived?" Makari slid off his stocky mount and rubbed his broad backside. None too sorry that he would not accompany the troops on the long hot trek into the far southern regions, he realized that he was aging, getting soft. It was time to think of retirement. After this campaign, perhaps, he mused.

The King and Ramose were assisted off their donkeys and

greeted Mekh in turn. Both knew the diminutive officer well and at once adopted the straight-forward language of the military men surrounding them. Soon, everyone was at ease, ready to concentrate on the tasks ahead.

"Colonel Mekh, this is the Archer Pase. He traversed the desert in seventeen days with a message from Barum. He should be able to give you information on the terrain. Question him about it later. Meanwhile, let him catch up on some well-earned rest. He only arrived yesterday."

Makari caught Mekh's quizzical look at Pase, sensing suspicion of the Archer, and appeased, "He won't be going anywhere."

Mekh understood and nodded. If the General thought the man was no threat to the well-guarded secret of the *Special Forces*, neither need he. But his years of training in this hidden environment had rendered him cautious toward strangers. Barking orders over his shoulder, he ushered his important visitors into the main building where cooler air welcomed them.

Before they reached the council room, Mekh whispered into Makari's ear, "The Lady Beeba has been told that you were coming, Grand General."

With a wink of appreciation, Makari took the lead and strode into a large room, ahead of his group; even of the King. This was his domain. Here, he was in charge. With both hands raised, he greeted three men seated around a large table. "General Saiss, I greet you; General Sekesh, good to see you again; and General Teyhab, having come all the way from Badari, I salute you for your timeliness. General Barum, as you realize of course, cannot be with us this time; though soon, you shall be with him."

"Grand General, we hail you," the three army commanders replied in unison as they rose from their seats.

As more newcomers spilled through the door General Sekesh was the first to recognize the King and the High Priest. Headquartered close to the capital, he was at court more often than his provincial counterparts. He pushed his chair back and kneeled, "Supreme Commander, Great Hor-Aha, we serve you."

The others understood and followed Sekesh's adulation of their King.

"Supreme Commander, Hor-Aha, we serve you to the death." Less reverently, they added, "High Priest of Ptah, we welcome you."

"Pleased to be among you." Aha affably indicated for them to get off their knees.

Ramose added his own greeting, "It is an honor for a servant of the gods to be among the bravest servants of our King."

The large table occupied much of the room. On it, watered wine, flat breads, seared meats, cold fowl, and luscious fruits were arranged. Formalities concluded, Makari seated his visitors according to rank, with Aha and Ramose presiding over the assembly from the two opposed narrow ends. Makari took one of the simple chairs on the wide side next to the King, facing the door, while his three army commanders regrouped across from him, with their backs to the only entrance. Colonels Khayn and Mekh took a seat next to their Grand General with Mekh closest to Ramose, facing the generals.

Two scribes squatted at low desks in a corner. Each wore a wide leather strap slung over one shoulder. On the front, a sling held two ink-palettes and in the back, a reed-brush holder was mounted. A freshly filled small water pot hung suspended. While the gum-hardened discs usually contained one of black carbon and one of red ocher, today the scribes carried two black discs. They had been warned to expect a long session and would need the extra supply of black.

To obtain their writing materials, many scribes kept their own work-slaves. The scrolls were made from the papyrus rush harvested in the Delta. Moistened strips of the plant's stem were laid side by side to form the longitudinal warp; then shorter strips were overlaid crosswise, after which the whole thing was pressed, dried and polished into the writing surface.

Despite their anxiety, the two scribes arranged their materials with great care. Several sheets, measuring one cubit each, were strung together side by side to form one continuous roll which then could be unrolled with the left hand as the scribe wrote, usually from right to left. Today, however, they would adopt a more expedient way. After moistening their reed brushes in the water carried on their back, they would write vertically in hieratic script. In this manner, they did not have to wait for the writing to dry before unrolling more of the scroll.

At last, everything was ready. With a double guard posted outside the door, the most important War Council under Aha's rule was about to begin. It would change the fate of The Two Lands forever.

"I trust that everyone was served a soldier's breakfast this morning," Makari prolonged civilian pleasantries for another moment.

The three army generals broke into wide grins. Their morning meal was tasty and most plentiful. In fact, the portions of stirred egg were huge. A bit on the gamey side, perhaps, with a faint aftertaste. But overall, most satisfying. At the time, some wondered where the ducks were kept as no squawking from tamed fowl had heralded in the dawn.

Aha, hungry after his long ride, broke off a chunk of bread and ripped a large drumstick from the steaming carcass of a duck before he passed the platter to his left. Makari followed his King's example. He had eaten little since his simple supper with Khayn the night before, and his morning meal with Ramose turned out to be meager. He also wanted to ease the tension in the room. Besides, he expected that their discussions would last long into the night. It made no sense to force his grumbling stomach into submission at this early stage. Chewing, he explained about the message from General Barum and its implications. Then he asked Ramose to present his Plan of Deception, as he called it not without irony, designed not only to deceive the enemy's many spies but also their own court.

When the generals realized that their King planned to arrive undetected at the Fourth Army camp ten days ahead of his official schedule, they cheered. This would catch the enemy off guard and add to their chance for victory.

Makari then detailed the planned troop movements. Each army was to push upriver to replace the one that had vacated those quarters. It assured immediate reinforcement should the Fourth be unsuccessful in subduing the enemy. He nodded at Khayn. His Aide handed him the three scrolls which had survived the previous night's planning session.

"Generals," Makari drew a deep breath. "These are the

outlines of your portions of the overall plan. Study them carefully. We will come back to each individual part later. Each of you will have the opportunity to fine-tune your own portion, as you see fit—once we have all agreed on the overall outline. Any suggestions thereof will be noted. Keep in mind that the strategy of the overall plan must be adhered to. Local tactics only may be reshaped as called for by unforeseen developments."

Without warning, Makari's voice became as hard as granite, "Any mistakes, and you will be cutting stone slabs in the quarries, wishing you were dead. For I shall descend upon you with the wrath of our Supreme Commander behind me. This, my friends, is not an exercise! It will be the most important engagement in our lifetime."

Aha beamed. His Grand General was invaluable. He caught the High Priest's eye. Ramose seemed to have something urgent on his mind. "Will you let the High Priest speak," Aha asked Makari who of course acquiesced to his King's request at once.

Ramose inclined his head thanking them for the opportunity. "In the wars before this, we left some of the enemy's lowly warriors alive to replenish our decimated forces," he said. "However, we always killed their officers for fear they might influence the captives, incite them into flight, or worse, into rebellion. In this war, I ask that captured enemy officers not be killed!"

Ramose heard the rising grumbles but persevered, "Our priesthood has developed a method by which a man's knowledge can be extracted from him. No, my valued friends, I do not speak of crude torture. Instead we, or at least a few of us, can read a man's thoughts and make him tell us all he knows without reservation."

He looked around the room. All eyes were on him now. "We can obtain valuable information from such captives. Enemy battle plans can then be relayed to our own commanders in the field."

Raised eyebrows met Ramose. He held up his hands, "Let me go one step further. After the captives are questioned by my priests, the most important enemy officers should be brought to Nekhen where I myself shall perform a delicate operation. It produces astounding results. After recovery of our—patients—we would encourage them to escape."

"Whatever for?"

"Never heard of such a thing!"

Despite the King's presence, the generals shouted their fierce protests. Their arms flailed about them as if someone was forcing them under water. They were military leaders, not traitors, they shouted. This was close to treason.

Even Makari found it difficult to retain his composure even though he knew Ramose well enough to anticipate a plausible explanation. He also knew him well enough to suspect that whatever Ramose told them was only a small part of what was really on his mind.

Ramose raised his arms. "I can assure you that these released prisoners would be the most docile beings on earth. With a little help from us, the gods are turning them into mindless court-jesters. Shadows of their former selves, they do not realize the extent to which they have changed. Nor does anyone who knows them. When they return to their own troops, they will be rewarded with a higher command. Leading their men back against us, their decisions clouded, with disastrous results. Unwittingly, they will sabotage their own efforts."

Ramose leaned back. Enough said. How else could he explain to these practical men the surgical experiments he and Badar had hopefully perfected. They had bored into a man's head through a small incision, disconnecting portions of his brain. Although early failures killed most of their patients, the outcome of the last few procedures was quite satisfying. Shrouded in secrecy, the two priests had practiced the delicate operation on some of the capital's criminals. After the unfortunate men had their noses lopped off by their jailers to mark them as convicts, they anticipated spending their short lives in the broiling stone quarries on the outskirts of Ineb-hedj. With the promise of a less painful existence, the condemned men had clamored to volunteer for the risky experiment. Most of them had become harmless imbeciles, with an occasional tick, perhaps. A few of these, however, had turned into raving lunatics leaving little choice as to their fate. Even so, their donation to science was not wasted. The priestly morticians were always grateful for new material to improve their knowledge of the preservation of the dead.

Traditionally, *Ka*-priests pickled the dead in a heavy saline solution, as they still did with Royal Placentas. The results were less than satisfactory until someone stumbled upon a long-dead miner who had fallen into a natron pit. While his skin was well preserved, his organs had deteriorated. This prompted the ever-experimenting priests to remove organs as well as the brain from fresh cadavers. They stuffed them with dry natron and wrapped huge quantities of linen strips around the corpse. Since the limbs were stiff by then, they did not bend them into the customary burial position. As far as could be gauged at the present, the method worked well.

Ramose turned his focus back to the assembly. He decided to recruit Tasar to hypnotize the prisoners immediately, when the enemy's extracted information could best be used to their advantage. His discussions with the young priest revealed the latter's excellent knowledge in medicine as well as his driving ambition to become a great surgeon. Besides, the youth should be eager to return to Nekhen.

With a nod toward the third general, Ramose continued, "This is meant for you, General Teyhab, as your forces will be involved in the sweep-up operations."

Makari confirmed the High Priest's suggestion. "All high-ranking enemy officers are to be captured alive. Upon capture, they become the property of the High Priest." His voice boomed louder than usual, perhaps to convince himself of the benefit of such unmilitary tactics.

Rumbling arose from the others until the war-tried soldiers could contain themselves no longer. Questions, grumbled statements, mixed with crude curses, filled the room.

Once more, Makari bid them silent. "Ramose has presented a plan with great advantage for the Two Lands. Imagine: One single enemy general captured alive," Makari's square face pushed forward, "...questioned to reveal their plans. Then, this officer returns to his command. With an altered mind. It would be worth more than a hundred spies."

Silence cloaked the room. They imagined how much damage the rearranged mind of an enemy general could wreak as he issued his deranged commands. Quite a lot, they admitted, before he was replaced—or killed.

"Remember: *No killing of enemy officers this time! Capture them alive!*" The practical Grand General knew that every warrior on a campaign craved extra rations almost as much as he longed for the sweetness of a woman's honey pot. He added, "I am prepared to sweeten the incentive for our troops not to kill the enemy. One cup of honey for a ranking officer, two extra rations of meat for the rank above captain, and five flagons of wine for any general captured. *As I said: Alive!*"

The faintest flicker of a smile appeared on Ramose's chiseled features. While he had dangled mysterious powers before these hardened men to ask for their compliance, Makari cunningly appealed to their basic instincts to assure obedience.

The discussions continued long after the sun sank below the horizon. The guards outside could hear raised voices, a fist pounding on the wooden table; chairs being pushed back as their occupants jumped up for emphasis, or in frustration, to present a heated counter argument.

While one of the scribes took down the hurled requests for weapons, supplies and re-enforcement, the other drew up the ever changing outline for the final battle. They would transcribe their drafts during that night and read them back to the group in final form in the next morning.

Makari sat back in his chair. He placed his square hands together, finger-tip to finger-tip. "Supreme Commander. High Priest. Fellow officers," he began. "I believe we have a final plan. I would like to go over it one more time." He glanced at the corner. "This will also give the scribes a chance to review their annotations. And, if it is agreeable to you, Hor-Aha, permit me to start with the First, moving on down the line, north to south. General Saiss, will you begin."

Among themselves, soldiers referred to Aha's armies not by their full titles but by numbers. Only when conversing with someone from civilian life, would they add the name of the region, though almost never by the name of its protector god. Their trust lay in their leaders, their plans, their weapons and their men. Not particularly pious or overly superstitious, they concerned themselves little with the gods, and the presence of the High Priest of Ptah made no difference to them now. The general of the First Army perceived his god-king's permission to speak as Aha gave him a nod.

"Most Supreme Commander, High Priest of Ptah, Grand General, fellow Generals, and Colonels," General Saiss, Commander of the *First Army of Sutekh*, stationed at Pe in the Delta, commenced feeling himself in a rare expansive mood. He supported his muscular body on the table by placing his strong hands on its very edge, his fingers turned under, white knuckles protruding.

"One fourth of my army shall remain in the Delta. The rest will move into the capital to form the last line of defense for Ineb-hedj. We will replenish our ranks with conscripts from the surrounding farms. With the inundation nearing, it is an opportune time for the fellah to drop his hoe and serve his King."

Saiss sat down and General Sekesh, Commander of the *Second Army of Ra*, headquartered at the outskirts of Ineb-hedj, stood up, "You will find my headquarters comfortable, Saiss," Sekesh nodded to his colleague. He annunciated every word as he addressed the assembly, "One fourth of the Second will accompany the King on the war barges. The rest will cross the desert on its drive to Badari, our next base. We are to remain at the ready for deployment there as a second front, should the campaign in the south fail to stop the enemy's advance."

As Sekesh sat down, he noticed the King frown. His reference to a possible failure in the south apparently displeased Aha. Sekesh vowed he would choose his words with greater care in future reports.

General Teyhab rose. His inflated ego was well known, and he always had a swagger about him. As the Commander of the *Third Army of Ptah*, which patrolled the middle section of the Two Lands, his headquarters were at Badari. His garrison was an important military presence along the river—heavily fortified, at the expense of its small temple. A handful of priests there practiced their healing on Teyhab's sick and injured.

"My troops cross the river and take the western desert route to move into position far to the south. Our main task will be to share in the sweep-up operations. I noted your command to capture enemy officers—*alive!*" He bowed to Ramose without much reverence and sat down, pleased with his own wit.

Makari rose once more and surveyed the group. "I shall speak for General Ali el'Barum of the *Fourth Army of Amun*," he said formally, mostly for the benefit of the scribes. The King nodded.

Makari continued, "General Barum is already in battle training near the Kharga Oasis. As soon as the King has joined up, the Fourth will push south. However, Barum's troops will not have to face the enemy with conventional weapons alone." Makari's remark raised his listeners' interest perceptively.

"My King, High Priest, Fellow Officers. The time has come to reveal the secret power of my *Special Forces*."

The Grand General looked at the seven men around the table. Five bored their eyes into him in surprise. The two colonels smiled.

Makari pointed a finger at Saiss. "Before I do so, however, let me ask our colleague if he has brought his own secret weapon with him."

The General of the First nodded, "As promised, Grand General. My donkeys came laden. We achieved our quota, barely though, before we ran out of the special material."

There was not a sound in the large room.

"Excellent. I will come to it in a moment. Now, back to my own surprise: For the past two years, I have trained my *Special Forces* with two major weapons, both of them outstanding. The first was perfected behind the high fencing you must have noticed coming in. This weapon is unequalled speed.

"The second secret weapon is a contribution from our colleague, General Saiss. He hit upon something so new that he was able to supply just enough for my *Special Forces*. A weapon of blinding indestructible hardness." Makari wiped a blurry eye. The air in the room was stifling by now and the wicks of the burning oil lamps belched acrid smoke.

"It is late. Allow us to keep our secrets from you one night longer. Tomorrow, you will be treated to a demonstration."

Stunned silence followed Makari's tantalizing revelation until, at last, Aha clapped his hands in unaccustomed delight. The Grand General only hoped that his impatient King would not ask for an immediate explanation.

"This is fantastic news, Makari. We look forward to your demonstration. It will be difficult to contain our curiosity until then, but I agree, the hour is late."

Pleased that the King did not reprimand him about his secrets, Makari declared the War Council adjourned. Gratefully stretching their limbs, the group exited the council building and spilled into a dark night, finding their way toward their assigned quarters with the aid of local guards.

Unnoticed by the others, Khayn, one of the scribes carrying the supply requisitions, and two furloughed garrison guards slipped away to journey back to Ineb-hedj.

* * *

Chapter Seventeen

Their morning meal was opulent. Loaves of unleavened bread, platters of chunks of charred tender meats, and pitchers of donkey's milk were set out, together with bowls of fresh figs, ripe dates, and juicy pomegranates. Honey pearled from glazed pots, and the portions of stirred egg were once again enormous. On this crisp desert morning, they did not linger over the generous offerings. Everyone impatiently anticipated Makari's promised demonstration.

Makari guided his excited group to a nearby hillock rising close to the west end of the high fencing from where they could look down into the vast corral. Before them stretched nothing but trampled sand and, at the far end of the enclosure, another broad hill blocked the view into the desert. Behind it the fencing vanished into the shimmer of the rising heat. Awe-inspiring, forever silent, the ancient colossus loomed in the distance.

The first faint rumbling quickened into the thunder of many feet, a beat too rapid for an advancing battalion. A merciless sun began to assault the group as they stared toward the ominous pounding. Suddenly, a blinding wall arose ahead and they had to squint. What was that? As brilliant as the sun, it advanced toward them with the speed of a comet.

The group huddled together as the swift apparition thundered past, hypnotizing the spectators as their eyes followed it in unison.

"By Horus! Ostriches! Those lancers are riding ostriches," Aha croaked, his throat bone-dry with excitement.

A cacophony of voices drowned Makari's answer.

The Grand General was slapped on the back, his arms were being grasped, his hands shaken. Questions bombarded his broad frame like an enemy force storming a battlement.

"And those shields? What are they made of?"

"They were blinding me."

"I couldn't see a thing!"

"What speed! Never thought these birds could run so fast!"

"Never saw one being tamed, much less ridden."

"Fantastic, Makari!"

His hands raised, Makari pleaded for silence. "This is what we have been working on for the last two years. First, we trained the birds to tolerate loads on their backs. Then we realized that with a man astride they could reach speeds not matched by man or beast. Except perhaps the cunning leopard. And no one I know would ride on one of those."

Laughter was followed by renewed exclamations of "Well done, Makari!" and "This is incredible!" As well as, "If I didn't see it with my own eyes!"

"Our colleague Saiss," Makari stepped toward General Saiss and clasped the smiling man's shoulder, "our colleague here has added another impressive weapon to complement my speed. You noticed the unusually gleaming shields?"

Nodding and murmuring from everyone.

"General Saiss!" Silence fell as the King jutted his chin toward the Commander of the First. "Have you squandered the realm's entire yellow nub to hammer out these shields? We haven't captured the enemy's new mine yet, you know!" Aha challenged, only half in jest.

"No, of course not, my Supreme Commander." Saiss bowed. "These shields have not been hammered from the yellow nub. It would have rendered them too soft to be effective. They are made from a new mixture which our smithy discovered. An interesting story."

"Ah, do tell."

"If there is time left this afternoon, I shall regale you with it, if I may. Foremost, I beg the High Priest's assistance to help reproduce more of this special metal. Temple smithies are well known for their innovations and craftsmanship."

Before Ramose could agree, Makari rejoined the group with three of the riders. Remaining astride, bowing from the waist, they reined their big birds in.

"Beware of those sharp toes. These birds can kill a man

with one swift kick," Makari cautioned as his visitors surged toward the lancers. He accepted a shield and offered it to Aha for inspection. It was as long as the torso of a small man, and wide enough for him to hide behind, with its sides curved inward. On the inside, an ample handgrip had been pulled from the still hot metal which was wound with braided leather to absorb a man's battle sweat.

Aha took the shield from Makari and looked up in surprise, "This is extremely light!"

"Yes, my King," Saiss smiled with pride. "And almost indestructible."

The shield was handed around and mock attacks were fended off, as they all had their chance to handle the amazing implement. Makari suggested that they return to the Council chambers for more in-depth discussions.

Aha thanked the three lancers, and then extended his raised hands toward the melee of riders who issued forth a single cry, "Great Hor-Aha! Supreme Commander!"

On the short walk back to the compound, Aha turned toward Ramose and said with a confidential undertone, "Did you know that I am almost as good as you are in foretelling the future? You see, I told my Steward to let the court know that I went into the desert to hunt ostriches. And here we are, amidst a whole flock of them."

Wistfully, he added, "Maybe I need to be more careful with my predictions in the future."

"We may all need to be more careful with our words in the future," Ramose replied.

Aha shrugged, somewhat annoyed. Why could the confounded priest not take a good joke without becoming pious?

General Teyhab pulled Makari aside to compliment his host. "A remarkable assembly, Grand General. And your morning meal was surpassed only by your surprises."

Then he added with feigned innocence, "By the way, how many ducks do you raise on your nearby farm to have harvested enough eggs for us?"

"None whatsoever." Makari winked at his strutting junior.

Teyhab swallowed hard and stole a glance at the hobbled ostriches as the taste of the gamey morning eggs rose bitter in his throat.

*

When the Council reconvened, the mood was high. Lightly watered date wine was passed around. A welcomed cool libation as everyone's throat was parched by the dusty morning outing and even more so from the excitement it generated. An air of camaraderie prevailed.

Aha felt a rare closeness with these high army officers. He relished their unadorned way of speech, the absence of false pretenses, and he actually began to anticipate leading his troops into battle. Provided they would be victorious.

On the way back from the demonstration, Ramose had briefly stopped at his quarters. When he returned to the council chamber, he carried a small flat ivory box which he carefully placed on the table in front of him. He then took his seat with a faint smile upon his lips.

Makari surveyed the room and noted that the remaining scribe was ready. He reopened the War Council with, "Much has been accomplished in a short time. We finalized our plans, you experienced the lightening swiftness of my new forces, and you were half blinded by a new discovery. I can honestly say that we are as prepared for a campaign as we will ever be." He raised his cup, "To our Supreme Commander, the Great Hor-Aha. To Victory!"

"Hear, hear."

Aha drank and then held his cup toward the assembled men. "To the Grand General for his excellent chairmanship and hospitality. That we may convene again at many future Councils. After our victorious campaign, of course."

"Hear, hear," echoed through the council chamber.

Ramose surprised everyone as he lifted his cup which had remained untouched so far. Some sighed and sank deeper into their chairs, some drank more wine. Teyhab tried to stifle a yawn.

"I have prayed to the gods and, soon, I shall consult the Oracle's infallible predictions."

The following obligatory 'hear-hear' had a less enthusiastic ring to it. Ramose continued undeterred. "There is a more practical application I wish to contribute to the war effort."

Suddenly, all eyes were riveted on the High Priest.

"Colonel Mekh, could I trouble you for one of your most miserable slaves so that I may free him from his earthly burden."

Makari nodded. Mekh stood up and went to open the door.

"Guards!" he called out. "Bring Hanni." He leaned against the door's heavy frame while everyone kept staring at the High Priest.

Outside, a faint scuffle arose and the short colonel opened the door wider. Through it he half pulled, half dragged an ancient slave. The old man's emaciated body was covered with oozing welts. Mekh pushed the limping man in front of Ramose.

"This is Hanni, the garrison's *Ostrich Egg Gatherer*. He won't be needed after tomorrow, and almost every bone in his body has been bruised or broken as our ostriches protect their eggs well. Hanni will only praise you for his *Ba's* release."

A faint glimmer flickered in the pitiful man's rheumy eyes. Was he to be set free at last? His toothless mouth widened into a hollow grimace as he tried to smile at his apparent savior.

"Are you prepared to be set free, Old Hanni?" Ramose pitied the wretch for his vain hope. It had to be done.

"Aye, My Lord. My broken body is eager for its well-earned rest," the old man croaked.

Ramose opened his small box. With extreme care, he took out a miniature lance tip and held its stem between two fingers, displaying it to the assembly. Then he stood up, towering high above the bent slave. Without warning, his hand shot forward. He only nicked the leathery skin of the old man's arm with the sharp tip.

The wretched slave shrieked in sudden terror. His eyes gaped wide at the single drop of blood oozing from his stringy forearm. Moments later, he collapsed. The tiny lance clattered to the ground with him.

"His old spirit has been freed. His miserable body is at rest. May Osiris welcome his *Ka,*" Ramose half-chanted.

The two guards who witnessed the incident through the open door sprang forward to drag the limp body away.

"Beware!" Ramose called out. "You are not to touch the lance tip!" With a piece of bread crust he pushed the sharp implement back into the flat box, securing the lid over the lethal tip. With the sole of his papyrus sandal, he ground the crust into harmless crumbs.

Everyone sat mesmerized. So, Ramose, their tempered High Priest, had a cruel streak in him after all!

The silence became so awkward that Aha felt compelled to break its spell, "Is this one of your magic tricks, High Priest?" His voice reflected awe rather than intended sarcasm.

"Not magic, Hor-Aha. Special knowledge. I would like to offer it to you, my King; to hasten your victory," Ramose replied evenly. "Tips like this one can be fitted onto longer lance shafts. Imagine the enemy's consternation after the first battle as they collect their dead lying slain apparently from nothing more than a slight cut. Felled just like the Egg Gatherer. Horror will spread through their ranks. Makari's swift riders, outfitted with these tips, will be invincible."

"And what about my men?" Makari thundered, jumping up. It was rare for the solid man to display his temper. "Handling those lances, they might kill themselves long before they reach Barum's camp!"

Ramose turned to Makari. "Grand General, your anguish is understandable. The tips are indeed covered with potent venom and you no doubt noticed how cautiously I handled the small tip before I freed the unfortunate Egg Gatherer's *Ka*."

"Expediently so, as we all saw," Makari growled.

Ramose continued, "No one will handle the treated tips lest they were coated with hot beeswax. I plan to have the entire supply of lance tips shipped to Nekhen on my own temple boats. Untreated, of course. In Nekhen, the tips will be dipped in fresh venom, covered with wax, to be trekked to Barum's oasis camp. This will ensure that the heat does not melt the wax as your ostrich riders push south through the western desert. Besides, I brought only one tip with me, and your *Amazing Forces* leave tomorrow." Ramose turned to the short colonel, "Are they not, Colonel Mekh?"

Mekh nodded.

Makari inclined his massive head, "I beg your indulgence, High Priest. I should have known better than to have doubted you." He added with renewed calm, "Please understand that the well-being of my *Special Forces* is paramount to me. As it will be to the entire war effort."

"Your concern for them speaks well of you." Ramose returned Makari's bow.

"Well, this has been a fascinating gathering," Aha said and stretched himself into a more comfortable position. "And there is still the story of the shields to be told. I want to learn about this metal which glitters like the sun, deflects hard blows like a quarry stone, and is as light as a falcon's wing. General Saiss, regale us with your story now."

"With pleasure, Great Hor-Aha." Saiss stood up, somewhat self-conscious, and cleared his throat, "At the headquarters of the First, no one ever rests."

His colleagues rolled their eyes. Saiss never missed an opportunity to aggrandize himself.

"The town of Pe has grown into a noisy trading center and many exotic wares pass through it on their way upriver..."

*

Black smoke bellowed from the large smithy of the Pe garrison. The clanging of hammers against stone anvils could be heard throughout the Delta. In this busy market center, skilled craftsmen and military personnel mixed with foreign traders from Babylonia and the vast continent beyond. Trading was brisk. Loud shouting accompanied each barter until a favorable bargain was sealed. Wine spilled in boisterous triumph as both seller and buyer celebrated their cunning victories.

In a backyard of the smithy, the chief smith sweated over a particularly intricate design. Grimy apprentices watched his powerful blows as others kept the underground furnace roaring. Above, an immense cauldron bubbled, its glowing rim level with the courtyard ground for easier pouring of the molten copper. A new batch of raw metal had just been added to melt into a consistent mass. Already, a thin crust of glowing matter layered the top and the chief smith eyed the hissing lava with calculated expertise. A few more minutes, he thought, and we can pour the rest of the molds and go home.

Shouts, loud enough to pierce the clanging of the smithy, preceded a figure that hurled itself toward the group of workers, followed through the narrow alley by gesticulating guards. The pursued man reached the courtyard and flung himself into its depths while casting wild looks about him. Trapped, he turned around. Without taking his eyes off his

161

pursuers he backed up to the bubbling cauldron. When his naked feet touched the searing rim, his back arched so violently that his hands flew up over his head. A pouch dropped from his fingers and plopped into the crusting copper.

"Eeejeh!" he wailed. Frenzied by fear and greed, blinded by pain, he dove after his precious loot. Steam hissed; the cauldron smacked its greedy lips; hot bubbles burped the human meal.

After the commotion died down and the courtyard was emptied of jabbering traders, stunned bystanders, and officious guards, the chief smith surveyed his ruined batch of copper. Listening to the excited babble in his yard, he had pieced together the dregs of the event. Apparently, the petty thief grabbed a heavy pouch from a rich trader which contained precious stones; blue and red ones, unearthed somewhere far away.

"Why did the stupid man jump! Now this batch is wasted," the apprentice wailed. He imagined himself working well into the night to stoke the fire for a repeated smelting.

"Not if we go ahead and pour it now," the heavy-set chief smith said. "If all of you keep your mouth shut for once, I say, we pour the molds."

The other smiths agreed. "Let's stir the mixture. Someone retrieve those specks of cloth."

They had a quota to fill. The Vizier's scribes were never late in tallying a new order.

Promising to keep their lips sealed, the smiths went about their business and poured the liquid metal. Instead of the usual brittle shields, however, the cooled molds yielded a feather-light, stone-hard substance that gleamed like rarified yellow nub.

"Maybe it was his bones," a stunned apprentice gaped. The chief smith kept his thoughts to himself. More likely, he suspected, it came from the thief's precious loot. What kind of stones were they? Diamonds? Sapphires? Rubies? The rich trader never said.

'Innumerable precious stones,' the crazed man had screamed demanding to be reimbursed by the smithy for his enormous loss. He was informed the Royal Army Smithy would do nothing of the kind.

*

"So you see, Hor-Aha, the mixture could not be duplicated since. We do not know the exact nature of those stones, nor can we guess at the correct proportions of copper to gems. Besides, it would be prohibitive to throw a pouch of them into each cauldron. We had just enough mixture to pour the shields you saw today. I brought every one of them with me, and I am gratified that it will be Makari's *Amazing Forces* to make good use of them."

Ramose's impromptu name for the riders had stuck. Everyone felt that they were more than special. They were indeed amazing.

Saiss turned to Ramose, "I hoped your metallurgists might help us with this puzzle, High Priest. Now that we know such a mixture is possible, experiments could be set up in your temple smithy. Your resources are so much greater, and my smiths have much to do to meet other demands. Surely, your knowledgeable priests can discover a less expensive additive than the one we used through our unexpected good fortune?"

"Good fortune for us, not the miserable thief."

Ramose's momentary compassion over the loss of a human life puzzled, if only briefly.

"I shall tell my metallurgists of this when I visit the temple smithy with the Venerable Badar to choose the special lance tips. Our priests can begin to mix different metals. I trust we will not have to furnish too many thieves for these experiments."

Ramose's audience smiled thinly.

*

Third Army General Teyhab was a good man, although among his colleagues he was known as a bit of a swaggerer. Having nothing spectacular to offer toward the war effort, he felt left out.

During the ensuing silence, as the others still thought about the High Priest's unhesitating human sacrifice, he perceived his chance and pushed his chair back noisily, "Since everyone boasted about their contribution, let me tell you of mine. Following our successful campaign, I invite all of you for good sport and celebration to my comfortable headquarters." He looked about, pleased with himself.

"Teyhab, my friend," Makari smiled, "have you forgotten

163

that by then Sekesh will be occupying your former Badari headquarters?"

Laughter shook the others. Teyhab turned crimson so that Makari felt compelled to come to the rescue of his bumbling general. "There is indeed something most important you will have to do. I sent an urgent message to your Aide-de-camp, Colonel Mayhah. He is to render a very special service in your absence."

"Oh? May I ask what that might be?" Teyhab was still flustered.

"He is to supply four special squads during separate on-shore encampments as Hor-Aha travels upriver. Needless to say, impeccable adherence to the outlined schedule is paramount. His flawless execution of these orders will be your most valuable contribution. I know we can count on the training of your officers."

Makari's reassuring words were balsam on Teyhab's wounded pride. Instead of being grateful, however, he pointed a thick finger at Sekesh whose laughter roared the loudest.

"And what are you going to contribute, eh, Sekesh? Other than making yourself comfortable in my quarters?"

Sekesh wiped his eyes with the back of his hand. He leaned forward and pointed his own stout finger at the General of the Third. "Teyhab," he hissed, "I gave my soldier's pledge to the King. My contribution will be the most unflinching, dedicated soldiering I can muster; from myself, and from my men."

"Very well put, Sekesh." Aha tried to clear the air of the thick acrimony that had crept into the room.

Makari jumped in. It was time to bring the Council to an end. "We are all prepared to lay down our lives for our King. Everyone is now ready for a victorious campaign. Victory to Hor-Aha." He bowed to his Supreme Commander, and then turned to his other guests, "May *Montu* be with you and your troops."

"May *Ptah* assure your safe return to Ineb-hedj," Ramose added as the scribe painted the last flourishes under his report.

It was early afternoon. They had shared a simple meal after which everyone prepared to leave Makari's Central War

Command. The generals Sekesh and Saiss headed for their own nearby garrisons while it was decided that General Teyhab accompany the *Amazing Forces*. He would catch up with Colonel Mayhah and his own Third Army somewhere near Barum's camp.

The King left with Ramose, his Palace Archers and the Royal Standard-Bearer. Meanwhile, Pase had given Colonel Mekh's adjutants valuable information about his desert route and Makari asked Ramose that Pase be allowed to return to his Fourth regiment on one of the temple boats.

The Grand General remained at his garrison to see his *Amazing Forces* off that evening, led by Colonel Mekh. General Teyhab and his small group would accompany them as they were to sweep deep into the western desert to avoid detection from the busy riverbanks. Jackasses had to be loaded with weapons, rations, fodder vetch and enough water for every man and beast.

Colonel Mekh was to carry special dispatches to General Barum. One of them outlined the battle plan. Another was Aha's *Authoritative Utterance* to be opened and read after the campaign, either by the King himself, if he was still alive, or by the next surviving commander-in-line.

*

Aha's group headed their rested jackasses toward the white walls of Ineb-hedj.

"I will inform my family tonight," Aha told Ramose, apprehensive about the inevitable dinner feud of his womenfolk.

"Remember, not a word of the deception, Hor-Aha. Especially nothing about the temple boats' early departure with you and Nefret on board," the High Priest warned.

Aha consented and then smoldered about the newest, audacious, and certainly most dangerous, of Nefret's suitors shaking his massive head to rid himself of his Vizier's distasteful face. Should he tell Nefret, and Hent, of al-Saqqara's latest impertinence? He certainly ought to tell Ramose. Perhaps tomorrow.

They bumped along the dusty route. Oblivious to physical discomfort, Ramose outlined the proposed switch between the King and Badar, between Nefret and her tall slave Zeina. Aha listened and resigned himself to an obviously unroyal and

165

uncomfortable river journey. He would miss his trusted Steward Beir. Not to think of Hent's willing maidens. Ramose better had good reason to take such unusual precautions.

Someone within his court had begun a subversive campaign. Aha could almost touch the undercurrent as he sat above the judicial assembly in his *Window of Appearances* during yet another boring audience. He could see it in the faces of his fawning nobles whose loyalty was somewhat less than unflinching. He would watch them closely from now on.

The faces of his courtiers appeared before his inner eye. The florid features of the *Privy-Councillor of the Two Diadems* melting into the desert heat; the old *Bearer of the Royal Scepters* shuffling noisily about. Aha could hear the uncouth shouts from his *Chief Keeper of Palace Slaves*. And, yes, oh yes, there was the ever-present stench of al-Saqqara's zealousness.

His court would be exposed to intrigue during his campaign against Nobatia. At least Nefret would be out of harm's way. Once in Nekhen, she might choose one among the eligible sons of that city's old noble houses.

Aha decided that al-Saqqara would make neither a trustworthy son-in-law nor a desirable consort.

"The gall of the ugly upstart," he growled boring his heels viciously into the sides of his plodding jackass.

* * *

Chapter Eighteen

And what is all this finery for?" Amma demanded when she saw her royal charge take off for the temple the following morning. "You are going there for your lessons, that is all!"

Nefret had chosen a wrapper that resembled the prior day's only vaguely. Where the other was fitted with solid wide shoulder straps covering her young breasts, this one had twenty single, tightly woven strands of silver hardly covering anything. With every turn, another strand fell aside to let a pink nipple escape. Over her shoulders, Nefret wore a finely spun ankle-length cape billowing around her like a summer-storm's cloud. Amma, beset by uneasiness, realized that she needed to have a special talk with Nefret very soon.

That morning, Chief Priest Wazenz ushered them into a different temple chamber. Furnished much simpler than Ramose's study, it did not open into a lush courtyard. While lessons were endured, two young people wished that the passing of time were matched to the rush of their blood.

Without Amma to watch their every move, glances were exchanged, and the lectures took on a lighter tone. Tasar noted Nefret's finery and smiled to himself, doubling his charm toward the other girls who enjoyed the quickened pulse of his teaching. With young adoration, they hung on every word the handsome priest expelled. Nefret asked Tasar to explain his drawings of the stars in greater detail. He bent over her, his long fingers tracing the kohl stars on her scroll. He felt the quiver of her mounds, saw the firming of her pink buttons, and his voice caressed her through unrelated words. So intrigued became the two by heavenly bodies that the handsome tutor brushed his lean cheek against his pupil's shiny hair and was compelled to guide her fingers across the papyrus sky. By day's end, Nefret hardly remembered what she had been taught.

As she had the prior evening, Nefret insisted on walking the short distance between temple and palace. Again, Tasar accompanied the four young women and Nefret enjoyed the innocent banter among their little group. Before they knew it, they had marched straight through the place gates. Tasar, aware of it, bowed deeply to his royal pupil and her ladies, reluctant to take his leave.

When he passed the guards on his way out, they recognized him and saluted lazily. Perfect, Tasar thought. All he had to do was to retrieve the indigo robe from Badar's rickety sedan. Then wait for the appointed hour to slip back into the palace grounds.

*

Chattering with excitement, Nefret and her women crossed the gleaming alabaster floor of the Great Foyer when a short figure sprang from behind a thick column blocking their way.

"Ha, there you are!" Dubar sneered. His sidelock bobbed up and down lending him a rather comical appearance. The slaves fell to their knees. The young prince ignored them and fixed his stare on his half-sister.

"Yes, here I am. What of it?" Nefret's cheery mood evaporated. "Get up, you three," she chided her women, poking the slow one, "Dokki! Get up, I said!"

"Who was that with you?" Dubar's legs were spread apart, his chin jutted into the musty palace air in a subconscious emulation of his father's more aggressive moods.

"Divine Prince, that was ..." Having scrambled to her feet, Dokki hastened to appease the young prince but a swift kick from Safaga stilled her in mid-sentence. As always when reprimanded, her fleshy lower lip began to tremble.

Sorry for the good-natured girl, Zeina put a consoling arm around her before the liquid eyes would spill over.

"A priest, as anyone could guess from his sash," Nefret snapped and tried to push past her annoying sibling.

A malicious gleam stole into Dubar's dark eyes.

"Father returned from his hunt," he blurted. "He called a family dinner for tonight. You better be there!"

"And why wouldn't I?" his sister retorted.

"Because you always act as though you have special privileges around here!" With a final snort, Dubar stormed off.

"Oh no! Not tonight! Safaga, what can I do?" Nefret breathed to her friend.

"You must attend the dinner. I'll wait for your handsome Tasar and tell him what happened," Safaga whispered back to her distraught mistress.

*

"There you are, Tasar. I wondered where you could have disappeared to. I almost suspected that you went to explore our House of Pleasures," Ramose said. "Its services are excellent, as was reported to me by others, of course," the High Priest chuckled.

Tasar had stolen into Badar's study to extract the cloak. The unmistakable baritone stopped him in his tracks. The High Priest's rare attempt at humor unnerved him. He did not wish to be perceived as a restless youth.

"Our young visitor from Nekhen seems to have developed a predilection for my old sedan," another voice broke in.

Tasar's eyes adjusted to the dimness and he saw Badar leaning against the wide door jamb between the old priest's adjacent chambers.

"You must have heard our mental summons, Tasar." Ramose's voice seemed to have an edge and Tasar had the distinct feeling that the High Priest spoke not totally in jest. Could he really read a man's thoughts without placing him into a trance?

"I trust you will not mind a simple supper with your elders for there is much work to be done, and you have already proven yourself skilled and a quick learner."

Tasar thought feverishly how he could get word to Nefret. There was no way out of this summons in time to meet her at the arranged hour. She would be furious. Which of her personas would forgive him? The strong-willed, spoiled Royal Heiress or the precious girl, whose innocence he had plundered without thought. And which of the two was to betray him if offended? There was no way of knowing. "Except that ..." he stammered, reddening, glad for the dim light.

"Any objections, my independent friend," Ramose laughed.

Tasar hastened to smile back, "No, of course not. I am completely at your service, Great Ones."

"That's better," Badar muttered.

When they settled down to work deep within the temple dungeons, Ramose took Tasar aside and placed his hands on the younger man's shoulders.

"I have observed you, young Tasar. You are of a special breed. Of course, Rahetep would not have sent anyone of lesser talents."

Tasar's heart beat quicker. He looked into the pair of piercing eyes and hoped he saw a kindly hue.

Ramose looked down at him, "Apply yourself with all your capability, continue your studies and, above all," his look took on a faraway, dreamy quality, "...above all, Tasar, keep yourself pure. Do not succumb to earthly pleasures with unworthy concubines. If you must do so, avail yourself of our temple chantresses. Do you understand?"

"I think so," Tasar croaked, his throat bone dry. His cheeks burned. He averted his eyes from Ramose's lapis lances boring into his soul.

"When you covet the highest calling, your discipline must be absolute. You have great strength within you, I feel. Though will it be sufficient to carry you to the pinnacle of your destiny?"

Tasar was about to proclaim his purity, when Ramose turned away to rummage among his dusty scrolls. Tasar's mind raced. Did the High Priest voice mere hope for a promising pupil, or was this a disguised threat to an apparent sinner against *Ma'at*? Had he guessed? His knees weakened and he leaned against a large offering basin. The coolness of its stone lent brief relief from his burning shame.

"Well, we better start. Tasar! No time to daydream. Let me explain what I need you to do." Ramose selected a scroll and unrolled its weighty length.

When Tasar was finally allowed to retire, dawn had almost broken through the night.

*

The King's family dinner started with a squabble, just as he knew it would end with one. They were still awaiting

Hent's arrival. No sooner had she pushed herself through the inner doorway did she begin to chastise Aha for his unexplained disappearance.

"To think that I had to hear it from a lowly servant," she whined and eased her bulk into a chair held out for her by Beir whose face remained impassive.

"Hent, dearest, you can hardly call Beir a lowly servant," Aha soothed. "I decided upon the hunt suddenly, and we left so early that there was no need to wake you."

"You should have taken me with you, Father," Dubar croaked. "Beir told us that you went ostrich hunting. Did you catch any?"

"We saw quite a few of them. And what a flock it was! Much too fast for us to catch." Aha smiled more to himself than to his stocky offspring.

Between the meat courses and the sweets, it was time to announce the planned journey to Nekhen. "It is high time that Nefret visited Nekhen. She needs to become acquainted with its noble houses." Aha looked at his Heiress almost kindly. "And their eligible sons," he added.

Nefret protested at once.

"Would you rather marry the Vizier?" Aha cut her short.

"The Vizier! How repulsive!"

"For Horus' sake, Aha. That is not amusing." Even Hent could not fathom to have her stepdaughter pawned off onto the disgusting man. Besides, she had learned from her disappointed slaves that the powerful man did not favor women.

"So, my pet, if nothing else, you will escape a rather unpleasant courtship." Aha took in his daughter's budding shape. After they returned to Ineb-hedj for his *Sed*-festival Aha would ask Ramose to have a talk with the Vizier to make the sniveling bureaucrat desist in his unwelcome pursuit of Nefret.

As Aha expected, Hent kept whimpering about the approaching birthing of their third child and he agreed that she should stay behind. Dubar, on the other hand, insisted that he be allowed to go to Nekhen. To Aha's surprise, it was Nefret who voiced the loudest protest to be taken on the journey. She dragged up one flimsy reason after another why she should not leave the palace.

"Nor its temple," Dubar croaked into the agitated melee.

Only seven-year-old Djer paid attention to his brother's sneered remark. "I like the temple," the small boy chimed in..

No one listened to him.

"It's settled then. Nefret and I journey to Nekhen," Aha signaled the dinner ended. Ramose could inform the family later of the timing of their journey. Beir, his trusted Steward, had already been instructed to tell the old Royal Head Nurse to start Nefret's packing.

Nefret immediately asked to be excused. Her stubborn half-brother was still arguing with his father when she fled the royal dining chamber.

*

Zeina had waited for her princess and the two hurried back toward their part of the darkened palace. Equal in height, with their hair the same length, a stranger might have taken them for twins. The hour was late and Nefret told Zeina that she did not need her anymore. She hardly dared to breathe as she slipped into her chamber alone. Would he be waiting?

Waiting instead was Amma. Alarmed, Nefret looked for Safaga who approached her just as Amma stepped out into the ante-chamber to call for Zeina and Dokki.

"Where is he?" Nefret hissed.

"He never came," was all her pretty co-conspirator could whisper back before Amma returned with the two other slaves. She asked all of them to gather around her, patting the alcove bed for Nefret to sit next to her. There was great tenderness in Amma's old eyes as she looked at her blossoming charge and the expectant faces of her young slaves. None of them appeared the least bit tired. Ah, sweet youth, she thought. Then she pulled herself together and said in her usual no-nonsense manner, "I have something extremely important to tell you. While Nefret was with the King, I was called to the temple where Ramose talked to me at great length. What a fortunate old woman I am to have gained the High Priest's trust." Amma surveyed the young upturned faces. "Our Princess is to journey to Nekhen. With the King."

"I know that already." Nefret pursed her lips to hide the high color of her cheeks.

"Not quite all of it, Nefret. The King told you that you would travel *officially* to the Court of Nekhen with him, on the Royal Bark. Further, Ramose is to question the *Oracle of Isis* on your behalf.

"Amma! How can Ramose question the Oracle on my behalf? He can do so only in Nekhen. As we all know, he is here. In Ineb-hedj!"

Nefret sat up so abruptly that she bumped into Amma. "Even Ramose cannot do such things long-distance."

"Calm yourself, child." Amma said. "Ramose is to journey to Nekhen as well." She clasped Nefret's cold hands in her own work-worn two. "Oh, child! Your hands are as clammy as a frog's hind legs," she fretted, instantly concerned.

"Really, Amma!" Nefret pulled her hands away. "I don't want to go to Nekhen to be cloistered in some stuffy old temple. I won't do it. I shall speak to Father tomorrow!"

She thought of her father's joke about the Vizier and shuddered. The ugly man always gave her the shivers. Not once did the high official smile at her with other than negligible respect. Not once did he give her to understand that he thought of her as anything other than a child. Nefret straightened up. She would defy the ugly man's intentions with all her might.

The sudden change from the innocent child into a haughty princess was not lost on the old woman. Amma let it pass. Adolescence was bound to bring mood swings, although this royal child did not cope well with them. It was time to have that special talk. Particularly, since the King was making inquiries for a suitable match for his willful daughter; one suitable for him. With the headstrong Nefret, most of the choices presented more of a problem than a solution. Best to dispel any of the girl's romantic notions soon, Amma thought.

As old as she was, Amma remembered those secret dreams young girls harbor in their heaving breasts. She also knew that the women servants spoke only too freely of their brief beddings with other slaves, or resident soldiers, even priests, who sported with them. Mostly though, the servant girls fantasized to catch and hold a free man's eye, and heart, so that he might free them from slavery or serfdom, or at least ensure a better life for the usually resulting offspring.

Priests in particular treated their sons well and initiated them frequently into the priesthood, while their daughters were trained as temple chantresses. The practice assured a growing number of *Keepers of the Secret Knowledge.*

*

It was a good many years since Amma gave in to the urges of youth. The old woman's toothless mouth widened into a bemused grin as she glanced at the pretty girls. Yes, even she was that young once. She had done well in choosing her lover, the priest Tuthmose. He was friends with Ramose who had far surpassed his older friend in ambition and position. Yet, with diplomacy and tact their friendship endured. Not in the least because Tuthmose resigned himself with grace to his lesser calling.

Her own small son had roamed on unsteady legs with the infant Lady Mayet when they still lived in Nekhen. After she chose to accompany the young Queen Mayet to the new court city in the north her lover Tuthmose was assigned to oversee the construction of a new Temple half a day's travel from Ineb-hedj. In time, Amma's and Tuthmose's son entered the priesthood and now served under his father as *Chief of Altar.*

To this day, Tuthmose sent occasional word of Khentika's well-being to Ineb-hedj. She tried to picture her son as a grown man of thirty-four and tears of pride placed a second veil over her rheumy eyes. Someone called her name. With dutiful reluctance, she pulled herself out of her distant musings.

*

"Amma!" Nefret shook her day-dreaming nurse by the shoulders. "Are we to stay at Nekhen's temple?"

"Yes and no."

Amma's answer perplexed Nefret. "Oh, Amma, don't speak in riddles."

"Nefret, you are to play a vital part in the safety of the Two Lands. This journey to Nekhen is such a deed." Amma's eyes filled with tears again. "You must be brave. It will not be an easy task. And, you will not travel in the comfort of your august station."

"Why not?" Nefret asked, alarmed yet excited. This had the makings of adventure. The bright girl was undecided

174

whether she was pleased with the possibility of a new diversion or displeased at the prospect of uncomfortable travel. Nefret day-dreamed until Amma boxed her on the arm to recapture her attention.

"The King told you that you would sail with him to Nekhen on the Royal Bark, with all the fanfare befitting a Royal Heiress. He said so for no one else is to know what I am about to tell the four of you."

The girls edged closer to Amma.

"You, my Princess, and you Safaga, and you too, Dokki, are to accompany the High Priest and the Venerable Badar." Amma raised her hand and they leaned closer to her still. "But it will not be on the Royal Bark."

"How then, Amma." Safaga asked.

"I know! Through the desert! Thus those excruciating lessons!" Nefret looked pleased with herself.

"No. You are to leave ahead of the official convoy on a temple boat. Secretly, in disguise."

With half open mouths, the young women gaped at the old nurse.

"In disguise?"

"As what, Amma?"

"As temple chantresses."

They giggled and jostled each other.

"Amma," Zeina held up a hand. "You did not mention my name." Surely, she thought, by oversight. Or could the old woman be punishing her? She was very careful in her nightly roaming. But Amma had spoken to the High Priest who knew everything.

"Zeina, my girl, you will be needed here a while longer and yours will be a most important mission."

The worried frown on Zeina's unblemished face made Amma feel sorry for the tall girl. "You will rejoin our Princess at Nekhen soon. I promise," Amma added, her smile little comfort for the trembling slave.

"Isn't Badar too ancient to travel? Even Ramose might be getting too old for such a long journey," Nefret pouted, trying to ambush the inconvenient travel plans. While she liked Badar, his magnetic eyes and his mysterious knowledge filled her with childish trepidation. The thought of his baleful look made her shudder. Ramose's presence would be a lot more comforting. She loved her tall mentor and always looked up to him as her trusted guardian.

"How can we be chantresses when we do not know the chants," practical Dokki chirped.

"Nor do we play the harp or the flute," Safaga grinned.

"I know! We are supposed to beat sistrums to make the rivermen row faster," Nefret joked half-heartedly, and the girls fell into their usual giggles.

Amma shook her head, "You won't have to do anything since the temple boats are being driven by the constant wind from the *Great Green* and do not require the rhythms of a drum for the rowers," she said. "There will be three boats, and no one must know that the Royal Heiress travels among the pilgrims."

"Us? Pilgrims?"

"You must appear as such." Now Amma really started to worry about the wisdom for such a small convoy. She had to make special offering to Osiris.

"Only three boats? Who will protect us?" It was as if Nefret read her mind.

"Well, there will be Badar and Ramose."

The girls grimaced and sighed, rolling their eyes at each other.

Amma grumbled them into renewed attention. "There will be a squad of temple bowmen and the capable boat captain with his well-trained rivermen. Also a messenger and another priest. Both are young and strong, and well trained in the use of arms."

Nefret sat up straight. "What other priest?"

"What messenger," Safaga echoed with a new alertness.

"Tasar, your tutor. He must return to his own temple." Amma had not missed the double intake of air as Nefret and Safaga exchanged a meaningful look.

"And you, Safaga, know the messenger, I believe." Amma turned to the blushing servant and winked. "I forgot his name. Wait. Pase—is it not?" She counted off the proposed travelers on her outstretched hands. "That makes fifteen. And then the three of you. Eighteen all together. Do you agree with that number?" When her simple mathematics remained unconfirmed, she added, "Zeina will travel with the official convoy."

Nefret had recovered sufficiently to argue, "Why? Zeina belongs with me. Has Hent asked for her? I do hope Hent is not going!"

Nefret did not hide her annoyance at the prospect. While she did not follow the convoluted reasons Amma gave for the journey, an element had just been introduced which changed her previous lack of interest. If Tasar went he would be close at hand for much of the journey. Then, if she was hidden away in the Temple of Horus, his temple, rather than the old royal palace, they would be nearer to each other still. *Heavenly Ptah!* He might be waiting for her in the secret passage!

She held her breath praying that he would not be bold enough to sneak all the way into her ante-chamber. Or worse, call out her name! *Great Ptah, don't let him come through the secret passage.*

On the brighter side, the journey was beginning to look promising. She would have to be very careful, and she definitely would need Safaga's help. What about that Pase of hers? Safaga had not told her much except admitted that he was not her first. Would Safaga be too preoccupied to watch out for her interests?

She tried to remember some of the things she overheard when the others teased Safaga. Had not Beir been gossiped about as well in connection with her? If only she could recall what it was. The more she knew, the easier she could bully Safaga into aiding her to meet with Tasar.

"Well, let's start packing, girls," Nefret cried and clapped her hands

"No, no. You must get some sleep, child. It can all be done tomorrow. Safaga, Zeina, come with me. You too, Dokki." If Amma sensed the change of heart in her young princess, she wanted to believe that she had awakened the girl's inherent sense of duty. Or was there some other reason? With travel arrangements preoccupying Amma, she pushed her uneasiness aside. Only the bare necessities could be packed to conform to the appearance as simple pilgrims. Ceremonial jewelry, mantels, new wigs, fine linens and cosmetica would be sent along with the royal convoy. Ramose had not left them much time to prepare themselves.

After Amma left with the slaves, Nefret waited for a few minutes. She listened for any sound. All she could hear was her own heart drumming against her ribcage. She jumped off her bed and slipped into the small ante-chamber. As if it were her lover's warm cheek, she cupped an oil lamp in her palm and slid behind the old wall hanging. The passage stretched much too long for her impatient heart. Rough ground tore at her bare feet. Unaware of any discomfort, she stumbled free of the passage at last and peered anxiously into the moonlit night. He was not there. Safaga had probably not waited long enough and he had left. Nefret pressed her lips together, angry at her seemingly uncaring friend. Unaccustomed to being disappointed, Nefret crouched down and put her head between her knees.

"I hate him," she sobbed with sudden fury. "How dare he not be here! Humbling me like a common slave on this freezing night!" She balled her fists together, "He shall be punished for his insolence!" Perhaps something had happened to him. Ramose could have found out and banished him to some horrid dungeon, or have him flung into the river as an offering to Hapi. On the other hand, the young card might be laughing at her this very moment. I will have him brought before me in chains and humiliate him!

Very well, she would marry the Vizier! Then he would be sorry. At last she realized how silly she was.

Even if she were deranged enough to give in to the ugly Ebu al-Saqqara—something she would *never* do—she could not take revenge in Tasar's transgression. It would only reveal her own unspeakable trespass of *Ma'at*. Then, her *Ba* could never cross the *Field of Rushes*. Instead, she would be forced to return as a *Ba-bird* to seek atonement in another life.

She sat there, a forlorn bundle, abandoned, wanting to die of shame and hopelessness.

Once the winds tugged too fiercely at her thin robe she crept back through the tunnel to seek refuge in her bed where she cried herself to sleep.

* * *

Chapter Nineteen

The next morning, travel fever swept through Nefret's chambers.

Bending over many open trunks, her women busily selected quilts, wraps and mantels. Cosmetica and the bare necessities were fitted into the trunk Nefret was to take with her. Ceremonial robes, wigs, and everything else would be carried along on the official royal convoy where Zeina and Amma were to watch over them as the tall veiled slave impersonated the Princess—ostensibly in seclusion to avoid detection of the secret switch. Zeina was determined to enjoy the respite from her subservient existence.

"Make certain that you wrap all of the new wigs," Safaga reminded Dokki who was folding ceremonial headpieces into woven containers to keep them from matting. The ornate wigs were for Nefret's return on the Royal Bark after her hair would have been closely cropped as part of her cleansing ceremony. Nefret liked the weight of her own shoulder-length hair although the constant fight against dirt and lice was bothersome. Vile concoctions were rubbed into her scalp by her slaves. Foul-smelling, they stung until Amma decided that all lice and nits were dead. Nor did Nefret look forward to wearing a wig during her sleep which necessitated the use of a wooden neckstand.

Slaves have it so much better, Nefret thought. She envied them as she looked over the chaotic scene with its promise of adventure. 'They are fed and well cared-for. I seldom beat them, and for the most part they come and go as they please, sneaking out to the market place, gawking at exotic goods, laughing at lewd gestures of the foreign traders.' She sighed with longing to be free of the prescribed court rituals. And

179

the many, albeit not always scrupulously heeded, restrictions to which custom bound her.

"Where is the blue robe?" she heard Safaga ask.

Nefret froze. "Why?"

"I just had a thought. You already told the King about it. So why not present it to him in Nekhen, at the *Festival of Opet*, rather than wait for his Jubilee back here in Ineb-hedj," the pretty slave suggested and began to search through yet another of the trunks from where her words emerged in muffled sounds. "It's not in here, Nefret."

"Dokki packed it! Dokki, have you wrapped all my wigs?" Nefret shot a stern look at the flustered slave.

The dark girl's mouth fell open. She knew she had not packed the blue robe. She most certainly would have remembered its delicate softness. And why did Nefret ask about the wigs again? Had she not heard her when she told Safaga that, yes, yes, and thrice yes, she packed the wigs. Why was everyone always picking on her? Tears stung her soulful dark eyes.

Poor Dokki could not know that Nefret hoped to divert everyone's attention away from the confounded robe. How thoughtless of her to have pressed Tasar into wearing it before he fled her chamber. She had to get it back. Safaga was the only one to help her but any opportunity to be alone with Safaga was lost in this madhouse of activity.

Thump! Nefret was startled from her frantic thoughts when Zeina slammed the first trunk shut tight. She secured the heavy lid by winding sturdy flax ropes around its bulk. Then she threaded the ends under the trunk. For this, she kneeled down, her firm buttocks performing a tantalizing dance.

Safaga was just about to signal Nefret to pinch Zeina, when sudden commotion arose in the anteroom.

A moment later, Dubar burst into the chamber, followed on his heels by Djer. The youngest prince wailed for his older brother to wait as his short legs pumped furiously in an effort to keep up.

Behind them, Queen Hent pushed her awkward bulk past the divider curtain advancing with a wide-legged waddle. No less noisy than her offspring, she admonished them, for *Mut's* sake, to mind their child-burdened mother. Her third pregnancy was advanced and her long wrapper ballooned unbecomingly.

The servant-girls sank to their knees, while Nefret turned toward her unannounced visitors whose entrance, for once, proved opportune saving her from further questions about the missing robe.

"Why are you already packing! Don't we still have many days before we leave!" Dubar spat his questions like commands. As of late, the King's oldest son had developed a most annoying stance. He would spread his stumpy legs and place his hands on his low hips in imagined self-importance.

You little bastard, Nefret thought unroyally. Her smile was tainted with annoyance at the uninvited trio's impertinence, but she controlled herself. "Many days still, Dubar? And what do you mean by 'we'?"

Nefret learned at an early age never to volunteer information. Let them spill their knowledge first! Was it Ramose who instilled in her such caution about ever-present court intrigues? No matter. It was wise to find out how much they knew before she admitted to anything. Did not Amma emphasize that no one was to know of their departure in the temple boats? Except Ramose, the King, Beir, and the old Grand General. And her slaves, of course.

"Nefret, dearest daughter," Hent's words pressed past her thin lips with great effort. "Surely you have been told by your dear Amma that I am to stay behind with Djer. He is too young to travel without me. Dubar will accompany you and the King for his first *Festival of Opet*. As the King will be occupied with graver matters, you, as the oldest of our children, must promise to watch over our precious prince."

"Dubar! Behave yourself!" Hent pushed her strutting son aside. Her thin lips stretched into a reluctant smile meant to be ingratiating. "Won't you, Nefret?"

Nefret did not miss the honeyed references to 'dearest daughter' and 'our children.' She held back a sharp retort. This grotesque woman was, after all, the Queen.

Hent, bloated and flushed, breathed heavily. "You are more mature than Dubar."

Her last comment gained her nothing except a disgusted sideways sneer from her oldest who glowered and swore silently that he would show them all. Very soon.

Djer stopped bawling and smirked. It served Dubar right, the seven-year-old thought and twisted his thin braided sidelock in his fingers.

Nefret and Safaga realized almost at the same instant that neither the queen nor her sons knew of their impending departure, days ahead of the official royal convoy. On the contrary, they seemed to assume that everyone would travel together aboard the Royal Bark. So Dubar had cajoled his father into letting him come along. Nefret was not pleased.

"My Lady, you are asking me too soon. In my excitement, I might forget my promise. You yourself have accused me of being scatter-brained."

If Hent was irritated by Nefret's impudent remark, she did not show it. Instead, she clasped her step-daughter's hands, determined to overcome the girl's resistance. "My dear Nefret! You poor child! Obviously, you have not yet been told! Let me be the first to break it to you, as a mother should."

Nefret grimaced as the Queen gushed on, "The High Priest has advised the King that you must go into seclusion." Sickeningly sweet, she continued, "From tomorrow on, after the temple ceremony, until you reach the Temple of Horus in Nekhen, only Amma will be allowed to serve you. No one may speak to you until *Opet*. However, then, during the festival, you must promise to protect Dubar. Promise me!"

It was difficult for Hent to beg favors from this haughty girl who soon would be initiated into court to sit beside the King in full regalia, with powers of her own. She needed to get on Nefret's better side.

Besides, it was time for Nefret to atone for a misdeed that occurred many years ago. It had cast such an ill omen over Dubar's future that the superstitious Hent was never without fear that some appalling fate would befall her oldest.

Unless, of course, doom was averted through the protection of the one who caused the calamity.

Nefret, hardly three years old at the time, had no recollection of the disastrous day in Hent's royal suite a dozen years ago.

*

Hent naturally aspired that Dubar, the first of her issue, inherit the Two Land's double crown despite Nefret's prior claim. When her time came to bear her child, Aha's second queen made elaborate arrangements to have its royal afterbirth preserved. As soon as she issued forth her son, the bustling midwife scooped the bloody membrane into thick natron solution curing in a clay jar. Under the well-established *Cult of the Royal Placenta*, a protective birth sack was invested with exceptional powers as the royal placenta was placed in a special shrine. Upon ascension to the throne, the new ruler's placenta was depicted on its own standard, to be carried aloft on ceremonial occasions. After death, this alter-ego would be buried with the deceased.

Should the placenta, however, be damaged or destroyed, great disaster was foretold. Because of this belief, Hent entrusted no one with this twin-god of her royal son and decided that his urn should not stand unprotected in a temple. She would watch over it herself. She kept the delicate jar with its pickled membrane in her bedchamber. Sealed with beeswax, the jar was topped by an exquisitely wrought lid of yellow nub. Its own small stepped alcove became Hent's premier place of worship. Dubar's royal placenta had assumed the status of a god and each day, the mother implored another deity to bring her son good fortune and longevity.

One day, while the Khamsin raged and the two small royal children could not be taken into the courtyard to play, Hent again kneeled before this shrine. Dubar was crawling about behind her and Nefret, barely three, annoyed the queen by pinching her fleshy arm in an attempt to lend her unsteady legs support.

Dubar's screams suddenly filled the hollow of the recess. The infant prince had stubbed his nose against a jutting corner of the alcove wall. In motherly haste, Hent jumped up to aid her howling son, shoving the clinging girl aside.

Nefret tottered toward the low-stepped platform. The tiny princess felt rejected. She was about to cry to regain the queen's sympathies when a glitter caught her eye. Curious about everything, the child reached for the glowing top of the amphora and pulled it toward her.

The crash almost caused Hent to jettison her son from her comforting arms. Aghast, she stared at the overturned amphora. Though it did not shatter, the beeswax seal split open. The lid clattered along the steps playing hop-scotch with itself. Like a lazy slug, a jellied mass escaped over the vessel's delicate rim to slither down the steps, onto the reed-covered floor. Before the horror-stricken Queen could react, a yellow flash streaked past her legs. As it seeped into the woven mats, her own pampered hound slurped up her first-born's quivering alter-ego.

"I never want to see that little monster again! Do you hear me!" The Queen's horse whisper turned a rushing Amma pale with concern for her beloved charge.

Hent's face was as white as her wrapper and her pendulous breasts heaved. "Do you hear me," she screamed at the mortified nurse. "And have that hound destroyed!"

No dog was ever seen again within the palace walls. Even the King was forced to leave his cherished hunting dogs in a kennel outside the royal compound. Hent insisted further that no dog would be buried in the royal tombs. Not with her, nor anyone connected with the royal family.

From that day on, Nefret was no longer allowed in the Queen's wing. Soon after the unfortunate incident, the High Priest brought a frightened slave-girl to the palace to serve the Royal Heiress and keep her company. More importantly, she was to keep Nefret away from the Queen's private chambers. Even Hent conceded that the young Sumerian discharged her duties well.

*

The Queen shook herself to dispel the ghastly memory of her son's Royal Placenta, spilled by pudgy little hands, ignobly lapped up by a hound! Only the culprit could avert a presaged cruel fate for Dubar. For this, Hent would gladly humble herself before the detested girl.

"If Nefret is to stay at the temple, I will too. I shall not remain alone in a musty old palace which has not been lived in for ages," Dubar announced.

"Oh, Dubar! You know very well that it is inhabited. The Royal Tax Collector keeps the place up for us," Hent soothed.

It was difficult for her to let Dubar go although she realized that his young blood was looking for adventure. But to rule one day, this journey was an excellent opportunity to get acquainted with the southern regions.

"All right, Lady Hent. I shall make certain that your son is returned to you," Nefret sighed and shook herself free of the clinging woman.

"Unharmed," Hent urged Nefret who had turned away.

Their presence no longer acknowledged, the royal threesome brushed against the kneeling servants and left the chamber as brusquely as they had entered.

A collective sigh followed their departure.

With the confusion of packing, Nefret forgot about the robe. Neither she nor Hent dreamed that, far from averting the cruel fate brought on by Dubar's spilled alter ego, Nefret would be the catalyst for the terrible omen to fulfill itself.

*

Time passed too slowly. And much too fast. Nefret and Tasar never found another moment alone when Amma decided to suffer through their lessons once more with them. When Nefret's eyes met Tasar's, she turned her nose up in the air, ignoring the plea in his eyes. He glanced at her as often as propriety allowed. He also noticed the frank looks from Nefret's pretty slave.

During the last hours of instruction on the fourth day, Ramose joined the studious group. Slowly, patiently, he unraveled his fantastic plan.

"Think of it as a pantomime. Only we are not in a play," Ramose warned. "Our lives and that of many others depend on the success of your execution of this deception." It was a heavy burden to place upon such young shoulders. Their agile minds reeled with wonder, anticipation and a little fear.

Because of the many preparations, the promised outing to Saqqara never took place just as the blue robe remained hidden in the old sedan.

*

"Saad! Saad!" Dubar grew impatient. Where was the sod? He would show him when he was king.

"Prince Dubar." Saad materialized from nowhere and bowed without enthusiasm to the stocky youth. "What brings you to the Vizier's working chambers?"

"I must see al-Saqqara at once," Dubar panted. His cheeks were flushed. Trying to catch his breath, he gulped for air.

"The Vizier is very, very busy, Prince Dubar."

Saad's calmness infuriated Dubar beyond reason. A red

haze filmed his eyes. With an unexpected lunge he pushed past the Head Scribe and made a dash for the working chambers of the powerful Vizier tearing the heavy door open.

"Uncle Ebu! Guess what ..."

Al-Saqqara's head jerked up. His face turned ashen.

As the over-excited youth stepped into the room, he saw the two men, half-hidden by the open door. Grand General Makari and Colonel Khayn looked up in surprise as Saad kept his place in the door.

"Gentlemen, I beg you, leave us for a moment," Ebu al-Saqqara whispered.

Makari and his Aide-de-camp pushed their supply tallies aside, stood up and left.

After Saad closed the door behind them, al-Saqqara rose slowly. Without a word, he approached the Prince whose rambunctious mood changed into fear.

Al-Saqqara's lips quivered and a fleck of spittle grew in one corner of his mouth. His eyes burned into Dubar and his bony fingers reached for Dubar's throat. A sob escaped the panic-stricken youth.

It was enough to bring al-Saqqara back from the abyss of his boiling rage. *The young lout is becoming a liability*, he thought.

"Dubar, my boy," he hissed from behind his pointed teeth as he redirected his hands to come to harmless rest on the Prince's shoulders. "Never, ever, do that again."

"Honored Vizier, you need to know." Dubar's formality was a plea for forgiveness. Regretting his impetuous disturbance of the Vizier's meeting, he still felt strongly about sharing his secret at once, just as he had shared many secrets with the Vizier as they had lain in the cushioned room of the darkened villa.

"Whatever it is, Dubar, it will have to wait."

Dubar opened his mouth.

"No, Dubar. I shall find time for you later. Right now, I have pressing business with the Grand General after which I must attend a special temple service as the High Priest is leaving for Nekhen tomorrow morning. Old Badar is to go with him. Glory be." Al-Saqqara bit his tongue.

"I was not aware of this," Dubar said. "Which makes it even more important that I tell you right now," Dubar sputtered, unaware of the Vizier's mounting discomfort.

"Dubar, I said: Not now! Come to see me tonight. I will listen to you then. While we have a cup of libation, eh? Would that please you, my Prince?"

Al-Saqqara propelled Dubar toward the door and pushed it open. "Saad, see that our impetuous Prince gets back to his own chambers. And ask Makari and Khayn to rejoin me, with my apologies for the interruption."

Dubar could hardly wait. *Tonight,* he thought, *I will astonish you.* Impatience tingled in his limbs. He yearned for the wafting images of Uncle Ebu's hot brew that made time stand still during the pleasuring by the older man. His mother's maidens never made him feel like that and he was no longer interested in them. Dubar was unaware of the forces that had begun to pull at him; nor did he realize that al-Saqqara's strong brew had become the mainstay of his existence. He only knew that he craved the dark liquid even more than the lascivious groping of 'Uncle Ebu.'

* * *

Chapter Twenty

Beir had laid out the King's ceremonial habit. Everything was perfect. As Aha stood motionless in his calf-length pleated kilt, his Steward placed a magnificent broad collar around his King's thick neck. Strands of hammered yellow nub were interspersed with beads of turquoise, carnelian and malachite. At last, Beir draped a light quilt over Aha's shoulders against the chill of the deep temple nave.

Four Royal Bearers stood by. Aha pressed himself into the cushions of his wide sedan. The old *Bearer of the Royal Scepters* handed him *Crook* and *Flail*. Then the *Privy-Councillor of the Two Diadems* entered and pressed the flat red crown of the Lower Region onto Aha's shaven pate while, on a plate of yellow nub, he would carry the high white crown of the Upper Region behind his King.

Aha averted his eyes from Beir. He had not yet told his trusted servant that the man returning in the veiled royal sedan after the temple ceremony would not be his King. Ramose had insisted upon keeping this part of their deception utterly secret. Any unintentional slip of the tongue by anyone could ruin everything.

As the procession crossed the Grand Foyer, Queen Hent's smaller sedan joined, its two bearers straining under her heaviness. The princes Dubar and Djer marched with uncustomary serenity beside their mother. They, too, were adorned in precious stones and wore calf-length pleated kilts, their sidelocks tamed by wide headbands.

From the opposite corridor, another sedan joined, borne easily by two muscular slaves. The Royal Heiress's chair took its place, followed by her women. Amma looked concerned and the three slave-girls appeared nervous. All of them feared the changes that the noon-time service meant for their lives. Only Nefret seemed unconcerned. Never permit your thoughts to reflect on your face, Ramose had warned her time and time again. At last, she heeded his admonitions.

*

The Temple of Ptah was filled to capacity. Everyone wanted to attend Ramose's last ceremony before the High Priest and the Divine Father of Ptah journeyed south. Priests along with their acolytes, temple musicians and scantily belted chantresses took up their places. Nobles and their entourage spilled into the last crevices of the columned nave. A hush descended as the royal procession entered. Everyone fell to their knees and remained so until the three royal sedans lined up in front.

As he drifted past his prone nobles, Aha's eyes roamed over the bowed heads. To his surprise, he spied the Vizier's tall headdress. The ugly man's presence alarmed him. Al-Saqqara was not an avid worshipper and seldom found reason to be at the temple. Aha prayed that Ramose's plan would work and was almost overcome by a desperate need for fresh air.

The sound of the huge gong vibrated through the temple. Heads turned as the High Priest appeared, followed by the *Divine Father of Ptah*, Chief Priest Wazenz, and a handsome young priest, a stranger still to most. The procession advanced slowly toward the great altar while the awed audience remained in solemn silence.

Ramose was draped in his purple robe, wearing his priestly headdress like a king, his mysterious crystal dangling from his neck. Badar, in an ankle-length white shirt, waved a smoking incense burner in front of him. It was attached to four gleaming chains. As the old priest swung it about, its heavy scent laced the temple air. Wazenz carried a tall staff in front of him with great reverence. At the precise moment, he was to hand it to his High Priest.

When the priests reached the royal sedans, Badar stopped and bent toward the Queen. Ramose did the same with the King, and Wazenz approached Nefret, who tried not to look at Tasar. In a harmonized sing-song, they showered the gods' favors upon the royal family until their soft litany lulled the worshippers into sweet day-dreams.

Badar swung his incense burner high above his head. A supplication to *Thoeris*, the Goddess of Childbirth, was in order. Entranced by the circular motion of the smoldering vessel, all eyes were on the venerable old priest.

It was the moment Ramose had waited for. He leaned close to Aha's sedan, half shielded by Beir and, from under his mantle, handed the King a tiny unstoppered vial, its few drops of bitter liquid holding the success of their daring plan.

Only minutes earlier, Ramose measured out the thick sap which he had drawn from the fruit of a stout plant he grew himself in a corner of his private garden. Its furrowed stem was spotted purple, the leaves fernlike and, once cut, could be mistaken for a bunch of parsley. It was the fruit that contained most of the poisonous oily fluid, its concentrate inducing paralysis of the muscles. Affecting the lower limbs first it extended upward to send the victim into stiff unconsciousness. If the affliction was not treated almost at once, the paralysis spread to the lungs. Death by asphyxia was certain. Timing, therefore, was crucial. Ramose needed to breathe life back into the King's lungs at precisely the right moment.

Despite Aha's revulsion to any unknown liquid, he placed the rim of the delicate vial on his tongue. Its contents trickled down his throat. He gagged and, gripped by sudden fear, started to pray. While his supplication was meant to be private, his fervent whispers reached the High Priest's ear.

"Great Ptah, truest of all the gods, let me live through this. Let my armies win against the enemy. Let me return to my city a victor. Take my most precious treasures in exchange. They are yours without question."

A chill ran down the High Priest's back. Only days ago, at Makari's camp, the King had jested, 'I may need to be more careful with my predictions of the future.' Striding toward the Altar of Ptah, Ramose steeled himself against that first wail he knew would soon burst out to be taken up by the multitude. Would it be Nefret's cry?

It was Hent's shrillness that shattered the adulation of the drowsy worshippers. Her ungainly body convulsed in terror, her eyes bulged in fear, as she stared at the stiffening body of the King. Aha's head fell to one side and the red crown crashed onto the stone floor. Then the two scepters clattered to the bottom of the chair where they shared space with the shards of a small vial.

Nefret wanted to jump out of her sedan when an iron hand restrained her. She looked into Senmut's steady eyes. The *Chief of Temple Bowmen* shook his head imperceptibly; she understood. This was the signal Ramose had talked about when he implored her to trust him. This was the diversion he spoke of. She leaned back and waited, finding it difficult to sit still. From under her lowered lids, she took a peek at Safaga, then at Dokki and Zeina. 'Now!' she urged them in her thoughts. Safaga! Zeina! Now! Where was Tasar? She tried to look for him when, with a small cry, Zeina sank toward the floor, her eyes rolled back.

Beir, who stood stunned by the King's sudden feint, caught the slave's light burden in his arms. "The slave too has fallen ill," he cried, terrified, loud enough for all to hear.

"Oh," Safaga sighed as she, too, slipped toward the stones. Dokki's strong arms broke her fall and Amma extended a wrinkled hand to help support the Sumerian.

"There falls another," someone shouted. The crowd pushed closer to the stricken group and all the priests surged down from the steps at once. Together with a squad of Temple Bowmen, they formed a protective shield around the royal sedans, opening their ranks briefly to admit Ramose and Badar into their midst.

"We must tend to the King immediately," Badar called. "Only then can we hope to bring him back to life."

"Wazenz, have our priests carry the royal sedan into my chambers," Ramose ordered. Then he turned to the pale Queen.

"My dear Queen Hent," he soothed the horrified woman. "Please spare your unborn child and return to your chambers. The Royal Heiress will stay here with the King. Also to keep herself informed about the fate of her women." He clapped his hands. "Make haste, Bowmen! Take the two sedans to my private chambers! And the slaves as well."

It all happened so quickly that no one had time to react. The royal sedan bearers relinquished their burdens to the Bowmen and Dubar and Djer trotted after the Queen's sedan jostling back toward the palace.

After being rushed along a dimly lit corridor, Aha's sedan

was deposited in Badar's chamber. Nefret, still in her chair, with Amma and Dokki holding up Safaga, and Beir carrying Zeina, were asked to wait in the High Priest's adjacent study. After the Bowmen left, Nefret jumped out of her sedan.

"Zeina, Safaga, you did well," she cried.

Safaga disengaged herself from Amma and Dokki. She glanced at Zeina whose arms were still entwined around the Steward's neck. "You can let her down now," she hissed at Beir who was still in shock. What was going on here?

"Amma, is Father alright?" Nefret asked.

"Yes, child," the old nurse replied. "I am sure he will be soon."

"What do you mean?" Nefret grew agitated. "Ramose promised me Father would not be harmed by his feint."

"Nor was he, my child," a calm baritone broke in. Ramose entered to assure them that all would be well by morning. "Aha suffered some dizziness brought on by the lack of fresh air," he explained. He omitted to tell them how relieved he was when his own breath restored the King's life. Either he was an expert or very lucky that the hemlock potion had not been too strong.

Ramose looked at a confused Beir and decided that he would not yet tell the King's long-time servant of their ultimate deception. Beir deserved his trust but this plan had to be concealed from all to the very moment the temple boats would leave their mooring.

"Beir, you better wait for the King in another chamber where you can recover from your own shock," Ramose suggested. "Later, you and I will accompany Hor-Aha back to the palace. It might be a few hours hence. Senmut will show you where you can get some rest."

The Steward hesitated and stared back uneasily but there was nothing he could do except leave as he was bidden.

The High Priest turned toward the excited girls, "Nefret, change places with Zeina quickly," he urged. His eyes came to rest upon the pretty Safaga and he told her, "Little gazelle, I am afraid you too will have to be assumed dead so that you will not be missed at the palace."

"What about Nefret's and the girls' things?" Amma asked and Ramose reassured her that a trunk was already loaded onto one of his temple boats.

Zeina thought of gentle Saad and her eyes filled with tears, just as Safaga's thoughts reached out for Beir. He looked so forlorn that she realized he had not been told about the deception.

"You, brave Dokki, will also be said to have fallen gravely ill, as you too will sail with us tomorrow," Ramose said and lifted the slave's quivering chin with a gentle finger.

"So I am to be dead as well," the dark girl whispered back, unflinching trust in her eyes.

Ramose tapped her on the shoulder. "May *Maat* be with you, child," he said.

Elated, she held his gaze. The great Ramose spoke to her directly. He touched her and his eyes penetrated into her very soul. He 'who almost never smiled' did just that at her, a slave. She could have fainted for joy.

Aha's head throbbed. He could not think of where he was. All he remembered were the fantastic dreams he endured. Harried hallucinations of monster birds with long swinging necks. Frenzied apparitions trampled his gleaming shield with cloven hoofs while he cowered in mortal fear. A funeral cortege floated down the swollen river. Temple chantresses wailed and flung themselves into the arms of a great storm, their shrill voices ringing out long after their images were swallowed by the raging Khamsin.

"Where am I?" Aha could hardly speak.

"Steady, my King," a whisper soothed. "I am glad you have awakened. It must have been a terrible voyage for you. Every small fruit differs in its potency even though we measured with great care."

"Badar?" Aha whispered back. "Is that you, my venerable old friend? What happened?"

Badar lifted Aha's head and held a cup of water to his lips. He recounted the events of the interrupted temple service. Soon Aha was awake enough to worry about their plans. He became agitated about the dangers ahead.

"Where is Nefret? Did you drug her too?"

"No, she is fine. She and her women are in the next chamber. The girls played their parts well. Remember," Badar warned, "none of them know that it will be you—and not I—who is carried onto the boat in my old sedan."

"Has Beir been told?"

"Not yet. Ramose thought it best so, great King. Now you and I must make the switch. Ramose will accompany you—actually, me in your place—back to the palace to placate Queen Hent. My old bones will be grateful for your sedan," Badar smiled while Aha winced at the thought of occupying the old priest's narrow chair.

"I trust you will have a comfortable night in my humble bed-chamber. May Ptah be with you, my courageous King," Badar said as Aha limped into the adjacent chamber to wait for morning.

Badar nestled into the royal sedan and closed the heavy curtains. It would be some time before the temple servants were to pick up the ornate sedan to return their supposed king to his palace.

Within hours, joyous cries spread over the expectant city.

"The King has been spared!"

"The King lives!"

The news flew out the temple doors, careened through the palace grounds, and lingered at the villas of the nobles. They touched down at the hovels of the poor, and invaded the craftsmen's humble work sheds. Ardent whispers carried the news to those who did not attend the worship. Have you heard? The High Priest and the Divine Father are to journey to Nekhen where Ramose will consult the *Oracle of Isis.*

*

It was late when Ramose decided that it was the right time for the King to be believed sufficiently recovered. The four temple servants took their places, the sedan's heavy drapes veiling its interior from curious eyes.

Ramose led the way as it fell to him officially to inform the court of the King's sudden illness and—praise Ptah—of the recovery. He could see the nobles scratching and pawing, pressed together in the Grand Foyer, scrutinizing him, weighing his every word. Vultures! He knew what they were like, these fawning nobles, steeped in their own duplicity. How he detested their underhanded jostling for power.

He wondered whether it would be appropriate for him to use the King's *Window of Appearances* for this important announcement. From there, he could look down upon them, humble them into submission before Ptah. It was tempting but he decided to stand under the small balcony, keeping the

Vizier and members of the *Kenbet* to his right. Let them crane their necks. How much should he tell them? A seizure, brought on by a fever from the swelling river. Not fatal, most fortunately, its ravages only to be halted by extreme quiet. No visitors, no light and, most assuredly, no court business. It was imperative that the King have complete rest. Only then would Aha not have to abandon his planned journey to Nekhen. Ah, and by the way, two of Nefret's maidens succumbed to the same dreaded fever, as has her dark slave. The Princess herself was fine although she, too, was to be kept in seclusion until her cleansing rites in Nekhen. That's what he would tell them.

Following the King's chair was that of the Royal Heiress whose face was also hidden behind heavy veils. Her dark hair glistened now and then under the light of a passing torch before it melted back into the blackness of the night.

Amma and Beir followed the procession with lowered heads. Both sent their secret supplications to Osiris. Amma prayed for her old sect-god not to covet the girls' souls. Beir asked for enlightenment. Something was not right, he sensed, confident that he would ferret out the truth.

* * *

Chapter Twenty-One

Only a few oil lamps lit the long hall of al-Saqqara's villa when Dubar crept through the half-hidden backdoor; by now, he could find his way blind-folded. Glancing up and down the dim passage to assure that he was unobserved, he slid toward a small door. Without knocking, he let himself into Uncle Ebu's chamber of dreams. Soft cushions invited to recline. From a shadowy courtyard, a lonely flute caressed the night. In a corner, a brazier promised warmth. On it balanced a copper kettle bubbling with a brew of exotic leaves. The pungent aroma of steeping hemp mixed reluctantly with the sweetness of burning incense. After Dubar's eyes adjusted to the reddish glow of the room he spied the reclining figure.

"So you have come at last." The prone Vizier motioned for his tardy guest to sink down next to him as he poured scalding liquid into two earthen cups. While their drinks cooled, the older man rubbed a moist palm over Dubar's stocky thigh. His mouth turned downward in unobserved disdain. He thought of the soft shyness of Hem, the pliable son of the *Privy-Councillor of the Two Diadems*. That would have been pure pleasure. Tonight was anything but.

All day, al-Saqqara was impatient over the ominous promise from this dark prince to share inciting knowledge. With luck, it would be something the Vizier could use against the High Priest, or against Dubar himself. His time was ripe; the seed of his success was to take root: To claim the two crowns from Aha and secure them for himself. With both hands, he would grasp them, holding on tight enough so as never to relinquish them; without having to debase himself by wedding the Royal Heiress.

"How is our great King," he inquired bringing his cup to

his lips, pretending to swallow deeply. "I was concerned and of course went immediately to see him. But they insisted that he was still too ill to receive me. Imagine! Me, the appointed Regent, not permitted to see the King!"

"We could not see him either," Dubar shrugged, then moaned, "Oh, this makes me feel so good." He gulped more of the steaming brew.

Al-Saqqara knew he had to do his gentle prodding before he let the youth slip deeper into his trance. "What did you want to tell me this morning, Dubar? I do apologize. It was important business." He kept massaging the stocky thigh, moving closer to the boy's filling center.

Dubar responded to the expert ministrations of the older man. He spread wide, straining upward. Instead of exciting the youth into release, al-Saqqara held the exquisite ecstasy just below its peak. He asked again, his face close to the preoccupied youth, "Dubar, what was so urgent this morning?"

Dubar looked up, his eyes glazed, "Don't stop, Uncle Ebu; I will tell you as soon as ... oh, don't stop."

"I won't, I promise. Now tell me, Dubar."

"Ramose! He went in as a young priest and came out as himself, in his robe. You know the one I mean." Dubar's stubby fingers groped for the Vizier.

Al-Saqqara had to bend closer to understand the slurred words. Even when he did, he had to prod the confused prince for their full meaning. Finally, it all made sense. Except for one thing. The wily Vizier was certain that Dubar was mistaken about the dark-cloaked apparition. The ubiquitous High Priest would never be foolish enough to expose himself to such danger. Not when he could move about the palace, including Nefret's private chambers, at any time, under any pretext. It must have been someone else who wore the High Priest's robe. Who? Why? It was not important. Al-Saqqara thought of a better way to discredit Ramose.

To escape Dubar's greedy handling he urged the excited youth into drinking more of the steaming brew. Despite his resolve, the boy's rough groping excited him and for a brief moment he wanted to give himself over to desire and its hot release.

Having summoned his self-control without success, he

grasped Dubar by the shoulders and turned him onto his hands and knees until the youth's broad backside was offered up to his urgings.

Just then, Dubar began to thrash about, working himself into a great fit of anger. "It is all her fault," he drooled and rolled onto his back again, his desire limp, forgotten. "I wish she were dead. Then I would be the next king. I hate her; she is not even my sister. Her mother was a worthless whore. One of these days, I swear, I shall kill her."

Al-Saqqara composed himself and listened to the youth's drugged ravings. He knew, of course, that the two siblings were not exactly fond of each other. Yet an outburst of such deep hatred surprised even the intrigue-seasoned Vizier. He rubbed his hands together. A plan firmed in his mind that would turn the upcoming royal journey to Nekhen fortuitous—for him.

"Nefret will always stand in your way, Dubar," al-Saqqara whispered. He brought his ugly features closer to the boy's perspiring face. "You can change that. Just imagine, without your sister blocking the way, you will be proclaimed king. It's a dangerous undertaking, you realize. Our very own secret."

Dubar nodded, eager to agree to anything, too entranced by his hashish-induced stupor to think about his father, the King, still alive. If only he could rid himself of Nefret.

Al-Saqqara's hand returned to the boy's seat of pleasure.

"Yes," Dubar rasped, straining upward again, his pillar thickening. "Something must happen to her in Nekhen, during the festival. What am I going to do about Ramose, though?" Dubar propped himself up on his elbows and squinted into the semi-darkness. "Tell me, what about the High Priest, Uncle Ebu?"

"Leave him to me, my son," al-Saqqara soothed. "He should be of no concern to you. It is your half-sister who has condemned your royal line with her trespass. She cannot be allowed to defile your father's semen. She must not inherit his throne. If you take care of her yourself, are you enough of a man to be our king? Keep a dagger at your side; the right moment will present itself."

"And I shall succeed." Dubar's eyes glowed with the unblinking hate of a fanatic. His words slurred again, he sank back, his mind exhausted by the nebulous images of the inciting brew. His head rolled back, his sidelock beckoning like a dwarf's gnarled finger. The prince's mouth fell open; he began to snore.

'Yes,' al-Saqqara thought, 'you just might succeed. I must arrange for an attendant to look after you on the long journey. He will carry the special leaves, brewing them for you, sparingly. In Nekhen, you will be maddened to the point of committing murder just for another taste. Of course, you will have to be punished for your heinous crime and I, the land's highest judge, will ensure that you, my dark Prince, will lose your worthless life.' Al-Saqqara's face glowed as he scratched his chin with a long curved nail. 'Still, it would be unwise to have my ultimate assent to power depend on your unstable hand, my lad.' The Vizier chortled and, reaching for a flickering lamp, he slipped from the thick-scented room.

Entering his private study, al-Saqqara gently pulled the door closed behind him. With almost sensuous care, he arranged his writing materials. After a moment's reflection, he drafted two messages, each equally fateful.

'To the Watch Captain Nebah,' he wrote. 'Fourth Army, Kharga Oasis...' He signed the scroll 'Al-Saqqara, Royal Vizier and Quartermaster, serving Hor-Aha, King of the Two Lands.'

When he finished, he did not seal the scroll. Instead, he pressed his personal seal onto the unrolled sheet, beneath the flourish of his name.

After Ramose announced his imminent departure, Makari had requested that the Archer Pase return to the Fourth with the High Priest. Al-Saqqara realized that the young Archer was an obvious choice to carry an official message for the Vizier to the Fourth. Together with another, addressed to the *Tax Collector of Nekhen*. He added a commendation for Pase to be delivered to his watch captain. Carrying his own praises, the pride-swelled archer was sure to deliver the scroll at any cost.

What the unfortunate Pase would not know was that the Watch Captain Nebah had long been recruited into a clandestine organization by one of the Vizier's followers. They called themselves the *Usurpers of the Two Crowns*, their traitorous ardor funneled by the fires of coveted power as they prepared themselves to serve their new master and proposed ruler of The Two Lands: King Saqqara.

*

Ebu al-Saqqara was the only son of a minor nobleman from the Delta who somehow had contrived to wed a wealthy, albeit ungainly, widow. Through his wife's connections, al-Saqqara's father obtained an appointment as *Overseer of the Royal Mastabas at Saqqara* where he raged over the slaving masses with intemperate ferocity. They said he could extract the last ounce of water from a man dying of thirst. Not once did he halt the advance of a run-away block of granite, even if one of the roller-placers stumbled into its path, weak from delirium. Nor did he tolerate the slightest murmur of protest, or heed heat-crazed pleas for an extra drop of putrid water. He did not need to. The ranks of his labor force were continuously replenished by captured enemies and condemned criminals.

What mattered to the Overseer was success. Because of the number of completed mastabas, he was elevated into grander nobility, taking the name of al-Saqqara.

The son, it soon became apparent, had inherited his father's relentless thirst for power. He was also burdened with his mother's extreme homeliness.

*

Young Ebu was educated with the children of other court nobles in Ineb-hedj. They teased him without mercy and, from an early age on, the boy learned to shun the boisterous company of his handsomer peers. He spent hours studying and plotting his meteoric rise within the court's growing administrative system. Unlike the carefree roaming sons of other nobles who came to know their households' women-slaves through youthful lusting, young Ebu developed the solitary habit of pleasuring himself.

By the time the comely youth turned into an even uglier man, his intimate knowledge of the Royal Court, its laws and inner workings, combined with his organizational abilities, came to the attention of the old nearsighted vizier. Young Ebu was appointed the *Reader of the Laws of Ma'at*. Before the ailing vizier relinquished his demanding position, shortly after King Narmer's disappearance in the river, he recommended young Ebu al-Saqqara as his successor. King Aha, himself young and new to Ineb-hedj, was more than glad to inherit the services of someone who knew his way around. Although Ebu al-Saqqara's power and influence increased, he rarely entertained in his riverside villa unless it proved unavoidable or lucrative.

To all appearances, al-Saqqara was consumed by his duties. He had never chosen a wife to give his home a gentler touch, nor was he known ever to have visited the local House of Pleasures. Initially viewed as the most eligible bachelor in the capital, scheming parents were prepared to overlook the Vizier's physical deterrents. His ugliness, however, brought on crying fits from their distraught daughters, and the nobles realized that they could reap even greater benefits by having their male offspring apprenticed in the powerful man's offices. Instead of being entertained to get acquainted with virginal daughters, al-Saqqara's working chambers became populated with the impressionable sons of Ineb-hedj's ambitious nobility.

However, the flagellating courtiers hardly imagined the kind of influence the Vizier was gaining over some of their offspring. Not over those sons who sought positions with him as Scribes, Keepers of Seals, Counters of the Grain Tallies, or Apprentice Quartermasters. Rather over their much younger issue, still engaged in childish play with the King's own sons with whom they shared their education. While it was not uncommon, or even frowned upon, for a bored noble to amuse himself with male slaves of a tender age, it was unthinkable for a minister of the court to engage in such pleasures with the sons of his peers. If exposed, he would have been charged with a serious crime, the punishment for which was castration.

Al-Saqqara was well aware of his dangerous gamble though he felt that the ultimate rewards were well worth the risks. He called himself 'Uncle Ebu' and told the boys that he was their co-conspirator in a delicious secret which they guarded with the intuitive cunning of children.

He would have preferred to be immediately pleasured by the proffered tightness of young boys instead of first having to ensnare his prey with games. He offered them a sip of sweet wine. Later, a cup of his special brew steeped from dried hemp leaves, imported from the cooler north. This soon rendered the healthy saplings into weak reeds. Through it, al-Saqqara hoped to cultivate a new breed of followers to populate his offices, following his every command in their addiction to the dark liquid. The Prince proved to be more susceptible than the scheming man could have wished for, given Dubar's stubborn disposition.

*

With deliberate care, al-Saqqara selected a second papyrus from the rustling stack. He wetted his reed-brush once more. His strokes flowed rapidly:

'To the Honorable Tesh, *Royal Tax Collector of the Great Southern City of Nekhen.*

I pray, lend me your support. Within a moon's cycle, the King, together with the Princess and the Prince, will arrive in Nekhen on the Royal Bark to attend the Festival of Opet.

I trust the royal quarters have been kept in readiness. Assure me that your own hand will guide the royal siblings during their stay; particularly the Royal Heiress Nefret.

I assume that you kept your grain silos filled for the King's use, for you are to re-provision the war barges. In great numbers, they are to stop in Nekhen from where they sail for the First Falls to replenish our troops' provisions. After our victory, they are to return to Nekhen with the King.'

Again, al-Saqqara signed his message to the Tax Collector with great flourish.

A surreptitious member of the *Usurpers of the Two Crowns,* Tesh had survived the small role he played during the last uprising against Unification. He had enjoyed the turmoil; feeding his own coffers from the collected levies which then found their way into the royal till sparingly. His greed did not go undetected and al-Saqqara sent him an ominous message: 'Join in my cause, or suffer the fate of a common thief.' Tesh agreed to unite with the Vizier and now aspired to renewed wealth and power as soon as his new master seized the crowns of the Two Lands.

Al-Saqqara chuckled. His plans forged ahead well. After Nefret's untimely death, he would present the model picture of the bereaved Regent. His King slain in battle, the Royal Heiress killed by her own half-brother. He and his *Kenbet* would be forced to condemn Dubar to death. He would then introduce young Djer to the special pleasures of his brew.

202

And poor Hent's was to be a difficult delivery. Women often died in childbirth. As might meddlesome queens, together with their newborns. The Vizier sneered; he knew the chosen midwife well.

Al-Saqqara's grasp for ultimate power was near fulfillment. Soon, nothing and no one would stand in his way. *King Saqqara, Ruler of the Two Lands!* No longer planning on Nefret to attain his goal, she was now only in the way. Of course, the High Priest and his flock of shamans still must be discredited. How ironic that the *Mastabas* erected under his father's whip and curses were soon to hold the bodies of those who scorned the son.

Al-Saqqara sat with his fingers steepled tip to tip. His eyes held the spark of fanaticism and small pearls of spittle foamed in the corners of his down-turned mouth. He unclasped his hands and leaned back stretching his thin legs before him. Languidly, he fondled himself into release at last.

* * *

Part III

Hapi, The Great River

Chapter Twenty-Two

The three temple boats pushed off their landing before first light, long before the sprawling court city of Ineb-hedj stirred into awakening. Nevertheless, hidden from view, there was one who watched.

Al-Saqqara stood alone atop a pylon, his mind in turmoil. His informer had just told him about the cunning switch Ramose had engineered between the King and old Badar. To think that Aha departed without declaring him Regent was shameful! He swore Makari was in on this. Unfortunately, he was unable to question the square goat-farmer without running the risk of revealing his invaluable source.

Al-Saqqara snickered. Such fools, all of them. If they could see how he had them by their puny *Mehyts*! How shocked they would be if they knew about his informer; the one they all trusted so implicitly. Still, he would have liked to confront Makari for his subversiveness against him. Outrageous! Al-Saqqara riled at the dawn, tears of anger impeding his sight. His plan could still work, though. Pity that he was unable to alter his messages. Nefret's fate could have been decided so much sooner. Especially if Tesh showed a little initiative. Al-Saqqara did not know the *Tax Collector* face to face but had learned enough about the greedy man to assume that Tesh would proceed with caution, if at all.

Nebah, on the other hand, would have an earlier chance

to execute his task and, because of his gambler's instincts, might act without hesitation. Whatever happened, and whenever it did, al-Saqqara would not forget the High Priest's sly deception. He was no one's yokel! Ramose would find that out with expediency. Al-Saqqara raised his fist toward the dark river.

*

In silent tandem, the three temple boats maneuvered through the reedbeds so as not to bump into dozing crocodiles or ill-tempered river hippos.

The vessels carried an emergency supply of fresh fruit, unleavened bread and date wine for the times when the travelers camped on shore. None of the nutritious beer was on board, however. It would only spoil during the long journey.

The meager provisions permitted a sparse existence at best were the travelers to depend on them alone. A day and a half ago, three inconspicuous river rafts had been sent ahead. Their hulls buried deep, they were loaded with three tents and bulging trunks containing cooking utensils and braziers, jugs of castor oil, quilts and earthenware. The sturdy rafts resembled ordinary cargo boats which treaded their way up the great river. They were to deposit their stores at designated overnight stops.

Already, the rising waters hugged the shoreline higher. As long as the great Hapi filled out gradually, their progress was assured. Even so, it would take up to twenty days to reach Nekhen, barring sandstorms. They were forced to round vast islands of flotsam which caused the wind to blow from the wrong direction. This, in turn, forced the rivermen to furl their sails and pole the boats past dangerous obstructions. At last, the boats reached midstream and the rivermen shook out their lateen sails. To a random observer, the three boats represented unarmed pilgrims on their way to take offerings to some upstream temple.

On the first boat, four temple bowmen stood motionless, wide sashes across their muscular chests proclaiming them to be priests. Bows and quivers with short precision arrows and several long throwing spears lay hidden beneath a pile of dirty sails. Seemingly lost in prayer, the men were alert for the slightest unusual sign. Their seasoned river captain stood on the high prow parting the water with easy grace. His eyes trained on the water, he hoped to spy submerged sandbars or a dozing hippopotamus in time to avert disaster.

The middle boat of the small flotilla boasted an enclosed shrine on its flat deck, the *Kariy*. Of all the travelers, Ramose alone knew the true identity of its less than comfortable occupant. Oppressive heat invaded the small superstructure and Badar's low-legged sedan provided little comfort for Aha who already detested his assigned role. Not a breeze reached the dark interior and the King grew hotter and angrier by the minute. At long last, he managed to doze off.

In contrast to his sequestered King, Ramose was seated on a platform behind the *Kariy*. Wrapped in his purple robe, he was visible to all under the woven baldachin proclaiming his sacred status. More practically, it afforded him shade from the searing sun. Ramose wished he could offer Nefret the same luxury. But this would arouse undue suspicions. Anyone observing them would certainly question why a temple chantress was singled out for such protective privilege.

Senmut, the sun-bronzed *Chief of Temple Bowmen*, stood behind Ramose. The unfamiliar priestly sash chafed his warrior's conscience. He envied his Bowmen blending well with the four toiling rivermen. He surveyed the river with sharp eyes. Dense clumps of high bulrushes were dangerous. A well-thrust arrow volley from such a vantage point could find its mark before he and his Bowmen could defend the tiny convoy. But they would try. To their deaths.

On the last boat, Nefret, Safaga and Dokki sat huddled amidships. Swathed from head to toe in long white robes, they were transformed into temple chantresses of equal station. The disguise further protected their tender skin from blood-thirsty gnats and mosquitoes that bred by the millions along the reedy shores. The maddening insects were as feared as *Seth* himself, their itching bites known to bring on high fever and delirium, even death.

Four rivermen, their rough unbleached waistcloths stained with sweat, toiled near the girls to take advantage of every breeze, while two more Temple Bowmen pitted against the unfamiliar tasks of handling chafing lines and heavy sails.

Tasar and Pase rounded out the third vessel's small complement. They also were wrapped in white kilts reaching just above their knees. Each wore a priestly sash across his chest, their spears hidden within reach. They and Chief Senmut knew of Nefret's identity though they had been admonished that they did not.

As the day wore on, the heat grew more oppressive and relief could only be obtained from the sluggish river. Dokki and Safaga changed places to dip a tight-meshed linen pouch into the gritty stream. Its rim holed, a rope was attached turning it into an effective scoop. The girls learned quickly not to let their pliable bucket fill to the brim. Trailing the fast-moving boat, it threatened to pull them into the dark water where *Sebek's* sentinels lurked for easy prey.

Now and then, a bulbous eye was spied between the reeds, protruding above the lapping waves, watching anything that moved. No one ever leaped into the river to help an unfortunate victim. Instead, it was hoped that the unintended offering might appease *Sebek* for another day.

Nefret fingered the slim leather sheath she wore tied around her middle. The ivory handle felt cool in her moist palm. Her mother's beautiful dagger would offer little protection were she to fall in. Sweating like a slave, she hated the silt-laden water. At least the moisture brought some relief from the throbbing heat. Too rarely, a breeze found its way across the river to billow her mantle around her, the sodden air mocking her slender limbs until all moisture was evaporated.

Under Safaga's watchful eye and guiding arm, Nefret was encouraged to handle the slimy bucket so as not to arouse suspicion from the rivermen. Their looks already belied feigned disinterest about the young chantresses. That tall girl held her head a trifle too high. And there was an imperceptible deference toward her from the other two. Whoever they were, the rivermen would have gladly dipped their throbbing pillars into any one of the women's honey pots, including the dark one with the perpetual frown. To them, a honey pot of any color was sweet.

Dokki detested the river, the lurking crocodiles, the treacherous reedbeds. She distrusted the unstable boat, hated the merciless heat, the blood-thirsty gnats and the general discomfort of this voyage. She cowered near Nefret in perpetual terror, to the consternation of her two companions.

Because of Dokki's obstinate nearness, Nefret and Safaga found no privacy to share their thoughts, much less their dangerous confidences.

Thinking herself unobserved, Safaga exchanged a knowing look with Pase who glanced at his pretty lover often, as if by chance. To be within an arm's reach of their handsome lovers excited Nefret and Safaga, and it frustrated them to feign indifference. Coy, furtive glances traced the river's reflections on the bodies of their men. Soon, delectable maleness became noticeable against the men's scanty waistwraps. Spine-tingling longing surged through Nefret, echoed by Safaga. A man's quick turn, or the squashing of a pesky gnat, revealed customarily well-hidden body parts sending even higher color into the cheeks of the young women. The men, too, pretended indifference as they envied the greedy wind caressing the slender female curves.

Their fantasies made Tasar and Pase nervous. With the High Priest's divine powers, he could read another man's thoughts like an open scroll. They re-draped their offending desire and adopted manly stances with far-away stares.

Pase looked forward to camping on shore where he might steal some time in Safaga's fulfilling embraces. He still regretted having been asleep when she washed the desert dust off his tortured body. While he could well imagine the sweetness of her ministrations the image alone was far from satisfying him. He needed her to satiate his hunger while he was awake.

Tasar thought about the journey's end, many days hence. Since he had been confronted with Nefret's identity, uneasy foreboding haunted him. He longed to touch her again; to breathe the intoxicating scent of her plundered innocence; to feel her silken tunnel close around him. With the ardor of youth, he anticipated a second, prolonged joining. Did he desire her because she was forbidden fruit? Hor-Aha's daughter was danger. Besides, the Royal Heiress was still annoyed why he had not come back to her that night.

Powerless to resist the temptation any longer he looked at Nefret. Her eyes locked into his. She stretched her long limbs in response to his swelling, not caring that their wordless exchange might be apparent to the others. When the girl turned away at last, her languid smile was that of a knowing woman.

With her, Tasar could envision a meteoric advancement in the priesthood. *If* he remained in Ineb-hedj, near Ramose. Near Nefret.

He would need permission for a permanent transfer from Nekhen to the pulsating new capital. Nefret could help. He would plant his seed. Tasar smiled at the double-entendre, his excitement surging. He had to win Nefret's good-will.

While his mind reacted, he willed his manhood to remain flaccid.

Many other craft passed the small temple convoy. Most lumbered sluggishly with produce destined for the growing metropolis of Ineb-hedj, its rapid expansion having grown into an insatiable burden on the fellah's harvest.

In the Fayum, freemen and farmers raised crops, fattened pigs and cranes, tended their livestock and trapped elusive waterfowl. Occasionally, they caught fish from the river's muddy waters which had been diverted to empty into these now fertile shallows.

The region was the Two Land's bread basket. During inundation, the women were forced to hand-feed the groups of cattle stranded on hillocks by the rising waters. It was a time when the men were conscripted into labor for the King.

Of all the rich offerings extracted by his hard labor, the fellah's meager allotment of bread, beer and grain was supplemented sometimes by catfish or an occasional fowl-fattened hyena. Both species were avoided by the upper class as unclean. All other foodstuffs harvested and caught were designated for the tables of the King, his fawning ministers, the priesthood and their gods. There was no way around it. The Vizier's unrelenting hordes of scribes kept careful tally.

* * *

Chapter Twenty-Three

The three boats pulled into the First Royal Mooring Place not long before the frogs chastened the waning day into night. Judging from its emerging outline, the new Temple of Horus promised to grow into a substantial shrine.

Ramose was glad for this first stop, for human habitation along the great Hapi would become sparse farther upriver when they depended on the overnight protection of the few army squads.

The boats thudded to a halt against the landing ramp. Huge stones had been hauled upriver by barge from the northern quarries. They formed a perfect slope that ran deep into the water. A poured gravel path led through caked mud, away from the river. Much of it would be swallowed once the river rose to inundation levels.

Ramose shaded his eyes against the setting sun until he spotted five figures on a knoll. Each man faced into a different direction, with the one in the middle extending his arms above his head; priests at supplication. A sigh of relief escaped Ramose. His travelers were assured a roof over their heads for the night. They would enjoy the hospitality of his old friend Tuthmose whom he saw pushing past the tight knot of priests rushing toward the boats.

"Ramose! The *One Chosen Among Us*, I welcome you," the hurrying man called out and waved. "I welcome you and your fellow-pilgrims to honor my humble temple with your presence."

"Tuthmose! May Ptah protect you! And may Horus favor you and reside in your temple," Ramose's sonorous voice easily carried across the water.

One after another, the travelers were assisted to disembark. Lastly, the boatmen carried the veiled sedan from the *Kariy* and lifted it off the boat.

Tuthmose glanced at the simple chair. Ramose's brief message had arrived the prior day stating that the Venerable Badar would travel with the High Priest. There was no mention of illness although it now appeared that the *Divine Father of Ptah* was unable to walk. Another glance toward the weary group, and Tuthmose recognized Tasar. He did not acknowledge his brief acquaintance with the young priest who had stayed at the temple for a few hours during his journey from Nekhen. The Chief Priest had offered the young messenger food and drink and his own son Khentika had found the younger man's personable manner refreshing.

Tuthmose recalled that at almost the same time another messenger, also from the south, was said to have stopped at the village sheik's house, requesting a new mount. Despite his dusty nomad rags the sheik's overseer had suspected the man to be a soldier.

Then, a third messenger, this time from Ramose, had announced the *High Priest of Ptah* and the *Venerable Badar* to be traveling upriver, planning to spend the night at the First Royal Mooring Place. Tuthmose sensed that something more than a pilgrimage was afoot. Already rumors abounded that the King, too, was soon to journey to Nekhen, ostensibly for the celebration of *Opet*.

The weary travelers were shown to a completed temple wing. Ramose, accompanying the sedan, chose a separate suite off an inner courtyard. The others were to occupy a series of chambers that led into each other through a main entrance. Safaga picked the last chamber in the row for the girls.

*

"Ramose. A request. Would you and the *Venerable Badar* pronounce the blessings of Ptah over this temple, to hasten its completion," Tuthmose asked of his old friend.

"The *Divine Badar* is ailing and requires rest lest he give up his *Ba* before we reach Nekhen," Ramose replied, and added, "I, on the other hand, feel perfectly well to ask for the *Blessing of Ptah* to invoke Horus's pleasure. And I would be delighted if your fine son assisted me as *Chief of Altar.*"

Tuthmose was more than pleased by his friend's gracious offer.

"After my invocation, I would welcome an hour of private

conversation, Tuthmose. It has been too long since we sat down together, you and I, like two old friends."

Elated by Ramose's words, he still had to ask. "How is Amma?"

"She follows with the Royal Convoy which will stop here as well," Ramose nodded. He realized why Tuthmose still cared for the old woman. Of all the willing maidens he had bedded, Amma was the only one to bear Tuthmose his son, Khentika.

*

To preserve his King's guise as the ailing Badar, Aha and Ramose occupied one chamber, with Aha sorely missing his competent Steward. He was a peace-loving man who enjoyed his luxuries. Someone entered. Aha looked up, unperturbed.

Despite his private doubt about the *Fighting Falcon's* alleged invincibility, Ramose approached his King with deference, his voice almost a whisper. "An early start tomorrow, my King. After our evening meal, Tasar will guard your door while I am absent. I promised Tuthmose to invoke the blessings of Ptah upon his new Horus temple. Please remember, Hor-Aha, no one must guess your identity. Not even Nefret. Here, you are the Venerable Badar!"

"I know it all too well, my friend; it is now apparent to me that he travels with much less comfort than I am accustomed to," Aha sighed. He glanced over the room's sparse furnishings and threw up his hands in despair. "They still use two-legged bedstands. I thought we abandoned those." Not unrelated to his complaint, he added, "Is my daughter comfortable?"

"I shall assure myself of it on the way out. Meantime, I asked Tasar to bring us something to eat."

Ramose had hardly finished his sentence, when he saw Tasar approach through the outer chamber. The young priest balanced a large tray in front of him and Ramose stepped forward to relieve the youth of his heavy load. "We appreciate this, Tasar. Please, wait for me outside. I shall be with you shortly."

"As you command, Ramose. I shall wait outside. With Khentika." Tasar was relieved that he was not asked to stay, sandwiched between the two old priests. There were times when even he, an educated man, was convinced that the ascetic temple servants divined a man's thoughts without hypnosis.

The fare Tasar had brought them was simple: fruit, cooked

grains and small pieces of seared meat, its origin indefinable. Ramose took the stoppered jar and smelled it. "Ah, unwatered wine," he smiled and filled two cups. Tuthmose apparently lived well. They seated themselves on two simple chairs after having pulled a stand between them, each thankful for the other's silence. Their peace was short-lived, however, for loud shouts jarred them from their private musings.

Ramose sprang to his feet. He pulled the door open and found Tasar splay-legged. His fist clenched the rags of an apparent intruder whose bony shoulders hung limp under the surgeon-priest's hard grip. A good head and a half shorter than Tasar, the wretched man trembled like a reed.

Khentika, who had been talking quietly with Tasar from an alcove nearby, waived his hands, "Tasar. It's the night-slave."

The unsuspecting servant's contorted face attested to his fear. Barely past the age of a boy, his stringy arms hung stretched by the weight of two large clay pots. White knuckles protruded from his bony fingers cramped around the wide rims in an effort not to drop the empty vessels. He had been ordered to put the pots in place for collection of the visitors' revered night soil. All the squirming servant wished for now was to leave the presence of these aggressive priests lest they wreak onto him some horrible plague. Was it not said that their eyebrows, raised in anger, could turn a grown man into a hyena? And their curses could hound a *Ba* so that it would never find its way past the *Field of Rushes*. In an unaccustomed show of self-preservation, the panicked slave dropped his jugs and ducked from under Tasar's grip. With a swift turn of his scaly heels he fled down the passageway for all his miserable worth. He would gladly take a beating from the slave-master for nothing was as bad as to offend a priest.

Imagining the poor slave's terror, the corners of Ramose's mouth curled in amusement as he reached for the pots and carried them himself to their intended nooks. But he became irritated what he noticed that Aha had not moved. The man's unshakable belief in his own unassailability was absolute. Such faith could raise havoc on the battlefield where spears were not guided by the gods, but lanced from the hands of trained warriors.

Ramose cursed the placid man's mental sluggishness even though he and Badar had turned it to their advantage on more than one occasion. While their counsel was mostly lent with benign forethought, the King's ensuing *Authoritative Utterances* more often than not proved advantageous to the priesthood.

Aware that Aha could never emulate the great King Narmer, Ramose vowed to increase his own vigilance. An ambush on their ill-protected little troupe would be calamitous for the Two Lands. Perhaps it was not wise, after all, for the King and the Royal Heiress to travel to Nekhen by his deceptive plans. So far, the ruse for the royal pair to pose as innocuous temple servants worked. But this was only their first day out, with many more ahead. Ramose trusted Tuthmose implicitly but most temples harbored spies. The night soil collector could have been one. If Aha was recognized, disaster further upriver was to be expected. They could be attacked from any of the steep bluffs bordering the riverbed. It was certain that word of their small convoy had already spread ahead.

While Aha had accepted the necessity for his disguise, he still did not understand why Nefret had to be part of the masquerade. Yet, it amused him to think of his strong-willed daughter as a humble temple chantress and he was confident that the imaginative girl managed to extract some kind of mischief from it. With his fatherly feelings ambiguous, he had avoided seeing too much of her at any one time. She reminded him too much of Mayet. Why could his young bride not have returned his burning desires! She might still be alive today. And he would not have to contend with the whining Hent. At least, the unpleasant woman gave him two sons; with a third child on the way. By the gods, there was no need to reaffirm his manly vigor through the confounded rituals of the *Sed*-festival! He sighed, and resigned himself to an uncomfortable night's sleep on the slanting bedstand. His lids were heavy and soon the rigors of the day and the wine claimed their toll. The *Lord of the Two Lands* fell asleep. Without a headstand, the wig slid forward, almost burying the thick nose, rendering this god-king's countenance less than god-like.

*

In the women's quarters, Safaga's practiced care turned the barren room into something akin to homey comfort. She spread soft quilts onto the two slanted platforms and sent Dokki in search of nourishment.

Nefret was drained. At first, she had been excited by the promise of adventure and by Tasar's constant nearness even though she pretended to be still angry with him for not showing up, and for not returning the indigo robe. Whenever she felt safe enough, she shot him tantalizing glances and enjoyed his obvious discomfort. With womanly satisfaction, she had watched as Tasar shifted positions, unable to restrain himself to glance back at her. After a lingering look into her eyes, he would gaze far out over the river, ostensibly unaware of her exulted presence.

Crammed together in the sparse chamber, Nefret tried to escape her bustling servants by pretending to be dozing. She wondered where Tasar was this instant. Would he invoke the help of his gods to be alone with her again? With astute practicality, Nefret doubted the assistance of the fickle gods. More likely, it would have to come about through Safaga's ingenuity. Her full lips pursed with an inner thirst.

"Nefret." Safaga's urging brought the dreaming girl back to their humble surroundings. "I have to prepare you for bed. You look exhausted. We rise early again tomorrow." Then, almost as if it were an unimportant after-thought, she asked, "What were you thinking of just now?"

"We are never alone anymore," Nefret complained and reached for her slave's hand. She realized how distant she had been with her trusted servant. She needed her friend now. Safaga always knew what to do.

Dokki padded in, balancing a heavy tray in front of her, unsure of her next step. "And where will I sleep," she whined.

"On the floor, of course," Nefret and Safaga echoed in unison. They giggled in harmless fun over the slow girl.

At once, Dokki's lips began to tremble.

Safaga took pity on the loyal slave as she led her to one of the nearby stands and helped her with the heavy tray. Then she pointed to one of the slanted platforms. "We'll sleep together on here, Dokki."

The cumbersome girl broke into a grateful smile.

During those times when the fun with the dark girl's apparent slowness went too far, Safaga felt compelled to take Dokki's side knowing that the timorous soul was being bruised by their careless teasing.

Poor Dokki. She becomes so easily confused, with Nefret

venting her bad humor on this patient girl.

The young women ate much the same fare as Ramose and the King were offered. They, too, sipped sweet wine.

Soon, Nefret fell onto one of the slanting beds. The dried leather straps across the frame sang under her slight weight. Safaga covered her mistress and Dokki extinguished the lamp's wick. A whiff of caster oil spoiled the air. How much better the oil smells at home, was Nefret's last thought.

Outside, two Temple Bowmen stood watch, wide awake, their young minds filled with images of alluring chantresses.

*

Ramose invoked the favor of the Falcon God, the protection of Ptah, for this newest Temple of Horus. The service was conducted without musicians, incense bearers or undulating chantresses.

After the simple ceremony, Khentika left. He sensed that the two old friends welcomed a private hour to reminisce when they were together at another Temple of Horus, in Nekhen.

"What happened to the Ancient Mats," Tuthmose asked Ramose. "Did you ever manage to penetrate their secret?"

"I did indeed. And I am going to tell you about it." Ramose paused, certain that his revelation would be safe with his friend. "Years ago, before I left Nekhen to be at Queen Mayet's side in Ineb-hedj, I was visited by *Isis*."

In breathless anticipation, Tuthmose drew closer as Ramose told of his long-kept secret.

*

As sleep eludes him, Ramose shakes the strange crystal from its pouch and takes it to the Altar of Horus at the great temple in Nekhen. From the empty nave, a moonbeam catches in the stone's depth. A thin green flash shoots toward the open ceiling, toward the moon itself. Ramose falls into a trance.

"Isis," he breathes.

"Ramose," the transparency sings out. "You will never learn their secret unless you look at nine squares at a time. Begin at the first mat's lowest edge, away from your heart. Count three by three. Nine squares. Each dark and light configuration is a different sound. When you wake up, you will remember what you already knew. My words only served to refresh your memory."

The image fades, and he remembers. He can unlock the secret of the Ancient Mats! He finishes his translation and keeps a papyrus copy with him, while the brittle originals remain in Nekhen to be copied and recopied by whip-driven acolytes.

*

"Isis handed me the key." Ramose said.

"The key?" There was not a trace of sleep now in Tuthmose's breathless voice.

"Well, it's more like a template. I had it fashioned from yellow nub. Here. It is now part of me." Ramose held up the precious disk that he wore on a chain around his neck.

Tuthmose had assumed that it served as a rest for the crystal nestling in the flat hollow.

"No, not exactly," Ramose smiled. "Here, I will show you its true significance. Can you provide some kohl and a shard?"

Tuthmose jumped up and led his friend into an inner temple chamber where he rummaged among a pile of broken pottery selecting a large flat piece. Papyrus was valuable and the bigger pottery shards were often used to jot down random thoughts or a brief domestic order.

Ramose drew a large square onto the ragged piece. The Chief Priest watched with fascination as Ramose divided this into several smaller ones, each two fingers wide, then still dividing those. He darkened several of the smallest squares with kohl. An asymmetrical design emerged.

"Let us assume this is one of the Ancient Mats which, as you well know, would have many more squares," Ramose explained. He slipped the chain with the gleaming disk off his neck and placed it over the lowest right-hand corner of the design. Three small rows and three columns showed through the cutout; a total of nine tiny squares, several of which were dark.

"I see," Tuthmose said, not doing so at all.

"Square Number One is dark." Ramose continued, "Next row to the left, Square Three is dark. Square Two of the third row is also dark. These nine squares present a particular word. This one here stands for *Mesedjer*, the ear. Or, to hear."

"Ingenious," Tuthmose marveled, thinking of innumerable possibilities such patterns could provide. "If you were to miss a row when copying a mat..." he mused.

"...Unimaginable chaos," Ramose laughed. "Everything would come out garbled. Now we both understand why it was imperative that the Mats were copied with such precision. And

218

why Rahetep used the reed whenever our attention waned for the blink of an eye."

"Did he know?" Tuthmose asked.

Ramose shook his head. "There was no way he could have. He solely knew that precision was paramount if the secret was ever to be unlocked."

"How then did you find out?" Tuthmose looked at his older friend with renewed admiration.

"With the help of this crystal—which, as you remember, was found together with the mats. Isis reminded me of the combinations of light and dark."

"She *reminded* you? Are you saying that the Mats are much more recent than we assumed?"

"On the contrary. They are older than you and I can imagine. As the translation progressed, I became aware how fantastic the contents were. Isis ordered me to translate them. Not for our people, but for a much later generation."

Tuthmose shook his head and leaned closer to Ramose.

"The first nine squares on the first mat translated into *Sebkeht* and *Djew*, and was followed by *Akhet* and *Imenet*. Thus, these people came from a 'Gateway in the Mountains over the Horizon to the West.' I assure you, Tuthmose, these were no recent travelers."

"You said Isis *reminded* you," Tuthmose came back to the word that had caught his attention. "How could you remember the hundreds of possible combinations?" Then he added, "Or did you have to call on Isis again to refresh your memory?"

"No, Tuthmose," Ramose smiled. "I attempted to speak to her after I arrived in Ineb-hedj. For other reasons. But I could not summon her. You see, *Isis* appears only in the empty nave of Nekhen's Temple. I have always suspected that it has to do with the green ray."

"What green ray?"

"When the crystal is held a certain way, a green flash shoots from its depths and soars toward the sky."

As Tuthmose listened to Ramose's unfolding story, he almost forgot to breathe.

Ramose ignored his friend's astonishment and spoke much like a tutor explaining a natural phenomenon to an awestruck pupil. "I already knew the patterns in my head. Do not ask me how. I always knew; although I had forgotten. Until Isis reminded me," Ramose finished his wondrous tale.

Way back, Tuthmose had sensed that his friend was a chosen instrument of the gods. It therefore did not surprise him that he was the one to divine the legends of the Ancient Mats. He stepped back a pace, thoroughly convinced that the tall man before him was an ancient *Ba* from another eon. Involuntarily, he sank to his knees. His voice quivered with emotion. "*Ancient One*, lay your hand upon this unworthy head of mine," he whispered.

Obliging his friend, Ramose invoked the added blessing of Isis. He then said, "We return to earth many times, Tuthmose. Each of us for a special purpose. I believe my foremost mission this time around was the translation of the Ancient Mats." Then he urged the kneeling man to rise. "There may be an assignment in all of this for you as well. The Mats speak of the *Guardian of the Desert*. My conclusions about the old legends startled even me. However, there is not enough time for this tonight." Ramose thought for a moment and then placed his hand on the Chief Priest's shoulder, "Tuthmose, come with us."

"Come with you?"

"To Nekhen. It would give me time to tell you all about my findings; about our colossus near Ineb-hedj. I am certain it is what the Ancient Mats refer to as the *Guardian of the Desert*. Someone besides me should know of this. Badar, of course, does." Ramose swallowed hard at the thought of his quickly aging mentor. "By the way, Badar plans to stay at the House of Life in Nekhen to write down everything he knows. How he came upon the Mats. They also speak of a treasure buried by an ancient people somewhere in the north, even though the Mats were found near Badari. I believe there is a lot more to this *Guardian of the Desert* than just the strangely carved outcropping we see today."

Ramose looked into his older friend's eyes. "Will you come with us tomorrow?"

"You honor me."

"Then it is decided. We will be in Nekhen for two to three moons at most. By the way, as I observed Khentika this evening I realized that he is more than capable to oversee your temple's progress here. And imagine Rahetep's pleasure seeing you again. Not to mention Amma's."

While deeply honored by the trust of the High Priest of Ptah, Tuthmose most cherished the intimacy Ramose shared with him.

"Tuthmose, do I remember correctly that you speak some Kush?"

"I did. A long time ago. Why do you ask?"

"It could be helpful." Ramose slipped the chain back over his neck and, lovingly, placed the crystal over the gleaming square. Then he took the pottery shard and broke it into small pieces. He had entrusted Tuthmose with a great legacy but decided not to tell him about the King until his friend was aboard and the three temple boats had pushed off from shore again.

* * *

Chapter Twenty-Four

The settlement of Badari gained importance as a river post so long ago that no one could say when it was settled although everyone still remembered when the Third Army built its huge fort choosing the small town as its headquarters.

Colonel Mayhah stretched and yawned. He relished the unrestrained power General Teyhab's absence afforded him. Conversely, he looked forward to Teyhab's return; the news from Central Command was bound to be stimulating. While he appreciated the small luxuries the well-supplied garrison offered, he itched for action and looked forward to the spoils of a victorious campaign. War along the Two Land's southern border was a matter of time.

"Colonel," the orderly's blare penetrated the ambitious warrior's thoughts. "An urgent messenger to see you. From Grand General Makari."

Hope leaped into Mayhah's head. His heartbeat quickened. Something had happened to Teyhab. "Bring him in," Mayhah said calmer than he felt. The news might be the worst. Or the best. Such as immediate advancement in case of Teyhab's death. In a flash, his inner eye saw an intricate carving carried before him: The standard of a general. His own. Mayhah devoured the proffered scroll. Suddenly, he found it difficult to mask his disappointment.

"Is this all?" he questioned the exhausted man.

"War seems imminent," the courier replied.

"Obviously," Mayhah snapped. As if he had not just been handed his orders to push the Third south. He glared at the annoying man. "What about these squads? It says in here that I am to dispatch four squads to different locations!"

"That is correct, Colonel. It has to be done without fail,"

the man mumbled, obviously familiar with the contents of the scroll.

Most inappropriate, Mayhah thought. He dismissed the reeking courier who must have sweated his way up the narrowing strips of hard river mud without availing himself of the river except to slacken his thirst.

'So I am to disburse four squads into different directions just to save some temple boats from their stupid superstitions! At a time when the Third is to march into war! Insane!' Mayhah knew he had no choice.

He assigned the first two squads to rush downriver from Badari. The third he selected to head into the opposite direction to meet the boats between Badari and Tjeny later on. Mayhah was about to draw several more men from the ranks for the fourth, and farthest, assignment between Tjeny and Abdju, when something occurred to him.

Although more of a barren necropolis than a settlement, Abdju did have a large temple. What was its deity? *Khentiamentiu*! No, that was the old god which the priesthood abandoned years ago. Unable, and too disinterested to recall the new patron god of Abdju, Mayhah sent for the resident garrison priest.

"The Temple of Osiris, Colonel," the older man explained. "Its Chief Priest Seka resides at Tjeny. But he also serves as *Hemu-ka* of Abdju. I know him well."

"Fascinating," Mayhah mumbled, his jaw set hard. Rather than deplete his own contingent of his best men to provide an escort for some foolish travelers, he would ask the garrison priest to dispatch one of his pious brethren with a message to this Seka-person. After all, this was temple business. It should be up to the priesthood to provide safety for their own. Besides, a Tjeny-group would take no time at all to reach the designated camp between Tjeny and Abdju. Whereas for his men, it meant pushing upriver from Badari for twice the distance, skirting inaccessible cliffs to boot. No, Mayhah decided, he did not have the days, nor the men, to expend on a fool's errand.

It was unfortunate that Mayhah did not see fit to share Makari's entire message with the garrison priest. Had the latter been given to understand that the High Priest Ramose and the Venerable Badar were the river travelers, he would never have chosen an inexperienced acolyte to rush Mayhah's request to Tjeny. Serving also as the garrison's chief medical officer, this priest concerned himself mostly with the healing of wounds, rather than the salvation of souls. He needed his better-trained assistants on hand.

Another task well delegated. Another step toward my own command, Mayhah gloated to himself, pleased by his quick-thinking ingenuity. Decisiveness separated a leader from his men. Satisfied with his course of action, he turned his attention to the enormous task of preparing the Badari garrison for its grueling push south. Their General Teyhab would catch up with them there. If he survived his journey through the desert from Central Command.

With his multitudes of men and loaded jackasses, Mayhah headed into the setting sun, cutting deep into the desert, away from a river that could not keep a secret long.

*

"How many did you count?" Colonel Mekh asked, concerned, and immediately ordered his *Amazing Forces* herded into a circle behind a steep incline.

"At least eight strong, Colonel," the scout reported. "No ordinary nomads, I'd say. As I lay hidden, I spotted no families, nor any nearby herds. They were headed for the river. As we are marching against the setting sun, I doubt they saw us."

"Let's hope so. We are far to the west of the river and should be as far south as Abdju lies on the Hapi. A few more days, and we'll arrive at the Great Oasis," Mekh replied. "Pray to *Montu* that Barum's outposts do not think us an enemy mirage," he added.

Mekh had to deliver his *Ostrich Riders* to the battlefield without exhaustion. He had set a reasonable pace, such as time allowed. They ran the big birds for a period of four hours, followed by two hours' rest, day and night. Only when the hot midday sun stung at its fiercest did they huddle beneath large strips of linen to catch up on much needed sleep.

They had left Makari's camp on the afternoon following the demonstration. Mekh had insisted that he be assigned a groom for every ostrich and he was glad for it. Each husbandman led his mount by a thin leather halter reining in his dancing charge when the urge for greater speed became too irresistible to the flightless bird. Water bladders strung across the birds' backs kept them accustomed to carry weight. The water was used sparingly and its scarcity urged on man and beast alike.

The assigned riders made the long trek on foot. Apart from sun-dried field rations, they carried lances and their gleaming shields. To prevent any reflection from the polished surface to betray their presence, their implements were wrapped in linen strips. Already, the sand-reddened cloth blended with the mottled desert floor.

Behind the swifter birds plodded the pack donkeys. Their heaped burdens were made up of provisions for the men, grains for the ostriches, and fodder vetch.

Mekh banged his flat palm against his shield, "We have rested long enough! Forward! March!"

One after the other, everyone found his place as Mekh's southward trek stretched into the approaching darkness. Each man followed in his forerunner's steps to assure himself safe passage. During the indigo desert night the lethal scorpion never slept. Neither did the giant cobra.

*

"I implore you, spare my life, for I am only a humble priest on a pilgrimage."

The pitiful cries of the young Badari acolyte drew derisive laughter from the grizzled tribesmen. They had descended like vultures on the lonely courier as he treaded his way along the river. Soon he was forced to skirt the cliffs, aware that he penetrated into the desert's unforgiving claws.

The marauders ringed the frightened youth stretched out in the red dust. Their dark faces hovered above his helpless form as wind-whipped streamers of grimy cloth fluttered behind them exposing their bearded grimaces. The sharp hoofs of a frightened pack-donkey cut the air close to the prone youth's head much to the amusement of the hairy lot.

"And what is this, priest? Your last prayer?"

Raucous laughter did not relieve the deadly threat.

A giant of a man stepped forward and ripped the leather husk from the felled youth's waist. His eyes triumphant, he shook out the scroll's length. Then he remembered that he could not read. In blind fury, his stone axe lashed out and crushed the ill-fated priest's skull.

The wild band's leader screamed at his over-zealous raider, "You son of a hyena! Now, we will never know! You are viler than the bent stinger of a scorpion!"

The others shrieked with laughter for 'Stinger of a Scorpion' was the giant's name.

Their leader was not amused and continued to foam his rage at the huge man in front of him, "Has it not occurred to you that the Ruler of the Kush pays nothing for spilled brains." He was beside himself with the imagined loss over his just reward. "He relinquishes his yellow nub only in return for spilled knowledge, you stinking turd of a he-goat!"

More insults were hurled at the stupefied desert raider. Their excited jabbering exhausted, the tribesmen climbed a bluff to survey the river. With luck, the waterway would be their telltale. Accompanied by lusty curses, they slapped their stubborn asses toward the cliff's edge.

"At least he can not betray our presence, Wadji," one of them tried to assuage their enraged headman as they squinted down upon the shimmering liquid band.

"There!" A marauder gesticulated wildly. Falcon-eyed, he had spied three boats sailing against the current. Shrieking triumphantly into the muffling wind, they sped away to lose themselves in the undulating desert where they would await their opportunity. The boats were certain to come ashore before nightfall.

Twirling clouds of dust were not the only thing that the marauders left behind. Trampled on the desert floor lay Colonel Mayhah's request for Chief Priest Seka to provide his temple's escort. Red sand thirstily absorbed the dead man's blood as it pooled around the unread scroll; hyenas soon would scent their evening meal.

*

The river travelers fell into a more or less bearable routine which did little to lessen the sweltering heat, the monotony of the riverbanks sliding by. Nor did it abate their anxiety about an expedient arrival at their destination.

On the second, third and fourth nights ashore, the boats were met by a squad from the Second Army.

As prearranged with General Sekesh during the War Council, the separate squads were dispatched from the Ineb-hedj garrison and waited at each designated mooring site.

Ramose, Tuthmose, their sequestered companion, and the girls claimed two of the three tents, whereas the third provided intermittent shelter for the others. The three sturdy canvases had been deposited along the shore by the cargo barges that had left the capital four days prior to the temple boats and were already ahead upriver.

During their fifth night, at Khnumu's insignificant Temple of Toth, an overzealous Head Priest seized the rare opportunity and insisted that the weary travelers be acquainted with his temple's Ibis-headed *God of Writing and Learning*. It took a firm rebuke from Ramose for him to allow the voyagers their sorely needed sleep.

On the sixth day, the small group settled in for another uneventful journey. Not so their seasoned crews; they knew what lay ahead. All at once, their mood sobered, their murmurings began to match the quickening current that rushed much fiercer against the graceful prows of the three faluccas. Steep cliffs soared upward from the river's edge. Soon, there was no shore. Only sheer walls, hemming the protesting river, squeezing its lazy waters into torrents.

They were entering the feared Narrows. Forceful downdrafts sprang upon them, reversing the water's flow. The wind howled eerily through the vast canyon. Here, spirits lived, and no self-respecting riverman remained within this fearful place longer than he had to. Terror doubled a man's strength as he pitted his oars against the roiling waters; the race against death ceased his happy chant.

"Furl the sails! Man the oars!" the captain shouted as the water pressed fiercer against their planks.

"Hold on for dear life!"

"Pray to Hapi for safe passage!"

The rivermen rowed with all their might. Still, their efforts did not prevent the first vessel from turning abeam to the rushing current. Even the Bowmen grabbed what poles they could find to help steady the runaway craft. The second boat fared better until it began to slip backward despite all hands straining at the oars.

The rowers on the third boat recognized the hazard and tried to avoid being broadsided by the second vessel when they were sucked into a large maelstrom. They were caught in a racing circle of water as their bow swung around. Faster, faster, the small falucca danced, twirling and jolting, slipping back downriver.

"Ramose! Ramose! Heeeelp!"

The High Priest looked back toward the terrified screams and saw Nefret standing in the middle of her runaway vessel, reaching toward him. He let go of the canopy supports he had gripped for better balance and cupped his hands around his mouth. "Sit down!" he shouted but his words were drowned in the commotion among his own crew. He extended his arms, raised and lowered them, hoping the girl would understand.

Nefret tottered to her own vessel's low railing for support when the stern heaved high out of the water. A surfacing herd of river-hippos gaped fleshy yawns, exposing lance-sharp incisors. Foul breath sickened the panicked travelers. The startled girl let go of the rail to cover her nose just as another bumping from the ill-tempered herbivores swamped the small falucca. The force of the collision flung Nefret backwards against the low rail-planking, catching her behind the knees. For a moment, she was held there by her mantle caught on a crossbeam. But her momentum was too great. She was flung into the murky river.

A scream shrilled. Dokki, more horrified than ever, pointed at Nefret's head bobbing among the river flotsam.

Safaga rushed to the railing and leaned out as far as she dared. She shouted for Nefret to keep herself afloat. A good swimmer, in the roiling maelstrom the girl's efforts seemed defeated.

"Someone! Save her!" she screeched.

The rivermen pretended to be tied to their rudder poles. To jump in after the girl was suicide. Besides, Hapi might be pleased with the offering of a temple chantress and deal gentler with them from now on.

Tasar stared, immobilized by the turmoil in his heart. He was a strong swimmer and the river held little fear for him. But if she did not make it back aboard, neither would her secret.

"Tasar! Save her!" Safaga's cry wrenched him from his thoughts. With one swift dive, he went over the low railing.

Pase watched him. No matter how much he would have

wanted to save this particular girl, knowing her identity from Safaga's whispered confidences, he was not able to. He glanced at his pretty lover, glad that she had appealed to Tasar; though also hurt that she had not turned to him. She knew of course that, just as he did not know how to read and write, neither could he swim. He shielded his eyes against the glare, against his shame. At least he could help locate the two among the reeds and floating debris.

The hippopotamuses were nowhere to be seen. Unconcerned with the troubles of humans, the heavy beasts had danced off in a graceful underwater ballet.

Nefret pedaled hard to keep from being swept downriver and to hold her head above water with her biggest fear that she could be carried off in an enormous stinking mouth.

"Ahgrrr," she yelped swallowing gritty water. There! It grasped her from behind! She swallowed another mouthful and kicked back with her heels. Now the beast's hot breath was on her ear!

"Nefret..."

Oh, Horus! It calls to me. She doled out another kick.

"Nefret! Stop kicking me!" Tasar sputtered behind her. "It's me." He grabbed her around the waist and forced her to turn until they faced each other.

"Oh, you!" Frantic with relief, she brought her fist down on the top of his head.

Tasar went under in the silt-laden water.

When he resurfaced, she screamed, "How dare you! You scared me to death, you clumsy oaf."

"Nefret. Stop hollering and hold on to me."

She did, treading water. "I hate you!"

"Will you calm down!"

"Go away. I hate you," she screamed louder.

"Start swimming or I shall let you drown!" Tasar yelled back. Their efforts to swim upstream got them nowhere.

"Leave me alone. That's what you do best." She pushed away.

So she was still mad at him for his not having been in her secret passage to pay homage. "There was no chance, my love. Ramose and Badar made me work all night. Otherwise," he gulped a clear breath of air. "Otherwise, I would have never let you wait. You must know that."

"Oh, must I? Well, I didn't. And don't call me your love."

"Nobody can hear us."

"That is hardly the point. I am still the Royal Heiress to you." She looked at him as haughtily as she could. Water ran into her eyes and dripped off her nose.

He grinned and swam closer. When he reached her, he pressed himself against her. She flapped her arms and sprayed his face. They were being swept further downstream when Tasar's toes touched something. Great Hapi, don't let it be one of your sleeping water-creatures, he prayed as he firmly planted his feet. At the same time, he reached for a bunch of reeds that protruded from the water. The sharp blades held and he was able to arrest their headlong rush downriver. Standing up, he groped for Nefret. The water barely reached under their armpits.

"Careful! It might not be stable."

"And what are you going to do now, Priest?" Nefret challenged. She shook herself. Her hair spun about her head and her firm breasts darted back and forth.

Tasar wondered if she just pretended to chastise him. He glanced over his shoulder for the boats. "Nefret, don't be like that. They'll be here soon." Her precocious mood endangered both of them. One slip of the tongue, a telling look, and Ramose would condemn him on the spot.

"You are hurting me," she pouted, but smiled at last.

He breathed a sigh of relief. Then, something she had said that first time, came back to him. If it was true, he could be condemned twice.

"Nefret?"

"What?" She jutted her chin at him yet did not reprimand him for addressing her so informally.

"Are you really promised to Ptah? To Ramose?"

She threw her head back and shook more water from her dark mane. The heavy drops glistened and she pealed with laughter. She looked radiant. And he knew that she was laughing at him, the little temptress. "It isn't true, is it," he smirked and he, too, laughed his relief across the river.

"You are forgetting yourself again, Priest." Just as easily as she laughed, her manner turned imperious. He tried to ignore his treacherous, no treasonous, thoughts before he had leapt into the river. Nefret was alive. Which could be dangerous for him unless he regained her confidence. He cupped her upturned face in his hands and tasted the river on her lips.

"Nefret! Taaasar! Where are you?" The calls sounded quite close now.

"Hang on to me," Tasar whispered. With her in tow, he pushed toward the approaching vessel, relief and regret intermingled in the crevasses of his pounding heart.

"Here," he called out. "Over here."

Before he and Nefret reached the swinging boat held in place by long poles, Nefret let go of him. He turned around. She was not there. Suddenly, he squealed like a woman. Hapi was reaching for him. This was his punishment. Tasar's eyes widened as a dark head appeared from under him.

"The next time, you better be there," Nefret smirked through strands of hair plastered against her fine features.

The little vixen swam better than he thought! He freed himself with a swift turn and groped for her under water.

"Careful, Priest," she hissed.

The boat maneuvered alongside them and Tasar fended off its looming hull as hands reached for them. Pase, Safaga and Dokki pulled Nefret up who giggled as Tasar pushed her from below. He knew he was forgiven. Pase proffered a steady hand and Tasar heaved himself aboard. The two men exchanged a quick look. Safaga squeezed Tasar's arm when she thought no one was looking. She rushed Nefret toward a stack of unused sails and after a swift punch from her, Dokki relinquished her dry mantle to her mistress.

*

Ramose had watched the terrifying struggle for a moment but then lost sight of the two swimmers. At last he saw them safely back aboard their vessel. His relief immense, he thanked the gods not only that Nefret had been rescued, but that Tasar was the one to do so. The young priest maintained a cool head throughout the journey, and once more proved himself worthy of the High Priest's liking. This one carries promise, Ramose thought. Should it become necessary, he felt that the young priest could also be told the true identity of the *Kariy's* occupant. For now, however, Ramose would keep that secret a while longer.

Again, he winced at Nefret's close call and shuddered as he remembered the grunting herd of hippos. He scanned the water for protruding eyes. Somewhere, they lurked and waited, ready to gnash incisors at easy prey.

*

The boatmen rowed all day. At last, the cliffs receded and the river widened from its narrow turbulence into a lazy expanse. More than once, they missed sandbars, and there were times when one or the other boat thumped hard against a submerged obstruction.

The captain felt as if he lost a kir-full of blood guiding his small convoy through the haunted canyon unscathed except for that silly girl's carelessness. Her plunge had frayed his nerves but with the mercy of the Great Hapi, he had conquered the fearful Narrows once again. He ordered his exhausted crew to turn the boats toward shore for a quiet night on land.

Ramose breathed an audible sigh as soon as he spied a company of stocky soldiers. The squad from General Teyhab's Third Army waited with the tents. Makari's organization proved flawless, and they set up camp under the emerging stars.

The presence of the first Badari squad meant that Colonel Mayhah had received General Teyhab's crucial message. It was a most welcome reassurance since they could now count on the other three squads. Just to make sure, however, Ramose planned to reassure himself of the arrangements at their eighth stop at Badari. In the absence of a proper temple, they were to take refuge in the garrison where he could speak to Colonel Mayhah in person.

When they pulled in at Badari, and after everyone was settled at the garrison, Ramose went to see Colonel Mayhah. A flustered aide told him that, unfortunately, the Colonel had marched deep into the desert with most of his garrison. The Army of Ptah was forming a second line of defense against an enemy break-through.

The garrison captain left in command of the small resident force gave Ramose to understand that Colonel Mayhah, indeed, took care of everything before he left. Why, then, did Ramose feel uneasy? Much as he tried to ignore the gnawing doubts, they would not go away.

The following day, they got under way with the rising sun. As the boats neared their ninth mooring site, soldiers were

232

indeed waiting for them. Ramose's concerns were allayed as this squad from the Third Army braced against the driving dust to pull them ashore. The men had had the initiative to erect the tents deposited earlier. All is well, Ramose thought.

During their tenth stop, at Tjeny, they were hosted at the Temple of Osiris by Chief Priest Seka whose realm included the vast cemeteries of Abdju.

Ramose arranged for Seka to come with them to be at the King's side during the forthcoming battles. For good reason. Seka's temple deity was, after all, Osiris, *God of the Dead*, whose insatiable appetite added one immortal *Ka* after another to his Netherworld. Seka's special supplications should guide the hungry god toward the souls of the enemy, away from the warriors of the Two Lands.

Chief Priest Seka of Tjeny and Abdju was flattered by Ramose's well-worded request. He offered to travel with them and camp one night in the wilderness when he could have reached Abdju within a day's ride to join the travelers there. Ramose trusted the earnest man. Still, as he did with Tuthmose, he confided the identity of the royal travelers to Seka only after he came aboard the following morning.

The distance between Tjeny and Abdju was short. Still, it had been decided to make camp between these settlements, for the rivermen needed the additional rest before continuing on to Hu from where several stretches of arduous rowing lay ahead.

A stop between Tjeny—under the protection of Colonel Mayhah's expected fourth squad—and its necropolis would further allow the pilgrims to reach Abdju during daylight hours, in time to visit the King's *Mastaba* which had been completed some time ago.

They could pray to Osiris, under Seka's guidance, for a plentiful afterlife. All of them would remember to ask the *God of the Dead* not to snatch them away too soon for there was still much to be accomplished.

* * *

Chapter Twenty-Five

The eleventh day faded into dusk to add another uneventful overnight stop, each having been made easier by the passengers' growing ability to cope. The rising river now soaked more of the dry shore turning it into mudflats.

Beyond Tjeny, red cliffs again crowded both riverbanks forcing the swelling waters into an ever deepening channel. While the boatmen welcomed the deeper draft they had to pit their oars against a swifter current as they left the sails up part-way for added thrust although this stretch was nothing compared to the Fearful Narrows. Here, at least, a strip of land enabled the vessels to be beached for the night.

The captain raised a sunburned hand to shade his eyes against the deep red glare of the setting sun and pointed at a small heap on the riverbank, the one thing to disturb the mud's monotone hue. *Our tents*, he thought relieved.

No gleam suggested a soldier's propped-up shield; no smoke attested to human habitation, however temporary. No animated figures ran about, stretching themselves into welcoming salutes. The narrow strip of land was empty.

Casting his eyes upward, the captain scanned the rugged cliff's edge. There! He caught a singular movement out of the corner of his eye. Perhaps a column of whirling dust drawn into the sky by the playful drafts frolicking around these cliffs.

A thin whooping cry pierced the air.

Everyone's eyes swept upward. Now they all saw the figures strung out against the sky, high on the cliff, motionless. An eye-blink later, the shimmering mirage vanished.

The river captain left his perch on the first boat's slender prow and balanced his way back toward the stern. Amidships, he ordered the sails dropped. Then he cupped his hands around his mouth and hailed the other two vessels. They drew alongside, held in place by a furiously poling crew. The nimble-footed captain readied himself to transfer onto the High Priest's boat. As he jumped, his own boat swung out and for an instant he clung to the low railing. His legs trailed in the water before he was able to heave himself on deck. Everyone was relieved to see him clamber aboard the other boat without his gift of a brown limb to Hapi.

"Great Ramose, all I can spot is a low heap. I believe it to be the tents. I saw no soldiers there, however. It could be that the men on the cliffs were your fourth escort squad from Badari. They must have scaled the bluff to spot us from up there. It will take them some time to make their way back down to shore."

Ramose hid his concern over the unidentified sighting as he gazed toward the western edge of the river. Beyond the narrow strip of land, walls of sandstone rose so steeply that the top seemed inaccessible. Already, the river was cloaked in shadows as the evening had begun its victorious descent over the yielding day. At the height of the flooding, there would be no more land left between the rushing current and the canyon walls. For now however, the strip of dry sand afforded them brief refuge from the night-darkened river.

It was not the lapping water, nor its lurking inhabitants, that Ramose dreaded most. His concern lay with the narrow shore where a raiding party could entrap them. Before their supposed protectors clambered down the cliff, his small group could be vulnerable to an attack by marauders. As he scanned the shore again, he spied the dark rock sluice between towering walls. A wadi!

If those had been Colonel Mayhah's men, his group could climb up onto the undulating plateau to set up camp there. They would be more exposed to the swirling dust but they would not be trapped between the river and the cliffs and Ramose preferred to entrust the safety of his small band to the openness of the desert. The wadi must have been carved into the sandstone eons ago when the savanna-like expanse was fed by an immense river. Now, its silvery band flowed merely through half-forgotten legends; with its long-vanished waters believed to have pooled beneath the porous desert sand to form an enormous underground lake. Believers said that it would reemerge in another time.

What if those men were not the expected escort? They could be marauders or, worse, scouts sent by the enemy to murder them. Did they know about the King? He had better be prepared. After another moment's reflection, Ramose issued his commands like a general.

"Do not empty our pots into the river. Carry them to the top. And, Captain," he called out to the riverman who was about to fling himself back onto his own boat. "Your men have to catch me a small crocodile. Have them extract the foul contents of its gut and add that to the pots."

How revolting! Everyone within earshot pulled a face. They imagined the stench that would issue forth from the gaseous hollows of the carrion-eater. Add to that their collected night soil! The girls dry-heaved theatrically at the disgusting thought.

"Never mind your sensibilities." Ramose feared that they would not be able to ward off an attack without sustaining crippling losses. But take an overwhelming stench, mixed with a little mysticism and handy poison, overshadow it with his own commanding appearance, and it just might induce a superstitious desert raider to prefer flight to a debilitating curse by a powerful servant of avenging gods.

The captain understood. As soon as they landed, he would dispatch three of his men to pounce upon the least alert of the vile river sentinels snoring in the mud.

The boats crunched onto shore. The rivermen jumped off and dragged their flat-bottomed vessels onto the hard mud. A few large boulders propped against the graceful sterns assured that the rising waters would not reclaim them. Everyone helped carry supplies and tents up the steep gully onto the open desert plain except for the rivermen who were to guard the boats.

The toiling group stopped to take a breath, and a quick look, when a shrouded figure emerged from the *Kariy*. With the sedan to remain on board, its veiled occupant had to conquer the steep incline on foot. Emerging from the cramped cabin, the freed man stretched his stiffened limbs and breathed so hard that his veil danced about his face.

For an old man, the Venerable Badar carries himself

surprisingly erect, Tasar observed to himself as he hauled another armload toward the wadi.

Having managed to squeeze close to him, Nefret followed Tasar's glance. She, too, detected something odd about the old priest. Not intending to stare, she dropped her gaze. Priests wore papyrus reeds on their feet. Those sandals were of leather. Finely crafted, decorative stamping along the straps, resembling hers!

"Safaga! Safaga!" Nefret rushed off to tell her friend.

"Not now, we have to hurry," Safaga whispered over her shoulder trying to gain ground against the steep terrain.

Dokki lumbered behind, her broad nose wrinkled against the heavy pots dangling from the straddling yoke across her shoulders. Her load seethed with a vile mixture of urine, decaying offal from a crocodile's gut, and human feces. The slave tried to keep the smelly pots as far away from herself as she could. For once, she chose her footing with great care. Neither she, nor anyone around her, wished for her to spill a single drop of the disgusting brew. When, at last, she reached the top, Ramose motioned for her to deposit the pots behind the large tent and she obeyed with such haste that she almost tripped.

"Dokki, Dokki," Ramose sighed and shook his head.

The travelers were more than ready to enjoy their respite, away from the incessant buzz of gnats, thankful for firm ground.

Once again, Ramose and the supposed *Divine Father of Ptah* chose the largest tent. Ramose invited Seka and Tuthmose to spend the night in its comfortable confines to help with offerings to the gods.

In the smallest tent, Nefret threw off her dust-laden cape. Borne by the wind, the fine desert sand knew no boundaries. It reached far into the river, and minuscule red crystals imbedded themselves into everything that barred their way. Nefret fingered her gritty hair. Sand ground between her teeth and clung to the insides of her nostrils. She wore almost nothing now. As the last of the daylight squeezed through the open tent flap, she noticed that the jagged mark on her left thigh had grown much darker than its surrounding skin. 'You will be as dark as Dokki,' Amma always scolded when she spent too much time outdoors. She placed her hand over the offending mark which was now easily swallowed by her palm.

"Do you think it will fade some day?" she asked Safaga who was shaking out their quilts.

Dokki left to climb back down to the river one more time to fill two water buckets. As she passed the third tent, Chief Senmut detached himself from his group. Offering the girl the protection of his muscled arms they left amidst the good-natured taunting of his envious Bowmen.

A stocky, dark-complexioned man himself, Senmut was drawn to the plump girl whose gleaming teeth brightened into such easy broad smiles. As they traveled on different boats he now grasped his chance to walk with the wholesome slave.

*

More than two hours passed and still the escort squad from the Badari garrison did not materialize. Ramose summoned Tuthmose and several Bowmen, and led the small procession back down the wadi. The shore was deserted and Tuthmose called out to the invisible boatmen. After much coaxing, the men crept out from cave-like hollows.

"Hear this, rivermen of the Great Hapi!" Ramose endowed his voice with its temple-service baritone. "Your duty is to Ptah. You have been called upon to take his highest servants to the city of Nekhen. Nay, to Horus himself. Together, we have faced dangers. We may have to face more. We must conquer our fears, endure the discomforts. Every last one of us!" He paused and fastened each man in turn with his blue gaze.

The men sensed that the High Priest was far from finished.

"However!" Ramose's voice turned thunderous. "Should your loyalty to Ptah weaken, should you escape during the night, great harm will befall your *Ba*. The one who harbors treason in his heart is already condemned. His *Ba* will never cross the *Field of Rushes*. For such a coward, there is no afterlife!" Ramose stretched himself to even greater height, his appearance now menacing. He pointed an accusing finger at his gaping audience.

For these superstitious men to think that their souls might never cross the *Field of Rushes* was horrifying. The mere suggestion of Ramose's curse upon their unworthy heads was enough for them to stand in obedient silence.

Ramose turned and walked back toward the wadi. Tuthmose followed him smirking into the darkness. "Impressive, Ramose."

"I can only hope that their fear of my curses is greater than their fear of staying behind unarmed. If I did not feel that we needed our Bowmen on the plateau I would have them come down here instead. Not only to assist these rivermen in case of trouble but also to prevent them from escaping," Ramose replied.

"They will obey you, Ramose. After all, how long have they been in your service?"

"Long enough to know that I make good on my promises. As well as my threats."

The two friends climbed back toward the dark plateau, followed by their Bowmen and, further down, by Dokki and Senmut who emerged from a hidden crevasse.

*

The High Priest sat cross-legged in the dimly lit tent. He could not find peace within himself even though their few guards stood in readiness. The vast plateau was broken up by gentle hillocks where every slope could hide a foe. To his two companions' amazement, Ramose suddenly jumped up and began pacing as much as possible in the confines of the tent.

"We have to split our group in two," he muttered, mostly to himself. He stopped to face Aha. "I beg of you, Hor-Aha, follow my advice. Let the women spend the night away from camp. A situation like this is precisely why I insisted that they be given rudimentary desert survival training. If our camp cannot be defended with success should we be attacked, they at least will have a chance to reach the river in the morning."

"What, alone?" Aha was astounded at the outrageous suggestion. Really, Ramose outdid himself this time.

"Of course not, Hor-Aha. The Archer and some of my Bowmen should be assigned to guard them. The girls never had a chance in Ineb-hedj to study the night sky. A perfect opportunity without frightening them unduly."

"What opportunity indeed! Really, Ramose!" Aha hissed. "Explain this great idea of yours a little better! Because, for the life of me, I cannot follow your reasoning."

"I fear uninvited visitors," Ramose said. "I think it best to send the women into hiding for the night. We sighted a group on a bluff. We now know they weren't the squad from the Third. They may have been harmless tribesmen. On the other hand, they could be marauders. The desert is full of these lawless bands who know no gods, no loyalty, and certainly no mercy."

"What about us then, eh? Are we to sit here until we are attacked?" Aha's sarcasm was evident. He had about enough of charades, the endless river, the uncomfortable camps. How he missed Beir's impeccable attendance.

"I have a plan," Ramose replied.

Aha's chin jutted out, "And might you tell us what that is?"

"Nomads are extremely superstitious, regardless of how strong and wild they appear. We have to make certain that they will not wish to linger here."

"Then why not have the girls stay?" Aha countered. Damned if he could follow his tall High Priest.

"There is risk involved. These marauders thirst for more than water."

"So be it," Aha sighed. "I shall abide by your fancy plans one last time, my friend." He sank back into his cushions longing for a good night's rest. Already half asleep, he mumbled, "I assume your malodorous concoction has something to do with these convoluted plans?"

Ramose smiled as Aha fell asleep. He turned to the Chief Priest from Tjeny. "I must find Tasar. Then I will tell you what I want you to do, Seka."

After outlining their situation and his plans to Tasar, Ramose added, "I want you to seek out the Archer. And, Tasar, if there is need, let Pase know who the tall chantress really is." He tapped Tasar on the shoulder. While talking to Aha, Ramose had decided to have the bright surgeon-priest from Nekhen escort the women.

Consumed with worry for the safety of his small troupe, Ramose, who could read the minds of seasoned men so well, for once overlooked to search the corners of a youthful heart.

*

Nefret stubbed her toe on a loose clump of clay as she stumbled through the starry night. She did not understand why Ramose had ordered her to be awakened together with Dokki and Safaga. Then Tasar and Pase appeared. Before she knew it, the five of them were trundling into the darkness wrapped in their quilts against the bitter desert night. The crunch of a footstep caused her to glance back. She almost jumped out of her skin at the shadow trailing them. The dark figure caught up and Senmut grinned apologetically. Relieved, the girls broke into nervous giggles while Tasar and Pase boxed their own fright away against the Chief's thick arms.

The six young people stayed within arm's reach of each other comforted by the sound of their footsteps. They found a low hill against which the girls spread their cloaks to huddle together in a hollow on the protected slope. The men braced against the wind in a brave stance to keep up their own courage.

"We should post a lookout at the top," Pase urged. He started to climb the steep side, then turned back to signal the pretty slave. Mumbling a brief excuse to her mistress, Safaga wrapped herself into her quilt and trailed off after Pase. Nefret, deprived of the warmth of her friend, shivered. Dokki put her big arms around her.

"I'll patrol the other side," Senmut announced awkwardly. He beckoned Dokki with a lingering glance. The dark slave, too, gathered her quilt around her ample shoulders. Leaving Nefret's side, she vanished into the darkness.

Tasar moved close to Nefret. "You are shivering."

"My women have lost their sense of duty," Nefret hissed through her clenched teeth. If she opened them they would rattle in the dark like a sistrum. She shook uncontrollably even though she was not that cold.

"Allow me to warm you, Princess," Tasar offered. Not able to gauge her mood in the dark he chose the formal address. He knelt down next to her. Without a word, Nefret leaned against him, her pouting abandoned. Tasar took her into his arms and she allowed his warmth to cover her until the fire within them burned hotter than any midday sun.

Nefret strained upward. She wanted him closer, deeper. From memory, she steeled herself against the sharp pain of their first intimate encounter. It never came. Instead, a sweet yearning surged up from within her. It lingered in her throbbing well; then spread to her heart. She felt like laughing, and then like crying. She had to hold on to him forever. Or she would die.

Tasar, too, remembered her fear when she had offered herself in virginal sweetness. He became gentler than he thought he knew how. He whispered honeyed words into her cascading hair, tongued the warm shell of her ear, and breathed his own life onto her lips. He relished the taste of her protruding nipples closing his strong teeth around them just enough to hold the firming buttons still. When Tasar withdrew from deep within her she reached down and touched his maleness. Shyly at first, she caressed the velvety head and sensed that it brought him a different kind of pleasure.

At last, they lay spent. She still cupped him, her fingers exploring his wondrous treasures as they floated within their cool confines.

That night, the stars shone as bright as they did every desert night. The young pair did not pay heed to the glittering firmament for what they discovered in each other eclipsed the heavenly glow above them. Intertwined, the young couple fell asleep. They were at peace; their predestined fates and their tenuous world forgotten.

The faintest shimmer heralded in a new beginning. An almost sensuous quiet prevailed over the seemingly empty expanse of the high desert.

Nefret stirred. Not yet fully awake, she shuddered and, with the undulating grace of a cheetah, fitted herself closer to her lover's perfect limbs loathe to relinquish him to the new day's reality.

Tasar, too, awakened. Instead of reveling in the night's stormy sweetness he craned his neck to spy the others as he lay next to the Royal Heiress in the growing dawn. Before Nefret could reach for him he leapt to his feet. "I must look for the others," was all he mumbled before he sprinted up the hill.

Trying not to wake Pase, Safaga wriggled from his embrace. Near the top of the hill, she found a suitable spot and squatted to pass her water. Thus preoccupied, she gazed toward the east expecting the sun to push over the horizon. Its tentacles had not yet reached above the cliff. The wind had ceased and the air warmed rapidly. A shuffling sound made Safaga turn. The dark slave smiled down at her. They nodded to each other as Dokki joined her in the hollow.

Relieved, they joined hands and climbed to the top of their hill.

"I shall call it my hill of happiness," Dokki smiled. "Did you notice our little Princess is a girl no longer." She clicked her tongue in the old way of her people.

Safaga was about to chastise the insolent girl to watch her mouth, when Dokki hissed like a cobra. Following her outstretched arm to the edge of the western horizon, Safaga squinted into the still dark distance where a row of men moved in unison, like a giant centipede. Safaga's eyes searched farther. There were no herds, no women, no children. Just a long line of men. Whenever nomads travel from one oasis to the next, they were surrounded by noisy families and bleating goats, with whistling herdsmen sending raucous curses over rough terrain. These men crept along in ominous silence.

'Danger,' Safaga thought at once. She reached for Dokki's hand and dragged the fear-frozen Noba off the hill. They tumbled down the slope and within moments reached Pase and Senmut and were joined by Tasar. The two girls competed with each other to explain what they saw, and all agreed that they needed to get back and warn the others. There was not one among them who did not hope that their sighting would divert the High Priest's attention so that he might forget to ask about their night in the desert.

Nefret was still stretched out on her quilt.

"Quickly! Get up!" A trace of panic crept into Safaga's voice. She waived her arms at the stirring girl shooing at her as if she were a fowl-hen to be scattered into flight.

Dokki's jabbering added further urgency. One last useless smoothing of their wraps and kilts was accompanied by blushing sideways glances before they fled back to camp.

No two needed their secret kept more closely than the young Royal Heiress and her ambitious priest from Nekhen.

* * *

Chapter Twenty-Six

As the six young people rushed past the camp guard, Senmut brushed Dokki's cheek with the back of his wide hand. Then he looked at Nefret and bowed from the waist. Pase followed his example.

Nefret's eyes narrowed. Neither Senmut nor Pase should have been told about her disguise. They knew through her slaves, she suspected. Should she scold the careless women? Or be grateful for the added protection that came with such knowledge?

Pase and Senmut left, and Tasar alone accompanied the three women toward their tent when he saw someone speak to Ramose. He quickened his step, fear parching his throat more than the desert had. When the other man left, Tasar approached the High Priest.

"Ah, Tasar. I was just told what you did out there." After a searching look into the young priest's eyes, Ramose held his heavy tent flap open, "Come in. There is someone who wishes to meet you."

Blushing deeply, Tasar tried to hide his guilt by lowering his head. The High Priest's words puzzled him. He already knew the *Venerable Badar* from Ineb-hedj and therefore Ramose's choice of words was ominous. Had this wily servant of Ptah sent a bowman after them during the night? If so, did the sentry report the Royal Heiress's sweet surrender to the common priest? A dense fog descended on Tasar's mind until he heard nothing except the pounding of the hammer that had replaced his heart.

"Here is Nefret's young priest, my King." The muffled words penetrated Tasar's racing thoughts. 'My King!' Tasar's head jerked up. By now, his pupils were dilated enough to adjust to the tent's dimness. Against the back wall, a reclining figure crushed numerous cushions. Tasar stared into the unveiled face. By the gods! It was the King! Oh *Maat, Goddess of Truth*, avert your eyes just one more time so that I may live, Tasar prayed with numb intensity and cursed his unrestrained youthful urges that brought him to the brink of death. 'Nefret's young priest.' That said it all! Tasar's knees buckled under him and he collapsed before Aha. Hiding his terror-stricken face in his hands, he waited for the swift crushing blow of a guard's avenging mace.

"Forgive me, my King," was all he could whisper, the sound barely squeaking through his trembling fingers.

"How could you know who she was," Aha said. "You had to hold on to her to save her life. And now you have done so twice. From what Ramose tells me, it must have been a good scare for all of you out there, in the dark, with the menace of an attack. You did well to bring the women back to camp. Who knows what would have happened otherwise. Now, tell us, young priest from Nekhen, could you see how many of them there were?"

Ramose, too, urged, "Yes, Tasar, tell us! How many did you count? First, let me remind you not to mention to anyone whom you met in here. As far as the others are concerned, this is still the *Venerable Badar*." He exchanged a glance with Aha before he continued, "Are those men headed in our direction?"

They don't suspect a thing! Tasar, delirious with relief, jumped to his feet and, babbling like a woman, described how he and the others spied the tribesmen. To rid himself of his excessive joy his gestures were exaggerated as he told them how the women cowered in fear; how the men calmed them down. He started to tell about Senmut suggesting this and that when he realized his mistake. In the nick of time, he bit his tongue lest it became plain enough that they had been paired into an equal number of men and women. Young healthy men, coy young women, spending a night together. A certain conclusion might occur even to a spent King. Just as it could awaken the imagination of a celibate High Priest.

Tasar forced himself to conclude his report calmly. "I suspected that this was not an ordinary caravan and decided to bring the women back to camp, my King."

*

"Great Ramose, they are a half hour's march away." The anxious voice came muffled through the sides of the tent.

Ramose recognized it and answered, "Thank you, Senmut. Caution your men not to attack without provocation. But keep your quivers within reach."

Almost before he finished his instructions, Ramose sank cross-legged onto a large cushion next to the King. A low murmur rose from within his chest and his eyes rolled back, open but unseeing. Tuthmose and Seka, who had been in the back of the tent, did not move. Nor did Tasar. Only Aha grew visibly agitated as Ramose slipped deeper into his self-induced trance.

"What is he doing?" the King whispered loudly. "This is hardly the time to escape into never-never land!"

For the first time since Tasar entered, Seka spoke. "My King," he said quietly. "The most advanced of our calling know a method that enables them to achieve total concentration. During this, the *Ba* leaves the body and flies into the realm of the gods. With their guidance, an experienced priest can compress many hours' worth of planning into a few moments."

"As Ramose does now. He implores the gods for a plan to save us from the raiders," Tuthmose completed his colleague's explanation.

"Of course, another plan," Aha sighed. He peered with some concern at his deathly pale High Priest.

"Tasar! Quickly! Bring the women here! Seka! Tuthmose! I need your help." Startled, they all looked at Ramose who issued the brief orders in his normal voice, every trace of the unearthly pallor gone from his features. "And send word down to the river to have the boats prepared for departure," he called after Tasar. Then he found his small ivory box. With great care, he took out two tiny stiletto-like tips and slid them between his index and middle fingers cupping his hands so that the miniature spears became invisible.

Aha rolled his eyes. What a journey! He would long remember it; if he survived this miserable trip. His thoughts turned to an imaginary scene: Old Badar enjoying unaccustomed luxuries heaped upon his ancient body by the capable Beir. How Aha missed his Steward's lavishing

246

devotion. As soon as Beir had caught up, in Nekhen, he would reward the trusted man with a new breastplate; just for having him around again. Beir would like the feel of precious ornaments around his powerful neck.

"Here, Hor-Aha." Ramose offered his King a cup of wine. Despite the early hour, Aha drank greedily. In a heartbeat the ruby liquid took effect. As reality faded from him, Aha tasted a faint bitterness. His lids, already heavy, opened in sudden recollection. Ramose had tricked him again! May the vultures pick his skull clean! He had tasted that same odd bitterness before he fainted into those disturbing dreams at the Temple of Ptah. Curses upon your head, Ramose! Aha slumped back, his body rigid.

When Nefret and her two slaves came into the large tent, the King lay unconscious. "Father," Nefret cried out and rushed to his side. "I knew it! As soon as I saw the sandals! I knew that it was Father!"

*

Swift-footed, they poured over the closest hillock like scavenging hyenas, their explosive rush brought to a reluctant halt when their leader raised his arms. Covered down to their scaly soles by flowing dust-reddened robes, their heads were wrapped in swaddling cloth with only a slit left for their eyes. In each pair, there was only cruel greed. The fanatic stares left no doubt that they would spare no one.

The marauders formed an impenetrable ring around the defenseless camp. Five men detached themselves from the main group and advanced with the apparent leader in their midst. He swung a long staff above his head. Usually, a warrior's greeting for his commander, this tribesman's motion exuded a whirling threat. Next to the ringleader, well over five cubits high and weighing easily as much as a young bull, stalked the biggest man any of the travelers had ever seen. His cold eyes bulged with lusty anticipation.

"I am Wadji, Cobra of the Desert," the leader called, his speech strangely accented. "The Cobra Goddess bids me to take what I find on her land. You are deep within its boundaries."

Pase, who had been asked by Ramose to stay close, dropped the corners of his mouth. The reeking man obviously had an inflated view of *Wadjet's* sandy realm. As there was nothing to be gained by arguing against the man's self-empowering assumptions, Pase waited. He sensed that he might not have to do so long. The High Priest's hurried instructions had prepared them. The two groups faced each other in coiled readiness.

A piercing wail rose high into the air. Women! As a single thought, unquenched lust lit the fires of desire in the deep-set eyes of the marauders as another keening joined the howling of the rising wind.

"In there," one of the tribesmen pointed out, and the five hurdled themselves at the largest of the tents. With brute force, the giant ripped the entrance flap away as he, Wadji, and the others rushed inside.

Sickening odor assaulted the expectant raiders like a mace blow. They gagged and reached for their flowing robes covering their faces to ward off the overpowering stench. When their dark pupils adjusted to the dimness, Wadji and his ,group stopped dead in their forward rush. They stared, horrified. The scene before them was pitiful to behold. Four figures, three men and a tall girl, lay rigid in apparent death while a pretty young woman writhed on the floor in agony, her half-naked body covered with fiery red blotches. A third woman, dark-skinned and plump, rocked back and forth on her ample haunches, wailing a stirring dirge. To one side of the square tent stood a very tall man staring at them in tearless shock. A much younger, handsome one, frothed at the mouth, his hands clasped around his throat, his eyes bulging in terror as if death was choking him.

The stench was enough for Wadji to feel that he would soon be next if he did not get out of there. Nevertheless, he called out again, "I am Wadji, Cobra of the Desert. And you are mine." He lifted his long walking staff and with a quick jab prodded the motionless tall girl. There was no movement. "Dead," he mumbled behind his covered face.

"The plague! It is the dreaded plague. By evening we shall all be dead. For death resides within this camp," the tall man with the frozen stare intoned as he approached Wadji. As if he thought that the tribesman could save him from a horrible fate, he reached toward the stunned Cobra of the Desert. Weakened by horror and grief, he stumbled. Without thinking, Wadji reached for the outstretched arms. Too late, he saw the disgusting blotches. Bile coated the desert-hardened man's dry throat. He jumped back two steps.

With great dexterity, and even greater caution, Ramose manipulated the tiny shafts firmly between his fingers. Then he raised his arms in front of him, careful to leave his hands below eye level of his adversaries.

"Advance no further, Wadji! The powers of Horus are greater than that of the giant cobra. I am the High Priest of Ptah and the Falcon-god is my protector. You, Cobra of the Desert, will die if you come any closer."

"And how will you kill me, Tall One?" Wadji cackled.

"By placing my bare hands on your shoulders," Ramose intoned, using the powerful voice of sacred supplication.

If Wadji was startled by this deep sing-song threat, he hid it well. For an instant he remained undecided, then laughed, "I don't believe you."

"I warn you," Ramose sang out and took a step forward.

Wadji turned to the big man behind him, "Stinger of a Scorpion, step up!" To Ramose, he gloated, "Not often is the scorpion stronger than the giant cobra. Together, however, they have greater power than the falcon. I wager your life against his that you cannot kill the Stinger."

I can, and I will. Ramose hoped that the sliver of a blade would penetrate deep enough through the brute's dirty clothes. Who knew how many robes this bull of a man wore heaped upon his rancid body. This task would not be as easy as when he had demonstrated the poison on poor old Hanni, Mekh's bent *Ostrich-Egg Gatherer*.

Wadji boxed his slow-witted man into position. "He is all yours, Priest of the Horus-god!" He laughed derisively certain to foil the priest's alleged power while being wily enough to volunteer another for the risky experiment. One could never tell what happened with the shamans of the foreign gods.

Ramose breathed deeply. His outstretched arms were growing heavy. He advanced with measured steps, not wanting to startle the giant whose fist could smash a man's skull.

The other three marauders stood motionless and held their breath partly out of curiosity, mostly not to breathe in the foulness of this tent.

Wadji stood coiled like his namesake ready to strike

should the priest make a move against him.

"Stinger of a Scorpion," Ramose soothed. "Are you ready to receive the great powers of Horus?" He locked his blue gaze into the fanatic's black stare and placed his hands onto the enormous shoulders. As tall as Ramose was, he had to reach up. Thankfully, the other's robe was thin and its threads parted easily under the penetrating tips.

The Stinger felt two bites. Sand fleas, he shrugged, his shoulders driving the exquisitely sharpened tips deeper under his dust-caked skin.

Ramose removed his hands, his thumbs sliding the tips back between his fingers, carefully so as not to nick himself. He stepped back just as the giant crashed to the floor where he lay lifeless, his eyes staring at nothing. The four marauders gasped. What magic was this?

Wadji could take no more of the stench. Nor of the tall priest who killed by a slight touch. He turned and pushed his way out. Back in the open, he unwound the strangling swatches from his face and greedily sucked fresh air through his nostrils. As he exhaled, he suddenly realized that the air itself might carry the awful plague. Hawking fiercely, he tried to expel the unknown harbingers of death. His followers tumbled from the tent equally crazed with avaricious fear for their miserable lives.

"Away!" Wadji cried and rushed toward the hillock, his three surviving leaders close at his heels.

The rest of the band could not fathom any reason for the sudden flight. Without their curiosity or their mounting lust satisfied, they crowded around the tent opening and, one by one, peered into it, only to stare at a scene of death, its overpowering stench quelling their greed. Great Cobra! There lay the lifeless form of the giant Stinger. Whoever slew him had to be more powerful than Wadji.

"Away!" they too cried and tumbled after their leaders, petrified that death might reach for them. As fast as their hardened soles allowed them to cover the rough terrain, they fled into the desert. When they felt safe at last, they reassembled.

Wadji thought it best that they should not report their horrifying encounter to anyone. He reasoned that there was nothing they could do. Unless they killed the rest of the travelers. But then they would have to breathe the putrid air again and thus might succumb themselves. Supposing, the plague spread further south and supposing they admitted that they knew about it; their masters would blame them for their lack of vigilance. Their roaming days as free desert spies would come to an ignoble end. The Cobra of the Desert did not relish the thought of being dragged off to some forsaken mine in the Land of the Kush, to end his days writhing under the lashes of sadistic overseers.

*

"What happened?" Nefret massaged her throbbing temples. Sitting up, she vaguely recalled the last hour.

"Dokki, promise me that you will never, ever, wail like that again! It sickened me. As does this ghastly smell. I need to breathe." She tried to jump up. Her head spun and a wave of nausea enveloped her.

"Not so fast, dear child," Ramose cautioned. "I led you into a deep trance which rendered you as stiff and as unfeeling as a board. Your body has to readjust to its natural state. You must move slowly now."

"It was incredible! I did not feel a thing when one of the brutes poked me, although I could hear every word," Nefret marveled. She examined the bluish mark the marauder's staff had left on her tender skin and then glanced shyly at her father who showed no sign of life.

"Ramose?" she asked with filling eyes. "Is Father going to be all right?" Her concern caught Ramose by surprise. The dangers of their unfortunate stop must have left their mark on this royal child. "Why does he not awaken?" she insisted.

"He will, my child. Now that you know who our veiled traveler is, I caution you to preserve his secret at all cost. As to his health, you need not be alarmed. He will recover without ill effect."

Safaga sat up and rubbed her aching hips. The writhing on the hard floor had chafed her skin half raw and with the angry red blotches on her limbs, she was quite a sight. Pase would not find her very appetizing right now. "I look disgusting," she moaned. Standing up, she stared at the lifeless King and quickly realized why the purportedly ailing Badar had never left the *Kariy* without being heavily veiled.

Thinking about disguises made her wonder about Zeina's

fate, the tall slave having gone into seclusion at the palace to travel with the Royal Convoy, posing as the Royal Heiress.

I wonder who is playing the King, Safaga thought, and suddenly missed even Amma's scolding. Hopefully, they would all be reunited soon.

Nefret questioned Ramose again, "Why are we awake so much sooner than Father?"

"Because you are much younger," Ramose said.

"Will you awaken Tuthmose and Seka now?" Safaga asked.

"Not yet. They are priests and possess special powers that enable them to stay longer under a trance," Ramose comforted. Judging by the self-examinations and rubbings of bruised skin, the girls were more concerned with their appearances than with the dangers of people emerging from deep hypnosis.

"There is little cause to concern yourselves," he smiled. "As to your rashes, they will fade soon after you have rinsed the acid off your skin."

"They are gone," a voice rejoiced outside the tent.

"You can return to your own tent now; however, stay inside. Go, little doves, for I must tend to the King and Seka."

Addressing Tasar, Ramose said, "You better rinse the froth from your mouth before you scare our own men into flight. After you call Pase to accompany our brave ladies back to their tent, have Senmut make sure there are no marauding stragglers left about. After that, I need your help." He turned his attention to his next pressing task. Once again, he worked with quick precision to coax his drugged King back to life. Seka and Tuthmose would also need assistance to reemerge from their self-induced trance.

First, Ramose straddled Aha, intent on breathing life back into his King's lungs. He pounded the hairless chest and after anxious moments, Aha took his first reluctant breath. With great gentleness, Ramose brought the vial containing the secret antidote to his King's lips.

Aha opened his eyes trying to focus as he allowed a few drops to trickle onto his tongue. "Not again, Ramose," he complained and pushed the High Priest's hand away.

"It was the only way, my King," his long-time advisor

soothed. "There, another few drops will bring about your full recovery." Ramose handed the small vial to Aha who shrugged and resigned himself to ingest another unknown potion.

After he was certain that Aha swallowed the last drop, Ramose said, "Something must have gone awry for the Third Army not to have sent their fourth squad. If we are to reach Abdju by mid-afternoon we must leave now. Only then, I predict, will we be safe."

"I mostly believe your predictions, Ramose. But never have I hoped for one to be truer than I do at this moment," Aha admitted. Then his face grew hard with indignation, "That Teyhab has much to answer for. Wait until I catch up with him at Barum's camp!"

"No guessing what could have gone wrong." Ramose sensed Aha's thirst for revenge. "In all fairness, Aha, remember that General Teyhab did not return to Badari after the War Council. He is trekking directly to the Kharga with Colonel Mekh. Responsibility for the mix-up rests with his Aide-de-camp, Colonel Mayhah."

"The Colonel and his men left Badari before your boats arrived at the garrison," Seka, fully awake now, interjected.

"Still, no excuse for Teyhab! We could have all been killed. Those responsible shall be punished," Aha growled, not satisfied with the priests' explanations. His head felt as if it had been split in two by a stone mace. The smell inside the tent grew intolerable.

"For Horus' sake! Get rid of this stinking mess! Best have it burned," Aha groaned and buried his face in a small cushion to escape the sickening stench.

*

The marauders rushed along the high plain until their lungs stung from gulping sand-laden air. Their breathing came in painful gasps. Only after they reached their hobbled pack-asses a ways from the doomed camp did they feel safe enough to halt their heedless flight.

Wadji forced himself to look back. Far in the distance, a dark pillar of smoke rose through the desert's iridescent heat. "They are burning their dead," he shuddered.

"May the sun scorch those who are still alive," the first leader added, his face distorted with disgust and fear.

"There! Another plume of smoke," the third man pointed, and the fourth added, "It is the Stinger's burning *Ba*."

* * *

Chapter Twenty-Seven

Pase and Senmut descended the wadi ahead of the others. They found the terrified rivermen squeezed into small crevasses along the cliffs where they became one with the few shadows the rising sun accorded the western shore. Perhaps the wind had whistled their approach through the steep gorge for one by one the boatmen crept into the open.

"At least they did not shove off without us," Pase said to Senmut pointing at the rising river.

"As superstitious as they are, they would not have dared. I heard what the High Priest told them," Senmut laughed. While he was attached to the temple just like the boat crew, his view toward the power of the gods was that of a professional soldier rather than the fearful beliefs of a pious servant.

Soon, everyone had come down from the plateau and Ramose, still gravely concerned, urged them to make haste.

Nefret knelt down and fingered her sandal straps while Safaga and Dokki were helped aboard by anxious rivermen.

The sun was already close to its zenith. The wind was becoming lazy and soon it would not fill their sails. The thought of having to row against the current did not faze the anxious crew. They wanted to reach the middle of the river and be freed of the shore's hazards.

"Hurry up!" Safaga and Dokki urged Nefret from aboard, careful not to call her by name. Nefret straightened up without heeding their beckoning. Instead, she approached the High Priest who was being assisted boarding his own vessel.

"Ramose?" Her voice was small. "Would you please ask my, ah, ask the *Venerable Traveler*," she caught herself, "if I might join him on this short trip?" While her upturned face appeared haughty her eyes were pleading.

Her request took Ramose by surprise. Perhaps the frightening experience had turned this willful, sometimes thoughtless, child into a caring daughter after all. Ramose held his hand out and she climbed aboard. He indicated for her to wait on deck as he vanished into the cabin.

Aha had settled down with a soothing cup of wine which he poured himself. Cautiously, he dipped the tip of his tongue into the cup to test the liquid for any telling bitterness.

"Ah, Ramose. I am not sure I want you near me when I drink my wine. Can you assure me that you have no vials hidden in your palm; in which case perhaps you wish to join me," he said, not without humor. In the dimness he missed Ramose's smile.

"Thank you, Venerable Lord," Ramose replied not trusting the soundness of the *Kariy*, addressing Aha as they had agreed. "I assure you that I am not here to add more potions to your wine." He paused and then whispered, "I come at Nefret's behest."

"Has she taken ill?"

"No, Venerable Lord, she has recovered admirably. She is on board this vessel now and has asked if she might join you."

"I cannot blame her for not wanting to stay out in the sun much longer," Aha chuckled.

"I do not believe that is the reason. She wishes to speak with you. Alone. Will you let her come in?"

"Not if she plans to be disagreeable. She usual is, you know." Aha recalled only too well their discomforting family scenes; the squabbles between Hent and Nefret; between Dubar and Nefret. Between even young Djer and Nefret. And himself always in the middle, beseeched by all to intervene. "Confound it, Ramose! She picks a fight whenever it suits her. And now I am trapped in here," Aha exploded.

Ramose shook his head, "I believe she has changed. When she thought you close to death she realized how little thought she gave to your well-being in the past. She might wish to atone. Away from Court. From constant distractions, and the Lady Hent's aversion to her." Aha looked up sharply and Ramose bit his lip. His reference to Hent's dislike of her step-daughter was a mistake. "A little humbleness from the girl might amuse you, Venerable Lord."

"All right, have her come in," Aha conceded. "You will stay

in here, with us?" he added, a supplicant rather than a king.

Ramose shook his head. "I think it best to remain on the lookout, my Lord," he said, glad to leave the stifling cabin. How uneasy this King was with his Royal Heiress. Ramose briefly pitied the lonely man. The willful girl's apparent change could be a promising sign of maturity. On the other hand, he knew gentle Mayet's daughter well and suspected that she was hatching something to amuse herself in Nekhen for which she required the King's consent.

*

"Come in, come in. How nice of you to keep your bored father company." Aha and Nefret scented each other like two animals, ill at ease, weary of each other's intentions.

She was reminded how he never used the words *my daughter* or *your father*. But after the morning's brush with disaster, she resolved that she should get to know this man whose two crowns she was destined to inherit. "Father ..."

"Shhh..." The sounds fluttered between them like wounded butterflies.

"I never have a chance to talk with you anymore. Alone, I mean. I hoped you would not mind." Nefret rushed her next sentences. "There is so much you can teach me. About my upcoming initiation. And all about the *Festival of Opet*. It will be my first time." She blushed at the thought of another 'first time.'

Aha was glad that she chose a safe subject. "Yes, yes, of course. Well. Come sit by me then. Bring a cup and join me in some wine—unwatered for a change. We won't tell Amma. And you are soon to be a Lady of my Court." He winked at her. "Now, let me look at you. You have grown into quite a beauty." Having taken control of the conversation, he allowed himself to be jovial. "Drink your wine, my girl. Ramose promised me it is not poisoned."

He peered at her again, perhaps for the first time seeing the fine features of his first queen duplicated in her daughter. While Mayet's softness was missing in Nefret, her resemblance to the dead queen was unmistakable.

"You look a lot like your mother."

"How about the eyes? Were my mother's as blue as mine?"

"No, they were dark. Like mine." Aha had not meant to bring up Mayet and thought he better keep in control. It

257

smarted to be reminded that his young bride never returned his passion willingly. Impatient in his youth, and in his new glory as king, he took what was his. If only he had been more tender, understanding. But her birth had robbed him of his one true love. Was it a wonder that he kept away from her?

Alone with her in this dark womb, the old hurt suddenly no longer consumed his heart. The child's blue eyes no longer fuelled his suspicions. Perhaps they could heal together. He would tell Nefret more about her gentle mother.

"Blue eyes were prevalent in Mayet's extended family. Several of her relatives had eyes the color of the sky. Your ancestors on your mother's side are said to have come from afar and legends tell that their homeland was surrounded by a great blue sea. After looking at the sky and the sea for many generations, their eyes took on those colors."

"Please, tell me more."

"Your mother was lovely, Nefret. And so very young when we were betrothed."

Renewed grief flooded Aha's eyes. He cleared his throat. "After I became king, I moved the court from Nekhen to Ineb-hedj. For political reasons. Of course, I took my queen with me. To my dismay, she never grew accustomed to her new surroundings." He sighed and fell silent.

"More, please. Tell me more," Nefret begged. She was settled at his feet and her dark head leaned against his knee.

Aha placed a hand on the luxuriant hair. He stroked it. Not absentmindedly, but with a father's tenderness. Then he talked about the noble house of Nekhen into which Mayet was born; his initial joy of having won so beautiful a bride. He touched on Nefret's astonishing birth, and how Badar's surgical skills saved her life yet were unable to save her mother.

"I never knew the whole story," Nefret whispered, choking back her tears. "You mean my mother would not have died if Badar had saved her, not me? Then it is my fault!" she cried and crumpled miserably at his feet.

"Shhh, child. Not so loud." Aha cautioned. "No, Nefret. You must not think that. Without Badar's actions, neither of you would have survived."

Nefret lay nestled in her father's arms, feeling loved by him. Her tears flowed freely as a great weight lifted from her young soul. At long last, she pulled herself free and smiled up at the man comforting her perhaps for the first time in her life. She wanted to keep their conversation going while she enjoyed his full attention. "Ramose, too, has blue eyes."

Aha grabbed her by the shoulders and held her at arm's length. The look she met was again hard. "Of course, he does," Aha barked. "He comes from the same stock."

"Then he and I have the same ancestors?" Nefret wriggled from Aha's angry grip. Why did her mentioning the High Priest bring about such sudden change? How had she offended her Father? Not knowing what else to do, she smiled bravely. She needed to discuss something else with him. Taking a deep breath, she groped for the right words lest she offend him further.

"Why does the Lady Hent dislike me so? As does Dubar. I try so hard to treat them with respect. All they do is put me down and sneer at me. Especially Dubar. He has been awful of late. I think he positively hates me."

"All boys his age hate girls," Aha laughed, glad for a different subject. "If they did not, they would discover much too early how delicious you girls are." A sensuous smile played his full lips and he winked slyly at her. Her eyes met his in such wide innocence that Aha was afraid his ferment-induced mood caused him to share inappropriate remarks with such young ears. He took another long sip of wine.

"I daresay that you, my lovely, will one day realize how pleasant young men are. Believe me, a lot more than you feel about them now." Aha snickered and buried his face in his large cup again, thus a sudden wariness on Nefret's face escaped him.

"When I return from the battlefield," Aha's voice had softened again, "we will celebrate the grandest festival this city has known and its nobles shall be presented to my daughter." As shall their sons, he appeased his conscience. "Back in Ineb-hedj, the *Sed*-festival will be even grander for the two of us."

The shadow of an ugly face crossed Aha's inner eye. He snorted the annoying intrusion away. Then he winked at Nefret and pointed his finger at her, "I remember that you promised me a new robe for my Jubilee. I shall wear your gift proudly, my beautiful daughter."

Joy, then fear, gripped Nefret. This was the first time she could remember that the King referred to her as 'his daughter.'

259

But he also remembered the robe! How long could she hide her unthinkable trespass from him? The same kind of trespass her mother was accused of according to the whispers of loose-tongued slaves.

Nefret wanted to cry out and ask for her Father's forgiveness. Instead, she smiled prettily up at him and took his limp hand in hers. "I must leave you to rest. Thank you for your great kindness." She got up, bowed and fled from the stuffy cabin.

Aha yawned contentedly and stretched out atop some quilts. "The gods be thanked. I have made peace. When we return from Nekhen ..." Sleep claimed the King in the middle of his promise.

*

On their twelfth day, in mid-afternoon, the boats closed in on the somber sentinels of Abdju. With the necropolis in sight, it was as good a time as any, Ramose decided, openly to reveal the King's identity to those on board the temple boats who had not already guessed it.

"He who so much as breathes a word shall have his offending tongue ripped out. Furthermore, Osiris will deny him entry into the afterlife."

There was no singing on deck during the rest of the trip and no tales were spun about previous river journeys. In a sober mood the boats were poled toward shore, their silent approach befitting the great necropolis.

Two cargo barges lay moored ahead having dropped off the supplies and tents along the way. Now their holds were empty as Abdju was their turning point. Still, the journey downriver would not be a wasted rush back to Ineb-hedj. They would take on the wrapped remains and death treasures of deceased nobles whose families had moved to the new capital long ago where they prospered. At last, they could afford to place their dearly departed in the new *Mastabas* at Saqqara.

Offerings to Ptah were to ensure that their dead were delivered intact. What they could not be assured of was that the death treasures would reach their new destination as plentiful as they had been when they were buried at Abdju.

Osiris always claimed the greater part of worldly hordings. It was a good life for the rivermen; as long as they were able to ward off marauders and pass safely through the Narrows.

"Ahoy there!" the captain hailed the barges. Their crews waved back.

"Ahoy there! Glad to see you made it. We trust you found everything along the way," a deep voice shouted back.

"That, and more," Seka answered cryptically. On familiar ground again, he would remember his experience as exciting. Especially, since not one of them had died. Osiris must have been satisfied with the great hulk of the Stinger of a Scorpion.

*

"This is where I shall enter the great afterlife," Aha mused as he, Ramose and Seka stood before his simple *Mastaba* built long ago. The mud brick tomb measured twenty-three by nineteen cubits, a modest size, considering.

"You will be our most honored *Ka.*" Seka bowed deeply in anticipation of the King's next, presumably permanent, visit to his extensive cemetery.

"I still might decree to be buried in my new *Mastaba* at Saqqara. It is much closer to my capital. With a lot more room inside," Aha added wistfully.

Ramose had implored the gods' protection for the new Saqqara structure which measured almost one hundred by forty-five cubits. Looking now at the humble Abdju version, he hoped that his King's *Ka* would not require a resting place soon. Abdju was much too close to their future battlefields.

"Let us offer prayers to my illustrious predecessor. Even though Narmer's body is not interred in here, I trust his *Ka* still welcomes our offerings." Aha moved toward an adjacent tomb of approximately the same proportions.

"King Narmer's *Ka* is always with us," Seka affirmed approaching the second monument with great deference. He thought about Aha's earlier remark. When news of the King's second *Mastaba* had reached Abdju, he was saddened that his established necropolis had been thus slighted. Seka believed that Abdju was the only rightful burial place for the rulers of the young dynasty and that only he and his *Ka*-priests should be its guardians. Saqqara was but an unworthy usurper.

*

A few hours after they had landed, the three temple boats slid back into the river.

"I am glad to get away from there," Nefret whispered to Safaga.

261

"The home of the dead is a dangerous place for the living. Osiris will do anything to obtain his souls," Dokki whispered and immediately covered her mouth with her dark hand as if to keep her words from reaching the vengeful god.

Safaga said, "Priest Seka seems to live quite well among the graves. He is ample proof Osiris does not reach for everyone."

"Perhaps he is unpalatable," Nefret laughed.

*

When the settlement of Hu came into view, the rivermen lashed the sails tightly to the booms. It was still early and they would enjoy the longer stop-over because the following day they would have to bring out the oars. From here on, the river was capricious and its deep bed turned due east so that the prevailing wind would be of no use to them.

After a good day's rowing, they reached Dendara, accepting the hospitality of its large temple. Then the river turned back on itself and more hours of arduous rowing were wrenched from the sweating rivermen until the river straightened south. Once more, they could shake out the sails and run before the wind.

"How much longer," Nefret complained. She and her women had just about enough of the reeking rivermen, their tuneless songs, and the cramped existence on the open deck. To their surprise, they grew tired of their ever-present lovers whom they had satisfied so passionately the night before the vile attack and who now feigned disinterest again

Aha was the only one who enjoyed the trip. After Abdju, he remained on deck to share a shady spot with Ramose under the canopy. Still, whenever they accepted the hospitality of small temples Ramose introduced them as simple servants of the gods, on a pilgrimage to Nekhen.

After the crews of the temple boats had been told about the identity of the well-fed man, their immobile faces never betrayed their thoughts.

Ramose's eyes roamed over the muscular backs. These men were the realm's true wealth. They, and the fellahin, would survive well into the future. The priesthood perpetuated itself through its temples; kings through their edifices, offspring and mastabas. But the simple people of the land and the river would endure throughout the ages.

*

The High Priest thought of the Ancient Mats telling of unfathomable achievements and extravagant wealth none of which were any longer evident. Then too, it had been the simple people who survived through their knowledge of the land, and because of their sunken Great River. They had woven the grasses of the verdant plains into a legacy of their vanished civilization.

Even though he had managed to translate the Mats into his own language, the origins of the ancient people still eluded him; just as the dire predictions for the end of their existence haunted his dreams.

* * *

Part IV

Nekhen, The Oracle of Isis

Chapter Twenty-Eight

At the end of the nineteenth day, the captain pointed ahead. Towering walls rose from beyond the dimming light. Relief, mixed with cautious expectancy, enlivened the travel-weary group. They knew not to expect cheering crowds; nor trumpets heralding their arrival; nor laden tables awaiting their parched throats as they were still assumed to be priestly pilgrims. Their true welcome would be safety itself.

At long last, they had reached the City of Nekhen, the old southern capital. Its sister city and cultural rival, Nekheb, beckoned from across the river yet the travelers had only eyes for the growing pylons of Nekhen. Its great houses were closely related to one another and the royal line. After King Narmer built his new court city in the north several decades ago, Nekhen's importance, and that of its wealthy nomarchs, waned considerably as the city's closeness to the tenuous southern border hurt its popularity.

Still, influential nomarchs, the governor of the city, and the King's chief administrators ruled the ancient nome from their great homes. Only the high-ranking *Royal Tax Collector* had his quarters in the old palace to maintain it in readiness for eventual royal visits from Ineb-hedj.

Already, the desert reclaimed the outlying corners of the ancient capital. Ramose feared that one day there would be nothing left except a windswept expanse. No Royal Palace, no

Temple of Horus, no Sacred Lake. No House of Life. What tragedy. Now, it was up to him to preserve the knowledge hammered onto the Tablets.

*

The entire city was highly walled. A second, smaller wall encased the palace and the adjacent Temple of Horus. Along the river, the two walls merged into one and, as in Ineb-hedj, a wide quay separated it from the river. The massive high pylons served as main entrance into the palace as well as the temple.

Ramose ordered all those who posed as priests to drape their sashes across their travel-bronzed torsos. The girls huddled together, again covered by coarse linen wraps. Before too long, the three boats reached the royal mooring ramp and thudded to a halt against great blocks of stone.

"Who comes alongside?" a lookout called from above. He leaned over a low parapet. His call awoke the day-dreaming palace guards below him. The river had risen enough for their station to be almost level with the landing site and the drowsy men jumped to the ready.

"Who comes alongside?" they loudly repeated the lookout's query.

"Priestly pilgrims, who have come to pray with the Chief Priest of the Temple of Horus," Ramose replied in his ritualistic sing-song usually reserved for godly invocations. "Go and inform Rahetep that old friends from the north humbly ask for his gracious hospitality."

One of the guards sprinted off and vanished through the forbidding entrance. Ramose soon expected a temple delegation and encouraged the travelers to disembark. The old sedan was carried up the brief incline by two rivermen their muscles bulging under the weight of the obviously well-fed occupant.

Several figures rushed out from the city entrance and trotted along the Great Road. Ramose recognized Rahetep spearheading his group. It had been a long time since they saw each other. Rahetep too recognized the tallest among the arrivals and stretched his hands toward Ramose. A cautioning look, however, put the intuitive Chief Priest on guard. Instead of calling out his illustrious friend's name, he simply said, "I welcome you to our humble temple, old friend."

"Rahetep," Ramose smiled. "It is good to see you. Do you

266

recognize your former acolyte, Tuthmose?"

"Tuthmose! Indeed. Welcome back to Nekhen."

"And this is Seka, Chief Priest of Tjeny and *Hemu-ka* of Abdju," Ramose continued the purposely superficial introductions.

Rahetep spied Tasar and nodded to him with a smile; the youth had obviously found favor. Well done, he mouthed. When he noticed the rickety old sedan he raised his eyebrows toward Ramose who whispered into his ear, "The namesake of your temple's deity is under your protection now." Nekhen's Chief Priest caught his breath. The reference to Horus, the godly falcon, could only mean one thing: Hor-Aha, the Falcon-King! He acknowledged the momentous news with a nod. Then he clapped his hands together and hastened his priests along, each reaching for as much as he could carry.

"Exercise great care and do not drop the large trunk from the third boat!" Ramose cautioned them as he and Rahetep led the way toward the gate. The cargo of the special tips weighed as heavily on the bearers' shoulders as the immediate procurement of their deadly coating weighed on the High Priest's mind.

Within the hour, the travelers were quartered at the temple. Bone weary, they gladly partook of fresh fruit and thirst-quenching juices heaped upon them by discrete temple serfs. Satiated and safe, all settled in for their first night's uninterrupted sleep since leaving Ineb-hedj.

Except Ramose. Emerging from a refreshing bath, where slender temple maidens oiled his sun-tortured skin and massaged his stiff muscles, he joined Rahetep for a light supper. "I feel reborn," he smiled as he entered his old tutor's private chambers. The document boxes were more numerous now and several chairs and stands had been added to the large room. Other than that, scarcely anything had changed.

"Ramose! At last!" Rahetep clasped his friend's hands in genuine delight. "How good it is to see you. You look well, and I am more than relieved that Tasar completed his mission. I knew you would realize at once that the discovery of the mine and the *Nobas'* advancing armies were of great significance. What takes my breath away, is..." with that Rahetep moved closer and, even in the privacy of his own chamber, continued in a whisper, "how did you ever persuade the King to journey with you in disguise?"

"I am pleased to be back," Ramose smiled, knowing that Rahetep dearly wished he would skip polite generalities and tell him about his plans. The rare opportunity to let the older man dangle a little longer was latent repayment for the lashes across his back when Ramose sat bent over the Ancient Mats, his thoughts far ahead of his studies. Wham! How often had the sting of Rahetep's sturdy reed brought him rudely back to his excruciating task.

"Tuthmose, too, is pleased to reacquaint himself with you. We assume we are safe from your admonitions these days."

"Have you not forgiven this old perfectionist by now," Rahetep mumbled. He screwed his face into mock humbleness.

"You are hereby absolved, Rahetep. And to prove it, I shall tell you everything."

Ramose took a good hour to relate the details of his plans, their masquerade, the King's hope to join his army unobserved by spies, foreign or otherwise. Then he outlined the great battle plan as devised by Makari. "Now you understand that Aha's identity must remain secret until he continues his journey to the Great Oasis in five days or so, to Barum's Fourth. Only Tuthmose, Tasar, the Archer Pase, and the Chief of my Bowmen, Senmut, know his true identity."

"Rest assured, Ramose, the King is safe within these walls."

"Horus willing," Ramose nodded. "And another thing, Rahetep, one of my young chantresses..."

"Oh?" Rahetep sang out, surprised.

Ramose shook his head. "No, no. She is the Royal Heiress, Princess Nefret."

Rahetep sucked his breath in, his eyes one great apology for the presumptuous thought.

"I brought her for safety reasons. She and her two slaves are to be kept in seclusion. After the Royal Bark arrives she will be taken to the palace as if she just arrived. Then her identity can be revealed," Ramose continued, a smile in the corners of his mouth.

"Tesh will have to be informed at some point," Rahetep mused, imagining the fawning Tax Collector's apoplexy.

"Tesh is to be told only about the official convoy. One of Nefret's slaves is impersonating her on the Bark while Badar poses as an ailing King."

"Pardon me for chuckling as I imagine Badar lying prone on deck having wine poured down his throat, with a slave fanning him for all his worth."

Ramose chuckled as well. Nothing was further from reality. He grew serious again. "By the time the royal convoy arrives in Nekhen, the enemy will have been engaged by our forces."

"Much to their surprise," Rahetep concluded.

"Soon after which," Ramose added, "victory is to be ours."

"Just in time for the festival," Nekhen's Chief Priest nodded. The *Festival of Opet* was an important event for his temple. To have the King take part in the opulent celebrations this year would awe the populace into renewed piety. Not to mention the added prestige from the presence of the High Priest and the Divine Father of Ptah!

Rahetep looked at Ramose, a question plainly in his eyes. Was the High Priest grooming a successor yet? Rahetep sighed. Pity that he was too old for the important post. From what Rahetep could glean, Tasar had gained the High Priest's confidence, perhaps the King's liking as well, during the long journey. Rahetep had chosen his messenger wisely.

*

"Tomorrow, we'll explore this rambling place," Nefret announced as she bedded down for her first night in the Temple of Horus.

"Tomorrow, we unpack. And then we rest some more," Safaga countered. "Besides, we need to await instructions from Ramose." She pulled at the quilt she shared with Dokki.

"Safaga, do you mind!" Dokki protested as half of her ample backside lay exposed.

"I didn't hear you protest when Senmut pulled your covers off," Safaga teased. The three giggled into their palms. Just as they had in Ineb-hedj. They missed Zeina.

Since womanhood discovered Dokki, she felt more accepted by the other two. Her bravery during their terrifying brush with the marauding tribesmen undoubtedly had something to do with it. It was further apparent that Dokki's already strong loyalty to the munificent High Priest of Ptah had turned into complete adoration.

"I wonder when Pase returns to the Fourth," Safaga whispered. Little did the two slaves realize how incessantly their young Princess day-dreamed of her own lover. She did not even tell Safaga knowing that a clandestine meeting with him would be disastrous if were they discovered.

*

When the sly Vizier had handed the two dispatches to Pase, he purposely had not sealed them. Hidden words arouse suspicion. Unsealed, the innocuously coded messages mirrored al-Saqqara's dutiful announcements. He knew that Pase could not read but correctly assumed that the simple man would give the scrolls to the High Priest for safekeeping during the long journey.

Immediately after their arrival in Nekhen, Pase asked Ramose if he could take the Royal Tax Collector's message to him. "Would you make certain that I take the right one, High Priest? And, if you have a moment, could you read the other one to me again?"

Ramose knew that the wished to hear the sweet sounds of his recommendation once more. He could not fault the diligent man for his small vanity. As he reexamined the words of both documents, his instincts still warned against a trap. But as often he read the messages he could not discern any unusual meaning in the words. He told Pase, however, to delay the Tax Collector's message for a few days and gave the archer to understand that there was plenty of time for the official to prepare the palace for the arrival of the Royal Bark. Ramose further wanted Pase to delay his own departure from Nekhen even though he was anxious to rejoin his comrades.

"You will guide the King to Barum's camp. I am sending Tasar, Tuthmose, Seka, as well as Senmut and his Bowmen with you," Ramose said. "I assume you know the way to the Oasis. And remember. Not a word about this to anyone."

Pase was more than flattered. Apart from the obvious honor, it gave him a little more time with Safaga. Back at his assigned quarters he laid down on his cot, confident that the Tax Collector's tardy message was Ramose's problem. The young archer yawned and quickly fell into the sleep of a happy man with a clear conscience.

*

"One hundred cobras? Alive! Ramose, do you really need that many?" Rahetep clapped his hands over his cheeks and shook his head in astonishment.

Ramose nodded, "One hundred, my friend. And I need

them in less than four days. Together with an ample supply of beeswax."

"That's an easier task. However, we are still in the dry season, and our keepers emptied their hives a number of moons ago. I shall see what we have left in our stores. May I ask why you need this curious mixture?"

"The spear tips will be covered with the venom of the mighty cobra. After that, we dip them into liquefied beeswax to seal the poison in. We wouldn't want to dispatch an innocent lance bearer to a mistaken death. The tips will be taken to the battle field where they are fitted. If handled properly, nothing should happen to anyone. Jab the enemy hard and his body heat melts the wax. The venom takes effect at once."

"Ingenious," Rahetep conceded, waiting.

"Quite. Imagine the terror among enemy ranks. They collect their dead after battle, but find no wounds deep enough to have caused the sudden deaths. Fear will gnaw at them like ravenous hyenas. Their hands will tremble. And as you know, an unsteady hand cannot deliver a lethal blow."

"Ingenious," Rahetep said again.

"I need acolytes to coat the tips. Send me only those you can spare. With the time available to us, they have to work fast. I will not have time to do this task myself, naturally."

"Naturally," Rahetep agreed.

*

Nekhen's Temple of Horus was not as large as the Temple of Ptah in Ineb-hedj. Its multiple chambers and hallways were just as confusing though. They laced through hidden courtyards into enormous libraries and crammed study chambers, secret laboratories and musty dungeons. Kitchens and storerooms alternated with verandas where huge pillars suddenly barred the way, redirecting a lost worshipper to half-hidden altar nooks. The main courtyard led past rows of large offering basins and, further into the grounds, huge grain silos burst with the annual harvest rent paid to the temple.

The *House of Life* stood apart from the main complex, secreted away behind the circular revetment of the Sacred Lake. A single path led past the water toward the House's entrance; and only a chosen few were allowed to enter through its heavy gates. Here, the Ancient Mats were kept, and carefully chosen acolytes copied the faint markings onto sturdier papyri.

'My precious Ancient Mats.' Ramose caressed the memory of his painstaking early years. Day in, day out, he sat bent copying the faint marks from the brittle originals onto new papyrus. Always under Rahetep's watchful eyes. His friend, Tuthmose, sat next to him, squinting as he traced the confusing squares with exacting care.

Their youthful impatience often elicited stern rebukes, the reprimands to be followed by sharp blows from a sturdy reed that Rahetep kept close at hand. Discipline was deemed of utmost importance.

Little did Ramose guess during those early days how all-consuming the translation of the Ancient Mats would become for him. Now, after so many years, he was back at the *House of Life*; with knowledge he could not share with anyone, his generation not yet mature enough to be entrusted with such portentous legacy.

*

The ancient priest waited as Ramose and Tuthmose came up the path to the *House of Life*. "High Lord of Ptah, honor me to open the gates for you." He bowed as deeply as his arthritic back allowed.

"How are you, Old Father," Ramose greeted the wizened man and bowed to his great age. "I am pleased to find you still so well."

"It has been long, Rama. Ah, and Tuthmose is with you, if my old eyes do not deceive me," the frail man whispered, his mind as sharp as ever. Tuthmose acknowledged the greeting with his own low bow.

The old lector continued, "You both have used your time well. I am proud to have taught you once." His toothless mouth widened with pleasure and he bowed again. "I am now the Overseer of your treasure, Great Ramose."

The two friends stepped aside to let the old Overseer pry the heavy doors apart. He struggled fiercely but neither of them lent a helping hand. This was the old man's task, and he was proud of it. At last, the wooden gates creaked wide. Within five steps was a second gate and, again, the old man strained with all his might, his tenacity at last rewarded.

Walking his visitors through the familiar passage, the Overseer stopped and looked up at his tall former pupil. "Forgive me, Ramose. I had hoped to welcome the Venerable

Badar as well. Did he not come with you?"

"You will see him soon, Overseer. Because the Divine Father has been blessed with a great age the river journey was hard on his health. He needed to rest. Be patient, Old One. You will see him within half a moon, I promise you."

The old man's leathery skin stretched drum-tight over his fleshless face in a toothless grin. He looked forward to the prospect of meeting the Venerable Badar again. He could be patient hoping that Osiris would be as well for his *Ba*.

They came to the end of the passage and turned into another. Suddenly, Rahetep stepped out in front of them, closing a hidden door behind him. "You are going to be pleased with our work," he smiled at Ramose and fell into step with them. "Our old Overseer has guarded your Tablets like a lion guards his pride. Here we are." Rahetep opened a heavy door.

"Ah!" Ramose and Tuthmose marveled at the magnificent display before them. A step spanned the length of the far wall. Neatly stacked on its ledge leaned a row of fifty gleaming slabs of yellow nub. Small carvings emerged as a distinguishable pattern of etched squares from the soft metal.

"Our *Great Sepulcher of Knowledge*." Rahetep gleamed like his tablets. Then he sighed, "Alas, the legends of the Mats are sealed to us. We still do not possess the key."

Ramose chuckled.

Rahetep caught the bemused look. He held up his hands, "Just one of my sayings, Ramose. Working first with the Mats and then the Tablets as long as I have, does it surprise you that I have great yearning to penetrate their secrets."

"High Priest of Ptah," the old Overseer whispered, his tired eyes watery from excitement and from regret. "The Tablets are completed. They are yours to take to Ineb-hedj." He always knew that the Tablets would leave the *House of Life* one day, just as he would have to once his task was finished.

Ramose laid his hand on the Overseer's shoulder. "I am grateful for the extreme care you have given our Tablets, Old Father."

Again Tuthmose marveled, "They are splendid."

"They are indeed," Ramose agreed. "Still, our work with them is far from done." He let his words sink in before he continued. "The yellow nub of the Tablets is thick enough for what I have in mind. Would you agree, Rahetep, that their blank sides cry out for a translation?"

"Ramose! You broke the code! By Horus, you found the key!" The Chief Priest's face lit up. After all these years, he was to glimpse the ancient past which had tantalized and tortured him long enough. He was jubilant.

"Yes, the gods gave me the key which, incidentally, is more like a template. You shall have a copy of it. I also brought a complete translation with me, written in my own hand. Badar knows which of the fifty scrolls translates which Tablet. I have told Tuthmose much of what I know. He, Badar, and you two, Rahetep and old Father, are the only ones to get to know the legends of the Ancient Mats."

"Who will stamp the translation onto the Tablets?" Rahetep asked.

"We will have to choose wisely. There is another matter of concern: Once the Tablets are inscribed with the translation, their gleaming surfaces must be obscured with something that will not ruin them when they are cleaned—in the distant future. They are to be numbered on the lower rims. In the correct order."

Ramose hesitated but then decided that he would like to be remembered in the future.

"And, Rahetep, make certain that a small winged scarab is stamped next to those numbers. I have chosen the *Khepri* as one of my personal seals. Maybe someone in the future wants to know who translated them. A small vanity, I know."

"What could be used to cover them?" Tuthmose asked Rahetep who was an accomplished alchemist and already had a mixture in mind.

"Give me a day or two to experiment. There is a pitch extracted from certain plants. It darkens as well as hardens over time and is soluble only in the sacred black liquid that bubbles up from the ground when it is mixed with natron."

"Excellent," Ramose nodded. Then, with a sly grin, he added, "Rahetep, I trust your laboratory priests will not confuse the pots of cobra venom with the mixture of the pitch."

"So do I," his former tutor chuckled.

It was good to have Ramose back to challenge him just as young Prince Rama had at an early age. Yes, Rahetep thought gratified, the return of his greatest of all pupils was exhilarating.

"The actual Mats are getting too brittle to be kept intact much longer," he said.

Ramose reflected for a moment and then nodded, "We shall burn them. And, Rahetep, from now on, no more papyrus copies."

* * *

Chapter Twenty-Nine

Psst, Tasar. Tasar! Psst!"

Tasar turned. A shadowy figure emerged from behind a pillar that had hidden the slim form when he passed it.

"Tasar," the soft voice urged again. The apparition pulled the hood of the white cloak back.

"Oh, it's you."

"Of course it's me," Safaga mocked. "You don't suppose *You-know-Who* would prowl these passages just to get a glimpse of you?" She pulled him behind the wide pillar. "Listen, Priest. Nefret goes into seclusion for her cleansing rites. No one can see her until the festival." When she saw Tasar's dismay, she added, "She told me how you rushed off with the robe. Did you bring it with you? It is the King's and he expects to wear it during *Opet*."

"By Horus, I forgot all about it!" Tasar hit his forehead with his palm. "Do you recall the second day of the special lessons? After Ramose left? I was to take the robe back then. But the High Priest bade me to work throughout the night. Remember?"

"I remember," Safaga mocked again. "That evening, the King summoned Nefret to dinner. She asked me to wait for you instead. Later, my trusting mistress waited for you herself. For hours." Safaga's lips pursed into a pretty pout, "As I recall, both of us did so in vain."

"I told you, Ramose kept me up all night."

Safaga recalled the tense hours she spent cowering in the dark passage, frightened that someone might discover her. "Nefret was furious. And so was I."

"I know!" Tasar cried.

"Shhh." Safaga put a slender finger to her lips.

"I remember," Tasar whispered. "I stuffed it under the cushion of a sedan in old Badar's study."

"In the *Venerable Badar's* study! That's where the switch was made. That old chair was on the boat with the King. Oh no! Hor-Aha sat on his own robe!" Safaga couldn't help her giggles. She looked at Tasar and they realized that the robe might be in Nekhen. Though was it still within their reach?

"Where do you suppose the old chair is now?" Safaga pinched Tasar's arm. When he shook himself free from her grasp, she stiffened at her breach of conduct. "Forgive me, Priest Tasar. I forgot my place."

"So you did, Slave. Now, let me think. It should be in the small temple suite with Hor-Aha."

"Shhh," the anxious slave cautioned again. "No one must know! Remember, everyone assumes that he is Badar. If we betray him he will have us killed."

Tasar's agile thoughts shaped into a feasible plan. "Leave it to me, Safaga. There is lots of time before *Opet.*" He moved closer to her. "Now take me to Nefret."

"Have you taken leave of your senses, Priest?" Safaga raised her arms as if to protect herself from him and Osiris, so shocked was she at the bold request.

"Safaga! Once Nefret transfers to the palace, I shall have no way to talk to her. I must see her while she is here at the temple. With only you and Dokki with her, this is my only chance. I beg of you!"

Tasar looked so desperate and smitten that the pretty slave could not resist. "All right then, come with me. But you'll only have a moment." She turned and hurried toward a dim passage. Tasar caught up with her as she opened a door. He slipped in after her—and looked straight into surprise-rounded black eyes.

"Tasar!" Dokki's full mouth hung open. No knowing what to do, she stared.

Safaga had dashed through to a second inner chamber and now returned pulling her young mistress behind her. With a smile, she pushed the Princess toward her lover and reminded them that their time together was brief. Then she dragged the dumfounded dark slave with her into the other room, and gently closed its door.

*

277

The two stood motionless. Their unexpected closeness stunned them, and they eyed each other in breathless wonder. Neither could think of anything to say.

At last, Nefret took a small step toward the man she hated childishly but yearned for as a woman.

Her movement broke the awkward spell and Tasar reached for her pulling her against his chest. Repeating his name, she sounded like a freed song bird twittering, as she clung to him; not with the eagerness of youth but with womanly longing for his warmth, for his protection. He sensed the change from girlish flirtations to soft surrender and desire welled up within him.

If only he could confess his love for her to Ramose; and if only she could tell her father. Those were steps he dared not yet for them to take. Not before he proved himself worthy. In the meantime, he and Nefret were toying with their lives.

They stood intertwined, holding fast, breathing each other's nearness, drinking in each other's breath. When she met his mouth, her lips responded ardently. He could hold back no longer and enveloped her with the urgency of youth. The world sank into oblivion. Time, however, does not stand still even for the deepest love.

*

"Nefret!" Safaga's hiss jolted the two back to reality. "Tasar, you must leave! Now!"

"Not yet," Nefret pleaded, but Safaga insisted. "I shall take you back," she said firmly to the young priest.

"There is no need, Safaga, I know my way around."

"Of course you do. But should someone see you in this wing, we must pretend that you have been with me." Safaga did not dare to give them another minute and pulled hard at Tasar's arm. This time, she was not rebuked for her lack of protocol. The perceptive slave could see his swelling and pulled harder at his arm. She saw how Tasar stole a last glimpse at Nefret before she pulled the door shut between them.

Following the slave along the empty passageway, Tasar did not care where their flight led them. He never felt like this before. Was his love for the young Nefret true? Or was this merely ambitious hunger for the Royal Heiress? They could achieve much if only they could proclaim their love openly. The dreaming lover almost bumped into Safaga who had stopped suddenly.

"I leave you here, Tasar. When will you bring the robe?"

He looked at her as if awakening from a dream. "Oh, the robe. Tell Nefret," he heard himself say, "...tell her that the next time she sees me, I will have the robe for her." At last, he smiled at the pretty slave. There was great tenderness in his eyes, and her heart danced faster though she knew it was not meant for her. Still, captivated by his soulful look, a sweet tingling invaded the very depth of her. She straightened to appear self-assured and when she spoke to him her voice carried a throaty undertone.

"Remember the robe, my priest."

"You need not worry, pretty one." Tasar cupped Safaga's face in his right palm. "I promise by the *Eye of Horus*, I will bring the King's robe."

Absentmindedly, Tasar continued to caress Safaga's cheek, unaware how sweetly his smooth palm burned into her skin, his long fingers a promise of his ample manhood.

The slave turned her head so that her lips rested in his palm and she could taste the salt of his skin. Tears of frustration filled her eyes. Her mistress trusted her, and depended on her. Ah, Pase. Ah, Beir. Where were her absent lovers now? So different from each other, and both so very different from this priest. Safaga stiffened with resolve and rushed off to escape his magnetism. The ambitious priest would never bed a lowly slave.

Tasar stared after the fleeing woman. How assured was he of her loyalty? Perhaps she did not approve of him. He must be more cautious with the headstrong slave. As useful as she was right now, her knowledge could prove dangerous in the future. He promised himself to search for the robe as soon as he gained access to the King's temporary quarters, most likely after the King had left for the Kharga. His mind returned to sweeter thoughts.

*

"There you are."

Tasar spun around and stared at the High Priest. Ramose strode quickly toward him and the young man's cheeks reddened deeply.

"Is something the matter?" Ramose inquired. "You jumped as if you were stung by a scorpion. You could hardly have mistaken me for a departed *Ba*. Or were you expecting someone else?" Ramose came abreast with the young priest and put a friendly arm around the younger man's left shoulder. "I have important work for you, young Tasar. Come. We need to discuss this in more privacy than this open space affords us." Ramose led the way through another long passage and then suddenly stopped.

Tasar thought the spot hardly more private when Ramose pushed an invisible panel, flush with the wall. He motioned and Tasar, puzzled, entered an empty chamber. How did Ramose find the unobtrusive entrance with such certainty? Of course, he remembered. The High Priest studied here, and most likely knew every nook and cranny of these old buildings.

Ramose strode across the hollow space and vanished through another door. Tasar hastened after him. The second chamber was large. Ample light spilled through wide openings from a walled courtyard. Leather-stripped chairs ringed a massive table. Intricately inlaid trunks bore signs of great age; their faience patterns peeling at the corners. Two huge ivory tusks curved upright in a far niche, behind them brilliant feathers spread into large fans. Most intriguing about this chamber were two leopard pelts hung spread-eagled across one wall. Tasar found himself in the inner sanctum of a *Sem*-priest. As far as he knew, no indication existed for this temple to have an officiating *Sem*-priest. No special rites were ever performed, no ancient verses chanted.

"You can see from these things how close we are to our exotic trading partners. Rahetep keeps this chamber for my special use. From the look on your face, I see that you have never been told about it."

Tasar shook his head.

The High Priest sat down in a comfortable chair and invited Tasar to take his place across from him. "I have been impressed by your deportment. And so was the King. Our young Princess as well, I might add."

Hot waves burned their way from Tasar's quickening heart onto his cheeks. Ramose took notice of the rising color on his new protege's face. Once more, his doubts strafed on Tasar's regrettable vanity; it detracted from the many other qualities of the likeable young priest.

"You know these grounds well, Tasar. Undoubtedly, you

are also acquainted with the palace court officials. I want you to take the Archer Pase to the *Royal Tax Collector* so he can deliver his message from the Vizier." Ramose's mouth pulled down a fraction. "We would not want to keep the high official waiting."

Tasar saw the hardening of the other's jaw; heard the sarcasm in the voice, and realized that for some reason, Ramose purposely had not allowed the archer to deliver his message right after their arrival.

"Pase gave me the Vizier's messages for safekeeping. One for Tesh. The other for Pase's Watch Captain Nebah. Read them and tell me what you think." Ramose handed two papyri to Tasar.

Handing them back after reading them, Tasar offered his opinion. "Too effusive for my taste. The Vizier tries to flatter both recipients. Then admonishes them needlessly to do their jobs. But I guess any slip-ups would naturally fall back on al-Saqqara's head."

"You discern nothing peculiar then? No hidden meaning?"

Tasar shook his head, "Nothing that I could detect."

Ramose pressed his lips together. He still sensed something sinister about the driveling words.

"Tomorrow night, the King leaves for the Oasis. Still in disguise, of course, among an inconspicuous squad of warriors returning to their camp. Rahetep promised his best donkeys. Seka goes along to become the regimental *Ka*-priest." For a moment, Ramose stared into space and then added slowly, "I pray that Seka's duties to Osiris will be few. By the way, he knows the language of the Noba. And," Ramose paused, "I decided that you go along as well. The , too, will ride with you as your guide. It is treacherous terrain."

"Of what use could I be, Ramose? I only know a few words of Wawat," Tasar interjected.

"Tuthmose is familiar with the dialects of the Kush. Between you three, you should manage quite well."

"Manage what, Ramose?"

Ramose's focus returned to the King's planned departure. "My Bowmen and Chief Senmut will provide protection," he said. "Also, they will carry the treated spear tips safely to Barum's camp. You and Senmut will be shown how to fit them onto the shafts. One caution: after you get there, do not handle

281

them yourselves. Instead, have a group of serfs do the fitting. And, Tasar, do not be slowed down in your other duties if one of them falls dead. It only means that he was a careless lad."

Tasar vividly recalled the marauder. At the time, even he believed that it was the High Priest's special touch which had dispatched the giant so effortlessly. He smiled. Ramose was human after all. Just more wily than all of his priests combined.

Ramose raised his finger to Tasar's face. "The purpose for you accompanying the group is different. Rahetep told me that you are well advanced in extracting a man's private thoughts."

Tasar looked up. What task did the High Priest have in store for him? Was it really true that Ramose could read a man's thoughts without availing himself of a trance? Perhaps he used the strange crystal he wore around his neck. He had better pay attention.

"After the first battle, you are to send all captured enemy officers into a deep trance during which you, Tuthmose, and Seka will extract their battle plans."

"Now I understand why you wanted to know about those languages," Tasar smiled. "And, I presume, after we learn of their plans, you wish me to tell the King."

Bemusement flashed across Ramose's lean face. "Informing General Barum or his aide will suffice." He took note of his disciple's dampened enthusiasm. "After you return to Nekhen, I will ask you to assist me in some surgical experiments. The procedures and their results are fascinating," he promised.

"How am I to get back?"

"On the supply barges, leaving from the First Falls. They will drop provisions there for our armies, and then carry our victorious King back to Nekhen."

"What if..." Tasar started.

Ramose cut him short. "We will be victorious! You are to bring the highest-ranking captives back with you." He looked sharply into Tasar's eyes as if to pierce the young priest's soul. Then his look softened and he added with something akin to concern, "Here is something to protect you on your journey. Use it in questioning the captives."

With deliberate care, Ramose opened a small box. Two amulets rested on fine linen. He selected one and solemnly placed the symbol of the sacred eye around Tasar's neck. "May this *Wedjat* eye protect you and those around you. I am choosing the left, the *Sacred Eye of Horus*. In your circumstance, it will give you better protection than the right *Eye of Ra*. Guard it with your life, my son. It may one day return the favor."

Tasar closed his eyes and felt the coolness of the finely wrought chain against his skin. He trembled with ill-contained excitement, so jubilant was he with his renewed good fortune. To be intimately close to Aha during a three to four-day trip! What opportunity to make a favorable impression on the King! The High Priest must have great confidence in his capabilities. Ramose was testing him for something great within the priesthood. Who was eventually to take The High Priest's place? Surely not Wazenz, Ineb-hedj's plump Chief Priest. No, the portly man would never do. Rahetep and Tuthmose were too old. Youthful smugness cursed through the young surgeon-priest.

Nekhen's elated surgeon-priest could hardly wait for his next adventure to begin. Two moons ago, he would not have dared to dream such lofty goals. Whole new possibilities opened up before him, including a chance at immortality. If Hor-Aha accepted him as his daughter's consort.

Once again, Tasar's ambitious daydreams caused him to forget his promise to retrieve the King's blue robe.

* * *

Chapter Thirty

That noon, Nekhen's Temple of Horus was closed for general worship. Not many of the townspeople minded; they much rather bedded down in the coolness of their villas to wile away the strength-sapping day's heat. Still, they found enough energy to pass on rumors that carried from the noble houses to the market place, from the old palace across the river to Nekheb, their less exulted sister-city.

'The High Priest journeyed here especially to seek answers before the High Altar of Horus. Awake, sleepy people. Today, he will consult the *Oracle of Isis*. Today, the mother of Horus will shape your destinies.'

It was not quite so, of course. Ramose prepared himself to query the *Oracle* only about the fates of the royal family. Nevertheless, anything concerning the royal house spilled over to the populace, its fate inextricable tied to that of the King.

A great hush descended over the city. Only the animals continued their endless baying, and waterfowl honked plaintively from floating reeds, with thousands of frogs joining in the cacophony. Hapi greedily lapped the ground higher each hour. The river, too, had an appointment with destiny. Its waters were to crest as Sothis, the Dog Star, climbed into the skies. Not during the darkness of the night but boldly during the brightness of day, to signal the beginning of the New Year, with five nameless days left over to be squandered by the careless.

In Nekhen, however, those spare calendar days were consecrated to the *Festival of Opet*. No one worked during the superfluous time which was followed by the river's inundation. As grazing lands lay awash, the fellah's woman fed his cattle by hand from his stores of fodder vetch while he himself was

284

pulled from his undemanding land and conscripted into labor for the King, either in the copper mines, the stone quarries, or to help build new palaces. He was allowed to return to toil his land only once the waters receded and the fertile black silt lay exposed.

*

Despite his admonishment at Ineb-hedj to the travelers to pack as little as possible, Ramose of course did not leave without his purple robe. He also brought his long staff gleaming in its precious box. These independent city nobles would likely not cower without his sacred implements.

Invoking the *Oracle* in search for a deeper truth called for different regalia. He had to discern subtle visions and expose them to the frailty of his own interpretation, a responsibility that weighed heavily upon him. Ramose implored Ptah and Horus to endow him with wisdom, with understanding and, above all, with humility.

*

Ready to discern the truth from the *Oracle*, Ramose implored:

"Isis, I heed your warning that we
not speak of woe too loudly
—for it could strike;
that we not to speak of victory too assuredly
—for it could prove elusive;
and that we not whisper of health and happiness too softly
—for my prayers might remain unheard."

As he intoned his entreaties to the *Oracle*, he had to strike the exact measure of certainty, assurance and supplication.

The bristling leopard skin clung to him like the live animal clings to its prey; muzzle gaping, yellowed incisors cutting into the back of the man's neck, his blood staining the killer's teeth, freeing the animal's cunning spirit to race through the Netherworld.

Ramose had transformed himself into a mystic *Sem*-priest so he might reach back to the forgotten origins of his ancient *Ba*.

From his neck chain dangled the crystal nestled atop the square hollow of the hammered plaque. Ramose clutched the translucent stone in his right fist, its edges cutting the soft flesh of his palm.

He opened his bloodied hand. The faceted plains caught a ray of light from above. Ramose brought a small vial held in his left to his lips. Even before the bitter drops reached his tongue, he willed his trance to take effect. His body swayed. Across his back, the leopard's tail swished back and forth as if the big cat were alive again, crouching, ready to pounce. He was pitted alone against the forces of the *Oracle*.

Not another soul was present in the cavernous temple to steady Ramose or to break his fall; he might not awaken from his trance. Rivulets formed on his thinker's forehead, his glazed eyes oblivious of the sting from his body's salt. A cry rose from deep within his soul. A bright green flash shot from the depths of the crystal toward the vaulted ceiling. If Ramose could see with a falcon's eye, he would have discerned the tiny hole seared into the uppermost beam of the nave. The crystal tumbled from his grasp. Ramose slid onto the slabs of cold stone, his mind no longer of this world.

*

Swathed in billowing transparency, white brilliance surrounds the Great Enchantress. Her hair streams behind her like a queen's standard. Her hands stretch toward him. No matter how he tries, he cannot touch her.

"Isis," he whispers. "What have you in store for your humble servant?"

She commands her gentle winds to lift him high into the skies from where he sees a field, strewn with slain hyenas, their bloated carcasses circled by stately birds. But they are not Nekhbet's vultures of the dead.

"Thank you Isis, you sent your Falcons!" Relief ebbs through him. Peace for the Two Lands and a long life for Aha.

The image shatters. Four ornate offering tables bar his way. On each slab, a Sati lies stretched out, face draped in heavy veils, feet protruding, clad in fine leather sandals. When he tries to snatch the shrouds away, Isis turns the fluttering cloth into stone. Unable to lift a single corner, he knows their names: Deceit. Tragedy. Murder. Condemnation.

Ramose cries out in pain.

Merciful winds carry him away to where the Hapi escapes into the glittering expanse of the Great Green, freed at last from the confines of its widespread Delta. Isis reappears next to him, her voice a melodious chant:

"Rama. You are not only to protect the innocent. You are also to rein

in the driven. Ma'at extracts harsh decisions. Understand those who have sinned. Above all, judge them from the depths of your soul.

Waves of helplessness crest over him.

"You are forced to endure a terrible truth. Do not confide in others. Or Osiris will claim the one you love the most. A lost Ba will depend on you to atone in another life."

Tears stain his ascetic features. Beyond her dire predictions, Isis had shown him hope.

*

Ramose's mind drifted back to the coldness of the temple floor. With great effort, he willed his thoughts to clear.

She had called him Rama!

Was he then not to judge as the uncompromising servant of Ptah but rather as a compassionate mortal? The spent man raised himself off the hard floor and groped his way toward the massive portal. Raising his fist against the heavy wood, he pounded on it once, twice, a third time. Before the weak sound could lose itself, the door swung open. Caring hands reached out for him.

"I am here to guide you back to life," Rahetep comforted. He, too, wore the skin of a leopard.

"Take me to the *House of Life.*" Ramose whispered, still trembling from his ordeal.

Rahetep guided him to the curved path where the old Overseer waited for them. As quickly as his bent legs allowed, the ancient servant led the way into a long walled yard adjacent to the *House of Life.*

A small pyre had been lit. Ten young acolytes stood motionless against a wall. Each held one of the fifty *Ancient Mats*, with the remainder of the brittle weavings piled high before the last. They stared at the two *Sem*-priests, never before having seen more magnificent or frightening apparitions.

Ramose stepped in front of the flames. Restored into the present, he lifted his arms and intoned melodious supplications to the patron god of fire.

Rahetep joined in with a strong bass-baritone. After several verses, Ramose reached toward the first acolyte who handed him his mat as the second youth handed over his to the first. As each mat journeyed closer to the pyre, the last acolyte replenished the long row from the pile at his feet.

The old Overseer raked the flames. One after the other, an

Ancient Mat was consumed. The acolytes remembered how they painstakingly stamped the shaded markings onto the fifty Tablets always praying that their eyes were clear and their hands steady. Now, their task was finished. They felt saddened. As Ramose threw the last of the mats into the fire the flames exploded hotly consuming the brittle grasses.

"I see not only sadness in your faces. But a tinge of fear," Ramose intoned as ten pairs of young eyes stared at him. With a gentle wave of his arms, he smiled, and the sadness lifted from their hearts, replaced by the eternal hope of youth.

"Just like you," Ramose said, "I once sat bent over those *Ancient Mats*. And, just like you, I shaded one confusing square after another, filled roll after roll of stiff papyri. Rahetep, not much older than his pupils then, was ever watchful that we did not err." Ramose saw the smiles creep up behind their eyes. It bolstered their morale that even the great Ramose began his steep ascent as an acolyte.

"Yours was the more difficult task; you stamped the squares onto the fifty Tablets. I inspected the gleaming result. Your work is flawless."

A collective sigh of relief escaped into the acrid air.

"However, those Tablets are far from finished. You are to continue your work on them."

They looked up in attentive curiosity. The first acolyte closest to the High Priest ventured quietly, "What more can we do, High Priest of Ptah?"

"I completed the translation."

The simple statement wrought wheezing astonishment from pouted lips. The lively youths abandoned their orderly row and crowded around the two *Sem*-priests, curiosity overcoming trepidation. Rahetep held up his hands in mock fear to be crushed. The Old Overseer strained from behind his smoking pyre. His hearing was no longer good.

Ramose spoke again, "I see that your enthusiasm has not gone up in smoke with the *Ancient Mats*. However, if you wish to continue working with the translation you know that you have to remain in the *House of Life* forever. I repeat: Forever. I want you to understand this before you volunteer. From then on, you will not be permitted to follow any other path open to others of the priesthood."

Hushed silence cried out for him to continue.

"You will never serve as *Ka*-priests. Nor become surgeons or royal tutors, nor teach the sciences as temple lectors. You will never serve as head or chief priest of a temple."

"Will the best of us ever become a *Sem*-priest?" A bright-eyed acolyte ventured forth.

Ramose shook his head. Deep silence ensued. "On the other hand," Ramose broke into their dashed dreams, "those of you who devote their lives to the Tablets, shall be known as the *Guardians of the Tablets*. Serving in solitude will turn you into revered sages."

The supple faces lit up with new ambitions.

"Remember: You will never share your limited understanding of the momentous truth revealed by these ancient writings with anyone. I say limited, because each will only be given five Tablets onto which to stamp the pertinent translation. You will never know the contents of the other forty-five."

Disappointment displaced new-found excitement. Yes, Ramose thought, I would have been just as dismayed.

"Question yourselves with utmost honesty: Is this what you want? For the rest of your earthly lives."

They knew it would not take them a lifetime to finish a mere five Tablets. And then what? The thought of uselessness weighed heavily upon the acolytes.

Rahetep sensed their torment, and added gravely, "Ramose and I return tomorrow to learn of your decision. Should any one of you feel that he cannot devote his life to the ancient legacy he will be permitted to serve the priesthood elsewhere. After tomorrow, your choice is irrevocable."

They fled the burning smoke, except for the bent *Overseer of the Treasure*. The old man could hardly contain his joy that his mission in the *House of Life* had not come to an end yet. To the dedicated servant more than to anyone else, Ramose's words heralded a miraculous reprieve. His precious Tablets were to remain at the *House of Life*. At least for a while, depending on the acolytes. He imagined that they would not be in a hurry to absolve themselves of their new task.

*

The Royal Tax Collector went into a great frenzy. Why was he handed al-Saqqara's message only now! The temple boats landed days ago! This now gave him ten days at best to prepare

289

the palace for the King's announced arrival. There were floormats to be rewoven, stores to be replenished, and lazy slaves bullied into unaccustomed haste. Moreover, the tallies had to be balanced. Without a doubt, the sly Vizier would send a scribe or two to check his ledgers. Tesh always meticulously collected the royal rents and taxes. Unfortunately, he was less diligent to record accurate numbers onto the appropriate scrolls. A pardonable oversight, he felt, with so many other tasks taking up his valuable time. Pardonable to him; surely not to al-Saqqara's bureaucrats. That was how his troubles had begun.

"Hang all scribes!" he swore under his breath. Above all, he had to get in touch with his hireling. If the Royal Heiress was to be 'guided by his own hand,' as al-Saqqara so succinctly wrote, he was to remain above suspicion. Luckily, a suitable assassin had long ago been wooed for just such an occasion. The greedy man should be eager to be of assistance. Naturally, Tesh would ensure that the despicable man was prevented from uttering a word, should he be apprehended.

Fuming, Tesh reviewed the last few days. No wonder, Rahetep hovered about the royal suites and, a day ago, insisted to perform incantations to chasten old souls from the long-empty chambers. Despite Tesh's objections, temple servants had carried the Chief Priest about in a rickety old sedan. Then, of all things, the meddling priest rushed off on foot, leaving the old chair behind. Tesh had a good mind to have it thrown out but became involved in other, more important, tasks.

The chair was stored in the outer room of the King's appointed suite where it stood next to an opening to a servant's chamber. Forgotten under an old cushion, a quilted robe waited to have the creases shaken out of its blue folds.

*

"Gone off? Gone off to where?" Nefret stared at her trembling slaves. Safaga and Dokki confronted her young fury bravely. Neither Tasar, nor the Archer Pase, nor Chief Senmut, could be found. Each looked as if she had lost her best friend.

"We don't know. They disappeared," Dokki sobbed. "I could not find a single Bowman to tell me anything." Since Senmut had lain with the dark girl, she blossomed into an almost handsome woman. Even Nefret, mostly preoccupied with her own feelings, noticed that Dokki held herself more proudly, grasped orders more quickly, and did not drop as many things, nor stumble quite as often.

"What is worse, I could not locate the old sedan in the King's temple chamber. Tasar remembered that he hid the robe under its cushion," Safaga fretted, recalling the young priest's promise. Despite her worries, she blushed at the mention of his name. "We cannot possibly sew another in time for *Opet*. Besides, we would not find any unusual cloth in the market of this provincial city."

"We have to tell Amma," Dokki wailed annoying Nefret who decreed, "We will just have to say that you forgot to pack the thing, won't we, Dokki."

"What do you mean, I forgot to pack it. I never saw it after we finished sewing it," Dokki defended herself.

"You can't blame Dokki." Safaga stepped between the two. She had crept for hours on end through the maze of passages and pathways that connected the vast temple. Nowhere did she spy Badar's old chair. Nor did she encounter Tasar as she hoped she might.

Dokki, meanwhile, had prowled the quarters of the palace guards to ask after Senmut's whereabouts. The delighted soldiers taunted and jostled her, and then sent her on her way for they could not tell her anything. It seemed that Tasar, Pase, and Senmut together with his Ineb-hedj Temple Bowmen had vanished overnight. She would try again tomorrow.

"Has anyone seen Father lately?" Nefret asked.

As if on cue, her women ventured, "They have gone off to war."

For the first time, Nefret envisioned the consequences of losing a battle. She suddenly thought she knew why she had been brought along. Not to be cleansed and initiated and shorn of her hair! Not to have the sons of Nekhen paraded before her! No! To claim her royal inheritance, so that no other could usurp the Two Crowns, should the King - her Father - be slain in battle! 'And when I am queen...' she had boasted to Dubar. How ill-prepared she was to carry the Two Crowns. Not yet. Not alone. Of course, there were a Regent and a Co-Regent to carry the worst of her weighty burden. Nefret's face turned ashen. A cry rose from her throat, "Oh no! Not them! Oh please, not them!"

"Not who, Nefret? We knew that they would have to leave

at some point." Safaga shook her mistress. She could not understand the sudden terror over what they knew was inevitable.

Nefret's eyes widened. Fury and terror rose within her.

"They will have me murdered! Where is my dagger?" Nefret pushed Safaga aside and rifled through their one trunk until she found the leather sheath. Her hands shook. She fastened the long thongs around her slender waist. But when she pulled her mother's dagger from its holder, her fingers no longer trembled. Her knuckles stood out white under her intense grip as she swung the ornate dagger high against imagined assailants.

Dokki stared at the choleric girl. Even quick-witted Safaga was unable to move for one awful instant, fearing that Nefret might turn the dagger's double-edge against herself.

"I shall kill anyone who dares to touch me!"

An indefinable mask of something more convulsive than hatred spread over Nefret's face. Her companions sensed the intensity of her threat. This frenzied being was not their beloved Princess, nor was she the childish, willful friend they adored. This was an avenging goddess. It dawned on Safaga that this outburst had nothing to do with Tasar or his disappearance. Nefret's terror was unfathomable, too deeply rooted within her tortured soul. As if an old *Ka* was strangling a young heart.

"Get Ramose. Run!" Safaga hissed.

*

Ramose could not extract much from Dokki's incoherent babble after she burst upon him. Her stricken face caused him to hurry after her without question. When he reached the girl's chamber, Nefret lay collapsed on one of the narrow daybeds, sobbing uncontrollably. Safaga shed tears of relief. She had been unable to calm Nefret who now sobbed in the High Priest's arms. The two slaves stood nearby, helpless, their heads bowed.

"Nefret. Child. Calm yourself. Nothing is going to happen to you. Not here. This is why I brought you. I admit that your cleansing rites were a convenient excuse for you to come to Nekhen. I believed, and still do, that you are much safer here, with me. It would not have been safe for you in Ineb-hedj." Ramose stroked the glistening dark hair.

"What about Hent! And our ugly Vizier! My supposed co-regents - ha!" Nefret's temper flared momentarily.

"Do not upset yourself, my child," Ramose soothed. "In ten days, the Royal Convoy arrives and you will be reunited with Amma and Zeina. Beir too." Ramose took a quick breath. "And Dubar, of course. You will have plenty of company, and you will be able to walk about openly in the royal palace suites."

"I am not looking forward to having Dubar strut about all day long, I assure you," Nefret balked. Then, putting on a calculated look of desperation, she pleaded, "Ramose, could I not stay here at the temple, with Amma and my slaves? Let Dubar have the musty old palace with the rest of the court. I promise I will not be in your way. Oh please, let us stay here, Ramose. Please."

Ramose had observed the two slaves rush about like butterflies. He also noticed his little Nefret blossoming into young awareness. For a brief moment, he envied but also pitied her. From now on, he would choose her lectors to be elderly.

"All right, my pretty. Until Amma and Zeina arrive. Then we have to switch you back."

"Ramose?" Nefret lifted her face shyly up to him.

"Yes, Nefret?"

"What did the *Oracle* predict for me?"

While the question from this curious child did not surprise Ramose, it caught him unprepared. The King had asked him the same thing but accepted Ramose's evasive answer with stoic fatalism and had drowned any unease in wine. This intelligent young woman would not be so easily deterred and a good part of the prophecies were about Nefret's future. Of course, he could not tell her so, particularly as he still had not arrived at a less ominous interpretation of the *Great Enchantress's* warning.

"I can tell you this much, Nefret." Was it wise? "The *Oracle* said that I must always protect you. Always! So you see, as long as I am here, you are safe. As long as you let me guide you."

Nefret sighed and snuggled closer to her beloved guardian, appreciating his warmth, his gentle wisdom, even his discipline.

'If only Father could have been like this,' she thought. 'After our talk in the *Kariy*, he is bound to want to know me better. I shall try to be nicer to Dubar and Hent.' Nefret sighed, content in her new resolve. Things would be different once they returned to Ineb-hedj where she would proudly sit beside her Father, and share his throne, a worthy heiress of his kingdom. 'What to do about Tasar though.'

"I shall find a way," she breathed onto Ramose's chest.

"A way for what?" Ramose asked, puzzled.

"A way for me to assure everyone's happiness," Nefret replied quickly and, lifting her head, she smiled up at him.

Ramose smiled back, loathe seeing this precocious child slip into the harsh world of adulthood.

* * *

Chapter Thirty-One

The darkening cloak of the night hid the departure of the small trek as it slipped undetected from behind the *Sacred Lake* through the back-gate of the temple. Pase and half of the Ineb-hedj Temple Bowmen led the way into the western desert. The priests Tuthmose, Seka and Tasar rode close to the disguised King with Senmut and the remainder of his Bowmen bringing up the rear. There were no standard bearers, no slaves to carry a royal sedan, and no fanfares heralding their progress as they sat straddled across Rahetep's best jackasses. The laden pack donkeys, following behind, left deep imprints in the sand. The poisonous spear tips for Colonel Mekh's *Ostrich Riders* lay tightly wrapped, separated from the provisions. Only one acolyte had lost his life during their preparation. As the rising sun overtook them slowly, Senmut looked back. Their deep tracks had already been swept clean. For once he was thankful for the incessant wind.

Tasar adjusted himself on his chafing saddle mat and fingered his *Wedjat* eye. A sudden impulse struck the irrepressible young priest. He glanced at Aha. The King appeared weary. Ahead lay a good three days' ride before they could hope to reach Barum's camp. Opulent court life had ill prepared his King for the rigors of a campaign. Tasar felt compassion for Hor-Aha having been reduced to this profusely sweating mortal.

"My King, if I may speak," Tasar bowed. Aha looked up with a wry smile on his cracked lips and scolded, "What is the use of my miserable disguise, if you keep shouting 'My King' for anyone to hear!"

Tuthmose and Seka grinned at the rebuke. They were far from the city.

"Forgive me,—ah—My Lord," Tasar corrected himself but dared to venture on, "If you would allow me, I have the means to insulate you from the strains of this arduous journey."

"Really!" Aha was less than convinced.

"Yes. Really. I can relieve your spirit from the earthly discomforts of your body."

"Spare me the suspense, priest, and speak your mind. And do not expect me to drink any of your bitter potions," Aha grumbled through gritty teeth. His spirit had been tampered with aplenty, and he was in no mood for another splitting headache. Indeed, he already had one. And a confounded chafe tormented him far below his pounding head.

Tasar shook his head, "No, you don't need to swallow anything—My Lord."

"Then enlighten me," Aha said without enthusiasm.

"We have new methods to separate the mind from the body. They have been tried on volunteers and were found effective." Tasar let go of his reins and took the amulet from his neck, swinging it back and forth, beginning a hypnotic sing-song.

"Your spirit is freed. It is carried onto a new plain. You feel no physical pain, no mental sorrow, nor the searing heat. Your spirit will be suspended."

Tuthmose, watching from behind, grew alarmed. He drew his jackass closer to Tasar and hissed, "Tasar! Not without his permission!" and slapped his donkey's flank so hard that the braying of the animal brought Aha out of his light trance.

"What were you saying? I remember. You have new tried methods. Can you swear that your 'volunteers' were unharmed by their experience?" Aha's voice reflected doubt; he might have trusted Ramose. But this young rogue?

"Yes, My Lord," Tasar insisted. "Our volunteers came from among the most honest of men. Their bodies were exposed to intense torture while they lived in that other realm. They reawakened in excellent condition, with no apparent discomfort or after-effects."

"And?" The King leaned closer.

"And they all vowed by the gods that they felt nothing during the suspension of their mind," Tasar's words pearled tantalizingly before Aha.

"Well, almost all." Tasar reddened at his wretched tongue.

Sure enough, the had King caught the inference.

"Dare I ask what happened to the one that got away?" Aha's voice rose in pitch. He glowered at the embarrassed youth. Ambitious young fool.

Tasar, not hearing the sarcastic tone, remained undeterred. "Oh, he was fine. Except that his mind was as blank as a newly pounded strip of papyrus," he admitted. "Of course, we later learned that the man's heart was treacherous."

"Is that what you propose for your King?" Aha roared. His backside was aflame and the insidious sand-fleas bit with ferocity. He kneed his jackass. The startled animal bucked and almost threw him off.

"First, you threaten to empty my mind! Then you infer that you will blame your blunders on my treacherous heart!" Aha's face exploded into an over-ripe pomegranate. "I should have your heart torn from your chest, charlatan, for foisting your preposterous attempts upon me!" Aha's rage only increased his insufferable torment. Insulted by this impertinent dolt, he wondered nevertheless if there was some merit to this young fool's proposition.

The others had become aware of the deteriorating exchange between the King and Tasar. While the priests pressed closer to their stunned colleague, Pase and his squad accelerated to place greater distance between themselves and their angry ruler, just as Senmut and the rear guard cautiously hung back. They rightly feared the King's wrath, but were even more concerned that the priests invoke calamity upon their heads to save their own hides.

"My Lord," Tuthmose tried to calm Aha's frayed temper. "Remember when a marauder poked Nefret during the attack? And she felt nothing."

Aha stopped his sulking and stared at the older priest. "Well, what of it? She was drugged by Ramose. Just as I was."

"Not exactly, My Lord." If he wished to turn the situation around, Tuthmose had better choose his words with exacting care. "You see, while Ramose entranced you with his special potion, Tasar dealt with your daughter by suggestion only, just as Seka did with the dark slave. And I placed the pretty servant into a trance the same way. It worked beautifully."

"He 'dealt' with my Royal Heiress?" Aha's eyes turned into mean slits. Tuthmose was on dangerous turf. "Then tell me,

Tuthmose, why was this painless method not used on me?" Aha pointed out. "Oh no, not on me," he sneered. "Instead, your King was forced to swallow a disgusting potion so he could suffer afterward! And I'll have you know, Ramose did this to me twice! Is that how your King's safety is assured!" Aha expelled great puffs of super-heated air.

He is like *Hapi*, the *Sacred Bull*, Tuthmose thought. Maddened, he paws the dirt, threatening but unsure of his attack. Aloud, the older priest continued in his soothing voice, "My Lord, your forceful spirit has more resistance than a girl's. There was not enough time to send you into a deep enough trance, as we still had to transport ourselves into deep unconsciousness."

"Charlatans!" Aha riled against the wind.

"Hor-Aha, ah, My Lord, we have been thoroughly trained..." Tuthmose renewed his soothing.

Tasar wished he never broached the subject. All he had wanted was for his King to be more comfortable. And, perhaps, to gain Aha's gratitude in the process. Now, the King's goodwill toward him had dried up like a drop of blood on a sun-baked offering table. Dashed were his hopes that he could please the King into accepting him as Nefret's consort. Through his own thoughtlessness, his lofty aspirations had been dealt a crushing blow.

"... and it worked perfectly. Because of this method, we escaped with our lives, unharmed," the older priest's voice broke through Tasar's self-effacing thoughts.

"Can you do it for a little while at a time? So that I can make certain it works as you claim," Aha asked with studied lassitude. It was much too hot to stay enraged.

"Yes, we can, My Lord," Tuthmose said. "It saps the energy somewhat. So I advise it for only once a day."

Slowly, Tasar became aware of the exchange between the older priest and Aha. The King seemed almost willing to submit to the experiment and Tasar wondered what was said while he lost himself in his disheartening reproach. His respect for the Fayum priest increased immeasurably.

"Well, what are you waiting for, my anxious youth?" Aha jutted his chin at Tasar. "Free me from this misery! Let me ride upon the clouds instead of this flea-bitten torture!" Aha hid his lingering apprehension behind a nervous laugh. If his body was to die from exhaustion, his spirit might as well have entered the pleasant realm of unreality prior to that. He hawked sand and laughed at his own recklessness. Far removed from his fawning courtiers, he was free to gamble with his life. And perhaps his death. After stealing a glance at Seka he tuned into Tasar's sing-song. The *Eye of Horus* swung back and forth in front of his red face, transfixing him. Not altogether unpleasant, Aha thought as he drifted high above himself—painlessly, weightlessly, as free as a falcon. Like Horus. He was Horus.

*

For three days, they rode, stoically bracing against the wind-driven sand, enduring the rays of an unblemished sun. And for three days, Tasar dispatched the King to soar through a wondrous painless realm. As promised, Aha's spirit remained unaffected by the arduous trek. His earthly backside, though, had not.

"You better bring him around," Seka whispered. "Pase says we are closing in on Barum's camp."

Awakened, Aha saw high palms dotting the horizon. He blinked three times. "A mirage?"

"No, My Lord. That is the Great Oasis," Tasar answered, just as Pase called out, "We have arrived. The Fourth Army of Amun lies ahead of you, Hor-Aha."

Being this close to his own regiment, Pase felt free to address his Supreme Commander with the respect due him. Surely, they could cast the tiresome charade aside by now. The loyal messenger longed to be a proud once again. He fingered his lower abdomen. The angry burn had healed though he would always bear the mark of his General's seal. He fidgeted with his woven saddlebag and produced the top portion of the King's battle standard, jamming it onto his long lance. Swinging it high above his head he noticed the King's frown.

"The Vizier handed it to me before we left Ineb-hedj," he called back. "The noble al-Saqqara said I must present it to my General. Of course, the Vizier was not aware that you, Great Aha, would join us before I reached my camp." Pase continued eagerly, "I thought we should approach the camp in style."

Their safe arrival made everyone giddy with anticipation and they saluted the standard and smiled at Aha, while Tasar quietly thanked Horus that fate had turned benevolent once more.

Pase and Senmut reached the first outpost. Sand-grizzled warriors appeared from behind every hillock, poured from every small depression. When they recognized the King's battle standard, they fell in behind the dusty group and cheered. Their Supreme Commander had arrived. The battle could be fought.

*

"Get up! Unhobble the goats. We are leaving." The tall tribesman started to pull down their tent. When the slender girl with the bronzed skin did not stir, he prodded her with a callused foot.

"You are a brute, Yadate," she chided, not minding his rough treatment. "Why don't you come and lie with me."

"If you don't get up, I shall bury you in the sand together with the tent," he threatened.

Realizing he was serious she nimbly leapt to her feet and started bundling their few belongings. "Where are we going in such a hurry? Did you inform my general about us leaving?" she asked, adding wistfully, "He will miss me."

"He will be too preoccupied," Yadate mimicked her high voice and grabbed her. "I saw something of great importance," he whispered as if he feared a scurrying scorpion to betray his words. "War is about to erupt. You and I, my lovely, are going to be richly rewarded as the Ruler of the Kush is bound to be generous when I tell him of my latest observations." He chortled. "Who says one cannot wrest a living from the desert." His own cleverness amused him and he brought his lips closer to her ear. A wisp of her raven hair caressed his wind-burned face and set his light eyes ablaze.

He reached roughly for her. There would be time, after all.

*

Pase was glad to be back with his battalion. Much had happened in two short moons. He survived the barren desert. He met the kingdom's most powerful men, even the King! He had reassured himself that he was more than a valiant warrior. He was still a man who could make his woman squeal. So what if the rowdy Palace Archers whispered sly remarks about the Steward? Safaga had tended to him, Pase, when he needed her, and pleasured him when he longed for her. Still, his true place was here among his fellow archers, in the service of his King. His mission, however, was not yet completed. He dismounted and took a moment to jostle with his friends.

Eager to report to his watch captain, Pase shook the sand out of his ears and dusted himself off.

*

"Captain Nebah, the Archer Pase reports back for duty," the orderly called out. Nebah stepped outside his tent.

"So, Archer, you have returned alive. And in such exulted company. What good fortune for you," Nebah grinned.

Pase froze into an exemplary salute. "Captain, I carry a message from the Royal Quartermaster, the Vizier Ebu al-Saqqara." Pase extended the leather holder to Nebah who was glad that he knew how to read. Around them, a widening circle of soldiers spread into a respectable crowd. In their sandy isolation, they felt entitled to hear news from the capital. Nebah pulled the scroll from its holder. While he ceremoniously unrolled it, turning it this way and that, his eyes scanned the text ahead. The fateful message was so cleverly coded that its wording was innocuous. He could read it aloud without fear.

"To the Watch Captain Nebah. That means me, brave warriors," Nebah jested. Those closest to him laughed dutifully.

"Fourth Army, Kharga Oasis," Nebah read on.

"That means us." The crowd began to enjoy this. Nebah held his hand up bidding silence.

"The courier Pase ..." Nebah paused. No one picked up the refrain; all eyes hung on his lips and he shrugged, "... carried out an important task with exemplary speed. He has rendered great service to our common goal. I wish that I could be the one to reward his valor. As he is under your command, I place my hand upon my heart and recommend him urgently for a promotion. Most assuredly, he will renew our trust in him during the forthcoming campaign. As Horus is with the Fourth, Montu will assure victory for our common cause." Nebah looked around. "It carries the mark of Ebu al-Saqqara, Vizier and Royal Quartermaster, serving Aha, Horus-King of the Two Lands."

After Nebah promoted Pase to Chief Archer, the boisterous crowd lifted the young warrior high on their shoulders and carried him away. Nebah stepped inside his tent and studied the coded message again. Transfixed, he mumbled to himself:

"...*with exemplary speed*... That means to act as soon as

301

possible. *...under your command...* I am to be the executioner. *...hand upon my heart...*

This meant he was to ram his sword through someone's heart. Whose, Barum's? One of the other generals'? *"...during the forthcoming campaign..."* 'The battle,' he thought. *"Horus is with the Fourth..."* "By my *Ka's* damnation!" Nebah blanched. "He means the King!"

All blood drained from the Watch Captain's face. Why did he ever join the *Usurpers of the Two Crowns?*

Nebah was a handsome man, compactly built, with strong straight limbs. Not violent, though he was given to heavy wagering. But the gift of winning eluded him and his mounting debts became a curse. When the winners pressured him too forcefully he asked for a brief furlough to seek relief from his tormentors. At Nekhen's oldest House of Pleasures, he was introduced to Tesh, the Royal Tax Collector. To his astonishment, the nobleman offered to take care of his debts. During the ensuing nights of revelry, Tesh enlisted Nebah to join a clandestine group. For a little favor now and then, the high official assuaged the soldier's qualms. If he betrayed one word of it, Tesh assured him that *Seth* would snatch his soul. At the time, the ominous words had been a whisper. Now, they pounded loudly in Nebah's ears. Disgust seared his throat. I have turned traitor. No, worse! I have become the harbinger of death. Nebah covered his face with both hands. Great sobs wrenched forth from within his tortured soul. "So be it," he whispered.

*

The combined armies of the Kush and the Wawat were positioned a day's march within the borders of the Two Lands, south-west of the First Falls. The region had just received some rain and the land's reddish brown mat sprouted into a green carpet.

Trampling the tender green belt, a vast enemy force made its base camp there, allowing their donkeys and goats to graze the grounds into bare dust again. They were waiting for the tall, dark masses of the *Noba* under the leadership of their legendary King Ogoni. The Ruler of the Kush looked forward to meeting the dark giant from the exotic regions to the south so that their combined forces could triumph against the *King of the Two Lands.*

The circular tent of the Kush Ruler was quite extraordinary. The large opening flap was fastened to two immense elephant tusks anchored in the ground. The sides of the tent were sewn together from wildebeest hides with the hairy side turned outward to provide insulation against the heat. Inside, soft leopard pelts covered the dirt. Basins and ornate cups of yellow nub glittered.

The Ruler of Kush towered over the writhing man swathed in dusty robes. He flung his cup aside and his voice rose to a thundering crescendo, "You miserable desert jackal! One of your own vipers just brought me different news. As we speak, the enemy king leads his troops from the Great Oasis toward us!" The raging man fought for breath before he could continue. "I rewarded you well to scour the desert and to report suspicious movements. How, then, did the *King of the Two Lands* come this far south without you having spotted him? Instead, you tell me that Aha's Royal Bark is still sailing toward Nekhen! And to top your impertinence, you have the audacity to ask for more reward!"

"Most honorable Ruler," Wadji stammered, "I swear to you, I identified the Royal Bark correctly with all its tenders and war galleys. Their laden troop barges crept along the Hapi like giant hippopotamuses wallowing in shallow water ..."

"The water is already rising, you imbecile," the Ruler hissed.

Wadji kicked himself for his ill-chosen metaphor. How could he convince the irate leader of his report's validity, and of his just reward, without revealing the unfortunate encounter with the plague-ridden pilgrims.

"Bring in the other two," the Ruler thundered to an aide.

A guard pushed a tall tribesman ahead of him while another tussled with an unruly woman.

"These two swore they saw a group of warriors not more than two days ago heading for the Great Oasis when their scout revealed the standard of the King of Kamt. My man here heard shouts of jubilation." The Ruler wagged his finger as if Wadji were a child. The Cobra glanced at the tribesman and shrank back from the man's blazing eyes. He recalled the blue glare of the magician who had willed the Stinger to his death. A bad omen.

"Cobra of the Desert," the Kush Ruler sneered. "Assure me that you saw no one alive stealing through the desert night."

Wadji's knees almost buckled. "No, Honorable Ruler," he wailed. "I saw no one alive, I swear. There is no need to worry. I saw their stinking corpses burn. And the desert surely killed those who did survive the plague." It slipped out of him before he knew it. At once, a lance prodded his loins with unkind persuasion, and Wadji hastened to retell his encounter with the plague-ridden camp, shuddering as he relived the terrifying scenes.

"So! Not only do you bring me bad information, you bring me the plague as well!" the Ruler of the Kush exploded.

Wadji swore the nomad's blue stare had caused his tongue to slip.

"We are mobilizing!" the Kush commanded to his aide.

It was the last thing Wadji heard. A long sword sliced through the air so swiftly that he never saw the glimmer of its blade. His severed head rolled to an uneasy stop at Yadate's feet.

* * *

Chapter Thirty-Two

The Fourth Army camp convulsed itself of its troops like a swollen termite queen expelling her myriad of eggs. Long before sun-up, every man was issued a wrist-guard for his throwing hand, a wide leather flap to protect his loins, and a tight-fitting leather helmet to deflect the crashing blows of a stone mace. Warriors with battle-axes and short spears mixed with those clutching javelins and hatchets. Some tested special slings and launched fist-size stones into the sky trusting not to maim too many of their own. Behind the melee of more than a thousand foot soldiers donkeys stood laden with dried rations and bladders bulging with fetid water from the Great Oasis. More beasts carried hay-like fodder vetch as animal forage was scarce until they reached the southern valleys. Supplies had been calculated to last five days. The battle should be won by then. If not, there would be no further need for provisions. While the Wawat were known as a peace-loving tribe, the Noba took no prisoners.

Aha marched at the very tip of his army, heralded by standard bearers, flanked by his highest-ranking officers. Whereas the regular army priests marched in the rear, the three priests sent by Ramose remained close to their King.

They, too, were issued protective helmets and leather flaps, and carried lances. Slung across their shoulders were woven bags that contained mysterious potions, healing salves and tourniquets, as well as their instruments for crude field surgery when called upon to perform amputations, extract imbedded lance-tips, or force broken collar bones back into place. Mostly, they would release the mortally wounded from their earthly agony.

Already, the Fourth pushed past the southern borders, an

endless human caterpillar worming its way deeper into enemy territory.

*

Night-darkened silhouettes hinted of high bluffs between Aha's army and the distant river as the convoy rolled to a tumultuous halt and struck camp for the night.

A scout rushed up to Keheb to report his last sighting. "Colonel, we spotted the advance camps of the Kush half a day's march to the south. They have many fires burning."

Informed by Keheb, Barum reflected why the Kush would light up the night sky like an offering altar. If they were this careless, an easy victory could be expected. On the other hand, the clever Noba could have cajoled the gullible Kush to serve as their human bulwark to exhaust Barum's forces. The General was certain that their first battle would be fought the following day. He called his officers together and went over the prepared battle plans once more.

"Hor-Aha stays at the command post. He must be protected at all times. Provide three squads. Two officers are to rotate throughout the day," he ordered. "However strongly their zeal might draw them into combat, those assigned must stay with Hor-Aha. Or lose their lives without going into battle. Understood!" It was not a question. "Tomorrow, we fight."

Barum dismissed the officers and spread his sleeping mat on the hard ground. He briefly thought of soft brown arms. Before he could conjure up further images of the tantalizing girl, he fell into a dreamless sleep.

*

Dawn grayed over the eastern plain. They had been on the march for hours when, suddenly, rumbling filled the air, not as urgent as water rushing over high cliffs. Neither was it as melodic. This distant murmur rang metallic.

Barum lifted his arms high. The ranks behind him repeated the warning to those further back. Before them, pierced by rocky hillocks, spread the timidly greening tentacles of the lower valleys. Unaccustomed humidity pearled on night-cooled bodies.

They squinted against the rising sun, barely discerning the undulating movements of the enemy's front lines. The masses of the Fourth rolled to a sluggish halt. At the rear, snakes of cooks and utensil bearers detached themselves with the supply

306

donkeys to seek a safer place where they could wait out the battle, start cooking fires, and dig sanitation trenches wide enough to serve as make-shift depositories for those slain in battle. Barum bade Hor-Aha to take cover. He signaled his officers. Trumpets sounded. Drums added their ominous roll.

Boom, boom, booom. Boom, boom, booom.

Ten thousand feet pounded in concert with the increasing beat. Faster, faster. Dust whirled. Standard bearers led waves of archers, spear throwers, lancers, and bowmen onto the plain, followed by battalions armed with maces, and battle axes. The last men brandished their straight swords. They would finish off what their fellow-warriors had left alive.

A signal flashed from Aha. A multi-throated chorus combined into a single battle cry.

"Victory to Hor-Aha!"

Boom, boom, booom, the drums incited. The warriors charged toward the enemy until their cries were picked up by Wawat sentinels scrambling back to their own encampment in surprised shock.

The Fourth Army of Amun sprung upon its multi-tribal enemy with stunning speed. Advancing bowmen met little resistance. Volley after volley, their missiles struck true. Screams of the wounded thickened the air. Shrieks of the terrified drowned out the moans of the dying. All during that hot day, Aha's troops pushed the valiant Kush and the weakening Wawat toward the First Falls. At dusk, the enemy's advance garrison lay underfoot, unmercifully trampled, skewered, sliced in half.

The battle ceased when night at last cloaked man's atrocities, its darkness a soldier's unintended peacemaker. The risk to engage friendly troops mistakenly would be too great. Bloody swords found shredded scabbards. Arrows slipped back into empty quivers. Exhausted men shook themselves amazed that they were still alive. Sweat and blood combined with red dust. Familiar faces had turned into ghoulish masks.

This was a time for the cooks; a time for the *Ka*-priests. A time when the thirsty were issued watered wine, and the hungry were given chunks of charred meat. It was a time for the army surgeons to keep the maimed from bleeding to death; a time when lancers swept the battlefield in search for a fallen enemy, only to massacre him if still alive, to throw his corpse into a nearby pit. Vultures and hyenas, dung beetles and lizards swarmed in droves. By morning, human bones would lie scattered to bleach under the unrelenting sun.

Captured enemy officers, unscathed enough to mend on their own, were forced to lie face down on the cooling ground before their weapons were snatched up. Then they were driven into holding pens where the sword-handlers tried to find the highest ranking among them. Barum's order 'The higher the rank, the higher the reward' had turned into fierce competition.

*

The amulet swung in front of his face with dizzying regularity. The prone Kush officer tried in vain to avert his gaze from the inlaid eye which stared coldly at him. An incessant chant caused his mind to float away.

Tasar carefully deepened the man's trance. "You are asleep. You stand before your commander to repeat tomorrow's battle plan. Repeat it now." He bent over the captive officer. With a flick of his wrist, he kept the amulet in perpetual motion while a translator mimicked the sing-song Kush dialect. The light-skinned Kush stared into space, his gaze remote, unresponsive to the translator's questions.

Colonel Keheb had insisted that he be present at the inquisition. Hovering about intently, he declared, "This is not working."

"I need Tuthmose," Tasar said, annoyed at the interference.

After Tuthmose took over, the Kush spoke at last. "The Black Noba will send reinforcement only tomorrow since our spies reported that the *King of Kamt* had not arrived in Nekhen yet. The *Cobra of the Desert* saw the royal convoy sailing upriver. We were told to have more time to prepare." Tuthmose translated and continued to prod the Kush.

"But the Puntan spy swore to a different story," the Kush said and fell silent.

Keheb shrugged his shoulders. Impatient, he ordered, "Tuthmose, ask him how large their forces are."

"The Noba number at least five thousand, with King Ogoni marching at the head. Some of them are said to come from as far away as the Sixth Falls. Our Kush lines are about two thousand strong. And the Wawat are so few that they might as well not be there." Such was the interpretation of the man's mumbling.

"Soon, none of them will be there," Keheb said with a sarcastic chuckle. He had heard enough and left the tent, grudgingly admitting renewed respect for the priesthood's powers.

"That is enough," Tuthmose said. "Tasar, call the guards." They waited until the squad arrived and Tuthmose snapped his fingers close to the Kush's ear. The man awakened with a bewildered look. By the time he recalled his ignoble capture, the guards had lashed leather straps around his hands and feet. They prodded him upright without respect and led him from the tent to the holding pen for captive officers.

"Thank you, Tuthmose. I only speak the dialect of the Wawat which did me no good," Tasar said and bowed. I hope the Kush lives, he thought. He will be an excellent specimen for the experiments.

The camp settled down. Well-fed troops succumbed to the sleep of the physically exhausted, the mentally devoid, confident that sentries would sound the alert before daylight crept upon them.

*

General Barum chose the site for that day's command post with long-practiced cunning. The hillock overlooked the vast plain of the intended battlefield. If a man strained his eyes he could discern the enemy's command post in the shimmering distance. It afforded the opposing commanders an equally excellent view of the wide valley.

Several tents were erected. High-ranking officers and battalion commanders grouped closely around Hor-Aha. General Barum, Colonel Keheb, and General Teyhab – who's Third Army had been left under the command of Colonel Mayhah - stood closest to their Supreme Commander.

Teyhab had traveled from the War Council as far as he could with Colonel Mekh's *Amazing Forces*. The *Ostrich Riders* were nowhere to be seen among the milling troops as their plan led them past Barum's forces so that they would swoop upon the enemy from behind his lines.

Most of Aha's group sat in folding chairs constructed by inventive craftsmen. Keeping as close as possible to Hor-Aha, without interfering in the art of waging war, stood Tuthmose, Seka and Tasar. Two tents were set up farther down for their use of which the smaller served as their interrogation chamber.

The second tent held the priests' sleeping mats and utensils. A larger third loomed even further away. From the emanating cries, it was evident that within it toiled the surgeons. Despite their efforts, a number of the maimed died from loss of blood, and Seka wandered tirelessly from one corpse to the next to commend its soul into Osiris's eternal care.

While Aha was Supreme Commander of his armies, he was wily enough to allow his knowledgeable generals to do the planning. At present, Barum conducted another of his open-air councils.

"This terrain is perfect. After the sun reaches its zenith, our front lines will fall back, sucking the enemy into a cauldron. The outer battalions circle the hills, drive over the crest, and noose the enemy. This circle has to be drawn tighter than an avaricious man's strings on a sack of emmer wheat."

Already sweating, Hor-Aha made an effort to nod vigorously.

Barum continued, "After yesterday's defeat, the Kush are desperate to regain ground. That's when Colonel Mekh sweeps in from behind with his *Amazing Forces*. He closes the bottleneck and spreads terror with the poisoned spears. Too late, the enemy will realize that he is trapped."

Enthusiastic murmurs swelled as the officers grasped the plan's brilliance.

"Remember! Like yesterday, enemy officers are to be taken alive. Their questioning by the priests provides us with valuable advantages."

Again, his listeners nodded vigorously.

"One last point: Count on a greater enemy force today. The Noba are joining the Kush. Their numbers are said to be great." He looked at his attentive audience. Even Hor-Aha sat up straight and paid attention.

"That is all. I trained you not to succumb to battle fever like common warriors. Your first duty is to Hor-Aha, and to assure that your men fall back when they are supposed to. Your second duty is to stay alive."

The battle-assigned officers bowed to Aha and left to rejoin their battalions.

General Barum turned toward the remainder of his officers. "Whose turn is it to guard Hor-Aha today?"

"Watch Captain Nebah, my General," Colonel Keheb

replied.

At the mention of his name Nebah, standing in the background, inclined his upper torso in a deep bow to the King. His eyes slid sideways. He neither looked at Aha, nor did he step forward. Instead, he remained half-hidden in the melee of lesser ranking officers.

Boom, boom, booom. Boom, boom, booom. Opposing drums beat another day into the travesty of human confrontation.

*

Scores of messengers scrambled up the sides of the hillock informing their Supreme Commander and General Barum of developments on the battlefield, sprinting back to the fighting battalion leaders with new orders. The runners bore no arms nor did they carry protective shields; speed was their defense. Unhindered by heavy implements they darted through the carnage like swift cheetahs hoping to avoid a large pack of ravenous hyenas.

The sun passed through its zenith. The forces of the Two Lands halted their forward surge. To the enemy's amazement, the *Fighting Hawk's* unrelenting assault ceased. Encouraged, the fierce Kush pushed the enemy back through the two hills into the valley from which Aha's forces had so fiercely advanced. With multi-dialectal cries of apparent victory, they pursued their uniformly retreating northern enemy.

Suddenly, as if commanded by a single voice, the *Fighting Hawk's* forces stopped their retreat to a man. The foremost battalions of the Kush, set upon by their own troops from behind, found themselves hemmed in by a natural cauldron. The clatter of spear against shield rang out. Maceheads thudded against human anvils to mingle with the last wails of the mortally wounded, the blasphemies of the defeated.

*

The Ruler of the Kush and the King of Nobatia had been elated over the midday's effortless advance. From where they stood, they observed their combined forces gaining easy ground over the Fourth Army. King Ogoni raised his arms to dispatch his *Black Noba*.

Drums pounded out their hollow rhythms. Dark bodies glistened in ritualistic dance whipped into frenzy by the staccato beat. Long-shinned legs kneed the air. Light-soled, splay-toed feet raised clouds of dust. Colorful feathers wafted above proud faces; white ibis-down fluffed around strong wrists and ankles. Lion-tooth necklaces clanged against sweat-beaded chests. Strips of sundry animal tails lashed out from strings tied around bellowing throats. Other than for their talismans, the *Noba* were quite naked, except that each man's dark penis was sheathed in a protective tube, pulled horizontal by the sinews of a lion, the long ends tied around the waist.

The *Nobas'* large zebra-skin shields were excellent camouflage for skirmishes in the bush. On the open plain, however, they called to a deadly hunter as loudly as a baying herd. But concealment from the enemy was not their aim. Today, he was to be taunted with eerie wails emitted from the horns of the ill-tempered buffalo. It was a spectacle that deserved viewing and applause rather than for its participants to be driven into defeat and annihilation. Even Ogoni could not help to marvel at the splendor of his exotic legions as they stomped into battle, each man the image of sustained virility.

Suddenly, the ebony-skinned king was aware that his command post was unprotected except for a handful of observers and guards, each craning his neck to follow the raging battle. Aggravated at such inexcusable carelessness, Ogoni turned toward the *Ruler of the Kush* when the air behind them exploded. They gaped in shock as long-necked birds raced toward them. Atop each, an unearthly avenger hid behind a blinding shield, effortlessly spearing the terror-frozen guards. Unnerved, Ogoni and the Kush Ruler bellowed frenetic orders.

"The two in the middle! Capture them alive," an *Ostrich-Rider* shouted, his cry too late to spare the *Ruler of the Kush*. A hastily thrown lance had nicked him in the thigh. The Ruler shrugged at his slight wound. His knees buckled. Ogoni stared at his fallen ally. The lance had only grazed the Kush's leg. Without taking a quivering hold in the fleshy thigh its tip clattered to the ground. Yet the Kush lay stretched in rigid death. Ogoni was so stunned that he could not lift his short dagger in self-defense. He was quickly taken captive.

"Look what I found," a rider boasted. He man-handled a tall tribesman from a nearby tent; another wrestled with an unruly woman who gathered her robes coyly to show her well-formed legs. She pushed her slender hips suggestively toward her captor who laughed, "Save it for later," as he lashed her to her hawk-eyed companion.

Having bound King Ogoni's wrists, Mekh's riders attached two long leather straps around his waist. Then they hitched him to two ostriches. Ogoni was forced to break into a trot until even his long strides threatened to become too short. He yanked hard on the straps in the hope of dislocating his tormentors but the riders sat well mounted. They laughed and increased their birds' odd gait. Soon, Ogoni's lungs stung and his vision became blurred. If he was to survive he had to cease his attempts to free himself. He looked up. They were headed toward several tents and he guessed that he was being herded toward the enemy's command post.

*

The cauldron's verdant ground was soaked crimson. The forward-surging Kush soon realized their predicament. Terrified, the first row of warriors turned back only to butt against the resplendent *Black Noba*. As they, too, turned to a man, all surged toward the two-hilled bottleneck.

Reinforcement from the *Red Noba* and the *Wawat* turned back much earlier. Instead of an unimpeded retreat, those troops suddenly faced a wide band of screaming whirlwinds. Nary an arrow could be placed into its bow, hardly a mace readied in defense. Terrifying lance-twirling, wing-flapping mirages, half man, half giant bird, swept toward them with tremendous speed. *Apparitions from the Netherworld*, holding the sun captive. Blinding rays shot toward the petrified *Noba*. Their shrieks pierced the air. In helpless terror, they threw their arms up, awaiting death.

In his finest hour, Colonel Mekh drove his *Amazing Forces* hard. His wiry riders rotated their shields sending the sun's brilliant reflection onto the stunned *Noba*. The blinded enemy was soon surrounded.

Kush warriors made a desperate last stand against the *Ostrich Riders*. When they saw the tall *Noba* felled by the slightest nick of a lance they too panicked. The deadliness of these bird-men sapped their courage. "Save yourselves! Over the hill," a bleeding *Noba* shouted. His cry was taken up by panicked *Kush*. They clawed the hard dust to gain against the steep incline.

General Teyhab had led his leather-capped battalion behind the hills to swarm over the low summit and wreak deadly havoc. The enemy tumbled back to surge west. This brought their desperate escape precariously close to Aha's command post from where his group followed the human river as it roiled through the valley. The carnage unfolded uncomfortably close-by.

The officers surrounding the King jumped out of their folding chairs as the combatants veered close enough for an errant lance to strike. Still, no one relinquished his precarious position, all eyes turned toward the slaughter below.

Watch Captain Nebah still kept in the background. With the outcome of the battle nearing, his breathing became erratic. To his dismay, Aha never joined the fracas where a quick thrust from anyone's lance could have felled him.

This was his only chance. The Guard Captain advanced one step at a time. His knuckles around his short lance turned white. Escape would be impossible. By Osiris, was there no other way? Nebah steadied his trembling hand. He gauged the distance, and took aim.

* * *

Chapter Thirty-Three

The loyal, the curious, and those who could afford to leave their homes to idle the time away, lined the banks of the river. "It's the Royal Convoy," one whispered to another. "The King," another added with importance. "Our King returns to Nekhen at long last."

Tesh, as well as Nekhen's Governor, and the powerful nomarchs were decked out in full regalia. Alongside them, lesser city nobles crowded and exchanged bits of gossip not caring that much of their knowledge was gleaned from household busy-bodies who lolled about the market place.

Those first in line eyed the water's lappings with caution as it forced them to edge further back against the palace wall. The Great Road was already half awash with the rising river.

Well past the noon hour, a roar surged upward in great waves as a smartly decorated prow rounded the last bend. The populace on both sides of the river cheered and hailed praise upon their King as the Royal Bark slid into view, driven against the current by muscled oarsmen.

"Hail Hor-Aha!"

"Hail the King!"

The convoy headed toward the palace landing and nervous pilots shouted for constant poling of the river-bottom while line handlers stood ready to make fast. A large number of troop supply barges followed the royal tenders. Heavily laden and seemingly unwieldy, the enormous floats lumbered past to tie up at the spacious city docks further up.

Aboard the Royal Bark was General Sekesh with one fourth of his Second Army, the remainder of his men from Ineb-hedj having stayed garrisoned at Badari. Only he, Beir and Amma knew that the man who waited patiently to be freed from the

315

Royal Cabin's hot interior was not the King.

Tesh, the Tax Collector, intended to welcome the royal family back into their old palace with proper pomp and circumstance. He hopped from one foot onto the other and stole quick glances at the Governor next to him who, traditionally, served as grand marshal during the opening procession of the *Festival of Opet*. Nevertheless, most of the sumptuous entertaining would fall to the Tax Collector.

Tesh stretched himself on his toes to see above the surging crowd. Rather small in stature, he often went unnoticed.

"May Seth bare his teeth at you!" he hissed.

The startled Governor looked down at Tesh. Had he jostled and thus offended the pompous little man? He followed Tesh's stare and found the reason for the curse. Equally bitter disappointment flooded through him. A solemn row of men spewed forth through the royal pylons, an imposing figure in the lead wearing an unusual purple robe. The *Ankh* glinted atop a high staff. The *High Priest of Ptah*, the Governor guessed, having recognized Rahetep. Shuffling behind them were the lesser temple priests and lectors.

"What? No undulating chantresses? No sistrum players?" With a trace of malice in his voice, the Governor leaned toward Tesh. "Nevertheless, exulted company, my friend. No doubt, they wish to wrest the welcoming honors away from us."

Tesh grunted. Rivals from long ago, each lusted after the rank and wealth of the other. So far, they kept a civil tongue in public. In private, they both solicited sympathy to their own cause from the southern nomarchs who proved infuriatingly reluctant to take sides. Their only common bond was their delight to discredit the priesthood. Always with sly caution, of course, so as not to incur the wrath the charlatans might invoke upon a careless man. To share their glorious moment with these irritating windbags was too much. Tesh fumed. He would not budge one step. Let them soak their sandals, he grimly smirked.

Ramose negotiated the last narrow strip of dry land easily. He and Rahetep were far from calm as they needed to act out their charade a while longer. He winked at Rahetep, grateful for his old tutor's loyalty, and steeled himself against the cold stares of the city nobles.

To his surprise, it was Tesh who addressed them with a

deep bow. "Chief Priest Rahetep. I beg of you, present me to your honored guest. I am aggrieved that I was not given the opportunity to pay my respects before now, High Priest of Ptah."

Mercifully, the Royal Bark docked and Ramose strode down the ramp with Rahetep in close pursuit, leaving Tesh and the Governor to wheeze after them. Bent over the vessel's railing, Ramose recognized Dubar who glowered down at him, chafing to escape the confines of the Royal Bark. The Prince seemed dazed, and Ramose looked for the Royal Steward. Instead, he saw an unknown servant hover close. When at last he spied Beir and their eyes met, he posed a silent question. Beir's lips split into a reassuring grin. All must have gone well, Ramose thought. Then he saw Amma's broad frame. As old as she was, she lent a firm hand to support a slender veiled figure and Dubar stepped aside to let his supposed sister pass. Zeina must have played her part well.

Ramose shifted his attention to the door of the Royal Cabin which Beir now held open. Four bearers emerged with an ornate curtained sedan. A bejeweled hand extended from the billowing strips of cloth waving to the waiting crowd in royal benevolence.

"Hail Hor-Aha! Hail the King!" the crowd cheered again.

Tesh could hardly contain himself. He rushed about and ordered people to make room for the arrivals.

The royal procession was soon swallowed by the palace entrance leaving the crowd outside the wall. With nothing else to do, speculation ran high and tongues wagged freely. There had been no sign of the Lady Hent. Just as well, they whispered, the traditional city still clinging to their dead Queen Mayet as the rightful Royal Wife. May her *Ka* rest safely with Osiris, and may her innocent *Ba* never have to return, they implored Horus on her behalf.

*

Tesh waived the Governor and the other nomarchs off. Playing the role of proud host, he ushered the arrivals on, "This passageway leads to the royal suites." To his dismay, the priests stuck to the royals like fleas to hunting dogs.

"The Royal Prince will be pleased with his rooms here," the eager Tax Collector pointed out, and Dubar left the procession with his slave.

Ramose again puzzled about Dubar's unknown servant. He drew Beir aside and was told that the man was pressed into Dubar's service by the Vizier moments before the Royal Bark sailed. The Prince had overruled Beir's objections with vehemence and there was nothing he could do, the Steward swore.

"This is an airy two-room suite for our Royal Heiress. Its second chamber leads into an inner garden. It connects to the sleeping chamber of the King's own suite," Tesh gushed. "And I noticed that the Princess brought only one old slave with her. I will send some of my own servants right away."

Amma stiffened and snorted through pursed lips. By Osiris, she was the Royal Nurse, and a freed woman. Not some 'old slave!'

Ramose saw her bristle and quickly stepped in. "No need, Honorable Tesh, thank you. I will send three of our temple maidens to tend to the Royal Heiress as she is to be kept in isolation until the festival to prepare herself for her initiation rites. Our temple slaves are instructed in the rituals. The Royal Nurse will bring them here from the Temple. By the way, this suite seems rather small. Will there be enough room for them?"

"Yes, of course, High Priest of Ptah," Tesh groveled. May Seth descend upon your meddling skull, he swore under his breath. If these priests and their pious servants were allowed to come and go as they pleased, he would have to act before they crowded the halls at every hour of the day. After he ushered Amma and the veiled Princess into their suite, he increased his speed leading the way toward the King's chambers.

To his surprise, the four royal bearers set the King's sedan down and bowed their leave at the priests. Tesh clapped his hands. Two palace slaves rushed to the fore. Before they could take the vacated places, the Steward and three of the priests clasped the sedan's handles and carried the ornate chair inside.

The High Priest turned. "I thank you, Tesh. The King needs to rest. Surely, you understand."

The door closed and Tesh was left surrounded by his slaves. His head pounded and hot anger spurted tears into his mean eyes.

*

Ramose rushed toward the sedan and drew the veils aside. "Badar! You are safely here at last!" He assisted the old priest climb stiffly from the chair. Despite its luxurious width, Badar was glad to be out of its confines, out of the suffocating cabin, away from the constant danger of detection. And away from Dubar. The youngster had behaved most distressingly. He had either hung about on deck sulking, or riled at the boatmen antagonizing them without cause. Even Beir had to endure the youth's violent outbursts. Then, inexplicably, great shivers had sent Dubar into a feverish stupor which only the taciturn new slave was able to control.

"It is an honor, Venerable Badar, to have you back in Nekhen," Rahetep bowed while Beir asked, "Ramose, what do you wish to do with the King's sedan?"

"I suggest we put it in place of the old one I had carried here so that we can take the Venerable Badar undetected back to the temple," Rahetep replied.

The old high priest threw up his hands. "Save me from yet another chair. Especially my own contraption," he begged. "I truly pitied Aha and he may never forgive me for his torturous journey."

Everyone laughed in mock assent. After weeks of worry, all had gone well.

"We could spirit you out of here without your chair," Ramose smiled. "I think you ought to come with us right now. Amidst us, no one will notice another priest leaving. And Beir will keep the curious away for another day or two while you, I mean, the King supposedly recovers."

"Have we heard from the Oasis?" Badar asked. Beir looked up and Badar thought he caught concern in the Steward's eyes. "Ah, loyal Beir," he smiled, "our King is fortunate to have you. I must thank him for lending me your excellent care during this journey."

The color on Beir's cheeks deepened. Was the trusted Steward that easily pleased by praise? Badar turned to the High Priest for an answer to his earlier question.

"No word yet from the battlefields," Ramose said. "It is too soon for a messenger to have made it back here from the Kharga."

"No enemy sentinels have climbed over the city walls as yet," Rahetep offered.

Concerned silence replaced the joy over their reunion.

*

Affronted by the High-Priest's off-handed dismissal, Tesh stormed back through the wide passage. When he reached Dubar's suite, he hesitated. Then, with a brief nod to himself, he waved his slaves away and rapped on the heavy door which opened up a crack. When the slave recognized their host, he pulled it wide and stepped aside. His bow to Tesh was brief. Not waiting to be addressed he spoke as soon as Tesh closed the door behind him.

"The Vizier sends greetings." The simple words jarred Tesh into caution. He was reminded of his task ahead of him. Before he could open his mouth, al-Saqqara's man spoke again.

"You must excuse the Prince. He is not himself. A touch of river fever. Could one of your servants bring a brazier? And a small pot of water with a cup. I carry medicinal leaves with me that, if brewed correctly, will drive the fevers down."

The man's demeanor was acceptably deferential. Still, something led Tesh to suspect that he was not a lowly slave. One of al-Saqqara's spies? Tesh sucked the air through his worn teeth. His skin began to crawl and cold perspiration broke out above his thin upper lip. He managed to nod to the rodent-like man. There was a noose tightening around his neck and Tesh vowed to send for his own secret hireling at once. He would offer the man a refreshing cup of wine to calm the assassin's nerves. Breathing in great gulps of air, he decided to invite the Governor and the scoffed nomarchs to a late dinner. Their presence this evening was his perfect alibi.

*

The door slamming behind Tesh brought Dubar from the adjacent sleeping chamber. His face was ashen and his movements uncoordinated. His hollow eyes were without focus and his lips widened into an angry sneer. "Hyena!" he riled. "Can't you see how I suffer! I know that you have more leaves. I can smell them on you." He lurched toward the slave who nimbly sidestepped the youth's drunken grasp.

"My Prince." The man's face remained impassive. "I was not able to steep the leaves more often on the Royal Bark. Too many to observe your need for them. But now, you shall have all you want."

"I detest you," Dubar slurred. He could hardly keep upright. The smallish man took Dubar by his fleshy shoulders and led him back toward the sleeping chamber. With amazing force for his slight build, he pushed the Prince onto the soft mats.

Heavy aroma filled the air. This would be his measly sixth cup since they left the capital. Countless bleak days and nights without Uncle Ebu's intoxicating elixir had been torture for the addicted youth.

"There. Only a while longer," al-Saqqara's man assuaged and left to answer a knock at the outer door.

*

Nefret, Safaga and Dokki crept into the palace in the guise of temple servants.

"Here you are," Nefret cried overjoyed as she shed her rough temple cape. "Never to be worn again," she laughed and rushed toward Amma flinging herself at the old woman.

"Where are your manners," Amma scolded her embarrassment away. Nefret dashed off to grab Zeina's hands. The two whirled around the room.

"How was it, Zeina? Did you enjoy being me? Did Amma treat you well?" Nefret shot a naughty look at the old nurse who cackled at the spectacle of the two together.

Helpless against their young exuberance, Amma wagged a gnarled finger at her royal prankster. "You are asking for it, child!" Tears of joy ran down her wrinkled cheeks as she gathered the girls around her.

"Just wait until you hear what happened to us."

"You will never guess."

"It was positively frightful!"

Dokki and Safaga had joined in Nefret's sputtering. While they served up disjointed bits and pieces of their adventure, the three were careful not to betray the memory of a certain night. Unable to learn anything about their lovers, they concluded that their men had left with the King. Every day, Safaga had prowled the temple grounds for arriving messengers, and Dokki stole off to ask the guards if they had any news, while Nefret tried to extract something from her elderly temple lectors. Now, with the impatience of young love, each counted off the lagging days and dreamed of the time when their lovers would return to them. By the time everyone relayed the events of their particular journey, sunlight had shadowed into early evening.

"Just look at these small chambers littered with our trunks.

321

There is hardly room for us," Amma despaired, her hands on her ample hips. "I have a solution," she brightened after she surveyed the clutter. "Since the Venerable Badar vacated the King's suite in favor of the temple, Nefret can take his sleeping chamber. Remember, the Tax Collector told us that the two suites connect through the garden. Beir's room is adjacent to the royal sitting chamber so he can prevent anyone from coming into the suite from the other side."

"How perfect. I shall see to Nefret in there," Safaga offered at once.

"What a clever little pet you are. You are not to neglect your duties to Nefret in favor of someone else," Amma warned, seeing right through the pretty slave's transparent plan to sidle into Beir's proximity.

Even though Safaga dreamed of Pase daily, the arrival of the Steward had rekindled her longing for his mature caresses. The older man offered different delights than did the soldier in his youthful ardor. If she felt slight pangs of guilt they lasted no longer than a heartbeat. There would be other times for Pase, she promised herself.

Amma clapped her hands together and announced, "All right. Safaga, you prepare Nefret for the night in the royal suite. And inform Beir."

Safaga caught the spark in Amma's eyes. Nefret, too, looked at her with the slyness of a cat, and the two young women grinned at each other before Amma dispelled the moment.

"Dokki, you and I will go to the kitchens to find something to eat. At this late hour, a light tray supper will suffice; we can eat in here. You, Zeina, put the veil back over your face, just in case."

* * *

Chapter Thirty-Four

Seka sensed the threat from behind. He pivoted and without a thought for his own safety threw himself back to back with his King. A whirring shadow sped toward him.

"Ahgrrr," the *Ka*-priest gurgled. Warm blood spurted from his lips as a strangling coldness stilled his heart. Seka slumped to the ground.

"By Horus ..." Aha turned. His eyes met Keheb's who also spun around. Before the Colonel found the source of the choking sound he spied Nebah just as the Watch Captain lowered his empty throwing arm, his fingers still splayed from the forceful thrust. Their stares locked. Then, with lightening agility, Keheb yanked the protruding lance from Seka's chest and lunged at Nebah.

"Die, vermin!" he snarled and rammed the dripping point through the Watch Captain's chest. Nebah hung in space, held aloft by Keheb's rage. With a sound of disgust, the Colonel released his grip and kicked the King's would-be assassin into his mortal fall. Nebah hit the ground face down, his dead weight forcing the lance shaft through his chest until the tip reemerged from his back; a bloody standard of swift punishment. Even Barum forgot the battle for an instant. At a flick of his fingers, Nebah's men were ringed.

Aha at last grasped the implication of Seka's sudden death. "He saved my life," he whispered to Tuthmose. "He will be missed. You shall serve as *Hemu-ka* from now on."

Tasar knelt down to pound life back into Seka's stilled heart. After some tense moments, he shook his head.

Tuthmose bent to close the dead *Ka*-priest's glassy eyes. Even in death, they questioned, Why? As if to answer them, Tuthmose said quietly, "Your soul was recalled by the god you served so well. May Osiris welcome your *Ka*." Then he added with a clearer voice, "Colonel, if the assassin is still alive I must question him. Others may be behind this blatant attempt."

Quick prodding of the outstretched captain confirmed that Keheb had stabbed true. The young colonel bit his lips in frustration that his better judgment had been blinded by his rage.

"How stupid of me to kill the man outright," he confessed and added in disbelief, "To think: one of our own! What would pressure a loyal officer into such desperation?"

"You did what you thought just, Keheb. Best question his men," Barum sighed.

The dead Watch Captain's squad of guards stood motionless, uncomprehending. Despite intensive questioning, it was apparent that the simple soldiers had no knowledge of their Captain's darker dealings.

"Was he in touch with anyone from the outside," Colonel Keheb asked.

"No one that we know of," one of the men offered after much prodding from his peers. "Except for the Archer. The one who brought the scroll. The Captain read it to us aloud. It contained a commendation to elevate the Archer Pase to Chief Archer. We all celebrated his promotion."

Pase? Barum wondered. The same Pase he had entrusted with his own vital message? He recalled having asked the man for his captain's name. 'The Watch Captain Nebah,' had been the reply. Barum looked at his aide. Keheb's brows were knotted in consternation. So, he too remembered.

"Fetch the Archer Pase!" Keheb bellowed. The runners sped away. An afterthought struck Keheb, "Search the traitor!"

They found the crumpled scroll deep in Nebah's quiver. Colonel Keheb smoothed it on his thigh to read it. An ordinary commendation, Keheb saw and let it flutter to the ground.

*

Pase returned with one of the runners. Having traveled with the King at close quarters for a good cycle of the moon, the young Archer stepped in front of his Supreme Commander in anticipation to be entrusted with another important task. He would welcome a leave from the battlefield where the dust was so dense that one could hardly distinguish friend from foe. Pase glanced at the two dead men, blood still draining from their fatal wounds, recognizing both of them.

"Chief Archer Pase." Barum's face was screwed into something akin to pain. "You gave a message to your Captain?"

"Indeed, my General." Pase looked again at the bloody scene. What message might they ask him to deliver in connection with this obvious calamity?

"Who entrusted you with that message?" Barum asked, and Pase thought: His stare is cold. Sweat broke through his pores. Not the sweat he shed freely under the sun but the kind that pours forth with numbing cold; it tightens the chest and parches the mouth. Pase ran his tongue over his lips but the salt of his perspiration only stung his tongue rather than relieve the dryness of his mouth.

"The message was given to me by the Vizier, my General. Just moments before I boarded the temple boat in Ineb-hedj. It was not sealed, so I asked the High Priest to read it to me in case the scroll was lost." Pase sought out the eyes of the young priest. "Please, Priest Tasar, attest to this."

Tasar picked up the scroll and stepped carefully over Seka's body to join the others. "The Archer speaks the truth, my King," he bowed. "The High Priest and I studied both messages several times as, for some reason, Ramose was uneasy about their text. However, we were unable to discern anything unusual within the profuse wording. Although," Tasar shook his head as if to dispel his own gnawing suspicion, "now I wonder why your name, Great Hor-Aha, would be mentioned in the ordinary context of both messages."

"What do you mean by 'both messages'?" Keheb jumped in and poked Tasar hard enough for Barum to place a restraining hand on his aide's arm. "Keheb! Let him explain."

Tasar did not waver under the rough punch. "The Vizier gave Pase two scrolls."

"What about the second?" Keheb now challenged Pase.

"I do not recall its exact words, my King," Pase's speech turned panic-strangled. This was turning into an inquisition. "I was instructed to deliver the other message to the *Royal Tax Collector*, which I did. A few days after our arrival in Nekhen. Like the High Priest told me to," he croaked, eyes popping.

"What did the High Priest have to do with your orders?" Barum interjected.

"I remember," Tasar broke in. "The second message was an

equally rambling litany for the *Tax Collector* to prepare for the arrival of the King and the Royal Heiress."

"The Vizier did not know about the King's secret journey?" Barum asked, incredulous.

"No one did," Aha interrupted. "Go on, Tasar. What else do you remember?"

"The message commanded Tesh to re-provision the troop barges and to dispatch them to the First Falls. And," Tasar squinted, trying to recall each flowery phrase. "Oh yes ... the *Tax Collector* was to see personally to the comforts of the Royal Heiress during her stay at the old palace. For security reasons, Ramose asked Pase to delay Tesh's message for a few days. What struck both the High Priest and myself as peculiar was that the Vizier emphasized so urgently for Tesh *himself* to take *special care* of the Princess. As if one would expect less. There was, however, no mention or concern about Prince Dubar; surely the Vizier knew that the Royal Prince went to Nekhen as well."

Tasar mused almost to himself, "I cannot fathom why both messages emphasized your royal names so strangely."

"It cannot be!" The vein on Aha's right temple reared like an angry cobra as he howled in helpless fury. "To think that the driveling swine had the audacity to ask me for her hand! Nothing must happen to Nefret!" Aha's outward explosion carried an inner prayer to any god who cared to listen. *Nothing. Not when I just started to love this child of mine.*

"Do you hear me! Nothing!"

Tasar's face lost all color. Nebah's message mentioned the King. And now an attempt had been made on his sacred life! The Tax Collector's message spoke of Nefret! His Nefret! In mortal danger at this very moment! Was she to die, ignobly, from the dirty hands of an assassin unleashed through a message delivered by the Archer?

"You are to blame for this!" he cried, overwrought by fear, ripped apart by pain. Before anyone could restrain him, he wrested his sword from its sheath and cleanly rammed it through the stunned Chief Archer. In vain clinging to the imbedded shaft for support, Pase dropped to his knees. His eyes fastened on his misguided attacker.

Tuthmose rushed to cushion the Archer's slow collapse. As Pase lay dying in Tuthmose's arms, the older man held Tasar's gaze with a long searching look. The others attributed the young man's precipitous attack to loyalty for his Royal Heiress whose life he had saved twice. Tuthmose, however, sensed something else behind the crazed loss of self-control, so unthinkable for a trained priest. "Watch yourself, young Tasar," he hissed at the capable youth he had come to like so well.

"Yes, you watch yourself, young fool! This was not the Archer's doing," Aha said between clenched teeth. He spat his bitterness toward the others, "Al-Saqqara is behind this treachery! The revenge of a slighted suitor."

Everyone was stunned at the open accusation against the powerful Vizier. Too late to have prevented the Archer's death, they could only pray for his *Ka*. The proud absolution of his duties had become the very cause of his senseless demise.

*

The sound of war clanged into focus. The raging battle could no longer be ignored. Nearby, stretcher bearers scurried toward the infirmaries, and submissive Kush were herded into captivity.

Barum was the first to find composure. He had to bring this sorry episode to its conclusion for them to return to the pressing business of winning the war. "We have no proof that the Royal Heiress is in any danger at this time," he offered to calm Aha's fears.

"No proof? No proof! What is it you want, Barum? My daughter's death mask on a platter?" Aha shouted and Barum stepped back a pace to escape the King's hot breath. It was a father's helpless fury against the nearest one at hand.

Aha tried to regain control and sighed, "All I can hope for now is that Ramose keeps a watchful eye on her in Nekhen."

"As will Amma. The Royal Convoy must have arrived by now," Tuthmose offered.

Aha looked up, a rueful smile on his lips. "Ah, my good Tuthmose. You remember Amma as she was when you and I first met her. During the days, when I courted my lovely Mayet. I was more afraid of Amma than I was of my bride's sharp-tongued mother. The years have taken their toll on our old nurse. Though even to this very day, I tend to mind her."

Tuthmose inclined his head and smiled, "Amma may have grown old, Hor-Aha, but I assure you she is still as fierce as ever when it comes to protecting her cherished Princess."

"Nevertheless, you must implore the gods that she is successful in her task." Aha looked at Tuthmose. The brief, almost intimate, interchange between the two men broke the tension at last, and everyone breathed easier. Except for Tasar, who was deathly pale. Unlike Aha, he could not cry out aloud in anguish. Nefret and the ugly Vizier! It pierced his heart with a thousand lances. How could that be! Al-Saqqara was not even interested in women! Tasar had heard the whispers of the Vizier's lustings. How could the disgusting man be so deadly offended by Aha's refusal? Tasar wished there was a way to alert Ramose.

Far to the east of the King's War Command, Hapi's First Falls rumbled over boulders ground smooth by the tumbling waters. Laden with fresh food for battle-weary troops the supply barges were to anchor there and wait to take the King back to Nekhen. They might board in three to four days from now, depending on the outcome of the battle. Oh, great Horus, let us be victorious, Tasar prayed. Then he looked down at Pase and thought of Safaga. How could he tell her of her brave archer's senseless death?

"Priest Tasar," a deep voice called to him. He turned. Senmut and his Bowmen restrained several captives. Very dark, and very naked, they held themselves proud despite their profusely bleeding wounds. Their ebony skin made the gaping cuts appear redder, deeper; somehow a grosser infraction against their perfect bodies.

Two of the captives stood out from the dark group by their lighter skin. Tribal dress proclaimed them to be nomads. The taller of the two had startling eyes the color of the sky. The other - Tasar's eyes widened in surprise - was a young woman whose flowing robes could not belie her slender limbs. She looked at Tasar with such defiance that he glanced at Senmut and, for an instant, felt that the other man, too, was thinking back to a certain starry night - when the Archer Pase had been one of them, so happy with his pretty lover.

"Yes? What is it?" Tasar asked in an attempt to break the enigmatic pull of the woman's liquid eyes.

"Mekh's *Amazing Forces* captured these," Senmut said and pointed to the dark group, one of them a good head taller. Tasar noticed that not all of the man's blackness was his own. A glistening black pelt lay wrapped around his upper torso. It fitted him like a second skin down to the waist. Below that, he was naked. Tasar's eyes strafed the curious tube and he wondered if it would be bothersome in battle. I'd rather wear my leather flap, he thought, bemused by the odd contraption. The tall man stepped into the fore.

"He could be one of their shamans," Senmut explained and pushed the tethered *Noba* toward Tasar. Something about the dark warrior caused even Senmut to manhandle him less roughly than the other captives. Soon, everyone from the War Command crowded around the exotic man who held himself with such noble bearing.

"Get me an interpreter," Keheb ordered.

Before someone could follow his command, the captive surprised them. "I know how to speak your pale tongue."

The King and Barum became aware of the exchange and they, too, approached the group.

"Then tell us, *Noba*! Where is your ally, the *Ruler of the Kush*? I might reward you for this information," Keheb said hoping the man understood.

Without hesitation, the proud man replied, "One of your over-zealous riders struck the brave Kush down." A disdainful sneer appeared on the fleshy, almost purple lips. Gradually, however, his arrogance evaporated as he recalled the negligible wound the *Ruler of the Kush* sustained. And still, he fell dead within an instant. To hide his fear of such awesome magic, he stared ahead. After some time, he looked at his captors with renewed insolence. His eyes came to rest on Aha. He guessed the King's identity and bowed. There was mockery in his reverence and when he spoke, it was with haughtiness.

"King of Kamt, hold me captive, torture me. You shall learn nothing from me. I am Ogoni, King of Nobatia."

"I greet you, Ogoni," Aha answered bowing negligibly, mainly to cover his delight over the opportune capture. "And I regret the death of your brave ally," he added and wondered why the light-skinned Kush, whose race was so closely related to Aha's own, had allied himself with this magnificent savage. Greed, he decided, for Ogoni's yellow nub.

While the others continued to stare at the man who proclaimed himself the feared Ogoni, Keheb prodded without ceremony. "We know all about your new mine. How far is it from here?"

"That, soldier, you shall never know!" A sonorous laugh rose from within Ogoni's muscular chest. He could endure their most excruciating torture and would rather die than divulge this information.

Ogoni could not guess the meaning of the brief smile that passed between the King, his general and a young priest. The latter nodded imperceptibly and fingered an amulet dangling from his neck. *Oh yes,* Tasar thought, *you will divulge it all too soon, proud warrior. And afterward, I shall obtain the King's permission to take you to Ramose. What a resplendent specimen for his experiments you'll make.*

"Put four guards on him. Give him food and drink, if he accepts it. Tasar will deal with him later," Barum ordered. He started to follow the King who had turned his attention back to the battle below.

Chief Senmut call out, "General, what about these two?"

In their exuberance to have captured the legendary King of Nobatia, they had ignored the rest of the prisoners. Barum looked again at the group of captives and was startled when he recognized Yadate staring back at him with sky-hued insolence. Then, Barum saw the girl.

When she felt his look upon her, she swayed her hips seductively.

"What now, my General?" she taunted. Her dark eyes bespoke of old promises. They also begged for a love-starved general to spare her life.

Barum stood frozen in place, his mind ablaze. While she had thrust her supple body toward him, and while he had dreamed aloud, she had listened, and betrayed him. Just as the sly tribesman had fed him unimportant bits of news and, accepting his generous rewards, the man had also spied for the Kush!

How could I have been such a fool! Disgusted with himself, Barum turned and walked away.

"General, what shall I do with them?" Senmut called after him, this time louder.

"Kill them," Barum growled back over his shoulder.

"The girl as well?"

"The girl as well!" Barum spat and pretended to shade his eyes from the sun to hide his shame-reddened face. Clenching his teeth so that his jaw jutted squarely out, he reassured himself, s*he meant nothing to me. Do you hear me, old fool! Nothing!*

The battle below seemed to command Barum's complete concentration when Keheb stepped up behind his general. For a long time, neither man spoke. When they finally did, it was business as usual. Their business of war.

* * *

Chapter Thirty-Five

Dubar jolted awake. Vaguely, his intermittent memory pieced together the royal convoy's arrival, the imposing city walls, and an annoying little man who ordered everyone about. He had to be in Nekhen. When he called for his new slave his own voice echoed back at him. Why was no one here to heed his princely wishes? The numbness in his mind gave way to increasing anger. Did he have to rise from this uncomfortable bedstand to look for the stupid slave himself! He swung his legs onto the floor. His temples throbbed; he saw a basin full of water nearby and without hesitation immersed his head. Shaking himself like a wetted-down hound, he felt better. After he surveyed the simple room he decided that his accommodations were intolerable. He was tired of being pushed aside by that ill-tempered, toothless Royal Nurse; tired of being placated by the inscrutable Steward; and tired of his arrogant sister ostracizing him. Worse, his own father had ignored him during the long journey. By Horus, he would remind all of them of his royal due!

Dubar stormed from his suite, his annoyance fed by renewed indignation, his reasoning obscured by the overwhelming hunger for al-Saqqara's brew. As he rushed past Nefret's suite he did not notice the shadowy form pressed into a recess; nor did he sense the cold stare that followed him. Dubar entered through a door. "Just as I thought!" he sneered. Recognizing his Father's sedan, he had to have found his way into the King's suite. His attempted shout turned into an adolescent croak that did not carry far.

Next to the ornate chair, Dubar saw another, far simpler one. Without much interest he yanked its curtains from their clasps. To vent his frustration he pounded the seat and with a last swift kick dislocated the worn cushion from the old chair's wooden slats. As if it had a life of its own, the indigo robe spilled toward the ground. The confused youth stared at it. Perhaps he was not in his father's suite. Had he blundered into the High Priest's chamber? But why was the royal sedan in here? And why would Ramose have stuffed his robe under the worn cushion of that old chair?

In a flash of lucidity, Dubar recalled that the High Priest's robe was of a different hue. Similar, but not the same. Still, he had seen such color once before. It hit him with searing clarity. Agitated, Dubar snatched the robe off the floor and draped it around his shoulders. Much too long for him, he fumbled to pull the hood over his sopping-wet sidelock until the deep folds obscured his sunken face. With malignant purpose, Dubar tripped toward an inner door. He guessed it to lead to the King's sleeping chamber. At long last, Aha would learn the truth about his unworthy Heiress; and would proclaim him, Dubar, as his rightful Royal Heir. He shook his head to clear the blinding fog. If only the pain would cease! Before he reached the inner door, madness clouded his mind once again.

*

Nefret untied her mother's dagger from her waist with loving reverence. How its blade glistened. How intricately the ivory handle was carved. Her mother's last protecting gift. Feeling safe at last, she could stop wearing it now. She dropped it on the bed. Content to have some time on her own, she settled in front of the small cosmetic stand next to the wide arches through which the courtyard's soft light enveloped half the King's bedchamber.

The young woman touched her beauty utensils and carved combs with relish. One after another, she picked up exquisite containers and inhaled the sweet aroma of precious oils. Never before had she appreciated her little treasures as much. It had been exciting to watch Safaga unpack the small luxuries after the long journey without them. Lucky Safaga. Off to spend an hour with the Steward. Nefret pictured them in amorous togetherness which brought Tasar to her mind. She threw her arms around her own slender body and imagined how, were he to appear suddenly, she would call out his name. Softly. Before racing to embrace him.

The heavy door creaked. Nefret turned and peered into the

shadowy interior, staring in joyous disbelief at the cloaked figure. "Tasar! You are back! And you brought the robe! Come to me, my love."

He did not advance a single step so that she had to bridge the gap between them. He also did not seem as tall as she remembered him.

The robe flung open; the hood was pushed back. A dark face pressed itself close to hers. Rough hands grabbed at her wrists. Sunken eyes glittered in deep hatred.

"Now I have proof, you whore! So it was that priest you coupled with!" It was the snarl of a rabid animal. The princely sidelock scythed the leaden air.

"Dubar!" Nefret fought to shake loose from his smarting grip. "Have you gone mad!"

The youth held onto her with great strength. He pressed into her until her forced retreat was stopped by the hard edge of the sleeping platform. Still he kept up his relentless push until she tumbled backward onto the low bedstand. He plunged on top of her. The indigo robe billowed around them as if to hide the dismal scene.

Nefret struggled trying not to inhale Dubar's stale breath as he fell into a belabored rhythm, riding her. An unforgiving sharpness pressed into her back.

"Get off me, you stinking hyena!" she gasped unable to dislodge the stocky youth prodding her with his hardness. Frenzied by disgust and fear, she tried to wriggle free from under him. Again, a cold protrusion dug hard into her. She freed her right hand from her incestuous attacker and slipped it beneath her arched back.

Dubar mistook her upward thrust and doubled his frenzied chafing. His thick lips covered her mouth. His white-mucused tongue pried her teeth apart as he settled his disgusting lips on hers.

Unable to breathe, Nefret clenched jaw loosened. Her frenetic brother took it as an invitation and furrowed deeper into the recesses of her mouth. Clamping her teeth down hard, she bit his tongue almost in half.

Spewing the sickening sweetness of his own blood, Dubar catapulted off her. "You whore," he lisped. Blinded by pain, he lurched toward the door.

Nefret grasped the carved ivory under her. Clutching it

firmly in her palm, she sprinted after him, outrage robbing her of her senses.

The blade tore through the light fabric as Nefret drove it deep into her brother's back. Determined to inflict more pain, she pulled the dagger from its fleshy seat.

Dubar gurgled, choking in his blood. Almost at the door he pivoted into a revealing collapse, his kilt bunching at his thick middle. Blood quelled from his gaping mouth. The red-smeared, ghoulish face only deepened Nefret's rage. She straddled the writhing youth. Her fist fused to her dagger and she drove its blade into her brother's chest until his groping fingers could reach for her no longer, and his thick chest ceased to shudder. Her fury spent with a last thrust, Nefret slid off the lifeless form.

Having stood still for to quiet her pounding heart, Nefret dragged the heavy body into the middle of the room. There, she pulled the robe out from under her dead brother and spread it over his obscene nakedness. Nausea felled her to her knees. In vain, she tried to spit out the taste of him. Still clutching the bloody dagger, she crawled toward the rays of light straying through the open arches. Still fairly intense, the light could not banish the darkness that had descended into Nefret's very soul.

*

Zeina sat still. As soon as Amma and the others came back she would no longer be treated like royalty. She rearranged her veil. She had enjoyed impersonating the Royal Heiress.

Someone entered the outer chamber. Probably a palace servant. Zeina smiled; she would act out her role one last time to perfection.

"You there! Slave," she called. "Hand me that wrap."

The man-servant must not have expected to find anyone there for he was startled by her voice. Recovering quickly, he found the cape atop one of the trunks and flung it over his left arm. In apparent reverence, he kept his right hand behind his back. Stepping into the inner chamber he bowed, muttering, "Royal Heiress," and advanced toward the veiled Zeina who reached for Nefret's flimsy shoulder cape. Instead of handing her the garment, the man's left hand grasped her outstretched wrist and pulled her toward him. His right hand emerged from behind his back. A dagger flashed toward the stunned girl and

335

was buried deep within her chest. Zeina sank to her knees.

"Why?" Her eyes widened in bewildered innocence. With a sneer, the villain let her slip from his grasp.

"Why?" Zeina gasped again. She crumpled to the floor.

Her attacker stood over her. "Because you are his Heiress," he hissed, devoid of any feeling although puzzled by the unusual numbness spreading through him. He felt a constricting slowing of his senses, of his very breath. Suddenly, he bellowed like a wounded bull. With great effort, he lurched into the depths of the room where he fell, eyes staring at flickering shadows on the ceiling. He could not move a muscle. *The wine,* he realized, before he spiraled into a dark void, *it had to be Tesh's offered glass of wine.*

The last glimpse Zeina could make out, was Nefret standing over her with a dripping dagger, wild-eyed, her face a frozen grimace. As the slave's life pooled at her young mistress's feet, she wondered why Nefret's mouth was smeared with blood. She inched her hand upward. With a throaty cry, Nefret sunk down next to her cradling Zeina's head in her lap, rocking back and forth, trying to coo life back into her dying friend.

*

Safaga placed a slim finger on her lips and longingly looked back at Beir. Sighing, she pushed the door to the King's suite open expecting an impatient Nefret. Her feverish reunion with the Steward had taken longer than she realized. Beir had been persuasive. He had taken his time with her.

"Stay out here," Safaga whispered to Beir and slipped into the inner chamber. Not finding Nefret, she hurried toward the open arches when her foot caught on something in the middle of the chamber. No, someone! She bent down. The robe blended perfectly into the room's increasing darkness. Holding her breath, she gingerly lifted a corner of the feather-light material. The light was not sufficient for her to see clearly and she prayed to Seth that it was not her mistress. When she recognized the distorted face she let out a great scream that brought her lover sprinting from the outer chamber.

"He is dead," Beir said quietly and at once thought of the implication for the two of them. "Where is Nefret," he whispered hoarsely as he placed the slithering folds back over Dubar's face.

The mention of her young mistress pulled Safaga from her

shock. "Merciful gods, let her be alive!" she keened and covered her face with both hands. Great sobs racked her small frame.

Beir took her sharply by the shoulders and shook his distraught lover. "Safaga! Stop! We must not lose our heads. Literally, my girl! You have to find the Princess." He propelled her toward the courtyard. "I shall fetch Ramose. He is the only one we can trust with this right now. Do not speak to anyone until I bring him back." He pressed the sobbing slave briefly to his chest and, after her shaking eased, he pushed her gently into the inner courtyard.

Safaga did not know how she crossed the gravelly space but she found herself entering the women's suite. It was all dark and renewed fear constricted her throat. The others should be here, unpacking, chattering excitedly, with Dokki laying out a simple evening meal, and Amma scolding ceaselessly, unable to dampen the girls' happy reunion. Safaga became aware of a soft murmur from the floor. Straining her eyes to penetrate the shadows, she whispered, "Nefret? Zeina? Where are you?"

The murmur grew louder until it turned to keening. Safaga fell to her knees and crawled toward the wailing, her heart pounding harder than ever. "Nefret? Zeina?" she urged. A seated form rocked back and forth.

"Nefret! Oh, my sweet. You know?"

A soft moan answered her. Safaga's eyes adjusted to the darkness and she noticed that Nefret held something in her lap. It was someone's head. Safaga's eyes followed the outstretched form, clad in fine linen, bands of yellow nub encircling the lifeless arms, a veil taming masses of dark hair.

"It's Zeina! What happened?" Safaga cried. Her arms encircled Nefret's heaving shoulders, the three remaining still; young friends, so vastly different from each other, now bound even more by tragedy.

*

Ramose, led by Beir, raced through the passageways connecting the temple to the palace. At the same time, Amma and Dokki returned with trays of food from the other direction. When they saw the High Priest, Dokki's eyes widened with open adoration, while Amma guessed from the men's grave faces that something was amiss. Her broad frame stiffened visibly. Most likely, the King had been slain in battle.

Nefret would have to be told. Without a word, she pushed the door to their suite open to let Ramose enter. Beir shot a furtive look down the long hallway before he followed.

Amma ordered Dokki to put the trays aside and to light some lamps. Steeling herself against great tragedy, she looked calmly at the High Priest. "Poor child. I am glad you came to tell her yourself, Ramose."

"How can you know already?" Ramose looked at her in surprise, and then at Beir, who shook his head.

"It is your hurried presence," Amma replied with quiet sorrow and went toward the inner chamber, then stood frozen in her tracks as the others filled the doorframe behind her. The group stared in disbelief at the scene splayed out before them, flickering shadows mimicking life where there was none.

*

"Safaga! What happened in here?" Beir was the first to find his voice. He rushed toward his pretty lover who held Nefret rocking in concert with her distraught mistress.

"Zeina was stabbed," the slave sobbed.

"Poor Zeina," Amma cried.

Ramose was the first to see the outstretched figure sprawled grotesquely behind the cowering group. "Who is that?" A familiar dagger gleamed next to the corpse, its ivory handle beautifully carved.

"A despicable assassin!" Beir pounced atop the lifeless man. The wide eyes stared up at him and the Steward thought he saw a flicker breaking the glassy gaze. He pressed his ear against the man's chest. "He breathes!" He grabbed the man's thick wrists. As he pulled the arms upward the hands flopped about heavily, without resistance.

Now Ramose bent over the prone man and looked into the wide pupils.

"He seems drugged rather than dying from loss of blood. His wounds are slight. I venture that he came in here after killing Dubar in the other suite. Having mistaken Zeina for the Princess, he thought he would duplicate his heinous task and slay another royal heir."

"What are you saying?" Amma gasped.

Ramose and Beir stared at her. Both realized instantaneously that they had been so stunned by what they found in the women's quarters they had forgotten about

Dubar, sprawled in indecent death next door.

"I rushed here because Beir told me about Dubar," Ramose said to Amma. "From what you said outside, I thought you knew."

"Knew what?" She gaped at him in toothless quest. "Ramose, when I saw you, I thought that the King had been slain. You came to tell his children. Now, what about Dubar?"

"He was stabbed to death as well by the assassin."

For the first time, Nefret lifted her head. She shook herself free of Safaga's tight embrace and gently placed Zeina's head on the floor. As if carrying a heavy burden, she stood up and looked at Ramose whom she loved like a father. He had always guided her like one. At this moment, however, he was the *High Priest of Ptah*, bound by sacred vows and by the strict laws of *Ma'at*. Could he still protect her now, she wondered.

"The intruder killed Zeina. I saw it. I crept up behind him and tried to stab him." Nefret looked down at the friend who had died in her place. She stretched herself taller, resolved to accept punishment for her own inexcusable crime. Her young voice was devoid of its familiar silvery bells. "This man did not assassinate the Prince. It was I who killed my brother. I did it out of hatred."

Ramose barely managed to catch her as she lost consciousness. He laid her onto one of the narrow beds, grateful for the simple task. He needed time to dispel the numbness descending over him. If only she had not said it out aloud. How could he protect her now? The blame for both killings could have easily been placed with the assassin. Only the gods and he would then have known the truth. 'I interpreted the *Oracle* correctly, after all,' he thought sadly. How could his sweet Nefret have harbored such deep hatred for her brother. 'And I never knew. Will I be able to forgive her? Yet I am bound to call for her punishment. Isis cautioned me that others must not know. The slaves already do.' There was not much time. If the truth became known neither he, nor the King, nor anyone else, could protect Nefret from the laws of *Ma'at*. Nor from the Vizier's unforgiving *Kenbet*, his Council of Judges.

"Quiet, everyone! Please!" Ramose raised his voice sharply. The wailing of the women had risen to a din. "Quiet, I beg of you! We must act quickly, and with great caution. Dokki!

Safaga! You two see to Nefret."

"Beir, is Badar's old sedan still here in the palace?"

"Yes, in the King's suite. There, through the courtyard."

"Good. Then you and I shall bring it here. We will carry Nefret to the temple in it right away. Dokki and Safaga, come with us."

"You cannot carry a sedan, Ramose," Amma protested.

The High Priest waived her off. "Amma, you alert the Tax Collector of this tragedy. Pretend that you just discovered the double murder. Tell him that you sent Beir for me. Make no mention that I already know of this. It will give the two of us time to return. Meanwhile, Dokki, prevent anyone from entering these rooms."

"By the way, where is that man-slave who came with Dubar from Ineb-hedj?" Ramose asked recalling the slave he had glimpsed with some misgiving upon arrival of the convoy.

"I have no idea where the wretched man has gone to. It is likely that he went in search of food for Dubar, just as Dokki and I had. He was not one of the regulars, you know." Amma had wondered all along about the strange slave who jumped hastily aboard minutes before they sailed.

"Listen, all of you. Dokki, stop sobbing." Ramose extended his hand toward the frightened slave. "Be still, child."

The shivering girl quieted down at once.

"If this assassin was someone's hireling, Nefret's life continues to be in danger here in Nekhen. It is paramount to make believe that she was killed."

A moan arose from the women. Ramose remained undeterred. "Do not remove the veil from Zeina's face. Since the poor child did not count on playing her big role to this sad end, at least she will have a grand burial."

"Ramose, this is impossible," Beir interrupted.

Amma, too, nodded vehemently. How could they pretend the dead Zeina was the Royal Heiress? "What about the death mask? It will have Zeina's features. And what about the dark birth mark on Nefret's thigh?"

"Leave all that to me," Ramose hushed urgently.

"What will happen to my little Princess?" Tears watered the old nurse's rheumy eyes.

Ramose looked at her with sadness, his own eyes suddenly brimming, "I cannot say, Amma. The gods will give me

340

guidance. In the meantime, not a word about this to anyone! While the girls will be safely isolated at the temple you, Amma, with Beir will have to face the official inquisition. I trust you both. Again, no one must learn that Nefret killed her princely brother; or that she is still alive. Your own lives depend on it!"

"No one, High Priest?" Amma whispered.

Ramose worked his jaw before he answered. "No one, Amma! Not even Aha can save his daughter now. No matter how much Dubar might have provoked her, which I suspect he did. You, as well as I, know that the Vizier will not hesitate for one ambitious moment to pronounce the harshest sentence upon this unfortunate royal child."

"No one shall know from us," Amma vowed and grasped Beir's hand. They both looked frankly into the High Priest's blue eyes and repeated in unison, "No one."

Ramose knew he could count on Amma who would rather die than break her promise. Beir, on the other hand, as the King's Personal Steward, enjoyed a special closeness with Aha. What would he do when he saw his King stooped in grief by his double loss? Would he weaken in his resolve, so that he might infuse a glimmer of hope into his King's broken heart?

Ramose liked Beir. But could he really trust him? For his own sake, he would have to assure himself of the man's silence.

* * *

Chapter Thirty-Six

The platform was shored up by loose gravel, with a temporary throne constructed from General Saiss's extraordinary shields. Amazingly, the strange alloy did not hold the day's extreme heat captive so that Hor-Aha sat on them without burning his royal backside.

There could be no doubt in anyone's mind: Hor-Aha was a god-king. Long measures of broad linen were strung above his head, their ends lashed to upturned lances spearing the hard sand. Not the slightest breeze disturbed the air and Aha welcomed the shade, sweating profusely nevertheless.

After every slain enemy's uncircumcised penis was cut off and added to Aha's victory pile, the tallying commenced in earnest. Their god-king had won his war by an overwhelming count. The yellow nub in Ogoni's dark realm was theirs for the taking. Of course, they had to find it first in the dense jungles of the unexplored south.

Aha's officers lined up in front of their Supreme Commander. General Barum's lips were stretched in a proud smile. His eyes, however, were not lit by the fires of victory, a deadened look mirroring the coldness in his soul. Colonel Keheb suspected that his general's sadness was not caused by the loss of so many of their fearless troops, for such was the price of war; nor for a love lost. Rather that it stemmed from anger over a betrayal, and from shame for his weakness. As Keheb lined up next to his superior, he hoped that the great warrior would triumph over the inner battle raging in his intrepid heart.

To Keheb's left, Colonel Mekh's slight build no longer belied this sinewy warrior's extraordinary capabilities. His *Ostrich Riders* had distinguished themselves bringing about the

342

turning point of the final battle. Next to them stood General Teyhab who had resumed command over the battalions from his *Third Army of Ptah*. His men had collected valuable weapons from the fallen, released the half-dead from their misery, and carried those who could be expected to live into the tents of the healer-priests.

Teyhab's Aide-de-camp, Colonel Mayhah, stood stiffly to one side. Despite the festive mood, the young officer lacked his usual bravado. When Hor-Aha's look rested upon him with knotted brows, Mayhah feared a latent reprimand about the missing fourth river escort. To his regret the priest Seka was no longer alive to be blamed for the unfortunate mishap. He feared the *Ka*-priest was the luckier of the two of them.

Behind the high-ranking officers crowded eager watch captains, proud brigade and company commanders, unflinching standard bearers, stocky squad leaders, the surviving runners, and the thousands of battle-fatigued warriors spilling into the vast cauldron of their bloody victory.

To the right of the King, Tasar and Tuthmose headed the contingent of exhausted priests. Their continuous attendance to the unending wounded had drained the last of their energies. Only their place of honor in this celebration half restored them. Chief Senmut and his expert Bowmen were lined up to the other side of Hor-Aha's throne representing the military power of the Temple of Ptah.

Closely guarded, leather shackles on his ebony wrists and ankles, stood the King of Nobatia, his nakedness accentuated by the bitter shame of his defeat. Several of his dark warriors, suspected to be officers, where two-tied with *Kush* mercenaries. While the lighter-skinned men had mourned their slain Ruler, they now bemoaned their own unsavory fate.

Barum glanced furtively in the direction of the captives. There was no sign of the tall tribesman, or his beautiful companion. Apparently, the Chief of Temple Bowmen had executed his orders without delay.

Apart from the assembly stood a broad-shouldered soldier, a great battle axe poised in mid-air as if to complete his strike at the slightest nod from the King. Who among them was condemned to die?

Colonel Mekh stepped up and proffered Hor-Aha a large scroll which he had carried from Grand General Makari's garrison all the way through the desert. Aha had dictated it after the council meeting, knowing that his royal decree would prove of significance only after victory.

Trumpets sounded four times. General Barum advanced from the row of officers and raised his arms.

"Hail, Hor-Aha!"

"Hail, Supreme Commander!"

"Hail, Fighting Falcon!"

"Victory! Victory! Victory!"

The salutes rushed along the lines of men in great waves as their triumphant cries undulated over the vast plain.

Aha raised his hands. Again, trumpets sounded. The jubilations of the multitudes were replaced by expectant silence. Only the distant baying of the pack donkeys pierced the stillness, as the air above rushed through the wings of the vultures circling their way toward their human banquet.

Aha stood up and ceremoniously broke his own seal on the tattered scroll, unrolling it slowly. Once again, trumpets blared admonishing the massed warriors, and General Barum raised his hands high over his head to command prolonged silence. At long last, their former battlefield seemed to hold its breath in anticipation.

"I, Hor-Aha, Ruler of the Two Lands, Supreme Commander of the four Royal Armies, Descendant of Horus, decree this to be my Authoritative Utterance:

"Through well-fought victory, the lands of the enemies are ours. The Ruler of the Kush lies slain. The King of Nobatia stands humbled here before us, his mercenaries decimated by your bravery.

"Therefore, I bestow the foremost royal commendation upon Grand General Makari who - as you know - remained as Co-Regent in Ineb-hedj. Our swift victory was largely due to his ingenious plans.

"At his own request, Grand General Makari, our Chancellor, is relieved of the burdens of his offices. He is hereby elevated to the *Honorable Lord Makari*, given ownership of the garrison farm which is to be exempt from all royal and temple rents. For the rest of their lives, he and the Lady Beeba shall receive a royal subsidy, along with my eternal gratitude."

Murmurs of assent swelled through the ranks.

"The next commendation goes to Colonel Mekh,

Commander of the Special Forces. From now on, the *Ostrich Riders* are to be known forever as the *Amazing Forces*, a name fittingly chosen by the High Priest of Ptah. Their ranks are to be expanded from among the most able—and the shortest and leanest—of our troops."

As smiles broadened many faces, Aha grinned to himself, amused by his own wit. Again, he raised his hands:

"The *Amazing Forces* shall come under the command of the new *General* Mekh," the King concluded, noticing how Mekh's short frame grew taller by the well-deserved promotion.

"Another, equally important commendation for great valor goes to General Barum, *Commander of the Fourth Army of Amun*. His tireless training near the oasis hastened our victory. From now on, you shall have to address him as *Grand General*, a most deserving successor to the Honorable Lord Makari."

This pleased the crowd to a man. Yet, the King had not assigned Makari's double-post of Chancellor to Barum. Who would be named to that important post? They did not have to guess for long.

"Lord Makari's Aide-de-camp, Colonel Khayn of Ineb-hedj, is hereby appointed as the new *Chancellor.*

"Colonel Keheb, who served most capably under his former General, shall be *General* Keheb, replacing our friend here, Ali el'Barum, as *Commander of the remaining Fourth Army of Amun.*"

Aha held the scroll up close, apparently trying to decipher its own dense words. All eyes hung on his lips and he relished the suspense of the well-timed pause.

"While General Sekesh of the *Second Army of Ra*, and General Saiss of the *First Army of Sutekh* did not participate in the battles directly, they protected the northern borders of the *Two Lands*. Special gifts of royal appreciation shall be awarded to them."

The sun rose higher beating mercilessly upon the assembly.

Aha's next words appeared rushed startling the officers from their expansive glory-wallowing into renewed attention.

"General Teyhab, *Commander of the Third Army of Ptah*, rendered great service far from his Badari headquarters. After each battle, his troops swept the plains. Innumerous enemy shields, maceheads and other useful implements were collected for future use.

"Thus, I am able to establish a *Fifth Army*. Its weaponry will come from those gathered enemy stores. I name as the new *Commander of this Fifth Royal Army...*" Aha paused again and stared at Colonel Mayhah whose face reddened, joyous anticipation threatening to strangle him.

"... I name as Commander of the Fifth: Captain Veni of the *Royal Palace Archers.*"

Eyes bulging, Mayhah forgot to exhale until his chest seemed to explode. Uncontrollable spasms shook his knees. The King held something else in store for him! Something unpleasant. Why otherwise that knotted-brow expression? He hardly heard his King's next words.

"Captain Veni, who is known to only some of you here, has served my Court faithfully for many years. His expert training produced many capable palace guards and archers."

Aha's brows knotted tighter over the bridge of his nose. He, along with everyone who had witnessed the attempt on his life, remembered the unfortunate Chief Archer Pase.

Aha cleared his throat and declared, "Now a *Colonel,* Veni shall take command of the new Fifth Army. An equal number of seasoned men will be drawn from our existing armies, with Veni's headquarters in the Delta town of Pe. There, the Fifth replaces the First as that army has moved to my capital. I hereby designate it as the *Fifth Army of Neit.*"

Aha let his words sink in.

"My greatest commendation, however, goes to all you warriors who fought so valiantly for the Two Lands! Extra rations will be issued tonight with another reward arriving on the supply barges awaiting us at the First Falls."

Word of the added rations spread rapidly among the troops.

"Hail, Hor-Aha!"

"Hail, Supreme Commander!"

Aha licked his dry lips. Ever alert, Tasar handed him a heavy gourd. With an appreciative nod, Aha reached for the bulging bladder and took a satisfying gulp, the tepid wine mixture refreshing him. Those nearest to their King vicariously tasted the ruby liquid wishing some of it would trickle down their own parched throats.

The commendations out of the way, Aha had not finished yet. Unexpectedly forceful, his voice droned over the joyful din. His eyes flashed.

"Two days ago, a despicable assassin, one from among your midst, made an attempt on the life of your King. Thanks to an alert priest, the traitor's worthless carcass has been left for the desert scavengers. I was spared only through the bravery of the *Ka*-priest Seka who gave his life for mine to Osiris; his name shall be inscribed on my *Mastaba* at Abdju.

"And then, there is the one among you who blatantly refused to follow my royal decree! His carelessness endangered the life of your King, as well as that of the High Priest and, worse, the Royal Heiress."

A sudden stillness descended into every man's soul and each quickly searched his conscience for possible trespasses. Thus occupied, none paid heed to the trembling young colonel, steeped in knowing agony. Anticipation was enough to kill Mayhah on the spot. He was short of breath and a sharp pain shot from his chest through his left arm. Cold sweat streamed down his cheeks like gushing tears.

The King's accusing finger sought out Mayhah as he addressed the young colonel's superior.

"General Teyhab, what says your man in his defense!"

The General of the Third recalled Makari's exacting orders. He himself was now at risk to be incriminated by his aide's unpardonable negligence.

"Colonel Mayhah! Colonel!" Teyhab's sharp command pulled the semi-conscious man from his stupor. Mayhah managed a fear-stiffened salute certain now that the man with the battle axe stood there for him.

"Colonel Mayhah, did you conspire with the enemy to ambush certain river travelers?"

The festive mood evaporated as an indignant rumble surged through the stunned ranks.

"I swear upon the *Ka* of my father, I did not, my General," Mayhah croaked, aghast at the accusation not of negligence, but of treason!

"Then tell us, how was it that our garrison's fourth squad never met the pilgrims as I had written in my orders?"

Mayhah's response came almost as a whisper, "Because I never dispatched it, General."

General Teyhab, taken aback by his subordinate's apparent insolence, managed to hiss, "And why, by Horus, not!"

Desperate to explain, Mayhah turned away from his general

toward the Fighting Falcon, his Supreme Commander. The King leaned forward in barely contained rage. At any other time, protocol would not have permitted Mayhah to address his god-king without a higher-ranking intermediary. In the field, however, they were all warriors and did not follow court formalities.

"Great Hor-Aha, I did send a messenger to the temple of Tjeny requesting that its Chief Priest provide that escort, that temple being so much closer to the chosen site. Remember, merciful King," Mayhah's words came with great difficulty, "I was told that we were to protect mere pilgrims from the Temple of Ptah. No mention was ever made of your most divine presence among them. I never knew."

"Seka never said anything about a messenger, or a request. He came aboard my boat at Tjeny, I have you know!" Hor-Aha cut in.

"Could it be possible, my King," Barum interjected, "that Mayhah's messenger never reached his destination? In which case Seka never learned of the Colonel's request."

"This man's disobedience placed my own as well as my daughter's life in mortal danger," Aha accused through Barum's intercession. Thankful that he and Nefret were not harmed, Aha decided to change his mind about the insolent young fool. He would put his condemned head to better use.

"Mayhah: You may not be guilty of premeditated treason. However, you are guilty of inexcusable negligence! Your punishment will be to lead our prisoners south. From far above the Fifth Falls, you will hack your way through the jungle to work in a new mine. You will dig there until your own reclaimed amount of yellow nub equals the weight of your body. Or until you die."

Mayhah swayed, near collapse. Vengeful Montu! Was he not a terrific warrior! To extract gleaming nub for as long as he survived the unknown ghosts of the southern jungles was a far worse fate than instant death by the executioner's clean axe. At last, his knees gave way. He crashed onto the jutting edge of a rock with such force that his head split wide open.

*

It took the army another day to reach the glistening Hapi where they expected the barges to be moored in one of the deeper channels. As the footsore warriors poured over the last

348

low hill, they saw the barges swing in mid-stream. The rivermen and crew had unloaded the supplies and stock-piled them on higher ground. Sacks of dried fruit bulged, mountains of waterfowl waited to be plucked and roasted, and neatly stacked grids with thousands of bread loaves perfumed the air while heaps of dried animal dung on the cooking fires stung the nostrils. One bellied amphora after another drew the parched troops irresistibly. Soon, freshly brewed beer and Delta wine slackened the communal thirst.

*

Those who had distinguished themselves during battle with particular valor were selected to share the King's triumphant entry into Nekhen by barge. As further reward, this honor was to be followed by a delirious week in the old city. The men expected tender welcomes by young maidens. In their arms, boastful recounts would be topped only by their manly prowess.

For Barum, the final departure was bittersweet. While one fourth of his troops were to journey back to Ineb-hedj to join the new Fifth Army, the rest was to stay behind. He himself, of course, was to sail on to the capital to assume his administrative position in the Fighting Falcon's court as the new Grand General.

Tasar and Tuthmose were also invited to accompany the King to Nekhen where their victorious return was to signal the beginning of the *Festival of Opet*.

On a separate raft, Senmut and his Bowmen guarded the roped King of Nobatia and several of his staff. Tasar had managed to obtain Aha's permission to ferry the ebony-skinned Ogoni to Nekhen's Temple of Horus for Ramose's experiments.

At last, everyone selected found his place on the huge barges. The moorings were slipped and the current caught the convoy speeding it downriver toward Nekhen.

Aha settled himself in as comfortably as he could. He looked forward to a quiet time for reflection. While he had not doubted victory, he was relieved that Montu had been on his side. With a shiver, he recalled his supplication to Ptah. 'Oh, great Ptah' he had frothed in fear, 'anything, just let me be victorious...' If Montu had watched over the generals, Ptah certainly had answered his own fervent prayers.

After wasted years of vile suspicions against his beloved first queen and heart-wrenching years of denying his young daughter, Aha found himself at peace. He would take Mayet's willful girl under his own tutelage to do her royal heritage proud. 'Ah, my lovely Mayet, why did I take so long to know that she was your special gift to me? I brought her home to Nekhen, to the city of your birth.'

As a new beginning, he and Nefret would preside over his court together. Aha looked forward to teach her how to rule, and she could show him how to be her father at long last. Just as he would combine his life with Nefret's, he would combine his two crowns into one. Ramose could design a Double Crown to signify unification of the Upper and Lower Regions, his dynasty's legacy. *Opet* was his opportunity to invite the local nomarchs to a feast to ensure their renewed loyalty. He and Nefret would get to know them. And their eligible sons. A prince from Nekhen in the family would cement his power in the southern regions nicely.

The victorious Fighting Falcon suddenly frowned at an ugly reminder. Once back in Ineb-hedj he would have to deal with the Vizier.

* * *

Chapter Thirty-Seven

Amma hurried toward a well-lit wing of the hastily rejuvenated palace when she met up with Dubar's new slave. He reminded her of a rodent; all furtive scraping and protruding teeth; beady eyes darting every which way.

"I need to find the Tax Collector!" she hissed and dragged the bewildered man by the arm rushing headlong through empty passages. Suddenly, Amma skittered to a halt. She must allow Ramose and Beir time to reach the temple with the unconscious Princess after which they had to gather some priests and return to the palace wing, as if summoned for the first time.

"Where have you been?" She questioned the squirming man who tried in vain to loosen her grip on him.

"I - I had to report to Tesh, the Tax Collector. By orders of the Vizier," the slave stammered.

"Then you know where to find him. Lead the way." Amma's step increased again.

*

Tesh was elated. City nobles who usually shunned him were not offended by his hasty dinner invitation, and now clamored for his favors assuming that, as the warden of the palace, he had access to the King. They dropped their names into Tesh's ears like generous offerings onto an altar.

Tesh stood up, ready to pronounce a boastful toast when the doors to the great audience hall were suddenly flung open. An ample woman burst in followed by a slave. The agitated palace guards crowded in behind the unlikely pair clamoring how they were unable to prevent the lamentable disturbance.

"What is the meaning of this?" Tesh commanded, wine cup half raised, eyes widening in contrived innocence. Obviously, the old witch had discovered her Royal Princess—presumably quite dead. Tesh hoped further that his poisoned wine had duly stilled his assassin's tongue.

"A terrible tragedy, your Honor! You must come at once," Amma wailed and fell to her swollen knees.

"What are you babbling about, old woman? Stand up and justify your bursting in like this," Tesh ordered, veiling the triumph in his eyes. He looked at al-Saqqara's slave and hoped that the Vizier had not taken the unappealing man into his confidences and revealed Tesh's own final role in the apparent tragedy. Best to eliminate this possible threat as well.

"Both the royal children have been slain, your Honor," Amma cried.

What was the old fool saying? Tesh stared at her and croaked, "What do you mean 'both'?" Had the assassin been carried away by his own zeal or had he been surprised by the Prince while he stabbed the girl? For a moment, Tesh was too stunned to move.

His guests were not. The dining hall reverberated with tumultuous shock. Chairs toppled, drinking cups clanged to the floor. The crowd surged toward the exit eager to hasten to the grisly scene.

When Tesh thought it best to take the lead, Amma was already ahead of the curious pack, her pace so driven that no one could press past her. Tesh, with Nekhen's nobles, reached the royal suites at the same time as Ramose approached from the opposite corridor that connected the palace with the temple.

Six of his priests were carrying three leather-laced stretchers, two for the dead royal children, one for the assassin. With Beir in the lead, more than a dozen temple guards gripped their short swords ready to strike out at the first suspicious move. Much to everyone's awe, Ramose wore his purple robe. In his left hand, he carried his tall staff. He appeared detached, unapproachable.

The two factions surged together in front of Dubar's suite, in the middle of the royal accommodations.

With his hands raised high, Ramose called out, "Halt!" His command produced an almost comical effect.

The first row of the curious stopped at once. Like a herd of stampeding antelopes before a dangerous river crossing, the onward-pressing city nobles bumped unceremoniously into the broad rumps of those now face to face with the priests. At last, the unwieldy mass jostled to a halt, with Tesh and Amma in the fore.

"Great woe has befallen us!" Ramose lifted his staff high above his head, his sing-song voice reminiscent of a temple service. In the light of the torches, his shadow loomed with foreboding over the hushed crowd.

"Tax Collector! The King's Steward informed me of a tragedy. Your presence tells me that you, too, have been apprised. You and I must bear witness. All you others, wait out here! No one is to leave."

Ramose looked at Beir who understood and threw the door to the King's large suite wide open. Tesh swallowed hard. He had no choice but to enter behind the High Priest, fighting the distinct sense of walking into a trap. While Beir kept watch at the outer door, Ramose and Tesh stepped through into the inner chamber.

This was the first time Ramose actually saw Dubar whose body was covered by a robe strangely resembling his own. Through a long tear, he noticed a glistening stain spreading onto the floormats. For a moment, he puzzled over the unusual draping that clung to the dead Prince. Then he pulled it off the lifeless form.

The two men recoiled, unprepared for the distasteful sight of an ugly mouth that gaped, filled with a curdled black mass, half of the dark tongue hanging down the jutting chin. Dubar's arms were flung aside in a vain struggle to fill his lungs. His legs were spread wide, the short kilt bunched around his thick waist. Even in death, Dubar's young manhood lay splayed disproportionately large in a flaccid reproach of his futile youth.

"It is the Prince," Tesh confirmed the obvious. He tried to suppress his disgust at the indecently displayed body. "He must have choked on his own blood," he mumbled. Glancing sideways, he mumbled, "What about the Princess?"

Beir, who ceded his watch to a temple guard and had joined the two men, motioned toward the open courtyard. "The Princess was struck down in her own suite. We can cross into her sleeping chamber from out there."

"I know that," Tesh grumbled wishing that the Steward had remained with the others. He disliked the meddling servant of the King. *The King! By the New Harvest Rent! Where was the King?*

Tesh grabbed Ramose by his robe, "This is the King's suite, not the Prince's! Where is the King?" Alarmed by the answer his question might evoke he fell silent. Had he become entangled in something larger than he had bargained for?

Ramose turned toward the paling Tax Collector, reclaiming his robe from the frozen man's grasp. This was not the time to disclose that the battles surely raged by now. He needed a few precious hours to decide upon the course of action to stave off further calamity.

"I was conducting a private worship for the King when Beir interrupted us," he said. "After the King was told the terrible truth, he went into seclusion at the temple, awaiting his dead children. We need to transfer their bodies immediately to Rahetep's embalming chambers where the death masks can be poured before their features stiffen."

Ramose looked down at Dubar. It would be difficult to take a decent impression from the distorted face. But it was not the boy's identity that worried him. He would have to obtain Nefret's impression so that her life-like mask could be placed securely over Zeina's face. Other than that, deception would be easy. Both girls' hair was the same blue-black hue. Their young bodies were of equal height and weight. Ramose thought briefly of Nefret's odd birthmark. He could work around that, too. The royal bodies were to be wrapped in linen and packed in natron so that the salt's preservatives kept them from decomposing. After that, Aha's supposed children would be ferried downriver to Ineb-hedj.

Despite the vagueness of his final plans, Ramose drew one inevitable conclusion. As far as the King, his court and the populace were concerned, both royal children had been assassinated. Prince Dubar and the Princess Nefret were dead.

"We have to hurry," Ramose urged and pushed past Beir to lead the way across the courtyard. In the women's suite they found Zeina where she fell, her face still veiled. The assassin lay nearby. Tesh prayed that he be dead by now.

"One of your servants?" Ramose faced Tesh. Towering over the Tax Collector, his blue eyes bored into the panic-stricken man.

"I never saw the man before," Tesh lied.

"You are awfully quick to draw such a conclusion," Beir

said. "It is dark in here and you have not even seen his face." He moved closer to the Tax Collector.

"I swear, I never laid eyes upon this vermin," Tesh stammered. He wanted to escape the stifling heat of the smallish chamber and hoped that the High Priest would accept the theory of a lone assassin. When he heard that Ramose wanted to transfer the royal bodies to the temple, he was relieved. This meant he himself would not have to face the King. At least not yet. Suddenly, a thought struck him. In his mounting panic, he did not weigh the consequences of his next suggestion.

"What about the Prince's slave? The one who came with him from Ineb-hedj? I did not trust the sly man from the outset." Tesh's innuendo was not lost on the High Priest.

"What about that slave?" Ramose looked sharply at the Tax Collector. "Why was he allowed on the Royal Bark to attend to the Prince? I don't recall ever seeing him at court."

Beir's answer was quick. "He was assigned to the Prince just before we sailed. The Vizier sent him after the Prince's regular attendant was taken ill. Dubar seemed to like the fellow. Frankly, Ramose, I was grateful. The boy exhibited insufferable mood swings on the river and only the new slave seemed to be able to calm him down."

"Where is he now?" Ramose asked, alarmed.

"Outside with Amma," Beir replied.

"He was with the old woman when she burst into my dining hall," Tesh confirmed. "We must question him immediately as to why he left his master's side this evening."

"No!" Beir countered.

Ramose turned to him and raised his eyebrows.

"I mean, the man was probably out looking for a late snack for Dubar," Beir hastened to explain, color spreading from his powerful neck onto his face.

"Perhaps," Ramose said and added, "By the way, where was Safaga during all that time?" And where were you, my lusty friend, he thought.

Beir dropped his eyes which told Ramose what he suspected.

"I cannot tell you how mortified we were. We assumed that Zeina and Nefret would stay together in their room."

"We'll talk about that later," Ramose said. Beir understood

that he should say nothing more in front of Tesh who looked at them wide-eyed, wondering if he could turn the servants' absences to his own advantage.

"I want Dubar's slave taken to the temple," Ramose said. He would deal with the man alone; and most assuredly explore the intriguing fact that the Vizier had engaged an unknown servant for such a long journey.

The waiting nobles stared through the half-open door of the King's suite in breathless anticipation. When the three men emerged behind them from the women's suite, the crowd turned and surged toward them. Questions were thrust upon Ramose like sharp lances. He raised his hands to quiet the babbling mob.

Beir's eyes sought out the new slave who was standing next to Amma. When he heard Ramose order his temple guards to take the Vizier's man into custody, he shrank back a pace.

The surprised man burst into terrified shrieks. "The Tax Collector, he is the one you want. He is behind this! I swear!" He was dragged off by the guards, his jumbled protestations echoing back toward the crowd.

Ramose motioned to his remaining guards. Tesh, who visibly blanched when the slave blurted out his accusation, was surrounded and led away as well. Once more, the now speechless city nobles bore witness to desperate protestations from one of their own, until muffled sounds offered no further information. A guard must have clamped a rough hand over Tesh's mouth.

The fetid air pooling in Beir's lungs escaped him with a whistling breath.

*

"I am on fire," Nefret moaned. She struggled against the hands that held her down as she tried to claw at the salve-drenched cloth covering her stinging face. "It hurts! My face is burning!"

"Calm yourself, child. The aloe's sap will soothe your skin."

Nefret stopped her thrashing and listened to the kindly voice. "Badar?" she whimpered. "Badar. Help me. What has happened? I cannot see."

"You are in the *House of Life*, my child. Try to lie still. You cannot see because your face is bandaged. Ramose will be here soon." Badar's old heart ached for the distraught girl.

He had lifted her from her mother's womb, and watched over her and guarded her, and cared for her more than she would ever know. Now she was beyond his help, her crime too severe. Its punishment, by law, was death. By hiding her in this isolated temple building, against all reason, Badar hoped that his brilliant successor would not have to act contrary to his beliefs, against their ancient teachings, against the stringent laws of *Ma'at*. Nor against the King, or the *Kenbet*. The old priest shook his head. In the end, the gods would judge Ramose.

"Where is Amma?" Nefret sobbed. She curled herself into a small bundle. "I want Amma."

"Nefret, we are here. Dokki and I," Safaga said.

Nefret sat up and, unseeing, stretched out her arms toward the voice, "Safaga! Hold me. You too, Dokki." The young women held on tight, each drawing consolation from the nearness of the other two. Each still in shock, terrified about their future.

Ramose slipped in unnoticed.

"Thank you, Badar. It is done," he whispered to his old mentor. "The wax imprint was perfect enough for the yellow nub to be poured. Here is the finished mask. It needs to be polished, of course, before it can be fused onto Zeina's face. Rahetep has started her embalming rites."

"Ramose ..." Meant as a hopeful call, it was a muffled whimper.

"Ah, my child, you have awakened."

Nefret struggled to free herself from Safaga and Dokki.

"Embalming rites? I am not dead," she cried. When no one answered, she sank back onto the bed. Had Ramose turned against her? Surely, he must loathe her for what she had done. Nefret sobbed out loud.

"Safaga, take the bandages off her face now," Badar said. "Be gentle," he reminded. "The wax was hotter than we anticipated. We were in a hurry."

Safaga's nimble fingers worked quickly on Nefret as Dokki caught the pieces of cloth freeing her mistress's young face from its imprisonment.

While Safaga unwrapped Nefret's bandages and removed the salve-stiffened eye patches, Ramose laid the death mask onto a stand. Then he and Badar went into a corner of the small room conferring with each other. The girls could not hear what was said. Still, they sensed grave concern in the priests' muffled voices.

Nefret blinked a few times until she saw the outlines of her slaves, and the two priests beyond. She tested her cheeks with her fingertips. The burning sensation had ceased but her skin felt tight. 'Wax too hot' indeed, she thought. How dare they do this to me! Instead of voicing her royal displeasure, as she would have done a day ago, she looked at her slave.

"Thank you, Safaga. I feel much better. You, too, Dokki. Thank you." Her voice was small and filled with anguish. Safaga and Dokki hugged her again and Nefret welcomed their comforting caresses, despite the pain on her burnt cheeks. Looking past her women, she spied the mask. While a perfect image of her features, Nefret did not see the peace pervading it. All she realized was that she was no longer considered among the living.

"But I am alive!" she cried. She stared into the hollow eyes of the gleaming mask. "I am alive! You cannot do this. If you bury Zeina with my mask, my *Ba* will never find me when it returns to earth!"

"Shhh, child," Ramose soothed. He returned to the daybed and took her into his arms. "Quiet now. A *Ba* always knows who it belonged to. It will return to you as your *Ba-bird*, with your own spirit, not that of Zeina's."

Nefret buried herself deep in Ramose's broad chest. His left arm around the sobbing girl, Ramose waved at the others with his right, "Safaga, Dokki. Go with the Venerable Badar. He will show you the *House of Life*. I wish to speak with Nefret."

"Yes, Ramose." The slaves stroked Nefret's hair and patted her slender arms as if for the last time. At last, they left Ramose alone with the unfortunate girl.

*

"Nefret, my child." Ramose looked at her.

The blue eyes, those same ones in which she so often had spied a twinkle even when he had scolded her, now looked pained and troubled. Her tears flowed again. A deep sadness seared her very soul.

"Nefret, my child," Ramose said again, his voice choked with emotion. "By your own admission, you have committed the gravest of crimes against *Ma'at*, and even I cannot save you from punishment. While your sin cannot be undone, the gods have shown me a way to spare your life. However, that means you can no longer be yourself. Do you understand? As far as everyone is concerned, you have been killed by an assassin."

"Is Zeina then to be buried in my *Mastaba*, forever thought to be the Royal Heiress? And what about her *Ka*? How will Osiris know that is not mine?"

"When Zeina is buried in your stead, Osiris will welcome her as herself. Your *Ka*, just as your *Ba*, belongs to you until you die."

"And after that?"

"Your *Akh*, your spirit of the sky, will travel through the *Field of Rushes* never to return to earth. Only then will you be transformed into a true *Akhu*, a Venerable One. Before this can be achieved, however, you have to find atonement for your misdeeds, or your *Ba* must return to this earth many times."

Nefret waited for Ramose to continue but he followed some thoughts he could not share with her. After a prolonged silence, she asked, "Ramose? Please tell me. When is Father coming back?"

"Soon," he answered. "Soon, my child."

A small flicker of hope stirred within her. "Ramose. You must let me speak with him. Please."

"That, my dear, will be impossible. The King is to be told that both you and your brother were killed by the assassin."

"Why?" Nefret grew agitated. She could not fathom how Ramose, who loved her since the day she was born, could deny her this last grasp at life. "Ramose! My Father is the King. He can overrule the Vizier and all his judges," she pleaded. "He can overrule you, if he chooses. And he will when we tell him the truth. Believe me, Ramose! He will!"

"True. He can overrule anyone. He cannot, however, usurp the will of the gods. I must abide by the *Oracle of Isis*. Or we are all doomed."

"Why, then, can you not speak to Isis again? You are the High Priest! Tell her that her *Oracle* was wrong!"

Ramose shook his head at the precious girl's desperate attempts to escape from her tragic destiny. "Nefret. It has been willed. The only way I can keep you alive is for you to flee from here."

She stared at him, aghast.

Ramose's voice was devoid of earlier sentiment. "Beir will take you across the Hapi to an isolated landing downriver. From there you can reach the Wadi Hammamat. It leads to the Crystal Sea. A willing sea captain is to be engaged to take you north to the Wadj, the Great Green, which lies beyond the many-tongued mouth of the Hapi. There, my dear, you shall board another vessel that will take you to a foreign island. To safety."

"For how long?" She asked, her twitter as tentative as that of a newly-hatched songbird.

Ramose took his time. "For ever."

"For ever? Ramose! No!" Nefret gasped and bowed her head. Tears streamed down her tortured cheeks. "Can Amma come with me?" It was but a whisper of hope.

"No, child. Not Amma. Not this time."

"What will happen to her? She is so old, and Hent hates her."

Nefret's sudden concern for her old nurse touched Ramose so that he almost wavered from his harsh decision. "Amma will be permitted to retire into the sanctity of the new temple, downriver. Do you remember? Where we spent our first night. I hope he comes back from the war alive."

"Who?"

"Tuthmose. He will take good care of her."

"What about Dokki? Let her come with me, at least."

"No, it has to be Safaga. Dokki's dark skin betrays her. She might be thought an enemy. Particularly now, when everyone is on the alert for *Noba* deserters. She will stay at the *House of Life* to serve Badar. He will treat her with much kindness."

Nefret sank deeper into herself. Was there no escape from this, except the one Ramose planned for her. So be it then, she thought. *If I follow his counsel now there may be a way out later.* She looked at Ramose, her eyes brightening.

"You said Beir is to accompany us and that our trek will bring us close to the capital? As the Royal Steward, he could smuggle me into the palace so I could talk to Father back in Ineb-hedj. Beir is devoted to him, you know."

"Yes, I know," Ramose sighed and a sudden hardness edged his jaw. The Steward's loyalty to his King caused some concern in choosing him as Nefret's guide. "Beir will take you as far as the Wadi Hammamat. Then, I think it best for him to rejoin the Royal Funeral Bark at Dendara."

"Are you saying that Safaga and I are to be left on our own?" Nefret's eyes widened in disbelief.

"Of course not, my dear. I shall send a second guide to join you with provisions for the rest of your long trek. He will have donkeys and enough of the yellow nub to assure a comfortable life for you and Safaga on that island."

"Whom will you choose?" Nefret asked.

"I am not certain yet. We need a few more days to gather everything. But you will leave a few hours after midnight tonight. You need to travel light to get away from here quickly. One of my temple boats has been readied. I myself shall sail upriver to meet the war barges. I think it best that the King hears the news from me."

The High Priest and the young woman remained silent for a while. They knew in their hearts that nothing they might add would make a difference now. Nefret had to come to terms with a fate decided by the gods. Secretly, she believed that it was her lifelong mentor, this all-powerful High Priest of Ptah, who had decided against her. Not his gods. Not Isis. He, Ramose; the surrogate father she loved. Tears of frustration stung her eyes. Her heart ached for an embrace, but she no longer craved Ramose's consoling arms. Her longing was for Tasar.

"Tell me, child, what really happened in the King's suite? How much of it was Dubar's doing?" Ramose hoped she might grasp the proffered reed so that he could absolve her *Ba*.

"It does not matter any longer," Nefret said and shook herself to dispel the image of Dubar's snarling face. "As you said, the Royal Heiress of the Two Lands is dead."

* * *

Chapter Thirty-Eight

Ramose shook his head.

There was such sadness in the eyes of the High Priest that Rahetep was overwrought with compassion for this noblest servant of the gods. Still, he could not agree with him.

"Rahetep," Ramose implored, "if I ever needed your help, it is now. You must assist me in Nefret's escape. You are the only one I can trust. Badar too, of course. However, you are the only one who can gather provisions and donkeys without arousing suspicion."

"I have never questioned your decisions, Ramose. But I must admit that I do not understand this. Why is it necessary to send the poor girl into an uncertain future? Possibly her death?" After a moment, Rahetep continued his supplication. "From what you have told me, Nefret killed Dubar in self-defense. We administered a cleansing potion to the vile assassin, and I should be able to question him soon. Tesh, too, is under guard, as is Dubar's slave. Listen to me! I believe Nefret is quite safe for now."

Ramose remained silent knowing that Rahetep was not finished.

The older priest continued, "Tesh has gravely implicated the Vizier, as has the slave. There shouldn't be others lurking about. Why then, do you need to send the Princess on such a dangerous journey? We can keep her at the *House of Life* until the King returns. Has she not pleaded with you to bring her case before him? Let Aha decide his daughter's fate. It is his right; you ought not to take that from him. He is her father!"

Ramose looked at Rahetep with such sorrow in his blue eyes that the older priest stopped his impassioned plea. Then, once more, the Chief Priest tried to reach past the cold remoteness of this venerated High Priest by adding, "Why, Ramose? I ask you one last time: Why?" Spent, Rahetep thought it ought to be Ramose pleading for his royal ward's life.

Ramose remained adamant. "Rahetep, if anyone understands me, it should be you. Need I remind you that the stringent laws of *Ma'at* forbid murder for whatever reason. At best, the King could permit Nefret to take her own life. And only following a demeaning public trial."

"Aha would not let it come to that," Rahetep countered still hoping to change Ramose's mind.

"Al-Saqqara would leave him no choice. More importantly, I, the *High Priest of Ptah*, must abide by the *Oracle* no matter how much I personally grieve. I feel I have been thrown into in an abyss. I love my child."

Rahetep's ears picked up the nuance. Years ago, court rumors had reached even remote Nekhen. It was of no consequence now. Except that, if true, he felt that it should have turned Ramose into an even stauncher proponent to seek the King's pardon for the unfortunate girl.

For the first time, Ramose admitted to himself that deep within his heart he believed differently than his unforgiving judgment demanded. Perhaps he did owe Rahetep an explanation. He forced himself to utter, "If I attempt to change the course of her fate, great turmoil will result for all of us. The King would be unseated and, with even graver consequences for our Two Lands, this will severely damage the unique power our priesthood has achieved at long last. We have worked too hard to let anything happen to it now."

Ramose paused. He was drained from the unaccustomed confrontation.

Rahetep could imagine the pain tearing at the High Priest's heart. With empathy for his troubled friend he said quietly, "I guess you have no choice."

*

The rhythmic splashing of the oars intermingled with the gurgle of the river's current. The palace guards had been told that the High Priest planned to go upriver to meet the King. Thus, they paid little heed when two temple boats pulled away shortly after midnight.

With hurried precision, the vessels maneuvered into midstream where they clustered. The flat-topped falucca caught the current, its three passengers, swathed in tribal robes, huddled closely together on deck. The second, baldachined vessel, however, turned south after its sails were hoisted. Several of its crew kept at the oars to assist the listless breeze to guide their craft upriver while one of the deckhands poled for dangerous shallows. The *Kariy* was empty now as Ramose sat on deck his eyes following the vanishing first falucca on its rush downriver. Sadness, greater than any he had ever known, pierced his well-guarded heart.

How could he let her go like this? Never to see her again, not even sixteen yet. Ramose sat partially hidden under his baldachin, just as he had during the journey toward Nekhen, only infinitely more perturbed. A handful of young priests were chosen to accompany him on this unhappy pilgrimage upriver. There was no telling when they would encounter the King's barges. Ramose dreaded having to face a victory-swollen Aha to tell him of the deaths of his two children.

After Ramose gave Nefret drugged wine to allow her at least a few hours of dreamless sleep, he had grasped his crystal and forced himself into a deep trance to attempt to find a less condemning interpretation to the *Oracle's* devastating judgment of his young ward. Isis never reappeared however hard he clenched his fist around the cutting edges of his crystal. No matter how urgently he beseeched the benign Mother of Horus, what appeared in front of his inner eye was a disturbing image of the vicious Seth, Isis' menacing other offspring.

Lulled by the rhythmic splashing of the oars, Ramose consulted his anxious heart. Should he have given in to Nefret's tearful pleading? Perhaps he should have entrusted her fate to Aha's stirring paternal concern. If he was wrong in sending her away, it would be he who had condemned her. Not the King. Not the powerful Vizier, nor the judges of the *Kenbet*. Nor Isis. But he, Prince Rama, the man who was her sworn protector.

Ramose sought solace in the cool sleekness of his crystal. It reminded him of the protective *Eye of Horus* he had thrust upon Tasar. He hoped that the young priest had not lost the precious object. Nor his life! He would know within the next few hours when his decision would become irreversible once he told the King of her supposed death. Then, Nefret's banishment would be final.

Despite his doubts, Ramose deeply believed that he had been given the divine right to choose this young sinner's penitence. *You are not only to protect the innocent, but are to judge and punish the driven,'* Isis had said. Had he followed her edict with wisdom? Or had he been too intent on protecting - What? The priesthood's sanctity? His own *Ba?* His blue eyes overflowed with a bitter river as he wept for Mayet's child.

*

"Boats ahead! Ahoy there! Identify yourselves," the pilot of the front barge called out. "Boats ahead," the mate of the second vessel took up the chant. The temple boat slid alongside the huge barge and was lashed against its planks. Tasar saw the *Kariy* and at once recognized the tall man beneath the baldachin.

"It is Ramose," he cried. Tuthmose echoed the younger priest's excitement. To cover his exuberance, he said, "Ramose brings us the blessings of the gods."

Closer to them now, the High Priest's serious expression caused them to refrain from further hailing of welcome. The two priests realized that he could well be the bearer of unpleasant tidings.

Aha, seated in the midst of his officers, stood up. If he sensed an unwelcome reason for Ramose's interception, he did not wish to learn of it too soon. Still triumphant from his great victory, he anticipated their grand entrance into Nekhen where cheering crowds would line the Royal Road. With contrived bravado, he called to the much smaller boat, "High Priest, did the gods tell you of our great victory? The enemy lies slain, once and for all. I even brought you a gift; a defeated king. Have you come to rejoice with us?"

Ramose did not reply. Neither did he smile. His cheeks hollow with grief, he kept his blue gaze fixed on the King and permitted two priests to assist him to clamber aboard the barge. Once before his King, a great sob rose from Ramose's throat. He sank to his knees.

The stunned barge occupants stared at the kneeling figure. Never before had the *High Priest of Ptah* humbled himself before anyone, except the gods. Cold foreboding clawed at all.

"I bear you great woe, most gracious King."

Aha thought of Hent. Had word from Ineb-hedj reached

Nekhen while he marched against the enemy? Had she succumbed to a difficult birth, like Mayet? Or did his third child by his second queen not survive the birthing?

"I beg for privacy, great King. It is imperative," Ramose whispered, still on his knees.

"Well," Aha said, "I don't think we will get much of that here on deck. The cabin in the hold below will have to do."

"Thank you, great Hor-Aha," Ramose replied with formality, his head bowed to his chest.

"But to reach it, you will have to get back on your feet, my dear Ramose," Aha attempted to lighten the barb of impending doom.

"I beg you, my King, let my two priests bear witness to my words," Ramose asked. Without waiting for Aha's consent he nodded to Tuthmose and Tasar to follow them below.

*

"Cursed Osiris! You greediest of gods! Did I not offer you enough young blood from the battlefields?

"Contemptible Isis! You caused this. Your *Oracle* guided the vile assassin's hand!

"A curse on all of you merciless vengeful gods! To make me victorious, only to hold horrendous grief in store for me!" Aha thought his heart would burst. He hid his face in his hands and tears seeped through his trembling fingers. "Seth! You misbegotten son of Isis! You took my children for no reason!"

Ramose did nothing to temper Aha's blasphemies. Nor could he soothe the terrible agony his words wrought for his King. He waited for Aha to cry himself out. Only then did he tell him the full story—the way it was to be told from then on.

After Ramose finished, he did not give Aha an opportunity to dwell on his great losses. He outlined funeral arrangements and spoke of glorious burials to be held at Saqqara. The present *Hapi* would be slaughtered as soon as they returned to Ineb-hedj; with the great beast to be buried and only its enormous horns were to protrude from the sand in memory of the royal children. Was the King listening?

"Buried at Saqqara," Aha mused. Suddenly, he thundered, "Al-Saqqara!" His fist hit the top of a nearby stand splitting the small piece in two. A feverish gleam flamed in his eyes. "He is behind it all! I did not tell you this, Ramose. That disgusting caricature had the audacity to suggest that he marry Nefret! Of course, I rebuked him. What impertinence, I told him! Little did I dream that my scorn would exact such merciless revenge."

Ramose long harbored his own suspicions against the Vizier which were confirmed through the questioning of Dubar's new slave and the whimpering Tax Collector. It was unfortunate that he had left Nekhen before the revived assassin was coherent. Rahetep should be interrogating him just about now.

"Al-Saqqara shall rot for this," was the King's solemn promise.

The two men gauged each other as if to force the other to reveal himself. Ramose could hear the hammer of his heart. The royal siblings had been under his care. By conjecture, the King might hold him accountable for their dreadful deaths. Instead of asking for his head, though, Aha had just offered up the Vizier's.

Tasar, who stood by silently with Tuthmose, cleared his throat, "I beg forgiveness, Hor-Aha." The young priest hesitated. "This was why I instinctively, and admittedly wrongly, killed the messenger after the attack on you. I remembered the wording the Vizier used in his text to the Tax Collector. I could not control my fears for the Princess Nefret that I struck out. Had I only voiced my suspicions then. And now...," Tasar's throat constricted from the helpless pain within him. He was unable to continue. The temperature in the cabin rose not only from the sun. The air became stifling. Tasar swayed, feeling faint.

Ramose steadied the distraught youth. "We know, Tasar. You revered her as much as we all did."

Tuthmose, meanwhile, formed his own opinion. How much did Ramose know, he wondered, about Tasar's youthful feelings for the Princess. To most, he was a promising surgeon-priest. Tuthmose, however, saw in him a healthy youth, in the prime of urging manhood. Much older, and much more in touch with the natural world, the First Mooring priest had sensed this from the beginning with his suspicions confirmed when he saw the youth's face after striking the Archer down. Such pain did not come from loyalty alone. It had to have surged up from frenzied fear for someone deeply loved.

No one voiced much grief over Dubar's demise and the King himself merely cursed the gods for having taken a son from him.

"Hor-Aha," Ramose said, addressing his King officially. "The worthless Tax Collector admitted to a subversive group called *The Usurpers of the Two Crowns*. I believe that Ebu al-Saqqara might be its surreptitious leader. Apparently, our ambitious Vizier has long entertained visions of proclaiming himself King one day."

"Preposterous!" Aha shouted and shook his fist at Ramose who retreated in shock at the ferocity in Aha's voice. Aha caught himself and added with more dignity, "I am not referring to your assumptions, Ramose. The thought of that man to fancy himself King when he carries not an ounce of royal blood is what I find preposterous. So you don't think that his heinous crime was committed solely due to my refusal."

"No. I believe it was a long planned coup," Ramose said.

"Then there must be others."

"Tesh is still turning himself inside out. The man started with petty thievery until his dishonesty was uncovered by the Vizier's scribes."

Ramose thought of the Tax Collector's admission of stealing whole silos full of emmer wheat. "Al-Saqqara apparently offered to save Tesh's reputation if he turned *Usurper*. Now, the Tax Collector is trying to save himself once more by naming others of this treasonous group. Before I left, he so much as admitted to having recruited one of Barum's minor officers."

"A Watch Captain by the name of Nebah," Aha snorted. "I got to know him only too well." When he saw the question in Ramose's eyes, he added, "Tuthmose will tell you all about his role in this."

Aha's eyes turned harder still. "We must build a watertight case against al-Saqqara. Not a word to anyone. After we return to Ineb-hedj we will let the despicable man gloat in his hollow victory - before he meets his miserable death." The King's eyes tightened into vicious slits and his tongue darted out to moisten his tight lips as he briefly savored the imagined taste of al-Saqqara's blood.

"What do you propose to do with him?" Tuthmose ventured.

"I? I do not propose to do anything. I shall leave that pleasurable task to *Nekhbet*. Let the vulture-goddess be al-

Saqqara's executioner."

They shuddered at the thought of ravenous birds tearing strips of flesh from the Vizier. The only sound in the stifling cabin was the gurgle of the water as it rushed past the planking.

When Aha spoke again his voice was firm, devoid of all emotion. "Ramose, you said Beir found my children. Who else was there?"

Ramose swallowed hard. His next words could spell disaster and he answered with great caution, "My King, Beir and the slave Safaga found the Prince in your royal suite. Amma and the two other slaves discovered Nefret in her assigned bedchamber."

"She had been left alone?"

"The royal convoy arrived late and no official supper had been prepared in the palace kitchens. The slaves went in search of a light evening meal," Ramose said, eyes downcast. *Goddess of Truth,* forgive me, he beseeched *Maat.*

"The Chief Priest Rahetep and I, together with most city officials, had welcomed the Royal Convoy, and after everyone was settled in at the palace, my priests and I took the Venerable Badar across to the temple. We did not wish anyone to suspect that the man on the Royal Bark was not you."

"Ah yes. I will have the slaves questioned when we get back."

"There is one other thing." Ramose hesitated.

"What?" Aha's chin jutted forward.

"Great Hor-Aha, Nefret's women-slaves were so distraught over what happened that they fled into the night."

"I don't believe you," Aha promptly said.

Ramose looked at him in shock. The King doubted his word? Did he suspect the truth?

"Amma would never do such a thing," Tuthmose protested as well.

"No, of course not," Ramose quickly agreed. "I was not referring to the Royal Nurse. I meant the others. They vanished by the time I left to come upriver."

"In that case, what are we waiting for? Put troops ashore from here to scour the desert further downriver! The women cannot have gone far given the harsh terrain."

"Temple guards were dispatched at once to look for them. As you said yourself, they could not have fled far. Beir did too."

"Beir did what, look for them?"

"No, he fled."

"Have you gone mad?" Aha was aghast. "Beir, acting like a superstitious slave! Never! He is the Royal Steward!"

"He was quite taken with Nefret's pretty slave Safaga," Ramose offered as a plausible excuse, again asking *Maat* to forgive him for his transgression against her laws of truthfulness.

Aha wagged a finger at the priests, "I am confident that once he finds the runaways, he will bring them back safely. Never, for one single moment, have I doubted Beir's loyalty. Admit, Safaga has turned into a striking little beauty. Can you blame him that he wants to find her?"

The Steward's safe return was not what Ramose wished for. It would pose serious complications, should Beir confess the truth to Aha at some later point.

Tasar had stood by silently, still numbed by secret grief. At the mention of Beir's name he looked up, his interest in the conversation renewed. "Beir and Safaga?" he wondered aloud. "I beg to differ, my King." He glanced at Ramose. Publicly to contradict the High Priest was unwise. He noticed Ramose's high brows knotting in consternation.

Nevertheless, before Ramose could reprimand him, he gushed, "It was the Archer Pase upon whom Safaga had bestowed her favors."

"You mean that messenger you killed?" the King asked, pitying the young priest who was obviously not aware that women often favored more than one handsome man. Poor bugger, he thought. Priests did miss out in life.

Ramose was astounded. "You killed the Archer? Why?"

Tasar reddened and lowered his eyes. "I stabbed the Archer to death because I believed him to be directly involved in the attempt on the King's life."

"Just how did you deduct his involvement?" Ramose prompted.

"If you recall, Ramose, the first message emphasized the King's name, the second that of the Princess. Pase had to be the link. Too late did I realize that he was merely the unknowing bearer of the treacherous words."

Tasar hung his head and Ramose studied him for some

time. Then, as if to himself, he breathed, "So, my studious young friend. You possess yet another talent: You are capable of taking a man's life without a query."

Tasar had expected anything from his principled superior except a hidden, yet unmistakable approval of his senseless killing of the Archer. Intuition pulled him from his remorse. He read Ramose well enough to realize that the High Priest gave him to understand that this 'other talent' of his was not met with displeasure. He glanced up at Ramose who had seemingly forgotten about the interchange.

A commotion on deck turned everyone's attention toward the door. Moments later, one of the guards knocked, "Another priest, my King! He insists to see the High Priest at once."

Ramose bowed to the King. "I shall see what this is all about. With your permission, Hor-Aha."

When Ramose emerged onto deck and after his eyes adjusted to the bright sun, they widened in surprise at the prow of his third temple boat rubbing against the barge.

"Rahetep?"

"Ramose! I must speak with you at once. In private." The Chief Priest appeared agitated and they retreated to an empty corner near the bow.

"I came as fast as I could. Something awful came to light while we questioned the assassin." Rahetep paused. He had to gather his breath - as well as his courage.

"What are you talking about?"

"The assassin was hired by the Tax Collector," Rahetep explained. "To perform what the Vizier had bidden Tesh to do. Unbeknownst to the Tax Collector, this man was also a minor member of the *Usurpers*."

"You came all this way to tell me that, Rahetep?"

"Unfortunately not. We learned of the identity of another important member of the secret group."

"For Horus' sake! Who?" Ramose saw his older friend swallow hard before he stepped closer.

"The Steward," the old Chief Priest whispered.

"Impossible!" Ramose called out. The shock hit him in the chest like a great boulder. "Great Ptah! Tell me you sent guards after them. And that they brought her back alive." The thought, that he had handed a traitorous Beir the opportunity to dispose of Nefret in the desert stunned Ramose. And

371

Safaga? Was she one of them as well? The grateful slave-child he had saved from cruel traders? Whom he had trusted? And Nefret now in their hands!

"Tell me that she is safely back!" Ramose shook Rahetep by the arms.

"We tried, Ramose. By the time I found out about Beir's treachery and sent my guards across the river, the three had vanished. It would take an army to find them in that vast emptiness."

It took Ramose a while to organized his racing thoughts. Then he saw a slim chance. For one thing, he could be sure that Beir would want to catch up with the Royal Convoy at Dendara to return to the capital with the King, probably to continue his shameful deception. For his journey back toward the river, the Steward needed fresh provisions. Ramose was certain he would wait for the promised second escort. It was worth a try. Besides, there was little else he could do right now. Disgust over Beir's long-time deceit gripped Ramose. What terrible twist of fate! Instead of saving Nefret, he had delivered her into the hands of her assassin.

"I must inform the King. Not a word of this to anyone. I suggest you return to your boat." Ramose turned away from his old friend and clambered back down below.

"Ah, Ramose. No more bad news, I hope," Aha ventured.

"Some important temple business. So many arrangements to be made, so much to do," Ramose answered with a sigh. Then, as if he was taken by a sudden idea, he said, "That's it!"

"What?" Everyone ask at once.

"Tasar should go in search of the slaves."

"Tasar? Alone? Somewhat unusual," Aha said. All this talk made him ill-tempered. "As I told you before, send troops."

Ramose had his answer ready. "Tasar is an expert tracker and is trained in desert survival. If anyone can, he will find Beir. I grant you that your Steward is most capable in many ways, Hor-Aha. I doubt though that he can read the stars or live off the meager fare the desert offers up grudgingly. Without such knowledge, anyone out there is lost."

Not waiting for Aha to assent, Ramose turned to Tasar, "I trust, young friend, that you will use every single one of your proven talents!"

Again the odd intonation. Tasar recalled the High Priest's

previous remark and sensed a connection. Ramose never wasted words. 'Proven talents. Desert survival. Killing Pase. Finding Beir.' Something to do with his 'willingness to kill a man without a query.' From his first day in the priesthood, he had been trained to abide his superiors' decisions without question. Today could be no different.

"If such is your wish, High Priest."

"It is." Ramose wanted to close the subject. "Provision from the temple stores! Start out tonight from Nekhen."

They looked at Aha who nodded, "All right. Do what you think is best, Ramose."

It was settled! Tasar was her only chance for survival. Her survival, Ramose mused. Not her return.

Their information and suspicions wove into a tapestry of ambition, intrigue and murder. All pointing to one man: Ebu al-Saqqara. After discussing required arrangements, the King asked everyone to leave. Alone at last, he gave in to his grief.

The royal tragedies had somehow seeped through the cracks of the cabin onto the decks from where the wind carried word across the water to the other barges. When the convoy at last sailed into Nekhen, the victorious songs of its brave warriors had turned into mournful dirges.

A few days hence, the Dog Star would rise and their New Year began. The river would crest as it always did. This year the legends, however, were to tell that Nekhen's *Festival of Opet* was not celebrated, nor did the King's Jubilee in the capital city of *White Walls* take place. Instead, the monuments and scrolls would tell of a royal double funeral at the new necropolis of Saqqara, and of Hor-Aha's Great Calamity, a king's bitter price for victory.

* * *

Part V

The Wadi Hammamat

Chapter Thirty-Nine

It took the falucca the remainder of darkness to cross the river. Despite the hour, many vessels laden with goods and livestock threaded their way up and down the swollen Hapi, the rivermen exchanging compassionate shouts as their boats slid past each other.

When the small temple craft reached the reedbeds on the other side its crew guided it to a quivering halt in the soft mud. Nefret, Safaga and Beir disembarked sloshing their way toward firmer ground. Behind them, the small falucca was already swallowed by the misty dawn.

Ahead of them stretched the craggy expanse of an arid desert. Each of the three fugitives carried a small amount of provisions bundled into a thin quilt. Water bladders, slung across their shoulders, would last them not more than three days. They wore long hooded robes to protect them from the sun and to lend some warmth during the chilly nights. The tribal clothes further served as disguises, and they carried the long digging sticks of frugal desert dwellers who long ago found many uses for such implements. An aid to walking over tough terrain, to dig for moisture-laden tubers or to crush a rearing cobra's head if one was agile and lucky enough. The long poles would also serve as fragile tent supports.

Neither of the three had their eyes ringed with kohl in court fashion, and instead of fine sandals their feet were encased in sturdy footwear. Already, the rough leather lashings chafed at Nefret's ankles, and her shoulder strap cut into her tender flesh. While a full waterbag was more than Nefret had ever carried physically, there was a much heavier burden weighing her down emotionally. During the river crossing she had sat on deck, huddled into herself, a trance-like look dulling her usually bright blue eyes. Gradually, with the rising heat, the numbness within her evaporated.

Beir watched his King's tall daughter with concern, ready to lend a strong arm should she stumble on the hard rubble that littered the uneven desert floor. Before they left, Ramose told him that Nefret had been given a calming potion to prevent her from falling into last-minute hysteria. When Ramose first suggested that Beir accompany this unfortunate royal daughter halfway into her banishment, the Steward was surprised. And pleased. To be handed this unexpected opportunity to complete the bumbling assassin's task was fortuitous.

Beir was glad that this assignment took him away from the oppressive atmosphere of the grief-shrouded palace. He liked and admired Amma, but now pitied her having to face the King; forever forbidden to whisper her consoling secret to the mourning father. Poor little Princess, Beir thought. He was actually quite fond of the precocious girl. Through her beautiful mother's dagger, she had become a fugitive from her hereditary land, having struck Dubar too many times to plead self-defense. What unrelenting hotness of spirit! The same that had festered in young Aha, and had consumed Dubar. Because of it, their kind was doomed.

When al-Saqqara tried to pull the Steward into his web of unsavory pleasures with his deceptive brew, Beir had steadfastly resisted. He imagined al-Saqqara's face with its mean eyes, and the spittle in the corners of the mouth, loathing the vile man. Would Aha ever be told the truth? Not by him. And certainly not by the Vizier, that was certain.

Once Nefret was dead, the High Priest's risky gamble to spare her life was over. The *Usurpers of the Two Crowns* would come into power and, in time, eliminate the High Priest and the Vizier as well.

When shall I do it, Beir wondered, returning to the present. *Tomorrow. Early.* He would dig a respectable pit so that the hyenas could not gnaw at the tender flesh. That much he would do for her. Beir only hoped that Safaga would see things his way after that.

"Beir?"

"Yes, Nefret?"

"Will it take us more than a day to reach the Crystal Sea?"

"Oh yes, many more, my Princess," Beir answered using her royal title to assure the stricken girl of his continued deference, and to appease her anguish.

"Then why did Ramose send us off without enough provisions? Now we have to wait for more in some dreadful place. What if we don't meet up with our new guide?" Nefret looked at Beir, her eyes bright again.

Beir explained, "Ramose knew that a heavily provisioned caravan would attract attention. Someone on the river might have looked more closely at us. Now, they can ogle at the new guide to their heart's content. To them, he is a farmer taking his produce to some village, or a pilgrim on his way to a distant temple."

"I guess," Nefret said, unconvinced.

"Besides," Beir continued, "it would have taken too much time to collect the things for your long journey. I shall wait with you near the Wadi Hammamat until that other guide catches up. It will allow us a good day's rest before we each continue our journey separately."

"Safaga and I toward the unknown and you back to the safety of my court and my Father. Oh, Beir," Nefret sobbed, "what is to become of me?"

Safaga rushed toward her distressed mistress and pulled her along by her loose robe. "Hush now. The two of us will be together." She gave Beir a long look. It felt good to have him near. Could she persuade Beir to flee with them? The well-provisioned guide would surely bring plenty of the yellow nub. She could imagine great possibilities. Not for her and Nefret, but for Beir and herself!

Shocked by the web she dared to weave, Safaga tried to expel the ugly thoughts only to realize that their sticky tentacles held fast. The pretty slave released her grip on Nefret and rushed ahead, again shocked by her own disloyalty. Out here each depended on the others. Their survival was assured only if they combined resources and energies to withstand the rigors of the cruel journey. After that, she and Beir could be free! A freedom gained through Nefret's nub; or something dearer?

"Safaga," Beir called after her. "Pace yourself, girl, or you will not last the day!"

*

They stopped to wait out the worst part of the searing day. Beir dug their sticks into the hard ground angling them so that they crossed at the top. He lashed the three ends together and draped two quilts over his tenuous tripod to provide some shade. They huddled close to each other under the puny shelter, sitting on the third quilt covering the ground.

A swallow of tepid water and some dried fruit constituted their noon-time meal. Their thirst not at all slackened, they laid back and, exhausted, soon dozed off. Had it not been for the hyena, they would have slept until the night's chill awakened them. The animal had scented the three humans since mid-morning and slunk after them. The ugly scavenger laughed a penetrating cackle to alert her distant pack.

Beir sprung to his feet. His head struck the gabled poles and he lifted the fragile tent off the ground. The quilted sides collapsed around him and entangled all three. The girls squealed and scrambled free. The chaos was too much even for the bold scavenger. She sauntered off with her uneven gait, trailing her hind-quarters in the dust.

"Good grief!" Nefret giggled as she and Safaga tried to disentangle themselves.

The amused Steward took advantage of the relief-giving hilarity. He moaned and clowned around pretending to be confused. Then he peered from under his tent-dress, standing wide-legged, imitating a snarling hyena. Nefret and Safaga cried out in pretended fright and he leaped forward to give chase as they eluded his clumsy attempts, laughing. Beir did not see the low clump of thorny brush and to the girls' delight he went crashing down, trapped under poles and quilts.

The girls pounced and straddled him, yelling like successful hunters, and the threesome laughed until tears streamed down their faces and their sides ached, the nasty old hyena long forgotten by the overdue release from pent-up fears and torments.

"I surrender," Beir gasped at last.

Still laughing, they sorted themselves out. Beir winced. A sharp pain seared into the back of his leg. Nefret and Safaga tugged hard at him again. They laughed and grunted and groaned pretending they were unable to help him to his feet and soon Beir was caught up in the merry-making once more. It was so good to be away from court intrigues and al-Saqqara. Out here, he could breathe, and think. He stood up, freed from his entanglements. Safaga took Nefret's hand and smiled, and Nefret looked at her two companions, grateful for such loyal friends. They shook out the quilts and bundled their meager possessions to take advantage of the cooler evening hours.

Beir hardly felt the second sting. The small nearly transparent creature dropped off Beir's leg. Joining the other, the scorpions scurried into the indifferent dusk.

*

"Let's stop here for the night," Beir decided after several hours following the sandy trail. His throat was parched and his joints ached. Heat consumed him from within. The fear of tomorrow gnaws at me, he told himself.

"We assume you build a better tent this time," Nefret giggled, recalling their dusty tangle. She did well on this first day. Tired out, she was not exhausted. Her young spirit had overcome the trauma of the previous day and she was proud that she was not a whimpering burden on her two servants. Servants? She should no longer think of them as such. They were her friends now. Without them, she would not survive.

They ate sparingly and each drank a few careful sips. When Beir left to seek out a suitable hollow away from the little camp, Nefret huddled closer to her companion. "Safaga," she whispered, "do you miss Pase?"

"Of course I do," Safaga whispered back, wondering what brought her other lover's name to Nefret's mind.

"And, you are lucky to have Beir. I will never see Tasar again. I should hate him for leaving me. Yet I want him so much I want to die."

"Nefret, you must not think like that! When he finds you gone, he might decide to come after you," Safaga soothed.

"Have you forgotten? Ramose has everyone believe that I am dead." Nefret's heartache overwhelmed her again.

The two sat quietly until Safaga's face brightened. "Tasar is a priest. The gods give him special knowledge! Surely he will be told the truth by Ptah or Horus, if not by Ramose."

Nefret never thought of Tasar as a servant of the gods, not

like she thought of Ramose. The idea of Tasar being told the truth by the gods appealed to her. It consoled her. She sighed and hoped her more mature friend was right.

They chose not to erect another tent. Instead, they spread one of their quilts on the hard ground and used the other two for cover. At first, it was awkward to decide on their close huddle. With renewed joking and giggling, the girls cajoled Beir to lie between them so that he could keep them both warm during the cold desert night.

"That way, you can protect us both at the same time," Nefret said. She yawned and curled herself into a ball on Beir's left, already half asleep.

"Which is all you should do at one time," Safaga whispered pressing her lips against the Steward's ear. His skin was hot and she could taste his salty perspiration.

During the next hours, Beir's thirst became overpowering. His jumbled thoughts raced back and forth. Was he doing the right thing? After his early misguided years as a secret Osiris-cult worshipper, why should he be forced to revert back to human sacrifices when he had long forsaken the brutal cult. Had he truly replaced *Sati*-worship with a better god? Or any god at all? Joining the Vizier's treasonous cause surely would bring the wrath of the misbegotten Seth upon his head, without any other reward.

He had started in the King's service when he was young and hotheaded, yet malleable. Aha's unprovoked outbursts were legendary and greatly feared among the servants even though the next moment, the King could be as docile as a tamed pintail duck. One day, Aha kicked Beir so viciously that he almost died. The Vizier came to his aid and saved him from Aha's unprovoked wrath. Was it surprising that he began to listen to al-Saqqara's suggestive murmurings?

Beir no longer believed that al-Saqqara spoke for the good of the common people. He tossed and turned. His heart ached. So did every joint. He grew thirstier by the minute. Beir saw through the Vizier's greed, the constant subversive plotting for his own advancement.

'I will not kill her.' Neither could he help her. He resolved that once he rejoined the convoy, he would talk to Ramose. Had he not assisted the High Priest in delaying his report to al-Saqqara about the over-hasty departure of the temple boats from Ineb-hedj? Surely, the High Priest would guide him toward better gods to worship. Beir was quite partial to *Ra*, the *God of Renewed Life*, rising into the sky each day.

The Steward flexed his aching knees to ease the pain. Safaga snuggled closer to this other man of hers who did not respond to the promise of her slender limbs.

*

"Beir! Wake up! Oh Great Ptah, what is the matter with him?" Safaga's frantic wailing awoke Nefret.

The sun stood high. They should have been on their way some time ago. Why did Beir not wake them? And why was Safaga kneeling over him, sobbing, shaking him? Nefret rubbed clinging sleep from her eyes.

"What is the matter with Beir?"

"He won't wake up!"

"Is he ... ?"

"Of course not!" Safaga cried, believing fervently that Beir was only fast asleep.

Nefret leaned over the motionless Steward. Beir's face was ashen and his skin looked wrinkled, like a used papyrus scroll. His breath came in belabored gulps, as if he was running out of air. Safaga shook him by the shoulders and again beseeched him to wake up. Beir's eyelids fluttered. He moved his cracked lips without a sound.

"Water," Safaga urged and Nefret grabbed the Steward's water bladder. With shaking fingers, she untied the knotted thongs and turned the bag upside down pointing the opening at Beir's lips. Precious liquid poured over the Steward's face.

"Not that way! You'll drown him!" Safaga snatched the bag away as Beir sputtered into semi-consciousness. She tore a strip of linen from her sleeve and soaked it with the last tepid water, patting his face, neck and chest. The moisture cooled him only temporarily before it evaporated from his burning skin.

"Oh, Great Ptah, do not let him die," Nefret pleaded with the omnipotent creator-god. "My life depends on him."

"He does not perspire any longer," she offered as a consolation to Safaga.

Deep concern coated Safaga's voice, "That is not a good sign, Nefret. Long ago, I saw a man die like this. On a caravan - when I was very young. They said that he was stung by a poisonous spider that had crawled inside his robe."

Nefret shot up off the ground. She snaked her young body like a temple dancer. Feet stomping, she shook her robe around herself. A chill ran down her spine at the thought of something crawling up inside her garment. "Are there spiders out here?" she asked.

"Of course. And scorpions. And snakes. A cobra is the worst. Its poison kills at once." Looking at Beir, Safaga whispered, "It was not a cobra or he would be dead by now."

"What are we going to do?" Nefret wailed and sat down again oblivious of the desert's small defensive creatures.

"There is nothing we can do. We have to wait," Safaga moaned.

"For what?" Nefret whispered. Her eyes widening in fear, she turned away. She hoped Safaga would not answer that.

*

Tasar was pleased with his progress considering the stubborn streak inherent in his jackass. At least the other three, heavily laden, followed willingly. He calculated that he should reach the designated place within a day or two.

When Ramose told him the truth about Nefret, swearing him to secrecy, Tasar did not know if he should laugh with joy, or cry in desperation. If she was still alive she was now stripped of her heritage. If he professed his love for her, would he be condemned to share her cruel fate?

And then, by Horus, a miracle occurred when Ramose entrusted him to guide her into exile. Tasar could have taken the High Priest's hands and swung him around in a joyous dance to life and freedom. The image they would have posed! Jubilant, he vowed to forsake his ambitions, those lofty goals paid for with human loneliness. If he chose to love her they could be free. Together. But where? On that island in the Great Green?

When Ramose further told him the suspected truth about the Royal Steward all elation drained from him. There was such tremendous pain in the High Priest's voice having realized that he himself placed Nefret into Beir's treacherous hands. Oh, cruelest of fates!

Tasar wondered how long before he caught up with them. If he was lucky to find them at all - before the Steward left her to die of thirst - or worse! Tasar fingered his double-belt and felt for the flat ivory box that Ramose had thrust at him, admonishing him not to touch the miniature spears. Properly used, Beir would fall just like the desert giant. What did they call him? Stinger! Stinger of a Scorpion. Tasar urged his balky animal into a jarring trot.

"Thank you, Horus, for this chance," he whispered and fingered the precious amulet around his neck, its long chain sewn into a double strip of linen. He prayed for the *Wedjat* amulet not to forsake him and looked up at the sky as if he expected a protecting falcon to soar above. By Horus! He gave a startled shout. One, two, no, five big birds drew ever lower as he watched their black circles against the brilliant sky ."Horus-falcons, indeed," he sneered.

"Away, vultures!" Tasar wind-milled his arms. Nevertheless, he changed direction to take a closer look at what unfortunate creature attracted the great birds. In the distance, a hyena laughed her foreboding cackle.

*

Nefret sat watching over Beir. The girls had managed to erect the poles creating some shade for him. For two days, there had been no change in the Steward's listlessness. She and Safaga tended the feverish man as best they could. Their water was almost gone, as were their provisions. Still, they clung to the hope of Beir's recovery. If only the disgusting vultures would fly away. Nefret's head dropped to her chest. Parched, discouraged and dead-tired, she dozed off.

"Nefret!" Safaga rushed at her. "Look!"

They squinted against the setting sun. On a distant ridge, a string of animals crossed in front of the fiery disk. "Too big for goats," Nefret decided. "Or perhaps antelopes," she said and looked back to see if Beir had moved.

"No! There! Don't you see? A rider! Nefret! We are saved." Safaga hopped from one foot to the other and waved her arms at the silhouetted small procession. Nefret too jumped up and threw her arms in the air. Then fear gripped her. Their camp might be too low to be seen by the distant caravan. "Safaga!" She tore one of the quilts from its flimsy rod. "Run up that hill and waive as high as you can reach."

Safaga snatched the thin quilt and scrambled up a low hill. Fearless with hope, she screamed at the two vultures that had alighted at the top. The big birds screeched back at her. Safaga twirled the quilt high above her head alternately shouting at the distant rider and begging the gods to save them from this parched inferno. When the small caravan vanished from her view, she sobbed in despair. It took an eternity before it reappeared from behind the last obstructing hill, near enough for Safaga to see clearer. She counted four donkeys, a lone rider astride the first. Was that all? She shaded her eyes as the shimmering image moved closer at a snail's pace. Not able to bear the suspense any longer, she broke into a run dragging the quilt behind her, shouting at the top of her lungs, forcing her legs to run faster, frantic the small band might vanish before her eyes like a cruel mirage.

"Over here. Please! Over here."

The rider turned toward her and spurned his donkey on. When he was quite close, he slid off his animal and pulled at his fluttering head covers.

"Safaga!"

"Tasar!" She sobbed and fell to her knees.

Tasar knelt down beside her and stroked her dust-caked cheeks asking her to stop her tears. She told him of their plight. Hers, Beir's, and the tall slave's.

The young priest scanned the sky overhead. How lucky that he decided to follow the telltale vultures.

"Safaga!" He shook the clinging girl. "Take me to Nefret!"

"You know?" she whispered.

"Of course I know, you silly girl. Quickly now, lead on."

"Poor Beir. He is so very ill," Safaga sighed. She stole a look at the handsome priest who caught her glance and smiled back at her. 'I pray she is not one of the *Usurpers*,' he thought.

*

Nefret took the second quilt off its supports and smacked it at the vulture. She hated to keep the unconscious Steward without protection from the sun but was more frightened of this harbinger of death hovering close by.

"Shoo! You disgusting thing," she hissed and snapped her quilt again. The sharp noise did nothing to discourage the wily bird. It sat patiently knowing that it would be feasting soon.

"Nefret," someone called her softly. She turned and stared. Her quilt fluttered to the ground. The next moment, she flung herself into her lover's arms.

"Tasar! Oh, Tasar! I knew it! You have come to save me!" Nefret pressed herself close to him, reassuring him of her love.

Tasar put his arms around her slender waist and lifted her upward with a joyous laugh. Thirstily, they sought each others' lips, the harsh world around them ceasing to exist.

Safaga's cheeks burned and her heart ached at the sight of the two lovers. "What about Beir?" she sulked.

"I am sorry, Safaga. You are right to chastise me. I'll tend to him at once." Tasar disengaged himself from Nefret's arms. "In the meantime, you could unload the donkeys and hobble them to let them graze." His endearing smile washed over her again.

Her feelings a confusing jumble, Safaga looked at the Steward languishing on his quilt.

"I can help you with the chores," Nefret offered. "Oh, Safaga. Isn't it wonderful that Tasar found us. Now we will survive for sure." She squeezed her friend's hand, overflowing with emotion. Safaga's pained expression made her realize that she was perhaps being cruel and she added, "Don't worry about Beir. Tasar is very skilled." Pride shone in her eyes. "He will get Beir well again. And then we can both be happy."

Safaga flung her arms around the younger woman and Nefret let her former slave shed her tears. She stroked Safaga's hair. How often had they held each other like this, only then it had always been the slave comforting the princess.

*

"Nefret! Safaga!" Tasar called into the desert.

The women hastened toward him. While they hobbled the donkeys, he had erected a proper tent taken from his packs, and built a fire. Acrid flames burrowed through flat cakes of dried dung carried in a sturdy basket by one of the donkeys.

"How is Beir," Nefret called out and settled herself close to the fire. Odious or not, the heat was most welcomed.

Tasar's face told them more than words would have.

Safaga did not rush toward the Steward. Instead, she approached the priest who cupped her drawn face in his hands and lifted it toward him. "I am sorry, Safaga," he consoled. "There was nothing I could do. The venom had reached his heart. The scorpion must have been gigantic." The slave's tears softened him and he took her in his arms. He looked at Nefret and they smiled at each other above Safaga's head. After a comforting interval, Tasar urged the women to stay huddled near the fire. He would attend to the Steward before nightfall.

"Tasar," Safaga whispered, "tell me, did you see Pase before you left?"

Tasar draped Beir's body over one of the donkeys and hesitated before he turned around to face her, aware of his quickening heartbeat. Why did she have to ask? Why now? Why at all? Anger welled up in him. As did guilt.

"Yes, Safaga," he said, "I was with him to the end."

"The end of what?" Safaga rushed at him while he leaned on his jackass for false support. Nefret rose from the fire and followed her friend. Her eyes never left Tasar's face.

The young priest swallowed hard. "Pase is dead, Safaga."

Safaga burst into wild sobs, the pain of her double loss emphasized by her confused feelings for Tasar. Nefret caught up to her distraught friend and rocked her in a tight embrace.

"He died a hero's death," Tasar said, uncertain whether the two heard him. He spurned the donkey on, its lifeless burden across its back, arms and legs trailing in the sand. Again disgusted with himself over Pase's senseless killing, Tasar selected a hollow for the pretty slave's second dead lover.

The vulture sat close by. Tasar looked at the gawking bird. "The rest is up to you, my sinister witness," he said to the bird. "For all I know, you are *Nekhbet* herself."

He raised his hands and intoned, "*Nekhbet*, Patron Goddess of this desert, I beseech you, let us pass through your harsh realm in safety."

Without another glance back, Tasar swung himself atop his jackass.

"Unfortunate girl," he murmured, "to have lost both men she loved."

He felt for his double-sewn belt. In it, together with many kernels of yellow nub, he carried Ramose's flat ivory box. 'I did not even have to use the tips,' he shuddered, remembering their lethal coating. What if the Steward had been well? It would have made no difference. He still would have died that night.

* * *

Chapter Forty

They climbed the *Black Hills* and looked down into the wide gully carved through the craggy desert mountains by an ancient river. Tasar decided to spend the night on the small plateau before venturing into the confines of the wadi. It was late in the day and the young priest built a lean-to with their tent cover under a granite overhang. He lit a low-burning fire to avoid attracting attention as the Wadi Hammamat was a well-traveled route that connected the Crystal Sea to the Valley of the Nile. The three travelers were bound to run into caravans or be hailed by the news-starved overseers from the quarries hidden in the many offshoot gullies that dissected the old riverbed.

Tasar asked the women to gather next to him. With an air of mystery, he pulled one of his saddlebags toward him and placed it squarely between his crossed legs.

"We could encounter those not kindly disposed toward desert tribes."

Nefret and Safaga waited and he continued, "You will need a new disguise."

"Not chantresses again," Safaga moaned and Nefret rolled her eyes. They giggled and jostled each other, happy for the welcome relief. It had been an arduous day.

"Bad idea," Tasar conceded. "The farther we travel, the less people worship our gods. And the less they would be inclined to respect us as temple servants." Tasar paused and pulled white linens from his bag. "I brought these wrappers. From now on, you are capable seamstresses who hail from ... Where shall we say?"

"Nubt," Nefret cried, the new game enlivening her.

"Dendara," Safaga chimed in. Tasar's nearness was giddying.

Tasar bowed to them, "Nubt it is," and they laughed, glad for each other's company.

"Who will you be, Tasar," Safaga teased.

"Ah," he said, "I am your trusted guide. Or I could be your older brother, Safaga. And, perhaps, your husband, Nefret." He shot a sideways glance at Nefret to gauge whether she was offended by his brazenness.

"Really, Tasar," both girls chided, Safaga in mock dismay, Nefret blushing furiously over his suggestion.

Taking up the light-hearted banter, Tasar continued, "Since you can no longer wrap yourselves in tribal clothes, I brought something that will protect you even better." He dove back into his bag and pulled out two dark wigs. "I vouch for a perfect fit."

"Of course, they will fit. These are my own," Nefret marveled. She quickly pulled one over her own hair.

"Where did you get these?" Safaga asked in astonishment.

"From Amma. I, ah, persuaded her to part with them."

Safaga doubted that the old nurse would hand over the ceremonial headpieces to Tasar without so much as an argument, and suspected Dokki to have lent a hand. "Aren't they a bit too fancy for mere seamstresses?"

"You can always roll them in the dust if that'll make them more suitable for your charade," Tasar countered and the girls beat his arm in feigned disgust.

Ever-practical Safaga had another question. "Why would these supposed seamstresses leave their comfortable dwelling on the plentiful Hapi to journey to the distant Crystal Sea?"

"Ah," Tasar held up his hand. "That will be explained as follows: Renown for their fine work, they are off to barter for bolts of exotic cloth from the foreign caravans gathering near the Crystal Sea."

He plunged his hands again into the depths of his bag and rummaged with exaggerated fury. Swaying back and forth, he murmured as if beseeching a reluctant cobra to rear its head. "I even have proof that you made this journey once before. Because this extraordinary piece," his arm arced wide, "can only have come from far away." He pulled up, and flowing folds spilled from their confinement, their indigo hue melting into the darkening sky.

The young women froze in disbelief, their stricken faces

hidden by the descending dusk.

"Did I not promise, Safaga, that when I saw our Princess next, I would return it to her?"

Nefret stared in speechless horror.

Safaga managed a hoarse whisper, "How did you come by this?"

"Not from Amma, I assure you," Tasar laughed, still unaware of their distress. "I found it by chance in the temple. It lay discarded in one of the underground embalming chambers, of all places."

Nefret leaned forward and reached for her father's intended robe. With trance-like slowness, she smoothed its creases until it spread over her as well as Safaga's lap. In the light of the low fire, kernels of sand shimmered through a long cut. Around it, marring the lovely material, was an ugly stain.

At last, Tasar guessed at the truth. "Nefret, I am dismayed. I did no realize that Zeina wore it when she was ..." His voice trailed off.

Nefret looked at him, her face a stony mask. "This is Dubar's blood." She flung herself across the garment. "Dubar's curse follows me! Will there be no escaping from his torment!"

After what seemed an eternity, Nefret ceased her anguished sobbing, having been persuaded that they should bed down for the night.

As Beir had before him, Tasar took his place in the middle to reassure and warm the two girls. He turned to Nefret and stroked her glistening hair. Then he kissed her cheek, and she welcomed his tenderness. Overcoming her inner torment she huddled closer to him.

As the night deepened, Tasar gave himself over to probing fingers that gently cupped his swelling *papyrus clump*. The tantalizing pressure around his *Mehyt* increased his desire and his pillar rose. He brought his face closer to Nefret's translucent features. Her breathing was deep and regular. She was fast asleep. Careful not to waken her, Tasar disentangled himself from the subconscious embrace of the girl and turned to the young woman on his other side.

*

Their progress through the wadi was steady. Several heavily laden caravans crossed their path without plaguing them with too many prying questions. The ancient *Road to the East* led them past numerous quarries and the hillsides were strewn with half-finished carvings and granite monuments. They passed the mines of the *Red Mountains* where armies of slaves were forced to follow even the smallest vein to extract the precious nub down to its last yellow fleck. Nearly everyone they met along the harsh route was helpful and disbursed advice.

On this day, though, they met no one. Since the incident with the robe, Nefret drank little of their tepid water and ate even less. She was withdrawn and Tasar found himself addressing Safaga more and more, in the hope that their conversation would pull Nefret from her depression. Neither he nor Safaga acknowledged their brief coming together.

Another seemingly interminable hot day past. As they stopped for the night, Tasar sniffed the air. It felt heavier, moister, and there was the slightest cooling breeze from the east. "We must be close. I can almost taste the salt of the Crystal Sea," he called to his weary companions.

*

Lateen-rigged boats looked more like small river faluccas, rather than their northern square-rigged ocean-going vessels plying the Great Green Sea beyond the Delta. The similarity was deceptive. The dhows from the large eastern peninsula were heavy vessels. A long stern overhang led to a crudely fashioned bowsprit that speared the constant northerlies with defiance; leaving the exposed deck unprotected against the elements.

Tasar fingered his double-folded belt to reassure himself that the knot held tight as its weight pulled at his middle. He carried a small fortune. In the Two Lands, the yellow nub had no commercial use and was mined to line temple walls and wooden portals, or for pretty jewelry and royal utensils. Foreigners, however, used it to trade for goods. He shook a few precious nuggets from the belt and closed his fist around them, steeling himself against the inevitable haggle with the bearded seamen. Animated barter was the custom along these shores and if he expected to seal a good bargain he needed to mimic their enthusiasm for it.

Several dhows skittered around shallow moorings. From the deck of one, shouting and the hectic shifting of cargo indicated that it was to shove off soon. Tasar hailed its captain expecting an onslaught of raucous foreign sounds. To his surprise, the fierce-eyed seaman spoke his tongue with eloquence and their deal was sealed with relatively little of the customary palaver. Within the hour, Tasar managed to exchange three of their worn-out donkeys for fresh onions, sweet dates and dried figs. He led the fourth animal to the slaughterhouse where he traded it for strips of dried goat meat.

The three travelers sorted and rearranged their few necessities which left them each with one large bundle. Tasar took on the additional load of their valuable tent cover. Carrying their parcels high over their heads, they waded through the gentle surf to the dhow anchored in shoulder-deep water. Strong arms hauled them aboard. At once, the dhow's odor assailed them with a vengeance. Nefret put her hand over her nose and shuffled across the rough-hewn planks slippery with rotting fish gut. The rancid crew gawked after her.

It took ingenuity by the three travelers to eke out a corner of their own among the high-stacked bales of trading goods. When the changing breeze brought a lusty whiff from a blackened cauldron, they were glad that Tasar had insisted on providing and cooking most of their own food. Several more nuggets changed hands before the young priest managed to arrange for the use of a smaller, equally encrusted pot. It teetered half-imbedded in hot embers in the middle of the open deck. At least, they would not starve. But they were low on drinking water.

Nefret looked at the immense crystal expanse. Never having seen so much water she scooped up a refreshing handful, startled and quickly sickened by its salt. How odd, she thought, that I cannot take the smallest sip from all this bounty. Hapi might be gritty with dark silt, yet it always quenched her thirst. In this liquid vastness, she saw neither the reedbeds nor the dangerous bulks of snoozing hippos, the river-pilot's scourge. Here, nothing impeded the onrush of choppy waves slapping against the sturdy planks. She did not see—nor could she know about—the coral reefs. Barely awash, they were the ocean-sailor's nightmare.

Nefret leaned her head against Tasar's shoulder. Half asleep, he pulled the quilt over both of them and she nestled deeper into his chest. Arms tightly wrapped around each other, they dozed off.

Leaning hard against the rail-planking, Safaga stared at the

---

flat horizon trying not to notice the two lovers. Not all droplets on her cheeks stemmed from the salty spray.

*

The violent motion of the dhow woke them with a start. They clawed at the low sides for support, holding on for dear life as the shallow vessel's bow reared toward the sky. The next instant, it pitched forward to bury the bowsprit in a churning trough. The wind howled and tore at the sail so hard that it threatened to bring the simple rigging down. The lateen boom scythed the air.

"This makes me ill," Nefret shouted.

Tasar and Safaga grimaced and gulped stinging air. They, too, were sickened by the boat's erratic motion, and hoped that deep breathing would help.

*

A low dark cloud, born in the western desert, came racing east toward the Crystal Sea. They were three days out when the squall overtook them.

"Rih al-Khamsin!" the seamen wailed. The captain screamed obscenities at his gesticulating crew. "It is an ordinary squall. You are worse than toothless women," he roared, unable to convince his seasoned men for they already bemoaned their inevitable fate.

The deck turned into chaos. Everyone was thrown from side to side. Huge bales and bulbous vats careened about like maddened bulls ready to gore the unwary. The caldron containing the sailors' smelly stew was the first thing to be swept overboard. With gargantuan effort, the seamen captured the slashing boom and lashed the whipping sail tight. Their efforts did little to steady the squirreling dhow. But no matter how much a night storm raged, daylight always brought new hope to every sailor.

"There are islands straight ahead, just before the sea splits into two. We will take advantage of their lee," the captain shouted to the huddled group. His hands were cupped in front of his mouth to be heard over the howling wind. "I know of a sandy cove. We'll anchor there to sort ourselves out from this rotten mess."

"Let it be soon," Nefret prayed, teeth chattering. The open sea now terrified her and she could not control her shaking knees.

Tasar bellowed out a shout but the wind ripped the words straight from his lips. Nefret never heard the warning. The loose plank, torn off the bowsprit, hit her squarely in the head.

*

The sun warmed her cheeks and a balmy breeze caressed her bruised limbs. Best of all, nothing around her or under her moved. Nefret pried her eyes open.

"About time you woke up," Safaga said. Careful not to cut her, she placed a hollow shard to Nefret's lips. Eager to catch every drop, she tried to sit up only to sink back with a stifled groan. Her head was a staccato drum. She still felt sick.

"How is our august patient?" At the sound of the pleasant voice, the pretty Sumerian turned with a smile, "I believe she is much better, Tasar. Now that she has regained her life."

"I am glad you are with us again," Tasar smiled. "The captain is ready to put out to sea. We must hurry, lest we be left behind on this forsaken shore."

"What happened?" Nefret whispered lifting her head. She winced in pain and fell back again.

"You have a nasty bump on your head, my lovely." Tasar stroked a wisp of hair from her pale face exposing a black-bluish mark on her left temple. "We anchored after the violent squall passed. For the last day and a half, we nursed our bruises while the seamen managed to repair most of the damage to their boat. You worried me, my beautiful."

Tasar and Safaga helped Nefret to her feet. Her legs would not support her so Tasar lifted her into his arms and waded toward the boat. Almost weightless, she smiled up at him, and like a trusting child, she closed her slender arms around his neck.

"Only a few more days," Tasar encouraged. "The captain promised me that, from now on, the sea will be as docile as Hapi himself. We will sail up the western of two narrow gulfs that stretch like fingers away from these cantankerous waters. You'll see, my precious, it will be much calmer there. Just hold on a few more days." Tasar held onto his own encouragement almost as fiercely as Nefret clung to him. The seamen had whispered that the squall was a forerunner of the dreaded Khamsin. If the dust-laden storm unleashed its fury upon the small dhow their survival through the desert might have been for naught.

Behind them, Safaga carried their two remaining bundles through the surf. Having lost much during the storm they still had their sturdy tent cover. The slave looked at Tasar's broad shoulders and thought of her brief moment with this man.

*

The dhow sea-sawed to windward, taking advantage of its lateen sail. They left the wide body of the Crystal Sea and as they plied the calmer waters of the narrow gulf, they never lost sight of land. The coastal mountains of the small eastern peninsula shimmered bluish through the heat, a harsh territory forbidden to the people of the *Two Lands*.

Local seafarers had a different reason to avoid the shores of the small peninsula. Wild tribes and renegades were rumored to eke out a pitiful existence there. A straying vessel was an eagerly awaited addition to their meager lives, its crew allegedly forced into hilarious entertainment, to be abysmally treated after that—or worse, for the free-roaming bands had murderous habits. It was even whispered that they ate their human captives. Reason enough for even an intrepid sea captain to stay close to the western shores defying its hidden reefs.

*

Oil lamps swayed at both ends of the dhow to avoid collision with other vessels crossing their path. Overhead, the stars were barely visible from the brilliant moon low above the water's silvery band.

The women huddled on either side of Tasar, Safaga acutely aware of the seamen's hungry looks; leering blood-shot eyes from behind bearded faces. Remembering those stares only all too well, she pressed herself closer to Tasar.

"Safaga," Tasar nudged her, "I would like to speak to Nefret. Would you mind giving us some time alone?"

"What about those men? They make my skin crawl," she protested.

"Stand near the bow," Tasar pointed, "where I can see you."

Safaga skulked away.

Tasar cupped Nefret's face in his hands, careful not to touch the large bruise. "Nefret, I love you, my sweet Princess," he whispered, passion constricting his throat.

She answered softly, "And I love you, my handsome

stranger from Nekhen. I loved you from the moment I saw you. Though I am no longer your Princess, nor anyone else's for that matter."

"You are forever a Princess," Tasar said pressing his palms to her cheeks. "Nefret, not only that. One day, you shall be the rightful Queen. Never forget: You are the *Royal Heiress of the Two Lands.*"

"Tasar, stop dreaming." She straightened up and looked at him, tired, resigned. "What will happen to me after we leave this awful dhow? Once we reach the Great Green?"

"Ramose has ordered me to arrange for your passage on one of the foreign merchant ships. The waters of the great *Wadj* are dotted with beautiful islands. You are to live on one of the largest, and richest, of them."

"What is it called?"

"I do not know, dearest. But I will find out before you sail. That way, I shall know where to find you." Tasar moved closer to her and looked deeply into her eyes. "Nefret, you must believe that we shall meet again."

She shook her head.

"Believe in yourself. And in me! I am to succeed Ramose."

Nefret pulled back from him. "Tasar!"

The young priest's ambition surfaced with unshakable certainty. He grasped her by the arms and repeated, "Do you hear me? I will be the next High Priest of Ptah!"

The silence between them deepened, and when she did not move Tasar said, his voice fervent with renewed conviction, "Ramose has to retire at some point. It is inevitable. Rahetep remains in Nekhen; besides, he is too old. And Wazenz is unsuitable. Should Ramose not retire, he cannot live forever. Nor will the King."

He felt her recoil as if he had turned into a viper, and forced her to face him. "Nefret! With Dubar dead, Djer is much too young to rule should Aha die. Therefore, the High Priest will be named co-regent. At that time, I expect to become the next High Priest. Then I can send for you, and restore your rightful throne to us."

"To us?" Had this clever young priest hatched his plans counting on her inheritance once he realized who she was? Anger rose at the apparent callousness. Before she could squirm from his grip, he swept her into his arms.

"Yes, my love, to us. You and I will live in greatness. Together. You as *Queen of the Two Lands*. I as your consort, and *High Priest of Ptah*. Just imagine having a husband to whom the gods speak."

With unshakable conviction, Tasar had rekindled the cooling embers of lost hope back into a small flicker. If he believed it, so must she.

*

"Too many reefs. We cannot risk sailing by night," the dhow captain announced late one afternoon. He guided his vessel toward shore. There were no more squalls although an ominous dark-yellowish band stretched ahead of them. Tasar calculated that they were a day's sail from where this gulf lost itself in the northern desert. From there, an overland trek would lead them to the expanse of the *Wadj*, the Great Green, and its seaport.

"Best take your provisions," the captain suggested when they disembarked to spend the night ashore. When he saw Tasar's raised brows, he explained that his men needed to scrub the slimy deck, the sea having been too calm to sweep it clean.

"I would not wish our buckets of seawater to spoil your food."

*

"Tasar! Nefret!" Safaga cried. She shaded her eyes against the rising sun, seeing nothing. At her feet, foamy surf languidly caressed the shore.

"They have gone," she wailed. "They sailed without us!"

The two lovers disentangled themselves and threw their thin quilt off. They stared at the empty sea.

Suddenly, Tasar howled like a wounded animal and fell to his knees. "They stole my belt," he sobbed. "Those stinking, fish-gutted hyenas stole the yellow nub!"

He pounded the hot beach with his fists and clawed at it as if it withheld the precious kernels from him. Shoveling up handfuls of sand he brought them to his rage-distorted face. The elusive grains trickled from his hands and quickly refilled the hollows of his anger, erasing all traces of his impotent fury against their new misfortune.

* * *

Chapter Forty-One

By all expectations, the royal convoy floating down the great Hapi from Nekhen toward Ineb-hedj should have displayed the proud banners of victory heralding a promise of renewed peace and conquered riches. Instead, the populace learned that the largest of the temple boats carried the bodies of Aha's two dead children.

Visible from shore on the baldachined platform, the shrouded royal litters bade all to weep. An honor guard surrounded the high platform and the added weight caused the temple boat to fetch a deeper draft so that the stern rudder sometimes grazed submerged obstructions.

The boat's *Kariy* now housed the *Per-wer* of Nekhen, the revered shrine with the King's royal placenta jar. Aha had not revisited his old capital but instead insisted that his alter ego be brought to him. When his time to *Join his Ka* came it would be buried with him at Saqqara. Until then, his jar would be worshipped in the *Per-nu*, in the Temple of Ptah. It was to take the place of Nefret's placenta jar to be buried with her in her royal *Mastaba* at Ineb-hedj's new necropolis. Whereas Dubar's missing placenta, having fallen prey to the hungry lappings of Hent's palace hound, now would cause his *Ba* to escape from his tomb without the prince's alter ego.

Following the funerary vessel was the Royal Bark. Ramose, having ceded his own boat to the royal dead, stayed close to Aha who sat motionless on deck. No one dared to notice that the Falcon-King's cheeks were wet. Even the painted *Wedjat* eye on the boat's curving prow appeared to shed tears as the Bark rushed headlong down the swollen river.

The second temple boat followed the Bark with Amma and Tuthmose onboard. It was loaded with Ramose's trunks holding his ceremonial insignia, purple robe, and one of the leopard skins from Nekhen.

At Nubt, the third, and smallest, of the maneuverable temple boats stopped briefly. There, Teyer, *Chief Priest of the Temple of Seth*, was appointed to succeed the heroic Seka as Chief Priest of Tjeny and *Ka*-priest of Abdju. He came aboard to be consecrated by the High Priest of Ptah and rode with them until he would disembark at Abdju, now under his care.

At Dendara, a day's journey before they would reach Abdju, Beir was expected to rejoin his King. A boat was sent for him but returned without the Steward. Aha, distressed, feared that his trusted servant had been lost to the desert. Ramose allowed himself to breathe a sigh of relief. He would not upset Aha further by the shocking revelation about his treasonous Steward. As soon as there was a chance, he would counsel Aha to take on another servant. Someone worthy of Beir's memory - as far as the King was concerned; as far as he, Ramose, was concerned, someone who was more inclined to visit his temple, to worship and to confide in Ptah; and - of course - in him. Tuthmose's splendid son Khentika came readily to mind for the delicate position.

On the third of Ramose's boats, Chief Senmut and his surviving Temple Bowmen stood guard over two special prisoners. One was Tesh, Nekhen's former Royal Tax Collector, charged with treason, who hoped he was kept alive so that his testimony could incriminate the sly Vizier; and so that his life would thereby be spared.

At the farthest corner of the stern stood the other prisoner: Ogoni, the conquered King of Nobatia. While the guards dealt harshly with Tesh, they treated the savage king with uneasy respect due as much to the *Noba's* blackness as to his regal bearing. Ogoni's haughtiness was little diminished by his capture; he held himself proud and straight, his dark eyes challenging those who dared to stare with too much curiosity at his ample nakedness.

Barum stood among the select few who had been invited to join Aha on the Royal Bark. As the new Grand General, he now commanded all five of the royal armies. He would miss the Kharga.

Huge barges, laden with troops, formed the largest part of the convoy. They held one fourth of Barum's former forces.

The tried warriors from the Kharga encampment were now part of the new *Fifth Army of Neit* to provide protection in the Lower Delta Region under the former archer captain, the newly appointed General Veni.

Two quarters of Barum's former army had remained in the south as a now much smaller *Fourth Army of Amun*. Their capable new general, Barum's longtime loyal Aide-de-camp Keheb, would ensure that any unlikely resurrection by the Wawat, Kush and Noba would never reach fruition. The rest of the heroic Fourth was, of course, dead, their bodies among the many nameless warriors whose clean-picked bones littered the abandoned battlefields.

The last of the large barges posed a curious sight. The bow was crammed with what seemed to be boys of barely medium height, yet with the powerful torsos of grown men. Even more startling was what could be seen above the coaming of the broad stern. Long necks topped by small heads with beady eyes undulated in the breeze. An unwary observer from shore might be terror-stricken thinking that he saw a hundred cobras swaying to the sounds of an unheard flute. An occasional flap of plumed wings soon conjured up the correct, but equally astounding, conclusion as the ostriches jostled for better vantage points.

General Mekh smiled at his *Amazing Forces*. The sinewy undersized riders had been his brain child, and he hoped that the new Grand General would be as supportive as wily 'Old Silver-Tongue' Makari had been.

The convoy slid past Badari where the newly quartered *Second Army of Ra* lined the eastern shore in a stiff salute to their victorious ruler. General Sekesh had advanced his headquarters from the capital according to plan and now occupied General Teyhab's old garrison. A royal messenger rowed ashore with a sealed papyrus copy of Aha's *Authoritative Utterance*. While it told of victory, it also confirmed the royal tragedy.

Mekh watched three of the huge barges pole toward Badari to take on those of Sekesh's soldiers who were assigned to the new *Fifth Army* in the Delta.

He then thought of Saiss' *Second Army* that was now to protect the capital. He would always be grateful to that general for the special shields. Everyone hoped that they might be duplicated. Surely, the clever priest-metallurgists were already at work analyzing their secret ingredients. Discovery could be close at hand.

Mekh glanced toward another barge. The stern was occupied by royal guardsmen pointing their lances at the naked enemy. Some of the dark-skinned warriors had lost their protective penis-sheaths, or they had been torn from them, and more than one of the young conquerors studied the enemy's uncircumcised genitals from under hooded eyes. Ample proportions more than confirmed the fierce reputation of a powerful opponent. It made victory doubly sweet.

*

Ramose looked toward the western shore where the proud buildings of the almost completed Temple of Horus came into view as the Royal Bark glided past the *First Royal Mooring Place*. He saw the small falucca being poled toward their convoy at great speed. Khentika's tallish figure stood out and Ramose remembered that the son was to join his parents downriver for the funeral festivities.

When the falucca closed in on the second temple boat, he could see the young priest stretching his hands toward Amma, overjoyed to be reunited with his mother. 'Young priest?' Ramose sighed, reminded that Khentika was his junior by a mere five years. Then he congratulated himself on his foresight. Khentika would do well as the King's new Steward. With his mother close at hand she could tutor him in the ways of the court. 'I wonder how Tasar is faring,' Ramose interrupted his own musings. He dared not think of Nefret. Her life was in the hands of the gods; with timely help from Tasar, he hoped.

After Khentika had boarded the temple boat carrying Amma and Thutmose, Ramose noticed that the vessel did not take up its proper place behind the Royal Bark again. Instead, its crew bent hard over their oars. Where did they think they were going? Did they want to overtake the lot? Ramose saw Tuthmose claw himself forward frantically trying to attract his attention. "Ramose, wait for us," he heard Tuthmose call out to him.

Ramose glanced at the King. Aha, too, had become aware of the undue rush of the temple boat and stood up. Ramose raised his eyebrows in silent request for assent. Aha nodded and they bade the crew to prepare for the temple boat to come alongside the Royal Bark.

"Come aboard, Tuthmose," Ramose called out and his older friend swung himself over the railing of the Royal Bark. He hastily whispered something to Ramose whose face remained impassive. "You too, Khentika," Ramose said, and the younger priest jumped across to the Royal Bark, falling to his knees before Aha, his forehead touching the wet planks.

"Hor-Aha, this is my son Khentika, Chief of Altar at the new Temple of Horus," Tuthmose presented his offspring.

"Yes, yours and Amma's, I know. And we already met, *Altar Chief of Horus*. Except that you thought me to be the Venerable Badar then," Aha said with a faint smile.

Khentika looked up at his King, compassion in his eyes. With trembling hands, he offered up a copper holder. "My King, a messenger arrived from Court an hour ago." Khentika's whisper was laced with such sadness that Aha recoiled.

'No more bad news,' his beating heart protested. He reached for the metal holder and peered at the seal. It was al-Saqqara's! His jaw set hard. His fist clamped around the holder so that the soft copper gave way under his anxiety. His chin jutted forward and the royal head jerked up. "Ramose! Follow me!"

Inside the Royal Cabin, Aha thrust the dented holder toward his High Priest, "You read it."

Ramose broke the seal and extracted the scroll from the twisted tube. He, too, feared bad news. With studied deliberateness, he smoothed the stiff papyrus, taking his time to step into the right light. More than once, he cleared his throat while his eyes skipped ahead in anguish for his already stricken King.

"Get on with it," Aha growled.

"Yes, my King. Al-Saqqara writes: 'Hor-Aha, great King of the Two Lands, Fighting Falcon-God ...'" Ramose, composed at last, feigned difficulty in deciphering the crinkled scroll so that Aha interrupted with vehemence, "Skip the traitor's drivel! The news, Priest, the news is what I need to hear!"

"...The Queen *Went to her Ka*. So did the child. It would have been another prince."

"Ahh ..." Aha fell to his knees, his ashen face buried in his hands. "Why? Ramose! Why?" he wept aloud clutching at the High Priest's kilt. "In my greatest hour of victory, why should

Ptah punish me like this? Did I not promise him rich offerings! Why has he taken my precious family from me!"

Sworn only two moons ago, the King's promise to Ptah was still etched in Ramose's mind. The words had jarred him then. A chill went down his spine now. 'Great Ptah, you only true god, let me live through this. Let my armies win against the enemy. And let me return to my city victorious. In exchange, you may take any of my most precious treasures. They are yours without a question.' Such had been the King's fervent prayers, and Ptah had paid heed. In exchange for victory, he had taken the lives of those most precious to Aha. Ramose shuddered again and bent down to assist the broken man before him.

"Aha," he murmured. "Do not begrudge what Ptah extracted from you. He, who has created all, took only what you offered. You asked and he led you into victory. The deaths were inevitable. Ptah took four lives—one for each of your four armies."

"Five," Aha corrected without thinking. "I have five armies now." He suddenly jumped up and stared at Ramose.

"Djer!" he cried. "There is still Djer!"

*

The convoy reached Ineb-hedj in record time. The war barges sailed past the whiteness of the high walls. The troops as well as Mekh's *Amazing Forces* would go ashore further downriver, closer to the military headquarters now under the command of General Saiss's First Army.

On the smallest temple boat, Bowmen concealed two captives from public view as they headed toward the temple landing ramp where Wazenz waited with a contingent of his priests. After a quick whispered conference with Senmut, Wazenz took charge of the two prisoners and, amidst a tight clump of temple servants, the traitor Tesh and the King of Nobatia were whisked to Ramose's underground dungeons.

The other two temple boats as well as the Royal Bark and its tenders headed for the royal palace landing that by now was practically awash with the inundating river.

The Great Road was lined with nobles, dressed in their finest, though they had abstained from wearing bejeweled accessories. They craned their necks to get a better look; nothing beyond fragmented whispers about war, victory and two dastardly murders had reached their burning ears. Most wept for their stricken King. A secretive few had spent their last night in fretful anxiety. One in particular should have had the good sense not to show his ugly face.

Al-Saqqara's entrenched belief in his own untouchable status allowed for no precaution. His conical headpiece elongated his like-wise shaped head, his ears as usual pointing outward. Saad and his scribes flanked their taciturn master. With great flourish, al-Saqqara bowed, hoping to attract the King's attention. Aha, seemingly preoccupied, never looked at the marked man.

Makari, Khayn, Veni and Saiss crowded close to the edge of the Royal Road, lined by Palace Archers. The officers bowed, first to Aha, then to Ramose, who disembarked with Barum. Tuthmose and Khentika helped Amma debark since the old woman found it difficult to negotiate the slippery planking. She was the only one who looked in the direction of al-Saqqara's tightly-knit group. But she did not acknowledge the Vizier. Instead, she looked at Saad with veiled compassion. She always liked the capable Head Scribe and had long known of his infatuation with her tall Zeina. Too soon, she thought, he would learn of his lover's supposed flight into the desert, never to know that the unfortunate slave returned to Ineb-hedj with the same royal pomp with which she had left, disguised, two moons ago. Except then, of course, she had been alive.

At last, the funerary temple boat carrying the salted royal bodies bumped to a halt along the ramp. Hushed silence enveloped the broad quay.

Aha, not wanting to have to witness his dead children being carried off, was about to wave his bearers on when he saw a pale face poking from behind the square frame of his retiring Chancellor.

"Djer!" he called.

The small boy crept forward.

"Come here, my son. Come, sit beside me."

With a gentle push from Makari, Djer propelled himself toward his father and climbed into the wide sedan. He snuggled up to Aha who put his arms around this youngest, now his only, child and pressed him to his chest so fiercely that the youngster winced.

"He asked to be at the quay, my King," Makari said. "The

403

Lady Beeba and I took the liberty to invite the prince to stay with us when we learned about the Queen."

It was then that Aha noticed the Chancellor's wife behind her husband: proud, capable, but always unobtrusive.

"Most gracious Lady Beeba, I thank you," Aha said, touched, and waived his free left hand at her with great regard for the remarkable noblewoman. He was filled with gratitude toward these two loyal people. Their astuteness to take his youngest son into their household possibly had kept the child alive.

Aha pulled young Djer closer. This time, the boy did not mind and gave his father such a delighted grin that Aha's throat constricted with overwhelming warmth.

The trust in Djer's eyes strengthened his resolve to avenge the deaths of his family without delay. Without mercy. His lips lost their smile and his jaw set in grim determination. He nodded to Makari, who nodded to Khayn, who motioned to Veni. The Royal Archers surrounded the sedan. The huge pylon portals swung open to swallow their returning King. Aha took a long look back at the river with a silent promise to Hapi.

On the quay, thirty priests formed ten tight rows of three abreast. There was the wizened *Prophet of Ptah*, flanked by a rosy-cheeked *Bearer of Floral Offerings*, and several Chief Lectors. Ptah's somber servants rustled along in their papyrus sandals and descended toward the baldachined funeral vessel. A royal honor guard lifted the first litter off the platform. With great care, it was handed over the sides where ten priests extended their arms to receive the remains of the Royal Heiress. Then followed Dubar's litter. In utter silence, the bodies of the royal children were taken home.

Ramose placed himself in the lead of the funeral procession while Tuthmose fell in behind. The cortege proceeded along the Great Road to vanish through the enormous temple pylons. That same night, Ramose would begin the extensive preparations for the official funerals. Together with the proper embalming, this was to take up to seventy days.

Aha had accepted Ramose's suggestion for Khentika to serve temporarily as his Steward much preferring the guileless upstream priest to any of his own fawning, two-faced nobles whom he no longer trusted.

Makari and his successor, Barum, were commanded to

follow the King's chair. The two military men took their places behind Khentika and accompanied Aha through the large audience hall into his private study chambers.

Left behind, al-Saqqara shrugged his shoulders. They would be swapping boring battle stories, drink wine and inform Makari of every gory detail. He had nothing but contempt for these crude and largely illiterate men of war. He turned toward his riverside villa. The evening was still young and he wished that young Hem were there, waiting with childish innocence for his Uncle Ebu. Thinking of the young son of the *Privy-Councillor of the Two Diadems*, al-Saqqara was relieved to be rid of Dubar's greedy fleshiness. Which brought to mind young Djer. He had seen how the youngest prince clung to Lady Beeba's wrapper. The time was ripe for the shy, stuttering Hem to befriend the seven-year old prince. At that age, little boys were most tender, and even more impressionable. Djer, after the King of course, was his final obstacle. How annoying, al-Saqqara thought, that he still had to contend with the meddlesome High Priest! So far, everything had gone right for him.

'Tomorrow, I shall obtain an audience with Aha,' al-Saqqara promised himself. He briefly thought of Hent's greedy midwife. The woman had been well rewarded.

Al-Saqqara did not see the Royal Steward disembark. Could the King have blamed Beir for his children's demise? If so, Aha would already have meted out his vengeance. Too bad. Over the past years, Beir had fed him valuable information. On the other hand, the man had come to know too much and had turned too secretive. Better for the Steward to be out of the way. Al-Saqqara rubbed his hands. He recalled the first time he approached Beir, a lowly slave, young and eager to please those in power. His duties consisted of interminable fanning of his equally young king. Aha was in one of his rotten moods. Likely, Mayet had once again rejected his crude lusting. He raged at Beir that an imaginary fly had defiled his royal skin and beat his slave until Beir collapsed into a bloody heap. Wronged, shamed, and near feinting, the slave dragged himself into an outer chamber. Believing himself alone, he swore crushing revenge. Aloud.

Al-Saqqara, summoned to the King's study on some tally matters, had been waiting in that ante-chamber and had overheard the foreboding mutterings. Arranging for the semi-conscious slave to be taken to his villa, he personally had taken care of him. While the handsome slave never warmed to his advances, he developed a liking for the special brew. Not given to excesses, however, he learned to control his thirst, and his hatred, and returned to his King to placate him with abject apologies for his unpardonable clumsiness. Regretting his hot temper, Aha made Beir his Personal Steward, forgetting all about the incident. But Beir never had. With great purpose, he strove to become his royal master's indispensable confidante.

Al-Saqqara wondered if Beir deliberately had not told him of the King's switch with Badar until it was too late for him to approach the royal sedan under some pretense. If Beir was dead, it was one less thing to worry about. 'I will relax tonight and enjoy an extra cup of wine,' al-Saqqara promised himself. 'And tomorrow—ah, tomorrow—I shall be reaffirmed co-regent. Yes. Tomorrow will be a glorious day for me at Aha's Court, soon to be called the *Court of King Saqqara.*'

As was his habit when he plotted his intrigues, the salivating man placed his bony hands over his genitals.

* * *

Chapter Forty-Two

During the deepest hour of the night, after the shrillness of the river frogs had ceased, dark figures crouched along the quay in single file hugging the palace wall. When its protective shadows no longer hid them, they sprinted past the open space toward the pretentious villa.

"Silence," a voice hissed as a weapon clanged. After a signaling tap on the next man's arm and a straining look toward their leader, they snaked into al-Saqqara's courtyard. A well-rewarded slave had overlooked to bar the doors that night.

Not until the five guards slipped into his bed chamber did al-Saqqara wake from heavy sleep, only slowly becoming aware of the intruders. With a startled croak from his parched throat, he attempted to jump to his feet but his legs disobeyed him. Rough hands pulled him from the bedstand. His senses dulled from the heavy wine he had so copiously enjoyed, he heard one of the guards bark at him to drape his puny body. Then, his hands were bound with chafing ropes.

At last awake, al-Saqqara howled, "Who are you? I demand to see your orders!" His legs threatened to give out from under him again.

The guards said nothing and grabbed him by the arms.

"You miserable wretches! The King shall hear of this," the stunned man fumed trying to keep his pointed teeth from chattering. "You cannot treat me in such a manner!" He squirmed to no avail.

Dragged from his villa like a wine-marinated pig, he quieted down for fear of drawing sleepy neighbors from their beds. After the cold night air cleared his mind some more, al-Saqqara envisioned his *Kenbet*. Surely, he could count on his judges. Still, there were always those who might turn against him. He knew his Council well; just as he knew most of their secrets. And since they knew what he knew, they should be easily persuaded to prepare his defense. Against what? Never mind. Most importantly, his *Kenbet* would surely side with him as none of his carefully selected judges were particularly predisposed toward the meddling priesthood. He sneered. Had Aha connected Hent's death to him? Nothing could be proven. Or had Nekhen's stupid Tax Collector spilled his stinking entrails? And what had become of the greedy gambler from the Fourth who had so miserably failed his mission?

Frantic for answers, al-Saqqara searched his mind what could have gone so wrong. It was debasing to be dragged along the Great Road, by night, like a common criminal. Where were these baboons taking him anyway? Most likely, Ramose had managed to discredit him. It would be his word against the detested priest's. Al-Saqqara shivered. It had to be that lying charlatan's doing, he riled inwardly.

They did not meet a soul along the way, and when the large palace gates swung open, no guards were visible. Al-Saqqara was relieved that they were headed for the palace rather than the temple. So he was to be brought before the King. Reaching the columned portico, the duty guards averted their eyes as the Vizier was dragged through the Grand Foyer. His captors headed for a side door. Al-Saqqara was only all too familiar with the small opening. From it, a narrow corridor led to several dank cubicles. These dungeons held the worst offenders against the laws of *Ma'at* prior to their public trial.

Locking his knees, al-Saqqara tried to dig his heels in. Acquainted with the tactics of desperate criminals, the guards grabbed him under the arms and pushed him before them like a stiff board. Faint pounding echoed from behind one of the hellish doors. Another prisoner! Al-Saqqara could not recall having scheduled anyone for trial. Who, then? Was the other's fate linked to his? Was it perhaps Beir? A chill ran down his spine as fear's bile rose bitter in his throat.

One door was less massive than the others. It led into a bath chamber lined with well-fitted stone slabs and a built-in waste trench. The mud-brick of the palace, excellent in a dry environment, did not stand up well to wetness. This way, water could cascade over the surface without harming it. A steady stream was fed from outside canals, the opening high enough for a man to stand under the wide trickle. At the same time, the run-off washed away human waste from the deep-cut trench. It was not often that criminals were given the privilege to avail themselves of these facilities prior to their accusation before the *Kenbet.*

A massive double-door at the other end of the long hallway led directly into the Grand Foyer. How many times had al-Saqqara sat in the middle of the long table, surrounded by his *Kenbet.* As criminals were led before him and his judges, they often had to appear in public besmeared with their own excrement and vomit. While an accused had the right to speak in his own defense it took an eloquent impervious man to plead his case as he stood there, defiled, debased, numbed by fear. Sickened by his own stench, the wretch usually hung his head and surrendered to his inevitable fate.

Cold sweat broke from al-Saqqara's pores with the smell of rancid wine. He struggled against being forced into the small cell. Once the door clanged shut, the darkness was impenetrable. There were no floormats to escape the crawling vermin.

"My defense!" he screamed and drummed on the heavy door. "I insist on counsel preparing my defense!"

When his fists could take their punishment no longer, he slumped onto the dank clay floor pounded into pungent slickness as each prior occupant had let his steaming water flow in terror. Alone in the terrifying darkness, al-Saqqara now did the same. He sat there, slumped against the rough wall. His stomach protested with unpleasant queasiness and he damned himself for having drunk so much the night before.

Suddenly, the door was flung open. A tall figure filled the dim frame and a sonorous voice intoned, "Al-Saqqara, I come to speak in your defense."

Of all the pissing nerve! "Out of my sight, damnable charlatan," al-Saqqara screeched and struggled to his feet. "To be defended by you is the last thing I wish for. I shall speak on my own behalf. As soon as my judges learn of the despicable untruths you have spread about me, my *Kenbet* will acquit me."

"As you wish, al-Saqqara. But you should know that I am not your accuser." Ramose, relieved, and ashamed of his harsh thoughts, turned and walked out.

Two guards appeared and motioned to al-Saqqara who was

still stunned by the High Priest's last remark. If not Ramose, then who presumed to speak against him? The guards prodded; it was time. Al-Saqqara looked down at his soiled appearance. One of the guards opened the door to the small bathing chamber. Relieved, Ebu al-Saqqara entered the cool stall. Folded on a low stool lay a fresh long shirt and, to his amazement, his official headdress. Fine leather sandals paired off on the floor. Things were looking up.

With a disgusted grunt, al-Saqqara ripped his filthy kilt from his thin hips and stood under the fresh stream gulping water in the hope to rid himself of the foul taste in his mouth. Unreasonably, he fretted that the *Shaduf* might cease its bowing to Hapi at this very moment. Water suddenly became the most precious thing to the filth-spattered man. He slurped another gritty mouthful and scrubbed himself down as fastidiously as he could.

After he had cleaned and clothed himself, he felt much better and even savored the moment when he placed his conical headdress on his shaven pate.

As if the guards knew that he had finished, they reappeared. "Ready, Vizier?" It was the first time they spoke to him and al-Saqqara noted with satisfaction that he was being addressed by his title even though the brief words hardly conveyed the reverence he should be accorded.

"Ready," he replied and stretched himself into defiant tallness, achieved only due to his headdress.

There was barely room for the three to walk abreast and one of the guards stepped his pace up to open the heavy door into to the Grand Foyer. A shoulder-high wall ran from it to an elevated circle, the holding pen for criminals on trial. Facing the *Kenbet*, only an accused man's shoulders and head were visible. While the stones hid his usually filthy body, the stench emanating from him never failed to hasten the judges' quick decisions.

The Vizier, however, was led along another passage until his guards shoved him through a narrow cut into the well-lit hall. The glare from the alabaster floor almost blinded him, its whiteness broken by a dark granite circle. It was into this ominous darkness that al-Saqqara was pushed by his guards.

*

Finally, al-Saqqara's eyes adjusted and he glanced toward

the holding pen. Above the wall, he saw a face he did not recognize. He looked around half hoping, half fearing, to see Beir among the throng. He recognized Chief Senmut. The guards behind the stranger were Temple Bowmen. He knew it! It did have something to do with that lying windbag Ramose!

The whole city seemed to have assembled in the crowded hall. At the long table to the left sat his *Kenbet's* full membership, with one chair remaining empty. Al-Saqqara's stomach knotted. It was where he should be, pronouncing final judgment over some miserable wretch!

To his right, a large contingent of priests shuffled about in stiff papyrus sandals. Wazenz, the portly Chief Priest, jostled for position with his lectors and younger altar chiefs, while an aging priest, heedless of the toes of others, tried to gain a better view over the proceedings. Ramose was not among them. Nor did al-Saqqara see the Steward anywhere.

Next to the detested priesthood, the army lined up, from the new Grand General to Veni and his Archers. Khayn was there, and Mekh had been pushed to the fore in deference to his small stature. Al-Saqqara knew them all, at least by sight or reputation. He found that it was strange for Makari not to be among them. He knew the old goat could not have been slain in battle as he had contrived to remain in Ineb-hedj during the campaign.

Preened in all their finery, the court nobles pretended that they did not see him. Al-Saqqara felt like spitting in their eager faces. Then he noticed Saad, the only one who looked at him with a mixture of sadness and sheer disbelief. Gullible Saad. He never knew. All those years of serving as his Head Scribe, and he never knew anything about the *Usurpers*. Al-Saqqara almost chuckled.

Loud knocking shattered the self-conscious silence and, as if relieved, everyone looked up at the *Window of Appearances*. Its doors flung open and Lord Makari appeared, clad in full war gear. He even wore his leather helmet. In his left, he carried the King's war banner and in his right, drawn from its leather sheath, he clutched his short sword. Al-Saqqara felt the copper blade gleam at him with malice whereas Makari's face was an impassive mask.

Next, Ramose entered. He, too, wore full regalia. A calf-length pleated kilt, topped by the wide precious belt, his sash across his chest. With the purple robe flowing behind him like an ominous storm cloud, the High Priest stepped out onto the balcony. The two men positioned themselves on either side of the empty throne.

Trumpet fanfares heralded the entrance of the King. This dismayed al-Saqqara. Never before had Aha attended a public trial, always having left this unpleasantness to the Vizier and his able Council, preferring to reserve his godly appearances for the more rewarding dispensation of special favors and the granting of new court appointments.

Aha took his seat with deliberate care. A steward arranged the rich pleats of the royal kilt; his face unknown at court. The King inclined his head briefly to the priesthood, his military officers and, lastly and even more briefly, to the excited nobles. Then he looked down at the *Kenbet* and acknowledged the judges with a brief nod. After that, he gazed over al-Saqqara's head, carefully avoiding the Vizier as the increasingly perturbed man's eyes pleaded for a sign of recognition from his King.

Khentika took his place behind the King just as Amma taught him. Aha could find no fault with the chosen kilt, nor with the pectoral, laid out by his new steward, down to the correct headdress: the *Red Crown* of the Lower Region. The *White Nefer* of the Upper Region was borne on a cushion by the *Privy-Councillor of the Two Diadems.*

The *Kenbet's* Head Judge stood up and pounded the table with his short staff. Its hollow sound echoed through the Grand Foyer. He had to clear his throat several times before he trusted himself to speak.

"The *Kenbet* of the Two Lands is assembled to judge Ebu al-Saqqara, Vizier and Quartermaster of Hor-Aha, our godly King. The accused has waived counsel. How, then, does he speak for himself?"

The Head Judge sat down and hoped that his part in this mock-trial would be brief. He, just as the other judges, had been apprised of the King's damning decree during the night by special royal messengers. Even though several of the judges were still sympathetic to the ugly man's plight, not one of them had entertained the notion of sending word to the condemned man. This was not a time to stand by dangerous loyalties.

Al-Saqqara's heart jumped at the unpromising start of the proceedings. Despite his resolve to fight for his life, his knees shook and he could barely think. After several attempts, he croaked, "What is the accusation against me?"

The Head Judge stood up again and tapped the table.

"Ebu al-Saqqara, you are charged with High Treason."

A collective sigh rippled through the stunned audience. Imagine: High treason, the gravest of all crimes!

The blood drained from al-Saqqara's face. He felt faint and knew that he had to challenge this abomination at once; he must proclaim his innocence with vigor and conviction lest he not see another dawn.

When quiet was restored, Lord Makari spoke from the balcony. "Nekhen's former *Royal Tax Collector* bears witness against you, Ebu al-Saqqara."

The Vizier's head jerked up in surprise. So that was Tesh, the thieving vermin! He should quickly point a finger at the stupid provincial's avarice, at his pilfering from the royal silos, and point out that his, al-Saqqara's, watchful scribes had caught him. The judges had to see that Tesh was trying to save his own hide by conjuring up false accusations against an alert Vizier. Why, then, had Aha involved himself? Just when al-Saqqara felt he had a plausible defense, he saw Ramose point a finger at the man behind the wall.

"The Tax Collector is not your accuser, Ebu al-Saqqara. He only bears witness against you. His eager tongue spilled forth the names of those who involved themselves in your treasonous ambitions."

Murmuring surged through the crowd, some laced with the fear of discovery by those with a guilty conscience. Some asked themselves with trepidation how much the King knew. The air in the Grand Foyer grew stifling.

Al-Saqqara wondered if he could turn things against the nobles. His voice nerve-shrilled, he summoned his reserves, and demanded much too loudly, "Then who dares accuse me? Who dares accuse the King's Vizier Ebu al-Saqqara?" He stared at the members of his *Kenbet*, ready to defy the next words which, however, were not uttered by his Council. Instead, they were flung down at him from the *Window of Appearances*.

"I do." The King's voice cut through the fetid air. Not a sound emanated from the sweating audience. One could have heard an ivory needle drop to the alabaster floor. The awful silence did not last.

Aha jumped up and shook his fist at al-Saqqara. His voice thundered down upon the quivering assembly.

"As if his treachery at Court was not enough! This despicable offshoot of a hyena, who still lifts his shifty eyes in brazen insolence, conspired to have me slain. And," Aha's voice threatened to break, "he is the murderer of my Royal Heirs!"

The brutal force of his King's loathing made al-Saqqara's skin crawl. He realized that long before the *Council of Judges* had been summoned to ponder his fate, he had already been sentenced by Aha, a king whom he had thought malleable and weak. He feared that had lost his lofty gamble and was as good as a condemned man. Al-Saqqara shot a hate-filled look at Ramose. This was his doing!

With a nod from the King, Lord Makari stepped up to address the Council.

"How do you speak, Lord Judges?"

Again, the Head Judge rose and tapped his staff three times on the sturdy table. He looked up at the *Window of Appearances*.

"We, the Judges of the *Kenbet*, find nothing in favor of the accused." He drew a heavy breath and added firmly, "We say: Guilty, my King."

Makari turned toward the High Priest. With studied formality, he asked, "High Priest of Ptah, how do you speak?"

Ramose answered just as formally, and as clearly, "I, High Priest of Ptah, find no remorse in the accused. I say: Guilty, my King."

The audience held its breath as Lord Makari bowed to Aha. Again, he asked in the same stylized tone, "Hor-Aha, King of the Two Lands, Protector of the Two Diadems, how do you speak?"

The silence in the Foyer deepened into a dark pit.

Aha spat but one word: "Guilty!"

*

Three Royal Archers dragged the two prisoners along the quay. Hobbled like lowly cattle, al-Saqqara and Tesh were forced onboard a crude unsteady raft. The oarsmen kept their eyes averted lest Seth sprang from the mouths of the condemned and put a curse on them for having been chosen to row this death float into the middle of the river. A small falucca followed them to take the two archers and their new captain back to shore. Al-Saqqara was stripped of his headdress and long shirt, and they ripped Tesh's kilt from his chafed hips, and threw the garments into the water. The rushing current swept them away, except for al-Saqqara's heavy headdress which instantly gurgled to the river's muddy bottom.

The new young Archer Captain who took over Veni's old post glanced at the naked man, once the most feared and despised official in the palace. 'His inflamed *Mehyt* is as unappetizing as his flushed face always was when he leered at me,' the young soldier thought in disgust, and stepped toward the condemned to get the unrewarding task over with. He ordered his archers to bind the prisoners together by their wrists and ankles.

The two condemned men were pushed down onto the slippery planks, face to face, so that they would witness each other's agony while swallowing each other's foul breath. Additional ropes anchored them to the raft so that they could not roll off. After all, the traitors had not been condemned to drown mercifully, nor to be honorably devoured by sacred crocodiles. 'Let *Nekhbet* and her winged harbingers of death be al-Saqqara's executioners,' had been the King's death sentence. The raft was to keep them afloat on Hapi's back until their stench attracted *Nekhbet's* vultures.

Along the shore, the crowds disbursed. No one was eager to observe the thrashings on the river raft. There would be no one to shudder in sympathy as chunks of flesh were ripped away by greedy beaks.

*

After two days, the screams from the small float ceased to foul the evening air and the watch-boat was able to return, its grisly vigil over. The King's once powerful Vizier had ceased to exist. His name would be stricken from every record, his villa destroyed. Ebu al-Saqqara was no longer. In fact, Aha decreed that he had never been.

A great gust of air sprung up with sudden vehemence, and the young captain urged his oarsmen to make fast. His eyes searched the sky but the descending darkness hid whatever brewed above. Ominous whistling pierced the thickening air and when the first fine grains of wind-borne sand stung their cheeks, fear spurned the Archers into haste.

"Rih al-Khamsin!"

415

They scrambled up the ramp. Driven by the howling wind, they ran toward the palace gates already being pushed shut against the threatening storm. It was late in the season, with the New Year almost upon them. Ptah willing, the feared *Wind of Fifty Days* would not be as devastating this time around.

* * *

Chapter Forty-Three

What are we going to do?" Nefret pressed closer to Safaga.

The pretty Sumerian was using the last of her own strength when she whispered, "This is the end."

Tasar's agile mind, however, did not allow him to spend his last energies in futile riling against misfortune. As soon as he had vented his frustration, he faced his companions with renewed resolve.

"See what we have left," he commanded them, and the girls were glad to be given something to do to take their minds off the dire situation. They spread the quilts and counted out their few provisions: a handful of sweet dates, a few sun-dried strips of ocean fish. Safaga held up a bundle of onions, and Nefret unwrapped a small melon-like fruit she had hoarded. They still had a few sips of tepid water.

With a flick of his arm, Tasar unfurled the creases of the tent cover. Out spilled the King's intended robe.

"Tasar, how can you!" Safaga cried and glanced at Nefret who simply shrugged her shoulders.

"We need it for protection," Tasar explained his accused callousness.

The girls had lost their wigs to the fierce squall and the heat of the rising day pummeled them mercilessly. They hoped to catch a cooling breeze off the water and were facing the surf when a ripping sound from behind made them turn. Tasar was tearing the robe into wide strips, handing each of the girls a remnant of the wondrous cloth.

"Cover your head and shoulders!" His brusqueness left no room for protest. He wound a strip around his own head pulling a deep fold over his tanned face. His features had a newly chiseled look. Safaga sighed.

Tasar took a mental fix on the sun's path. Above, the sky was cloudless, though a dirty-yellow stripe obscured the horizon ahead. Bending down, he bundled their pitiful provisions into the two quilts for the girls to carry. He himself shouldered what was left of the heavy tent. He turned north, parallel to the shore. The girls fell in behind him.

"Do you know where you are going?" Nefret called to him, without true curiosity.

"To the end of the Crystal Sea to some trading settlements, the largest of which has a temple dedicated to one of our gods, I believe," Tasar called back and the two girls hastened their stride to come abreast with him.

"Then the priests can give us more of the yellow nub," Nefret stated, rising hope and thirst thinning her voice.

"I doubt it," Tasar answered. "I shall arrange for you two to stay there while I go back."

"Back to where?" Nefret was alarmed at the prospect of being abandoned once again - this time by Tasar - which would be much worse than having been put ashore by the lecherous men from the smelly dhow.

"To Ineb-hedj. To see Ramose. A small wadi runs from the Crystal Sea toward the City of White Walls. It should not take more than, oh, three to four days."

"You mean we will be that close to home?" Nefret's interest picked up. "I am going with you," she announced.

He shook his head. It was too hot to argue.

"Tasar! Answer me!"

"Ramose should be at Ineb-hedj by now. He will be relieved that you made it this far, Nefret. He will help us reach the *Wadj*," Tasar said economizing his breath.

There was not the slightest breeze and shimmering images evaporated into the searing air. They were fortunate to have worn their sandals when they disembarked. Ahead lay a long even stretch of shoreline. If they waded in the shallow water it would cool them down. Tasar took his sandals off. The girls followed his example and welcomed the mild relief. The wet sand made the going more difficult and they fell quiet again, wearily searching ahead to avoid slippery rocks and small crevasses. On the distant horizon, the yellow band grew darker.

*

They walked single file. Occasional boulders and rocky

outcroppings prevented them from traveling during the dark though it would have been much cooler. This close to the water, the nights did not turn as chilly as on the open desert. But the days grew just as hot. On occasion, they spotted a boat as it slid past with tantalizing slowness. Either the crews did not see their frenetic waving or they preferred not to. The three travelers would have to reach the northern settlements on their own - or die on this forsaken shore.

"Tasar!"

Pushing the soft material out of his eyes, he turned and saw Nefret on her knees, her face close to the last tentacle of foaming surf. Her cupped hands pressed against her lips, she licked salty wetness from her palms.

"Nefret!" Tasar's shout echoed along the empty shore. He ran back to her. "Stop that at once!"

With the strength left in them, Tasar and Safaga pulled the struggling girl away from the water's edge. Finally, they succeeded. When Nefret's last fist opened onto nothing but wet sand she looked at it with glazed eyes.

"No!" Great sobs racked her thin frame.

"How much did she drink?" Tasar asked Safaga, horrified.

"I don't know. I thought she was going to splash some water on her face. Instead, she kneeled down and drank and drank. Despite your warning." Safaga, close to tears herself, held on to Nefret who lay stretched out on the hot sand alternately begging for water and riling at her two heartless companions.

"You want me to die! I saw the way you look at each other." Nefret buried her face in her salt-encrusted hands.

"Safaga! Hold her head from behind to keep her face out of the sand," Tasar instructed. He turned the delirious girl onto her stomach. With Safaga astride Nefret's back, he squatted down and his fingers pried her teeth open. Then he stuck his middle finger deep down her throat. Nefret retched, bringing up most of what she had ingested. Tasar sat her up and reached for a tellingly flat bladder. Gently, he held the opening to her cracked lips.

Nefret gulped the last of their water and Tasar pulled her head to his chest. He held her there and rocked her while she cried more salt from her exhausted body and all her anguish from her reeling mind.

Safaga watched them, and unjustly kicked the empty waterbag. She walked into the surf where she sat, the water racing toward her. Only when the playful waves threatened to engulf her did she crawl back to shore where Nefret still lay in Tasar's arms, pale and lifeless; yet her eyes hung on his every whisper. "Just one more day, my sweet," he cooed. "Then we are safe."

Safaga hoped that he believed it and put her hand on his shoulder. Weary to his bones, he smiled up at her. "We'll camp over there for the night," he said over his shoulder. "Help me carry Nefret. I will come back for our things."

His mouth felt dry and he was more than concerned about their lack of drinking water. How long would it take until he himself, against his better judgment, succumbed to the deceptive sea bending down to drink from it, knowing that it brought delirium and, soon thereafter, death. He looked at Nefret, and a painful cry escaped his cracked lips. "Merciful Ptah," he sobbed, "do not let her die."

"Tasar." Safaga shook the crying man. "Whatever happens, you still have me."

"It is not the same," he answered without thinking.

"But I love you."

His muscles stiffened and he pretended not to hear, not to feel the softness of Safaga's touch. A heavy stillness hung between them.

"Tasar!" No longer the plea of a scorned lover, Safaga's cry jarred him.

His eyes flashed annoyance. "Nefret is not going to die! Nor do I intend to run off with a slave."

Safaga pulled at his hair and forced him to follow her outstretched arm. Her pretty face was filled with fear. "Look! Out there!"

To the north, the yellow band had mushroomed into dust-laden clouds bearing down on them. The ominous sight brought Tasar to his feet and he instantly forgot his anger. He had never experienced the full-blown horror of the Great Wind. Instinctively, he knew these were the outcroppings of the dreaded Khamsin.

"We must dig in!" He shouted against the wind beginning to tear at them. "Safaga! Cover your face with the blue cloth! And do the same for Nefret. Over there is a hollow protected by a rocky ledge. Help me to get her to it. Quickly, girl!"

The two dug side by side while Nefret sat propped up against the rock, as lifeless as a statue, unconcerned about the chaos fomenting around her. Safaga tied a blue strip around the lifeless girl's head to cover nose and mouth.

"Faster, Safaga! Dig faster! I am going back for our packs."

"Don't leave me!" Safaga pleaded and clung to him. He tore loose without much effort and pushed off into the yellow brine. Safaga looked at Nefret. What good would it do her if her mistress survived? Now that there was nothing more to trade.

"Safaga! I told you to dig!" Tasar shouted from behind. "What have you been doing, girl? Our lives depend on shelter from the Khamsin."

"The Khamsin?" Nefret cried. "Tasar! Help me. I am drowning." She sputtered the choking grit from her dry mouth.

"Cover your face," Tasar called out and dropped his heavy bundles. Pulling out two shards, he gave one to Safaga and started to dig the natural hollow deeper.

Preoccupied with their survival, he did not see the tears pouring from Safaga's burning eyes. If he had, he would not have spared the time to ponder the hurt feelings of a slave. She had held up well after the death of both her lovers, though. As the Two Lands were not her native home she should adjust reasonably well to a new beginning somewhere else. He looked at her as she struggled to keep up with his forceful digging. There was no denying it: she was pretty, even after the hardships of the past moon. He glanced back at Nefret who had quieted down and sat listlessly watching them over the rim of her shroud.

The air thickened with tiny particles of sand and the setting sun, as red as blood, became obscured by darkening dust. The storm clawed and groped and tore at them with a high-pitched howl that turned into a deafening roar. No longer was the tumultuous wind satisfied to make the sand dance. Its devastating breath toyed with larger pebbles, skipping them across the water until they sank, capriciously abandoned.

They were huddled together, their backs rounded against the raging wind, their heads tucked deep into their shoulders. Tasar had placed Nefret onto a corner of their cover leaning her against a rock. He and Safaga huddled next to her pulling

421

the rest of the rough tent material over their heads. To keep a firm grip on the outer corners they tucked them under their thighs. While the ledge lent some protection against the fiercest blasts there was no escaping from the intrusive sand. The incessant howling above posed no danger to them physically, but it was so nerve-wracking that Tasar feared they might lose their mind if it did not abate soon. He pulled the girls closer to him until he felt their breath on his encrusted cheeks. He turned his head and sought Nefret's mouth. Although her lips were dry she weakly pressed closer and he tightened his arm around her. Then he turned the other way. Safaga met his mouth with such fervor that he had to pry himself loose. He patted the slave's cheek and hoped that she understood. Once more, he turned to Nefret and blew softly into her ear. She did not respond.

Hour after hour passed without the tearing and the howling letting up. Tasar felt a mounting wall of sand claw at him. He groped for the amulet around his neck, its brilliance hidden in the smutty cloth.

"Heavenly Horus, keep us from being buried alive," he sobbed at his *Protective Eye of Horus* before blackness enveloped him.

*

Soft light bathes everything. The air smells clean, the breeze soothes. There is no need for the cloth around her head. She unwinds it and looks up. A billowing green brightness gives vaguely shape to a translucent form. The woman is beautiful; streamers of honeyed hair flow behind her like a banner.

'Come, child. I am your spirit's guide.'

'Isis.' Nefret stretches her arms toward the apparition. She no longer feels her thirst. Nor her earthly fear.

Lifted from the sand, she joins the goddess's wafting image. Their fingers touch.

She now knows that her sinner's Ba will have another chance to atone and to find peace; in another time, in another life.

*

The eerie stillness jarred him awake. His knees were stiff from being pulled close to his torso, the way the common dead were wrapped for burial. He blinked repeatedly in an effort to open his eyes against the sandy crust. And still, he stared into darkness. Perhaps he was dead. He could not recall passing through the *Field of Rushes* to reach the Netherworld. Great Horus, his soul was lost in the Dark Void!

Tasar shook himself. The hard casing of compacted sand began to trickle down his back. Once more, he wriggled and again everything around him crumbled until he could finally free his arms to throw off the sand-laden tent.

Dawn had broken with a bluish-yellow light that tortured the landscape. Tasar tried to breathe and spat out the grit between his teeth. There was slight movement from under the mound next to him. He knelt down and dug, using his hands as shovels. Taking hold of a corner of the half buried cover he tore at it with all his might and then dug again, brushing armfuls of sand away as fast as he could. Though he grew hot no beads of perspiration formed on his forehead. He had hardly enough moisture left in him to keep his tongue from sticking to his swollen palate.

There, a strip of dark blue! Tasar pulled at it not daring to work any faster for fear of strangling its wearer. Anxious moments passed until a wrapped head appeared. Relieved, he unwound the cloth and pummeled the sand from dark hair. Safaga sputtered into life.

"Oh, it's you," he breathed.

Before the pretty slave could extract herself from her sandy tomb, Tasar went back to digging. His fingers found another strip of indigo buried too deeply to be pulled free.

"Safaga! Under here," he called. "Help me or she'll suffocate!"

He dug faster. Then he stopped and sobbed, imploring every god he knew. Again, he dug calling Nefret's name as he clawed at the rubble until his fingers bled.

"Here is one of her sandals," Safaga cried pulling at the badly worn leather. "How did she get so far from us?"

Tasar doubled his efforts. "She must have crawled out of the hollow. Why did I not notice? I should have stopped her!"

"You must not blame yourself." Safaga dug feverishly at the shifting ground.

"Nefret!" Tasar cried. Frantically, he followed the blue strip hand over hand as it snaked into the sand.

"Nefret! My one and only love! Hold on!"

The flesh from his fingers wore away as he unraveled more of the once beautiful jubilee robe. She had to be under there!

"I will do anything. Anything! If only you will live.'

Youthful hopes of prominence and power were meaningless to him now. It did not matter that Ramose might not choose him as the next High Priest of Ptah. Only her survival mattered now. He vowed to stay with her; and prove his worth to her. Again, he vowed to protect and love her for all eternity.

"Hold on, my love," Tasar sobbed as he dug deeper into the sand, and into his soul.

* * *

Epilogue

At last, the *Great Wind of Fifty Days* subsided, and the people of the river valley could breathe anew without inhaling mouthfuls of dust. Hot sand, however, still covered all the wells and canals, the body of a careless brother, the carcasses of suffocated livestock. Donkeys lay bunched together with hyenas, and crocodiles caught snoring on shore lay bloated next to drowned cranes and rotting fish. Losing no time, survivors started digging, mourned their dead, and prayed to Ptah for a kinder future.

After al-Saqqara's trial, many of the Two Land's nobles were rudely awakened during the middle of the night and dragged toward crude rafts. Members of the clandestine *Usurpers of the Two Crowns* who once shared their leader's lofty ambitions were now to share his ignoble demise.

The Royal Funeral Cortege was a grand affair, and the wailing of the official mourners carried far into the desert. In endless lines, the remaining unscathed nobles and their gift-bearing servants snaked past the four new royal *Mastabas* at Ineb-hedj's wind-swept necropolis where the monuments were to bear eternal witness to King Aha's tragedy.

*

To support his faltering strength, Ramose leaned on the *Per-nu*, where Nefret's Placenta Jar once stood. It had been thought to hold the Royal Heiress's alter-ego. Empty, as only he and Badar knew it was, the small shrine had been placed at the unfortunate Zeina's feet in the royal sarcophagus. The High Priest wondered if its ill omen would fulfill itself despite the tall slave's ultimate sacrifice. After the Vizier's mock trial, Ramose and his *Ka*-priests unwrapped the natron-packed murder victims deep within the caverns of his great temple. It took them two moons to empty the bodies of their organs and the brain, and to repack the cadavers with salts and fragrant herbs before they were rewrapped with huge quantities of fine linen for their last earthly journey.

Ramose recalled the day when the bodies had been unwrapped following the long trip down the Hapi. Through Tuthmose, Amma had asked that she be permitted to view the body of her beloved royal charge. Ramose suspected what she was looking for. When the old nurse could not find the dark uneven mark on the dead girl's left thigh she had locked eyes with him. Despite his vow of silence, he nodded briefly. Then he handed her a small vial. The next morning, a palace slave found old Amma on her sleeping platform. An oddly contented smile played around her fallen mouth.

*

Alone in his temple, Ramose pressed his aching forehead against the cool granite of the enormous offering basin. At last, even the *Bearer of Floral Offerings* had left. Ramose's face was drawn and his brilliant eyes were dulled by a great sadness that threatened to strangle his heart.

His ears still rang from the protesting screeches the heavy granite blocks sent against the cloudless sky as they were slid across the top of the royal *Mastabas*. He prayed to *Ptah* and to *Maat* forever to safeguard his deception of his King. If Nefret was still alive, he would gladly endure the gods' wrath.

There was little else for him to do now. The temple butchers had slaughtered the Hapi bull and dressed it for burial next to the royal tombs. He had dispatched *Sem*-priests to scour the land for a suitable young calf to be prodded and shaped into the new sacred bull. Ramose glanced at the offering basin still caked with the heart-blood of the sacrificed old Hapi.

For the first time at odds with his calling, he was disheartened by Isis' cruel prophecy. His dark musings wrapped around him like a cloak so that he remained unaware of the insistent pounding.

"Boom, boom, boom!"

The dull sound reverberated through the nave's vaulted emptiness.

"Boom, boom, boom!"

Another desperate clamor for admittance.

Wazenz emerged from a side door. What noisome racket, he

inwardly chided the unknown intruder. With a concerned look at his motionless High Priest, he ambled toward the huge temple doors and opened them a crack. Indignation blanketed his face when he saw a tattered stranger.

"Wazenz."

Barely audible, the beggar's word took the rotund Chief Priest aback. The man's eyelids were burned to the sockets. The flaking skin on his forehead and nose exposed patches of raw flesh. But mostly, it was the stranger's filthy strips of clothing that perplexed Wazenz. The parched apparition's wrappings bore faint shades of royal lapis lazuli. Who was this then? Only Ramose was permitted to wear colors of any kind. Was this beggar mocking the sacred cape of the High Priest? Or was he an ignorant foreign trader who had fallen on hard times? At any rate, how dared the emaciated stranger disturb the midday peace and boldly seek admittance before the *Altar of Ptah* in such affronting tatters.

"Wazenz, you do not wish to know me then?" The strangled plea for recognition was a mere croak from a parched throat.

Wazenz remained unmoved.

"It is not a question of wishing to know you or not, Stranger. I simply do not know you. Nor will I guess who you might pretend to be."

With surprising strength, the dust-caked man pushed the temple doors wider and lunged past Wazenz who stepped back, disgusted, trying not to be touched.

The commotion pulled Ramose from his reverie. He stepped up to the *High Altar of Ptah*, waiting for the stranger to approach. Sun-blackened hands reached for him before the emaciated man crumpled to his knees, a reddish-blue bundle of abject misery.

The dirty shreds struck a chord within Ramose.

"Have you committed some heinous crime to seek refuge in the Temple of Ptah, Stranger?" he asked, not without compassion.

When the gaunt man looked up something in his eyes drew Ramose closer. Maybe it was the haunting plea of the spent creature.

The man's heat-swollen hands fumbled with a strip that hung around his scruffy neck. Fingers trembling from exhaustion, he managed to rip the double-sewn rag apart. A finely crafted chain lay exposed. Reaching deeper still, a faience amulet spilled from a second wrapping. The carnelian and lapis *Eye of Horus* stared up at the High Priest.

"How did you get this!" Ramose demanded, his heart pulsing faster.

"You gave it to me," the filthy man whispered.

"Never!"

"Ramose! Recognize the man you called 'son' not long ago. I am - Tasar!"

Wazenz, who had joined them, stared in disbelief.

Ramose reached down and pulled the sobbing man to his feet.

"Tasar?" he asked in wonderment.

Relieved that the High Priest recognized him at last, Tasar leaned against the blood-stained offering basin while the High Priest searched the tortured face for traces of its former handsome features.

"Wazenz, quickly! Some wine," Ramose bade the shocked Chief Priest and repeated, as if to assure himself that he had heard correctly. "Tasar? Tasar? It is really you? What terrible fate has befallen you to have robbed you of your youth. Was it the Khamsin?"

"The Great Wind was not the worst of it," Tasar whispered.

Ramose wished he did not have to hear much else. Yet he had to know. No matter what the truth was.

Wazenz returned with a small amphora of the temple's hardy date wine and Ramose cautioned Tasar to sip it slowly. After the wine worked its enlivening effect on the exhausted youth, Ramose nodded to his Chief Priest, "Leave us."

Wazenz resented his dismissal. Unlike Tasar's thirst, his curiosity would now remain unquenched.

"Now, Tasar, tell me everything that happened." The two men knew the one question the High Priest hungered to ask yet feared to have answered.

Tasar described his journey from Nekhen to catch up with the fleeing travelers. When he mentioned the Royal Steward's death, there was a sudden glimmer in the other's sky-blue eyes.

After a while, Ramose could not contain himself for another anxious moment. His look bored into Tasar's very soul. He had to ask. "Nefret?"

Tasar's eyes glazed over as if he had gone blind from too much sun. After another small sip of wine, he summoned up his courage. "At long last, the Great Wind subsided. I managed to free the slave from the sand. Frenzied with fear, the two of us dug for Nefret. Safaga showed me a blue strip of cloth snaking into the packed ground. We dug until our fingers bled."

Tasar broke into great sobs. It took him a moment and another gulp of wine before he could continue.

"I called to Nefret to hang on."

"And?"

"Safaga and I pulled at the cloth."

"And?"

"The sand gave way. The strip broke free."

Deadly coldness blew down from the temple's rafters.

"And!" Ramose's very breath turned cold.

"She was not there."

Ramose reared up.

"You scoundrel!" he roared and pounced upon Tasar like the great spotted jungle cat. "Do you take me for a fool? Now I remember where I saw the color of your shreds." Dubar's discarded death shroud wafted before his inner eye.

"You stole the cape from the embalming chamber. Then you and the Sumerian plotted together. To think that I trusted you with all my yellow nub only for you to steal it. So that it would last the two of you for life!" Ramose gulped for air. He never knew such heartache. Except, when Mayet had died. To prevent total collapse in front of this unworthy *Ba*, he roared again, "So you and that ungrateful slave decided to go free!"

Again, he had to fight for his next breath before he thundered on, "You killed Nefret! You killed my child!"

"Ramose! By the Great Ptah! Believe me! We looked everywhere for her."

"Did you now?" Ramose brought his wrath to within two fingers' breadth of Tasar's face forcing the trembling man to his knees. "And where is your shameless accomplice now? The truth, you miserable wretch!" Ramose stretched to his full height, towering like an avenging *Seth* above the sunken figure.

Tasar's whisper barely reached him.

"Safaga died of thirst. She was loyal to the end. By the great Ptah, I speak the truth." With the last of his remaining strength, Tasar issued forth a cry that was not quite human any more. "I searched everywhere. The Khamsin must have taken her."

With great restraint, Ramose overcame the furor in his heart, and his words took on a gentler tone. "So you really tried, young Tasar?"

"I really tried, Ramose. You entrusted her life to me, as a

429

priest. But I also loved her. As a man. How can I ask you to understand?"

The great rage at last drained from Ramose, the High Priest, as compassion and memories flooded back into the heart of Rama, the man.

"I do understand, my son," he said at last. "Did you ever find her?"

"No, Ramose. Nefret had vanished without a trace."

Safe at last from the raging wind, and the rage of Ramose's grief, Tasar's own pain became too much for him.

"This is the end," he sobbed and collapsed.

Ramose gazed at the crumpled form at his feet. With the gentleness born of a great soul, he touched the distraught youth and lifted Tasar's face toward him. The two men looked into each other's eyes, no longer weary, no longer in anger, their mutual loss drawing them close.

"I do understand such love more than you can know, young Tasar."

The young mourner grasped his great mentor's hands and buried his sun-ravaged face in their forgiving coolness.

Ramose knelt down to be at the same level with the young sinner.

"Tasar, my son, if you must show your grief now, I understand. But bear your pain silently thereafter, and bury your heart's longing forever in your calling to serve Ptah. Most of all, Tasar, console yourself and remember that the end is but a new beginning for the eternal *Ba*."

# # #

Appendix A
Ancient Lands and Cities
(Modern Names in Parentheses)
Time: About 3080 BC

Two Lands (Egypt)
Lower and Upper Egypt from the Delta
to the First Cataract after Unification - 3100 B.C.

Ineb-hedj "City of the White Walls" (Memphis)
Built ca. 3090 by Narmer (supposedly the legendary
Menes of the Greek historian Manethos).
On the West Bank of the Nile, its great temple was
consecrated to Ptah, its necropolis was Saqqara.

Kharga Oasis (also called The Great Oasis)
Battle Field for Aha's campaign against the Noba and the
Kush in the Western desert;
a 3-4 day's donkey ride from Nekhen.

Central Command
Makari's Garrison-Farm, 2-3 hours' ride west of Ineb-
hedj; Training ground for Makari's Special Forces
overshadowed by the "Guardian of the Desert"
(Sphinx).

Abdju (Abydos)
Vast Desert Cemetery for the Ancient City of Tjeny.

Badari (130 Miles north of Nekhen)

Crystal Sea (Red Sea)

First Falls (First Cataract)
South of Nekhen - ancient border

First Royal Mooring Place - (Herakleopolis)
Temple of Horus in process of being built.

Khnumu (Hermopolis - near the later Amarna)
On the Westbank; 100 miles north of Abydos,
with its Temple of Thoth, the Ibis-headed goddess of
Writing and Learning

Nekhen (Hierakonpolis) - Old Capital of the South
On Westbank of the Nile; the combined palace and
temple grounds were surrounded by an enormous wall

Nubt (Ombos) Important Ancient Trading Center

Tjeny (Thinis) Possibly in or near modern Girga.
Ancient capital of the Eighth Upper Egyptian nome.

Wadj (The Great Green - Mediterranean)

Note:

Iwun (Heliopolis, in the Delta)
as well as **Thebes** and **Karnak/Luxor** were built too late
for this story. Even the great **Pyramids** had not yet been
built.

Only an unknown early form of the Sphinx existed, its face
later supposedly fashioned under Chafre to resemble him.

* * *

Appendix B
Main Characters

Mayet (Dead)
Was 19 when she died in childbirth. First Queen of Aha. Mother of Nefret. Born in Nekhen.

Narmer (Dead)
First King of the First Dynasty - 3100 B.C. Credited with building the City of White Walls (Ineb-hedj, later called Memphis by the Greeks) and with the Unification of the Upper and Lower Regions into one realm - The Two Lands. His consort is buried in Nekhen.

Ramose (38)
High Priest of Ptah. Born in Nekhen as Prince Rama, he enters the priesthood, but remains in the service of King Aha. As Badar's successor, he resides at the Temple of Ptah in the City of "White Walls"

Nefret (15 1/2)
Royal Heiress of the Two Lands; daughter of King Aha and his deceased first Queen Mayet. Born in Ineb-hedj

Dubar (barely 15)
First Prince of the Two Lands. Son of Aha by his second Queen, Hent, who despises her step-daughter Nefret.

Aha (35)
Second Horus-King of the First Dynasty.
Father of Nefret, Dubar and Djer.
Born at Nubt, Aha first ruled from southern Nekhen. Moved his capital to Narmer's northern court city of Ineb-hedj (City of White Walls=Memphis)

Hent (30)
Born in the Nile Delta region. Second wife of Aha who bore him two sons: Dubar and Djer.
Was elevated to Principal Wife and Co-Regent with Nefret, Aha's daughter by Mayet.

Djer (7)
Second Prince of the Two Lands, Aha's youngest son by Hent.

Tasar (20)
Brilliant surgeon-priest from Nekhen. Protege of Rahetep, Chief Priest at the Temple of Horus. Lover of Nefret.

Amma (48)
Royal Head Nurse. Wet-nursed Mayet when Amma herself was barely 16 after bearing a son, Khentika, fathered by the priest Tuthmose. Princess Nefret's nurse since birth.

Safaga (21)
Pretty Sumerian slave. Brought to "White Walls" at the age of eight. Nefret's closest attendant.

Zeina (18)
Nefret's Second slave. Bears a striking resemblance to the tall Princess

Dokki (19)
Nefret's third slave, a Black Noba. The plump girl is slow to grasp things; extremely loyal to Nefret.

Ebu al-Saqqara (36)
Vizier of the Two Lands. Born near Saqqara.
He serves as Quartermaster of the Royal Armies.
Second most powerful man in the young kingdom; harbors secret enmity toward the priesthood and longs for Aha's throne.

Badar (60)
Born Abou al-Badari at Badari. First high priest-surgeon under Narmer, continued to serve young King Aha. Now retired and known as The Divine Father of Ptah, also often addressed as The Venerable Badar.

Pase (20)
Courier from the Fourth Army camp in the Kharga Oasis. Former Royal Archer of the Palace Guards in Ineb-hedj, at which time he was the lover of Safaga.

Beir (28)
King Aha's implicitly trusted Personal Steward. Some-time lover of Safaga after Pase's transfer to the Kharga Oasis.

Saad (25)
Personal Scribe of the Vizier.
Likes the tall slave Zeina.

Yadate (approx. 30)
Blue-eyed tribesman from the Land of Punt (Ethiopia). Provides his own mistress to General Barum for profit; rewarded from several masters whom he feeds information.

Makari (55)
Aha's Chancellor and Grand General; a military genius, he trains the Special Forces (Ostrich Riders) on his farm near the Sphinx.

Ali el-Barum (35)
General of Fourth Army of Amun. Usually head-quartered near Nekhen. Encamped around the Kharga Oasis to prepare his troops for the Annual War Games.

Keheb (25)
Aid-de-Camp to General Barum; Regimental Seal-Bearer of the Fourth Army and Barum's scribe.

Veni (30)
Captain of the Royal Palace Archers at the palace in Ineb-hedj.

Khayn (30)
Colonel, first Aide-de-camp of Grand General Makari, headquartered at the Palace in Ineb-hedj.

Mekh (31)
Colonel; Makari's second Aide de Camp.
Heads Special Forces at Makari's garrison-farm near the Guardian of the Desert (early form of the Sphinx).

Senmut (26)
Chief of Temple Bowmen.
Accompanies the Temple Boats to Nekhen.
Develops a liking for the dark slave Dokki.

Tuthmose (50)
Chief Priest at the Temple of Horus being built at the First Royal Mooring Place (the later Hermopolis); he has a son with Amma.

Khentika (33)
Born to Amma and Tuthmose shortly before Queen Mayet's birth in Nekhen. Now, he serves as his father's Chief of Altar at the First Royal Mooring Place.

Nebah (29)
Watch Captain at the Fourth Army. Pase's superior. Given to fierce wagering, he becomes a secret member of the *Usurpers of the Two Crowns*.

Tesh (36)
Royal Tax Collector at the royal palace in Nekhen; was forced to become a member of the Usurpers of the Two Crowns after caught stealing from the King's grain silos.

Wadji, Cobra of the Desert.
Leader of marauding tribesmen; a hired spy of the Ruler of the Kush.

Ruler of the Kush, allies himself with King Ogoni to do battle against the Egyptians.

Ogoni,
King of Nobatia.
Ruler of the fierce Black and Red Noba tribes.

* * *

Appendix C
The Priesthood

Ramose
born Prince Rama of Nekhen,
High Priest of Ptah, Temple of Ptah at Ineb-hedj
(Memphis)

Badar
born al-Badari at Badari.
Founder of an organized, strengthened priesthood.
Now retired Father of Ptah, Temple of Ptah at Ineb-Hedj
(Memphis)

Wazenz
Chief Priest, Temple of Ptah at Ineb-hedj (Memphis)

Rahetep
Chief Priest, Temple of Horus at Nekhen (Hierakonpolis)

Seka
Chief Priest, Temple of Osiris at Tjeny; Ka-priest of
Abydos

Teyer
Chief Priest, Temple of Seth at Nubt (Nagada/Ombos)

Temple of Thoth at Khnumu (Hermopolis)
(no chief priest)

* * *

Appendix D

The Royal Armies

(Each army was named after the main deity worshipped in
the Region under its protection)

Central Command

Makari
Grand General, and Chancellor
usually works out of his desert camp near the capital
(his wife Lady Beeba tends a farms there); Often resides in
Ineb-hedj, the capital; Trained the Special Forces. (After
the battle, retires).

Colonel Khayn
Aide-de-camp to Makari (After battle, becomes
Chancellor)

Colonel Mekh
Commander of Special Forces (After battle, becomes
General)

Captain Veni
Captain of Royal Palace Archers (After battle, becomes
Colonel; and Commander of the new Fifth Army of Neit

First Army of Sutekh
(East and Lower Delta)

General Saiss
Headquartered in the Delta - in Pe (Buto)
(Battle Plan: to move headquarters close to Ineb-hedj)

Second Army of Ra
(Upper Delta)

General Sekesh
Headquartered close to Ineb-hedj
(Battle Plan: to move headquarters to Badari)

Third Army of Ptah
(Middle of the Two Lands)

General Teyhab
Headquartered at Badari – (journeyed to Makari's Central
Command)
(Battle Plan: to move headquarters to Kharga Oasis)

Colonel Mayhah
Aide-de-camp
(after the battle, is condemned to Overseer of the
captured Nobatian gold mine

Fourth Army of Amun
(encamped near the Great Kharga Oasis for War Games)
Usually Headquartered around Nekhen
General Barum
(After battle, replaced Makari and becomes Grand
General)
Colonel Keheb
Barum's Aid-de-Camp and Scribe
(After battle, he becomes a General and Commander)
Nebah
Watch Captain; (Superior of Pase)
Traitor (slain by Tasar)

Fifth Army of Neit
(newly formed army after the victorious battle)
Veni
Archer Captain, appointed Commander, advanced to
Colonel.
Will occupy the First Army's old headquarters in the Delta
city of Pe

* * *

Appendix E

Egyptian Gods

(As Referred to in this Novel)

Hapi
Sacred Bull (Greek: Apis bull),
another form of the Nile God.
Also, a name for the Nile itself

Horus
Son of Osiris and Isis. Heavenly falcon whose wings
protected Egypt against chaos. Sign of the King.
Kings had throne names, birth names and—in the case of
the Horus-Kings—Horus-names.
King Aha is often formally addressed as *Hor-Aha*

Isis
Wife of Osiris, Mother of Horus and Seth

Khnum
Lord of the Cool Water.
Ancient God of the First Cataract on the Island of
Elephantine, where the Nile was said to emerge from the
Underworld of its subterranean Ocean of Nun through
two caverns

Maat
Goddess of Truth (vs. **Ma'at** – Egyptian World Order)

Montu
God of War

Nekhbet
Vulture-headed Patron-Goddess of Upper Egypt

Osiris
Supreme God of the Underworld. An ancient Osiris-cult
practicing Sati – human sacrifices at burials

Ptah
Worshipped primarily in Ineb-hedj, the City of White
Walls (Memphis); ancient Creator God

Sebek
Rivergod, God of the Sacred Crocodile

Seker
God of Saqqara.
Also fetish deity of Ineb-hedj (Memphis)

Seth
God of violence and confusion
(second son of Osiris and Isis)
Wadjet
Cobra Goddess of Lower Egypt

* * *

GLOSSARY

Khamsin
The Great Wind of Fifty Days (between Easter and Pentecost); a hot southerly Egyptian wind blowing in from the Sahara

Sirocco
A hot dust-laden wind of cyclonic origin blowing from the Libyan desert into the northern Mediterranean Sea and Coastline

* * *

Ak-ieb
One who has entered the heart; close friend, sweetheart

Authoritative Utterance
Royal Decree

Ba
Part of the soul of the deceased that returns to earth for atonement often in the form of a **Ba-Bird**

Bark (also spelled Barque)
Royal boat

Falucca
Lateen-rigged river boat

Fellah
(Farmer, Peasant; plural = **Fellahin**)

Hemu-ka
Servant to the Ka (Ka-priest)

Ka
The spiritual double (soul) of the deceased which has to be fed and nurtured after death;
looked after by the ka-priests

Ka-Priest
Hemu-ka, Ka-servant; officiating death-priest;
guardian of any necropolis

Kamt
Ancient name for the Two Lands (Egypt)

Kariy
Enclosed sacred shrine on a temple boat

Keftin
Cretans - Ancient People of Crete

Kenbet
> Advisory Council;
> assisting the Vizier in his duty as chief justice

Khepri
> Sacred Winged Scarab
> (Ramose used it as his personal seal)

Ma'at
> (as distinguished from Maat – Goddess of Truth)
> World Order—suppression of feelings, decreed by the gods.
> Anyone acting against Ma'at was severely punished.
> For the most serious crimes, only the King could allow the perpetrator to commit suicide

Nomarch
> Powerful rulers of the numerous nomes

Nome
> Autonomous district prior to Unification in 3100 B.C.

Nub
> (also: Yellow Nub) - Gold

Opening of the Mouth
> Ceremony before burial, to let the soul (Ka) escape

Opet
> Festival of Opet (later held mainly in Thebes)
> Occurred in the second month of **Akhet**, the Season of Inundation

Per-nu
> Lower Egyptian Shrine at Ineb-hedj (Memphis) where jars with the Royal Placenta were stored after birth, to be kept there during the royal family's lifetime after death.
> The jars were usually buried with them

Per-wer
> Upper Egyptian Shrine at Nekhen (Hierakonpolis), built within the heart of the temple, containing the amphorae with the placentas of the originating royal family

Pharaoh
> An additional title for the king.
> It came into use only during the New Kingdom
> (It is therefore absent in this novel)

Rhyton
> Ancient Cretan vessels

Sati
Practice of human sacrifice (especially at burials) at the beginning of the Dynastic period.
Later, the practice died out as a waste of human resources

Sed-Festival
Held by early kings after several years of reign.
Involved ritual re-coronation aimed at rejuvenating the King and reestablishing his rule

Sem-Priest
Officiating priest at animal sacrifices, they were the Guardians of Hapi, the sacred Apis Bull; the only ones allowed to wear leopard skins, intact with head and tail

Sakieh
Water Wheel - has clay buckets and was drawn by oxen (a later invention - not used in this novel)

Shaduf
Water Lift (preceded the **Sakieh**. Still used to this day)

Sothis (Greek: Sirius)
The Dog Star, which rises annually on the horizon in the morning approx. July 19th, at about the same that the Nile begins to rise rapidly each year. The day was thus held to be the true New Year's Day. The heliacal rising of Sothis was thus immensely important to these ancient people

Sphinx
Recently purported to be over 7500 years old; referred to in this novel as the "Guardian of the Desert"

Wedjat
Symbol of the Sacred Eye
Worn in amulet form, often painted onto the prow of Nile vessels
Left Protective Eye of Horus
Right- Eye of the sun god Ra (or Re)

Window of Appearances
Royal Balcony with its own entrance
Overlooks the Palace's Grand Foyer.
From it, the King dispenses special favors and rations.
Announces his "Authoritative Utterances

* * *

Ancient Egyptian Seasons
(Three Seasons of four months each)

Akhet – Inundation
Peret - The land reemerges from the flood
Shomu - The water is at its shallowest

Day
    divided into 12 hours but varied in length according to the season
Year
    measured in Lunar Months, each averaging 29 1/2 days

# # #

Will the Legends of the Winged Scarab
ever be re-discovered?

ABOUT THE AUTHOR

Ms. Borg lives in a diversified lake community in Arkansas, where she continues to write fiction.

* * *

If you enjoyed *KHAMSIN, The Devil Wind of The Nile*, you surely will enjoy the second book in the *Winged Scarab* series, **SIROCCO, Storm over Land and Sea,** a present-day thriller with tie-ins to *KHAMSIN* through the Golden Tablets. However, *SIROCCO* is a stand-alone novel.

Another connection to *SIROCCO* appears in the novella **Edward, Con Extraordinaire.**

* * *

SIROCCO, Storm over Land and Sea

Egyptologist Naunet Klein and her two Boston colleagues arrive in Cairo to assist museum director Dr. Jabari El-Masri in deciphering golden tablets inscribed with dire predictions from an unknown ancient culture predating the Egyptians.

She never dreamed that she would meet a handsome stranger.

Nor had she and her colleagues expected to be embroiled in Egypt's political upheaval, and an audacious theft that culminates in kidnapping and murder.

During a perilous sailing trip from the Red Sea to Crete, Naunet learns the truth about the ancient writings and the dapper Edward Guernsey-Crock.

Time is running out.

* * *

Made in the USA
Lexington, KY
21 January 2014